The Gabriel Extortion

Harlen Campbell

Cover Art by Amanda Campbell

ISBN 978-0-9832055-9-3
Print Edition

Red Hand Productions
Www.teletale.com

For the innocent victims

of our ancient dreams

PART ONE

Threat

Chapter 1

When Danny slipped into his *Science and Society* class, Simon Foreman scowled. "Did you lose something over the weekend, Mr. Murphy?"

Danny froze halfway into his seat, unsure if the professor was actually upset or merely amusing himself. "Sir?"

"Your shadow? Your twin? Mr. Massini's presentation is scheduled for this morning." Foreman shook his head. "I realize you aren't his keeper, but since you usually arrive together, I thought—"

"Oh!" It finally snapped that the desk beside his was empty. No shadow meant no Tony. Danny forced a smile. "He was coming in early to set up his presentation so I didn't stop for him today. You want me to text him?"

"When did he tell you that?"

"Last night. He was ready except for some graphics, but he wasn't feeling too great. He had the . . . well, he had a stomach problem, sort of. Maybe he got worse."

Foreman nodded, then made a decision. "Let him be. He'll get here or he won't. If he makes it, he can present at the end of class. If not, we'll discuss the effect of artificial intelligence on social stability without his insight. Until then. . . ."

Foreman turned back to the white board and resumed his lecture.

Danny opened his laptop, but instead of taking notes, he checked his media. He found nothing new on Tony's Facebook page, but there never was anymore, and nothing on Instagram except a couple of selfies at the concert Saturday. He was laughing and looked like he'd been through an explosion at a paint factory. Nothing on Twitter, of course.

He shot a text to Tony's number: *Dude, Foreman seriously busted you in front of the whole class. You gonna make it in?*

Nothing.

You tight today?

Nothing.

He tuned in to the lecture for a while. Foreman paced back and forth in front of the class like an aging lion, trying to coax a definition of social stability out of his students. Danny decided he could manage that on his own and tried an email. He had no luck there either and started worrying. Tony blew off a couple of quizzes early in the course while he was trying hook up with Rosa Baca and he was seriously counting on this presentation to bump his grade. Something major must have happened.

Danny swallowed his anxiety as well as he could and tried to take notes between his increasingly nervous texts. When Tony was still a no-show with ten minutes left before the bell, he jammed everything in his backpack and headed for the door as quietly as possible. Foreman watched him leave without comment.

Once in the hall, Danny changed his mind about calling his friend. If something was wrong, Tony wouldn't want his parents busting his ass for skipping class. It was better to just drop by the house. Play it cool. See what happened. He was probably worked up over nothing.

It wasn't nothing.

Tony's brother, Mike, answered his knock too quickly and seemed to sag when he recognized Danny. He stepped out of the house and closed the door with a backward glance, then leaned against it, a tall, dark headed young man in a tee shirt and jeans. He apologized softly. "Sorry, Danny. Mom's trying to rest. We can't disturb her."

"What's wrong? Is she okay? I can't connect with Tony at all. Is he here?"

"He's at the hospital. Dad's with him."

Danny was alarmed. "Your Dad is in the hospital?"

Mike scrubbed his face with both hands and sighed. "They took him in around three. The diarrhea kept getting worse. He got weaker and weaker. When he started having trouble breathing, we drove him to the emergency room at Mercy. I just brought Mom home an hour ago. They said there was nothing she could do except pray and she could do that here. Dad wouldn't leave."

Tony, then. Not his dad. It made no sense. Tony was barely nineteen. Danny said, "I just talked to him last night."

"I'm sorry." Mike reached for his shoulder but pulled his hand back before he connected.

"What room?"

"They won't let you see him. He's in the ICU. It's family only."

"I'm going to try." Danny ran to his car and whispered, please, please, all the way to the hospital. The lot by the emergency entrance was full of ambulances. Most of them were parked with their lights flashing and engines running, and a patrolman waved him away from the lot. He found an empty spot in the employee lot and ran back to the emergency room. The cop was busy waving other cars away and didn't pay any attention to him, but an orderly wearing a white mask met him at the door and wouldn't let him enter because he wasn't sick.

Danny said, "It's okay. I'm family. My brother is in there."

The orderly shrugged. "It doesn't matter."

"But my father is with him. I just took my mom home and Dad is expecting me back. He'll want to know how she is."

"So call him."

Danny swallowed and tried another tack. "My brother is Tony. Anthony Massini. Do you know him? How he is? What's wrong?"

"Call your father. If he's with your brother, he'll know as much as anybody. Maybe they'll let him out to talk to you."

"Maybe? What does that mean?"

"Maybe he's not quarantined. Look, you can't get in, and if you did you might not get out. Go home. Take care of your mother."

5

Behind Danny, two ambulances turned on their lights and sirens and edged toward the street. The patrolman blocked traffic while they made a left turn and sped off. Danny walked over to him and waited until he could get attention. He didn't recognize the man, but maybe he would be recognized. He said, "I'm Danny Murphy. Chief Murphy is my father."

The officer nodded cautiously. "How can I help you?"

"My friend is in there and they won't let me see him. We started school together. I've known Tony my whole life and now something is wrong with him and I have to know if he's okay. I have to."

"I can't help you." He actually looked sorry.

"At least tell me what's going on here."

"What's going on is I'm directing traffic and no one gets into the emergency lot except ambulances unless they've got a patient or a body. That's all I know."

"A body?" Danny felt sick. "People are dead?"

"I didn't say that." Another ambulance turned on its siren. The officer glanced quickly over his shoulder, then added, "Look, if the Chief is really your father, talk to him. He knows a hell of a lot more than I do, and he might be free to talk about it. Now move along. I'm busy."

Danny gave up. He took a place on the sidewalk about twenty feet from the emergency room door. When the orderly noticed him and stepped in his direction, he moved back another ten feet. That seemed far enough, or maybe the orderly was just distracted. An ambulance pulled into the lot and backed toward the door. Two nurses came out. Both wore plastic isolation gowns, masks, and face shields. One opened the ambulance door and a man jumped out. He was wearing a mask and a worried expression. He stood aside while the nurses extracted a gurney with what looked like a body on it.

Danny shivered and jogged back to his car. Twenty minutes later, he walked into his father's office in the City Admin Complex. He'd had to show his ID twice to get into the building and two cops in the chief's outer office eyed him suspiciously until Brenda waved him to a seat. Her phone rang constantly but she ignored it most of the time.

He picked an empty chair and settled in for a wait. The room filled slowly, then emptied into his father's office. He was still waiting an hour later when the door opened and a small group of councilmen left. A couple of minutes passed before it opened again, this time to release a mixed group of uniformed and plainclothes officers. His father followed them out. They were talking quietly about some sort of search. The conversation died when they noticed him. His father started to approach him, but Mayor Baca entered the room and the Chief changed direction.

"Dad!" Danny intercepted him. "Tony is in the hospital and they won't tell me anything."

"Tony? What's wrong with him?"

Baca stopped to give Chief Murphy a moment, but he was obviously impatient.

"I don't know. He got sick last night and his dad took him to Mercy. I went to see him, but there are cops and ambulances everywhere. I couldn't get in. I'm worried!"

The mayor broke in. "What kind of sickness, Danny?"

"His brother said diarrhea and he got real weak. He had trouble breathing. It sounds serious, but nobody will talk to me."

Baca gave the chief a measured look and shook his head, then stepped into the office. Murphy looked torn, but he only said, "We'll talk later."

"But, Dad—"

"Later, Danny. Find your sister and get her home. Stay close to your mother. I'll have someone call the hospital about Tony."

"But—"

"It's the best I can do, son. Now get out of here. Get Emma home." He disappeared into his office.

Danny looked at the receptionist. They were alone for the moment. He asked, "Could you call the hospital? Say you're calling for the Chief of Police?"

She just shook her head and bit her lips. She looked pale.

"Do you know what's going on?"

She took a deep breath, then shot a nervous glance at the inner door before whispering, "Do what he said. Get your sister home safe."

Since he had no better plan, Danny texted Emma on the way to his car. A few minutes later, she replied that she was having coffee with her friends at the mall and what was the big emergency. He fired back an order to get home immediately, adding, "Dad says," to keep her from ignoring him completely.

When he opened the front door, his mother called from the den. "Ben? Is that you? What is so damned—"

"It's me, Mom."

"Danny?" She appeared in the doorway. "Did Brenda call you too? What's going on?"

"I don't know." He never hugged her anymore, except maybe at bedtime, but now he needed the comfort and went to her. She held him until he took a deep breath and said, "Something happened to Tony. He's at the hospital and I went there, but I couldn't see him. There were ambulances everywhere and they weren't letting anyone in, not even family."

"Ambulances?" She stiffened. "Where's Emmie?"

"I texted her. She will be home pretty soon."

"You texted?" She pushed him away and dashed to her purse. "Texted? I'm calling her. I want her butt home now!"

"Take it easy, Mom. I told her Dad said. She'll come as soon as she can."

His mother was too busy dialing to hear him. She said, "Maybe there's something on the news," and put the phone to her ear with her left hand while pointing at the TV with her right.

That was a good idea. Danny turned it on and flipped through channels until he saw a shot of a parking lot full of ambulances. A woman standing in front of them with a microphone spoke breathlessly about food poisoning. He backed slowly to the couch and sat down. His eyes never left the screen.

"Turn it up." His mother sat beside him, close enough for their shoulders to touch, and said, "She didn't answer."

"She doesn't talk on the phone. She texts."

"I know. I'm going to strangle her if she doesn't start answering the damn phone when I call."

Danny nodded. "That'll work."

The screen switched to another reporter, another parking lot full of ambulances, and another Emergency Entrance sign.

This time, Danny recognized the hospital. The same orderly stood guard at the door. He'd been joined by a second orderly and a uniformed policeman. All three wore surgical face masks. A small crowd of men and women stood off to the side. "That's Mercy," he said softly. "That's where Tony is."

The new reporter started working his way through the same story. The picture abruptly switched back to the anchor room. A man and woman sat behind the desk and the woman began speaking. "If you've just joined us, at least sixty-three people have been taken to local hospitals with symptoms of food poisoning. The type of poison has not been identified, but unconfirmed reports say that the symptoms are consistent with botulism and a spokesman for Mayor Baca has announced that food samples are being collected from the homes of the victims."

The picture cut to the male anchor who continued, "So far, neither the victims nor their families have reported any common foods or restaurants, so it is hard to determine the source of contamination, but both doctors and investigators from the county and state health departments are—"

The front door slammed and Emma entered. She demanded, "What's the big emergency?"

Her mother waved her over to the couch and started telling her about the story. Ben shouted, "Quiet, damn it!"

They both glared at him and his mother opened her mouth, but he jabbed a finger at the screen and hissed angrily, "Listen!"

The picture had switched to a third emergency room. The anchorwoman was speaking in a voice over. "We have just received an updated report. At least six people have died in local hospitals from this tragic case of food poisoning. Health officials, assisted by the police, are doing everything they can to identify the source, but—"

"That's ridiculous!"

Both Danny and Emma turned to their mother. He asked, "What's ridiculous?"

She pointed at the screen where all of the hospital personnel waiting by the emergency entrance were masked. She asked, "Why the masks? If it's food poisoning, why the masks? Those are for airborne diseases."

"Do you think it's a gas?" Danny asked. "Some kind of gas attack?"

She shook her head. "Gas would go right through surgical masks. They're worried about bacteria, or maybe viruses."

"How do you know about masks?" He sounded doubtful, even to himself.

"Your aunt is a nurse. I'm calling your father." She grabbed her phone and hurried toward the kitchen.

Emma took her place beside Danny. She leaned against him and he put an arm around her. They watched the screen in silence for a few minutes. The count of affected people went up to 87 while the number of confirmed dead held at six. She asked softly, "Do you think they might cancel my soccer camp?"

Danny forced himself to take a deep breath instead of snapping at her. He remembered how hard she'd worked to earn her spot on the Freshman soccer team and his expression softened. "I don't know, Emmie. Probably not. Camp is sixty miles away and you don't leave until Saturday. They have five days to figure this out."

Emma nodded. She asked hesitantly, "Why are you so upset?"

He pointed at the screen. The death toll had been updated. It stood at nine. "Tony is sick. They took him to Mercy."

"Oh." She waited a moment, watching his face. "Does he have that food poisoning?"

"I don't know. They wouldn't let me see him."

Their mother came back into the room. She said, "I finally got through to Brenda. Your dad couldn't talk, but he sent a message. I'm supposed to feed you and get some rest. She said it will probably be after midnight before he gets home. They're waiting on some kind of report."

"So we just eat and pretend nothing is happening?"

"I guess. We can watch TV."

"That won't help."

"Why don't you call Tony's mother. She may have heard something from her husband by now."

"Good idea!" He grabbed his phone and started for his bedroom to make the call. As he left he heard Emma ask what was for dinner. His mother said she didn't know. She said that

Brenda suggested sticking to canned goods, old canned goods, until she heard different.

Chapter 2

Danny's father shook him out of a fitful sleep. Silhouetted against light from the door, Ben Murphy rubbed his closely cropped hair and waited impatiently. Danny groaned and asked, "What time is it?"

"After three."

"What...?" Memory came back. "Tony?"

"He was still hanging in there at midnight. Get a robe on." He rubbed Danny's cheek. "I need everyone downstairs."

"What about Emmie?"

"Her mother's getting her." His father disappeared.

When Danny padded downstairs, he found his father sipping a cup of coffee at the kitchen table. A second cup sat in front of the chair beside him. Danny poured one for himself and, after a moment's hesitation, made another for his sister. Hers got a healthy splash of almond milk and a spoon of sugar. He put them on the table and sat, watching his father silently. He looked beyond tired.

"What's up, Dad?"

"Wait. Let's just do this once." It was a short wait. His mom and Emma showed up almost immediately. His mom looked worried and Emma confused. As soon as they were seated, he sighed and began, "You know what's happening at the hospitals. Some of it anyway. What you don't know is that a package was delivered to Mayor Baca's office Monday morning. In addition to some other stuff, it had a note in it."

He closed his eyes and quoted from memory. "This killed a few citizens. 5 K-Au will save the rest. Expect my call." He took a deep breath and added, "It was signed Gabriel."

Emma glanced from her father to her mother, then asked very hesitantly, "What is a kau?"

Murphy ignored the question for the moment. He focused on his wife and continued, "The package sat in the mail room until after lunch and then it didn't get opened for another couple of hours because people were beginning to call with questions about food poisoning. The first call was from county health, but someone there must have called one of the radio stations. People were showing up at urgent care centers all over town with the same symptoms. Botulism."

"Did they confirm that?"

"Not yet." He swirled the coffee in his cup and sighed. "All hell was breaking loose and nobody had even died yet. And then someone in Ed's office got around to opening the package. They saw the note and ran it over to my office. Part of it anyway."

"What did they keep?"

"Besides the note, there was a sealed tube with warning labels on it — poison and biohazard stickers — and a baggie with some colored powder. They sent me the note and mailer and called the department of health to pick up the rest. Ed told me the guy who picked up the tube showed up in full hazmat gear. Scared the hell out of everyone in his office."

"It should," his wife said quietly.

Emma took advantage of a pause to repeat her question. "What's a kau?"

Danny started to answer her, but he got embarrassed and shut up. Ben Murphy looked at his son and asked, "You have a guess, Danny?"

"You said K-Au. Not 'kau.' Au is the chemical symbol for gold and K stands for kilo. Thousand. He wants five thousand dollars in gold."

"Pretty close, but we don't think he wants dollars. It's way too little for what he is threatening. We think he means kilograms. That would be worth over two hundred thousand dollars."

"Oh." Danny was embarrassed, then angry. Very angry.

"This Gabriel guy poisoned Tony for money?"

"That's what it looks like."

"We've got to catch him!"

"We will, son, but it won't be easy. He has some very deadly poison and we don't even know how he's giving it to people. Nobody ate at the same restaurant or went to the same grocery store. They don't seem to have anything in common except their symptoms and they're all pretty young. Under forty, anyway."

His wife asked, "Did you get anything back from the lab? Anything at all?"

He nodded. "The powder was calcium carbonate and some kind of red dye."

"Chalk?" She was surprised.

Emma was impressed. "How did you know that, Mom? Calcium whatever?"

Anne Murphy smiled. "I work for the school system, dear. If there's one thing teachers know about, it is chalk."

"That's it! I bet that's it." Danny felt dizzy, then excited. He jumped from the table, dashed up to his room, and ran back with his phone. He opened Tony's Instagram page and showed it to his father. "Tony took these selfies Saturday night. See the colors? He went to that *Hue and Chroma* concert. They throw bags of color at each other during the performance. See?"

The Chief saw. He pulled his phone and walked out of the room, dialing urgently. A few minutes later he returned to the table looking grim.

Danny's heart sank. "Was I wrong?"

"No, you were right. Everyone they've traced so far was either at the concert or spent time with someone who was there." He looked directly at Danny. "You didn't go, did you?"

"I was working on my report. It's due Wednesday."

"Have you seen Tony since then?"

Danny shook his head.

His mother asked, "What about his family?"

"I talked to his brother after class. That's all."

"I meant, how are they, Danny? His family?"

"Oh, God!" He hadn't thought of that. He grabbed his phone and dialed Tony's home number. There was no answer.

He hung up and tried again.

No answer.

He started to dial a third time but his father stopped him and said, "I'll have a patrol stop by the house. Do a wellness check." He started dialing.

Danny nodded. He felt numb. He glanced around the table. His mother looked as worried as he felt. Emma was just staring at him. Her cheeks were wet.

His father hung up. "I should hear in half an hour or so. Maybe a bit longer. The patrols are pretty busy." He cleared his throat and addressed his wife. "I want you and the kids to start thinking about what you'd take if you had to leave suddenly."

His mother cried, "Ben? No!"

"I'm not saying now, Anne. I'm saying if, but call your sister in Denver and let her know she might have guests."

Emma said, "We're not going without you, Daddy."

"This is just in case, sweetheart. Besides, your soccer camp starts Saturday. All this will all be over by the time you get back."

"Promise?" She walked around the table and hugged him. "I love you, Daddy. I don't really want to go to that stupid camp."

He patted her back and said, "You're going to be a hit, Sweetie. You're going to make the team and have a great freshman year in high school."

Danny watched them together. He saw his father and mother looking at each other over Emma's back. They didn't say anything, but they were communicating.

His mother finally nodded. "Okay, Ben. I'll call Margie."

"Tomorrow is soon enough, I guess." He turned to Danny. "Take your sister upstairs. There's nothing more to do tonight. I'll wake you when I hear anything."

Danny nodded, but Emma wouldn't leave until her father slapped her butt and assured her everything would be okay. Then she followed Danny upstairs and made him stay in her room until she fell asleep. The companionship helped them both. He drifted off while rubbing her back and didn't wake until his father shook him just after dawn. He was already dressed for work.

In the hall, Murphy put a hand on his shoulder and said, "I didn't wake you because there wasn't any news about Tony's family. The patrol checked their house three times. It was open and empty. They locked up and left a note on the door but no one called them back."

"Okay." Danny felt empty.

"Look, there are lots of reasons the house could be empty, Danny. Maybe they're at the hospital. Maybe they decided to leave town."

"Without Tony?"

"That's the other thing." Murphy cleared his throat. "We had a bad night at the hospitals. The count is up to nineteen now."

"Tony?"

The chief hesitated, took a breath, and shook his head. "I'm sorry, son."

Danny started trembling. He felt like throwing up. "I better get dressed."

"Are you going to class today?"

"I might as well. I'll stop at Tony's—" His voice broke. He finished, "—at the Massini's on my way. I should talk to Mike if I can find him. His Mom. And I forgot about Parker. He needs to be fed. But I don't know what to say to them. You know I shot Tony with one of those dart guns when we were playing war one time and he stuck his head up and my dart, the kind with a rubber suction cup on it, got him right in the middle of his forehead and he wore that thing around the house all afternoon. It kept coming off and he kept licking it and sticking it back on, telling me he was going to tell mom and get you to whip my butt. And I kept saying I was sorry whenever I could stop laughing."

"Are you okay, Danny?"

"Yeah. But I'm going to . . . to . . . ."

"Right. Well, keep all this to yourself. We don't need to start a panic." With that, Ben Murphy squeezed his shoulder and left for work. Danny showered and dressed. He stopped in the kitchen to say goodbye to his mother and found her sitting with what looked like the same cup of coffee, a middle-aged blond with tight lips and a fresh set of lines around her eyes, working on a list. He looked over her shoulder. *Insurance.*

Clothes for a week.   Passports. Medicine. Vaccination records. Wills.

"Jeez, Mom. Wills?"

"It's just in case, Danny."

"Don't show it to Emmie."

"Of course not." She bit her pen and stared at the paper. "I'm forgetting something. What?"

He looked again. "Money? Do we need some cash?"

"That's it." She nodded absently. "I'll get to the bank this morning, but there was something else. . . ."

He left her staring at her list and drove to what had once been his second home.

No one answered the bell or his knock. He found the spare key and cracked the front door just far enough to call Parker, Tony's flop-eared black and white mutt. He got no answer. He should have. Parker was almost as much his dog as Tony's. They'd raised him together since the day Mr. Massini brought the puppy home on Tony's eleventh birthday. Parker should have come to his voice. Danny didn't want to go in. The house was too quiet, so he sat on the front porch and waited.

Mike drove up a bit after nine. He sat in the car, staring at the dash, for a long time. Then he walked slowly over to Danny and sat beside him. He said, "I guess you heard."

"I went to the hospital last night but they wouldn't let me see him and they wouldn't tell anything, so I asked Dad to call. He just told me."

Mike rubbed his eyes. They were very red. "Being the Chief's kid is good for something, I guess."

"I don't know what to say, Mike. I sat here since seven trying to think what to say, and I've got nothing."

"Same here, Danny. I don't know what to do next. I don't want to stand up and I don't want to lie down."

"Yeah." He took a deep breath and asked, "How's your dad taking it? Is he still at the hospital?"

"He's still there." Mike's voice went completely flat. "He's not coming back. You really don't know, do you? You don't know a god damned thing."

"What?"

"Dad collapsed in the emergency room while they were putting a tube down Tony's throat. That's when Mom got hysterical and the nurse told me to take her home. I got her back and put her in bed and that's when you came by. She was okay, kind of okay, for a few hours, but then I got a call that Mike was getting worse and Dad was unconscious, so I went in to tell Mom that I needed to go back to the hospital, and she was having trouble breathing. I got her in the car and took her back to Mercy and they checked her in. I've been there ever since."

"Christ! You should have called, Mike."

"Tony went around four. Dad lasted until almost six. Mom just passed. They gave me a bunch of tests, but they said I'm clean. No problems." He put his face in his hands. He said, "I'm just fine."

Danny put an arm over Mike's shoulders. When they stopped shaking, he stood and pulled him up. "Come on, buddy. You're going to my house."

"No!" Mike jerked away and opened the front door. "This is where I belong. Someone has to look after the house."

"You need to get out of here, Mike. It's just for a day or two. My folks will know what to do."

"I'm staying here, Danny. Thanks for coming." He closed the door firmly.

Danny knocked a couple of times, but when the house remained silent, he went to his car and called his mother. She said she'd get his father to send someone or she'd come herself. He told her not to go in the house. The line went quiet. He couldn't even hear her breathing. He drew a breath to explain, but she said, "Of course. Do you think it's safe to have him here?"

"The hospital checked him out. He's clean. At least he was a few minutes ago."

"I'll ask your father. Are you coming home now?"

"I've got class."

He drove to the university through streets that were unusually empty and walked into a classroom less than half full only twenty minutes late. Professor Foreman lifted an eyebrow when Danny showed up but he didn't interrupt the lecture and he made no comment about Tony's non-appearance. In fact, he seemed determined to rush through the lecture as quickly as possible. Danny sat through it numbly, but he heard little of the lecture. A sense of emptiness overwhelmed him. He felt hollowed out, lost, and barely in control.

Foreman saved him. Just before the scheduled end of class, he slammed his course book on his desk and snapped, "Enough! Let's talk about something interesting. Let's talk botulism."

He had the full attention of the class. He stared over the students, but his eyes seemed to linger on Danny. Or possibly on the empty desk beside him. He asked, "Who can tell us how botulism poisoning is connected to technological change?"

The silence was deafening.

Foreman grinned fiercely: reddish complexion, heavily lined face, curly gray hair a couple months past its cut-by date. He cleared his throat. "All right. Does anyone know what botulism toxin is?"

A girl near the front row said, "It paralyzes muscles, doesn't it? Doctors use it on your face so you don't get wrinkles."

He nodded. "That's one use. Where does it come from?"

"Spoiled food." She sounded positive.

"Are you saying it comes from the food itself? From bad potatoes or cabbages?"

Danny thought he saw where Foreman was going. He lifted his hand. "No, it's bacterial. Bacteria on spoiled food make the poison. The toxin."

"Excellent. Now, do you think modern technology makes botulism more common or more rare?"

Danny had no idea. "Maybe we keep left-overs around longer, so there'd be more chance of spoilage, but it's easier to cook and that should kill bacteria." He shrugged. "I guess I don't know, professor."

"Another result of technology is population growth. Could that effect the incidence of botulism poisoning?"

Silence, then someone suggested, "Maybe it'd get worse? More patients at a time?"

"Good, but why?"

"More people would be eating together?"

Foreman nodded. "Let me give you some statistics. Most outbreaks of botulism poisoning are limited to one or two

19

patients. In the last 40 years, only six involved more than ten patients. They affected a total of 188 people. Any guesses how many of those people died?"

The room was still, focused. Foreman waited for a guess, then said, "Two. Only two."

He let the students wait before continuing, "How many people have died from our local outbreak?"

Another silence. Someone said, "I heard a dozen on the radio." Someone else said, "No, it was only nine. It was on TV last night."

Foreman focused on Danny. "What about it, Mr. Murphy? Your father is the chief of police. Surely you have a guess?"

Danny felt a flash of resentment that Foreman had put him on the spot. He didn't want to answer, but at the same time he knew that the situation was serious. His classmates needed to know. Unable to deny knowing the number, he mumbled.

"What was that?"

Danny took a deep breath and spoke up. "Nineteen. Just a guess."

A soft gasp circled the room.

Foreman nodded and asked the class, "Has anyone heard anything about the source of the poisoning? Was it potato salad? Cheese dip? Something else?"

When he got no answer, he cleared his throat. "Okay, two last points. First, another consequence of population increase is political violence. Conflict. That's something we should think about. Second, I received notice this morning that your classmate, Mr. Anthony Massini, was among the casualties of the recent outbreak. On behalf of the university, I want to extend our condolences to his family and of course to his friends and fellow students." He sighed and added, "That's all. Class dismissed."

Chapter 3

Danny didn't notice Rosa Baca until after Brenda told him he'd have to wait to see his father. A quick scan of the crowded outer office told him to expect a long wait. That was when he noticed Rosa sitting uncomfortably among a knot of staffers from her father's office. She saw him about the same time. When he pointed at the door and lifted his eyebrows, she nodded.

Once in the hallway, he didn't know how to begin. She solved his problem by saying, "I'm sorry about your friend, Danny."

"Yeah, it sucks." He hesitated. "He was your friend, too."

She looked surprised. "I didn't really know him that well."

"He asked you to go to the *Hue and Chroma* concert with him."

She shook her head. "He didn't."

"Wow." Danny tried to laugh. "He must have chickened out."

"Maybe. I'd have said yes, just to see the concert."

"You didn't like him?"

"He wasn't even on my radar that way. I see more of you because we have to go to the political things with our families." She shuddered. "If I'd gone to that concert—"

"You might be dead." He finished the thought for her, then added, "Tony's dad died. And his mom."

"Both of them?" She swallowed nervously. "Is Mike okay?"

"You know Mike?"

"We dated a lot when I started at the university. He was a senior then. He broke it off after he was accepted to law school." She focused on the wall and finished, "It didn't matter even then. It certainly doesn't matter now."

"It sounds like it meant something to you," Danny said softly.

"Maybe toward the end. When we met, I was a Freshman looking for an experience and he qualified. It took awhile to realize that I couldn't even offer him a decent conversation. When he figured that out, he ended it."

"That's pretty harsh. It doesn't sound like Mike."

"He wasn't cruel. He just ended the relationship. He didn't start it. I did that." She shrugged. "I just didn't realize that the stakes were so high, or so different for us. I picked him to be my first. I didn't think he could be my last."

"Really?" When she nodded, he asked, "Did Tony know?"

"Probably."

"Maybe that's why he didn't ask you out."

"Maybe it's why he wanted to. It doesn't matter any more." She glanced at the door. "What do you think they're talking about?"

"Our dads?" He thought a moment. "The attack. Terrorism. What else?"

"Terrorism?" Rosa looked shocked. "Papa said it was food poisoning."

"My teacher doesn't think so. I'm taking a survey course called 'Science and Society' this summer and Professor Foreman talked about it in class. He thinks it was terrorism."

"What does the chief think?"

Danny wasn't sure how much his father told him was a secret, so he just shrugged.

Rosa looked thoughtful. "Do you want to know what I think they're meeting about?"

"What?"

"How to get us out of town."

"Yeah. That too." Danny closed his eyes for a moment but when he opened them again nothing had changed. He said, "I guess you came with your dad?"

Rosa nodded. "I'm interning in his office for the summer.

He was going to take me to lunch so I was waiting when he got the call. Your dad needed to see him so we stopped on the way to our restaurant."

"A bunch of people from his office are in there." Danny nodded at the waiting room. "Are all of you going to lunch?"

Rosa shook her head. "Just Papa and me. The others started showing up after he went in with your dad."

"Something is happening." Danny reached a decision and opened the door. "I'm going in. Do you want to come?"

"Brenda won't let us in."

"She doesn't like a scene." He took Rosa's hand. "We'll look ready to make one."

The scene wasn't needed. The waiting room was mostly empty and Brenda was on the phone. She just nodded at them when they slipped past her desk and into the Chief's crowded office. The mayor's staff and a collection of uniformed and plainclothes officers were scattered around the office. The senior mayoral staff had taken all the chairs. Everyone else formed a loose crescent centered on Murphy and Baca, who stood together in front of the chief's desk. Murphy was talking when Danny closed the door softly and pulled Rosa to an inconspicuous post near the wall.

". . . so the count, as of two-thirty this afternoon, stands at twenty-three dead and approximately eighty infected. That's only four more fatalities than this morning, which sounds like we're making some headway—" A hopeful murmur crossed the room. He quelled it with a raised hand. "—but the bad news is that three of the fatalities were found at home in bed. We have no idea how many other victims are still out there."

Baca asked, "Can't we get an estimate? How many kids went to see that band?"

"They sold six hundred tickets."

One of the staffers interrupted. "Six hundred? What's the occupancy rating on that club?"

Murphy looked at one of the uniforms and asked, "Phil?"

"Three ninety-seven. They over-sold by a couple hundred."

Mayor Baca made a sour face. "You mean we could have another five hundred casualties?"

Murphy shook his head. "Not everyone at the concert was affected. We've been interviewing the people we can identify.

That's how we found the three new dead. But most of the people we found were okay or just a little nauseated or had the runs."

"So you think we've got most of the victims?"

"The health department says we're probably looking at another ten to fifteen fatalities and maybe another fifty hospitalizations, depending."

"Depending on what?"

Danny peered over the shoulders in front of him and recognized the questioner as Phil Posner, the city Fire Chief.

"Depending on whether we can find the ones who are seriously sick before they die, and depending on what the hell is killing them," Murphy said quietly, "and there is one other factor. At least two of the dead weren't even at the concert. They died because their kid went to see the band."

Danny leaned against the wall. He felt light-headed. Rosa grabbed his hand and squeezed it. She whispered, "We should go."

He nodded and she pulled him to the door. Brenda was still at her desk in the outer office, still on the phone, and she paid no attention as they passed. Danny started for the parking structure. When Rosa followed him, he stopped and asked, "You need a ride anywhere? Are you living at home?"

She nodded. "Just for the summer, to save money. Then it's probably back to the dorms unless I can share an apartment."

"Tony and I used to talk about getting a place together." He sighed. "I guess we waited too long."

"You couldn't have known." She gave him a sharp glance. "You're going to see Mike, aren't you?"

He nodded. "He was spending the summer with his folks. Tony figured it would be their last summer together. I want to talk about what happened, what he's going to do."

Rosa announced, "I'm going with you."

Danny started to argue, then realized he didn't care. He shrugged and led the way to his car. Their drive was silent. When he parked and opened his door, Rosa didn't move. He asked, "Are you coming?"

She shook her head and leaned back into her seat. Her eyes closed. He gave her a moment, then nodded and walked to the house. He rang the bell without expecting a response and was surprised when the door opened immediately.

Mike looked haggard. Barefoot. Dirty jeans. Rumpled white t-shirt. At least two days worth of stubble. Red eyes. Ratty hair. But he managed a tired smile when he recognized Danny. He stepped back and waved him into the darkened house, then looked past him and asked, "Who's with you?"

"Rosa. She's staying in the car."

"Might as well get it over with." Mike sighed. He stepped into the doorway and shouted, "If you don't come in, we're going to talk about you." Then he shot Danny a sidelong glance, said, "There's coffee," and led the way into the kitchen.

Danny's mom said that Mrs. Massini swept a floor twice just to get it clean enough to mop. She'd never have let anyone see her kitchen in this condition. A half-eaten cheeseburger lay on its flattened sack surrounded by most of an order of fries. Worse, several brown rings of coffee circled an empty cup on the Formica table. Even worse, a bottle of Patron, Mr. Massini's favorite tequila, the bottle he opened only for birthdays, weddings, and funerals, stood between the coffee cup and a shot glass.

Danny couldn't think of anything to say about the bottle so he ignored it. He took a seat while Mike moved two clean cups and a carafe to the table and filled all three cups. When Danny raised his eyebrows at the third, Mike offered a weak grin. "She'll be in," he said. "It'll just take her a few minutes."

Danny nodded and looked around. "Where's Parker?"

"Parker? He's gone too?" Mike took a deep breath and released it slowly. "I forgot to feed him. I was so worried about Mom. I thought I saw him in the rear mirror when I drove her to the hospital, but I couldn't stop. She was having trouble breathing."

"We should look for him."

"I guess." But Mike didn't move. He closed his eyes and said, "Maybe he's with Tony."

"That sucks." Danny shook his head angrily. "I'm going to find him."

"Good. He was a good dog."

"I have to go home first. Take care of Mom and Emma."

Mike nodded. "Watch your rear view mirror, Danny. If you

see him, stop."

"That's a crappy thing to say." He picked up the shot glass and sniffed. He set it aside looking puzzled.

"I couldn't," Mike said. "I got it out last night, sort of a goodbye to Pop, you know?, but I couldn't, not until all this is over. Tony and Mom and Pop and all those people at the hospital."

"I want to ask about that." Danny took a deep breath and said, "I understand about Tony. He was at the concert and got whatever it was there. Poison, whatever. But your mom and dad got it too, and you didn't. How did that happen?"

Mike sipped at his coffee. "You know how Mom is." He swallowed painfully. "Can't stand a mess. Starts washing your shirt before it's off your back. You know?"

Danny nodded and glanced around the kitchen.

Mike nodded. "I know. She'd have a fit if she saw her kitchen like this, but she. . . ," he shook his head violently before continuing, ". . . anyway, I was in my room, studying, when I heard the garage door open and Pop went out to see him. When they came in, they must have been a sight because she had them stripping in the laundry room, before she's even let them in the house."

Rosa slipped into the third chair while he was talking. She asked, "You didn't see them?"

Mike shook his head. "I was kind of pissed that I had to study. The last thing I wanted was to listen to him raving about what an awesome time he had, so I just hid out. He went on about the light show and the music and the colors. You know about *Hue and Chroma* concerts, right? How everyone brings these shakers full of colored chalk and they throw colors all over each other? Well, apparently—"

"That doesn't sound like Tony," Danny interrupted. "Did he bring chalk too? Where did he get it?"

"Let me finish," Mike said impatiently. "He said there was a guy passing out the shakers to anyone who didn't bring one, so things started getting crazy the minute the first set started, and it must have been really crazy. Tony was pretty hyper from what I heard, and even Pop got excited. He must have—"

Danny interrupted, "We think the chalk was poisoned."

"It had to be something like that." Mike didn't look

surprised. "Pop helped Tony clean his car and Mom must have been exposed while she was washing up. If Tony brought a souvenir home from the concert, I can't find it. That leaves the chalk." He shook his head and stared at his hands. He folded them on the table and said, "If I had gone, at least I'd be with my family now."

"Don't say that!" Rosa covered Mike's hands with hers. She bent over them and peered up into his face. "You're in a bad place now, Mike, but people love you and things are going to get better. You'll see. We'll help you. Take care of you. . . ."

Mike started, "Look, Rosa—"

"No, you look! You're alive, and where there's life. . . ."

Danny didn't want to hear about life. He was stuck on where there wasn't life. Alive, Tony couldn't work up the nerve to invite Rosa to a concert. Probably just as well.

He felt sick. He stepped out of the room and wandered to Tony's door. He pushed it open and stood awhile, staring into the room where he and Tony discovered Super Mario, Grand Theft Auto, Lara Croft, and puberty.

Tony's desk was neat, just the way Mrs. Massini liked it. His textbooks and reading material were neatly stacked by the wall, his laptop squarely centered on the spotless surface. His bed, however, was a mess by his mother's standards. The blanket and comforter had been tossed loosely over the mattress and, even more alarming, his pillow lay on the floor.

"Looking for something?"

Danny looked over his shoulder at Mike. Rosa was nowhere to be seen. He'd been vaguely aware that their discussion reached a crescendo shortly after he left the kitchen. He shrugged. "I thought I'd take his last paper to Professor Foreman, but I guess it doesn't matter."

Mike sighed. "Guess not."

"What are you going to do, Mike?"

"No idea. I tried to make arrangements. No one will tell me when they'll release my family."

"Maybe Dad can find out. I'll ask him." Danny hesitated. "I meant when this is over. You should stay with us. You'd be welcome."

Mike shook his head. "I'm going to find who did this."

"The police—"

"No!"

"Okay." Danny tried another tack. "Have you checked Tony's car?"

"I looked in the windows. There's still a lot of that colored chalk on the seat. I started to open the door, but then I didn't. I don't know how to clean it up."

"I'll ask Dad."

Mike nodded and walked back to the kitchen. He emptied all three untouched coffee cups and left them, dirty, in the sink. Then he sat in front of the bottle of Patron and the shot glass and stared at them. Danny stood in the doorway for a moment. He asked, "Will you be all right?"

"Sure. I'm not going to open it until I can bury them. Then I'll probably drink it."

"I'll help you."

"Thanks." Mike's eyes didn't waver. "You should go now."

Danny started to repeat his offer of a place to stay, but it seemed pointless. He let himself out and found Rosa waiting in his car. She did not feel like talking, so he drove her home in silence. She didn't thank him for the ride, but her quiet nod felt like acknowledgment of a conspiracy.

His sister screamed when he opened the door. She threw herself at him shouting, "Mom! He's home! Mom!"

Danny hugged her while looking over her shoulder for the emergency that justified all the noise. A skinny, long-legged blond girl around Emma's age stood by the couch. She looked nervous, but not panicked, so he ignored her and turned to his mother, who rushed in from the kitchen demanding, "Danny! Where have you been? Are you all right? Have you seen Rosa Baca? Why didn't you call?"

And so on.

He turned slightly to keep Emma between him and his mother, who seemed on the verge of joining the attack, and said, "I just took Rosa home. Is Dad here yet?"

His mother shook her head and began to relax. "He's going to be late again. He called when Brenda said that you kids were waiting to see him and Eddie, but then you disappeared. What happened?"

"We drove by Tony's to see— I mean, we went to see how Mike is doing." Danny swallowed uncomfortably and released

Emma. "What's the big deal?"

"You need to call your father."

Emma whispered, "It's up to twenty-nine, Danny."

"Twenty-nine?"

She nodded, her cheek tight against his chest. He looked at his mother and mouthed, "Dead?"

She nodded. "Call your father, Danny. Emma, why don't you take Janis upstairs. You've got a lot of packing to do."

Emma nodded but she didn't release her hold. Janis knew an order when she heard one. She helped Danny peel his sister's arms off and led her upstairs.

Danny stepped into the den for a bit of privacy, dialed his father, and reached Brenda. She hadn't finished telling him the Chief was still in conference when his father came on line and demanded to know why he left, then said, "Never mind that. What is the name of that professor of yours? The one teaching about science?"

"You mean Dr. Foreman?"

"That's him. You think he might have any idea what's going on with this poison business?"

"Well," Danny felt a little off balance, "he mentioned botulism in class today."

"He did?" His father sounded surprised.

"He was telling the class about Tony. He made it part of the lesson, I guess, but it sounded like he cared."

"What did he say about botulism?"

"He said there were six mass poisonings in the last forty years and almost two hundred people were poisoned, but only two died. But that doesn't sound right if twenty-nine people are already dead. Isn't that too many?"

Chief Murphy was silent. He took a deep breath and asked, "You have class in the morning?"

"Yes."

"Can you bring Foreman to my office before noon?"

"I'll try."

"Don't just try, Danny. If you have any problems, call Brenda. She'll send a patrol car." He hesitated, then added, "Make it eleven-thirty. At the latest."

Chapter 4

Danny slept poorly and woke early Wednesday morning. He found his mother at the kitchen table with her hands supporting her head. She didn't look up when he greeted her. He poured a cup and sat beside her.

"Is he gone already?"

"He left around four." She shook her head slowly. "Home at midnight and gone at four."

"Did something else happen?"

"He got a call just after two. It sounded like more people are dying."

"At the hospitals?"

"Everywhere. He was too tired to talk about it, but he got very quiet after the last call. Are you going to see him today?"

Danny nodded. "He asked me to bring my professor to his office before noon. What's happening at noon?"

"I have no idea."

His mother looked directly at him for the first time. "If you find out what's going on, will you tell me?"

"Of course. Do you want to come with us?"

"I have to work. The school admin office is opening for a couple hours. We're still trying to get the curriculum changes settled."

"Okay." He finished his coffee and stood. "What about Emmie?"

"Janis will be with her. She's staying until Saturday and

we're taking them both to the bus for soccer camp."

"She's staying here? What about—"

"Her mother is a doctor. She can't leave the hospital. If Janis weren't here, Emma would be alone."

"What about when her Mom's shift ends? Won't she want to see Janis?"

"It isn't a matter of shifts, Danny. The whole hospital is locked down. When we arranged for Janis to come here, Pam said the ER and all critical and urgent care centers are in full quarantine. Unless they present with botulism symptoms, all new patients are diverted to Children's Hospital, out by the freeway. Only the poisoning patients are being accepted at Mercy and University Hospitals."

"You mean she can't leave work? She's trapped there?"

"Yes." She sighed. "Janis hides it well, but she's really scared."

"I bet." Danny made a decision. "I've got to go."

"It's too early for your class."

"I can't stay here."

"Then go." But she stopped him before he reached the door. "Remember, if you learn. . . ?"

"I'll call you," he promised.

It took longer for Mike to answer his door than for Danny's drive to the house. He looked more tired but a little neater than yesterday. At least he'd shaved. When he recognized Danny, his expression became resigned. He said, "Come on in."

Danny pushed past him and entered the kitchen. He saw no sign of Parker. His dish was in the corner by the utility room. It was full.

Mike saw him looking and shrugged.

Danny felt empty. He glanced at the Patron bottle. It hadn't been opened. He leaned against the refrigerator and looked Mike squarely in the face. "Did you mean what you said about finding the guy who did this?"

Mike tensed. He met Danny's gaze and nodded.

"You can't do it alone."

"I know." Mike dropped into a chair and crossed his arms. "I've been talking to people."

"Like who?"

31

"I've got a friend at the paper. She does background research for the writers. I know a guy at a medical lab. There are some others."

"Do they have names?"

Mike shook his head slowly.

"Okay." Danny changed tactic. "What happens when you find him?"

Mike shrugged again.

Danny took a breath and released it slowly. He said, "You know somebody close to the police, too."

After a long pause, Mike asked, "You know what you're offering?"

"Tony was like my brother. He was a really nice guy and Gabriel made him into a killer, shaking that poison over all his friends, and then he came home and killed his mom and dad. No matter what they do to that bastard, it won't be enough." He swallowed with difficult and added, "I need to be part of it."

Mike sat up and leaned forward. His eyes flashed. "Who is Gabriel?"

Danny pulled a chair for himself and leaned close to Tony's brother. He lowered his voice and began, "The mayor got a note. . . ."

They talked about the threat, what it might mean, and how to proceed for so long that Danny was almost late for class. It didn't matter much. Half the chairs in the room were still empty when Foreman walked in and set a small notebook on the front table. His eyes swept the room before settling on Danny. He said, "I'm going to have to apologize to the class. Mr. Murphy's presentation on . . . what was your subject again, Mr. Murphy?"

Danny stuttered, his face burning. He'd completely forgotten his paper was due.

Before he could form a response, Foreman let him off the hook. "Never mind. We won't have time for it." His demeanor became graver. "The university president called an emergency meeting of the staff and faculty at seven this morning. She announced some changes to our operating procedures in response to . . . well, to what's been happening. Most of the changes affect dormitories, food services, library hours, administrative and service staffing, the campus police, and so forth, but one, in particular, will affect our class." He pulled a sheet from from his notebook and read:

"Effective immediately, faculty will minimize contact among students and between faculty and the student body. Classes will meet on line wherever feasible. Instructors are encouraged to reduce work group, study group, and other interaction associated with classes. On line or email meetings will replace office hours until further notice.

"So. What does this mean for us?" He paused a moment, then continued, "First, classes are canceled until further notice. I'll need current email addresses for everyone. As soon as I have a site for the class set up on the university server, I'll email you." He looked around the class, then asked for questions. Almost every hand went up.

The girl who knew botulism was used for cosmetics didn't wait to be called. "Why, professor? If this is just food poisoning, why is she canceling classes?"

Foreman rubbed his face tiredly and said, "Obviously, the president thinks it may be more than just food poisoning. That is the only conclusion I can draw from this. I have no information beyond what's in the directive. I will post the document on line sometime this afternoon, so you will all know everything I know. Any other questions?"

Another student waved and said, "I heard over fifty people are dead now. Is that true?"

"I don't know. The radio said thirty this morning, but the number might have changed. As far as I know, only Mr. Massini from our class has been affected. Has anyone heard different?" When no one answered, he asked, "Mr. Murphy? What have you heard?"

Danny shook his head. "Twenty-nine, but that was last night."

"So no one knows for sure."

Someone said, "The hospitals are full. My cousin had a car accident last night and they couldn't even get an ambulance to come."

"Was it serious?"

"Her neck and shoulder hurt and she's got a big bruise, but she'll be okay."

33

Foreman nodded. "Then she's lucky. For the rest of us, the lesson is clear: be careful. Until this is over, we can't count on public services."

Another student asked, "If it isn't botulism, what is it?"

"I have no idea." Foreman began handing out sheets of paper. "Here is a list of useful email and web addresses. It includes access instructions for the on line learning center and the university servers for those of you who haven't bothered to sign in yet. Since we're already gathered, I'll talk to anyone who needs me face-to-face for the rest of the class. After that, in the spirit of the president's orders, you can only reach me on line. If I just happen to be sitting at the Campus Corner Cafe between four and six, Monday, Wednesday, and Friday, you are welcome to chat for a minute, but only about subjects that aren't specifically mentioned in the school curriculum." He cleared his throat and added, "Of course, the curriculum does not specifically mention anything we've discussed in class."

Danny sat back, grinning, while his fellow students clustered around the professor. Foreman dealt with them patiently and sent only an occasional glance toward Danny, until eleven, when he abruptly ended the meeting and chased everyone but Danny away. Then he asked, "Are you ready to go, Mr. Murphy?"

"Yes, sir." Danny stood.

"Shall we drive separately?"

"I can take you."

Foreman smiled. "I suppose my other choice would be a squad car?"

"It's not like that," Danny said quickly. "Anyway, they're called patrol cars here."

"Tomato, tomahto." Foreman started walking. "Is this your father's command performance?"

Danny nodded. "But I'm not sure what it's about."

"I can guess."

The Mayor and the Chief of Police both stood when Brenda ushered them into the chief's office at eleven-thirty. Danny fumbled through introductions. When he started to leave, Foreman stopped him. "I'd like Mr. Murphy to stay," he said. "He's had good insights in class and most of the victims

34

have been from his generation."

"Victims?" The chief shot a hard look at his son. "What did he tell you?"

"Less than the radio or the television," Foreman assured him. "Common sense tells me more. It says you've got people dying with symptoms of botulism poisoning and no source of the toxin. It says you received a threat of some sort and you don't know if it's real. It says—"

The Chief interrupted him. "Look, Professor—"

"Call me Simon," Foreman said. "We're well beyond formality, don't you think?"

Chief Murphy raised an eyebrow at the Mayor, who nodded slowly. Then he asked, "Can you keep this confidential?"

"Of course."

Murphy looked at his son. "That goes for you, too, Danny."

"I know." He glanced at Foreman, but the professor's face was expressionless. He didn't say anything about the casualty numbers Danny had leaked in class.

"Right." Murphy led them to a work table near his window and handed Foreman a sheet of paper. "This is a scan of a note the mayor received Monday. The note and envelope went to the lab, but we got nothing from them. No DNA, no prints, no special paper or ink. The envelope was postmarked in town. It also contained a baggie with under an ounce of colored chalk and a sealed tube covered with warning labels. The chalk could have come from any kindergarten school kit. The sealed tube went to the state lab. The preliminary analysis came back yesterday afternoon. The material tested positive for botulism toxin, but not for botulism bacteria." He waited a moment to let all that sink in, then continued, "When the package arrived, all hell was breaking loose because of the casualties. That's probably why it wasn't opened until later in the afternoon. Just an explanation, not an excuse. Anyway, no one could figure out where they contacted the poison until Danny heard about the colored chalk and remembered some selfies his friend took at a concert. We followed that up and confirmed that all the original casualties were either at the concert or knew someone who was there." Again he fell silent. He seemed to be thinking about how to proceed.

Foreman took the opportunity to ask, "What other bacteria did the lab find?"

"What?" the question surprised the Chief. "Staph and E. coli. Those are everywhere in the environment. The lab suggested that the sample might have been contaminated."

"Or the author might be infected."

"That was another possibility."

The Mayor added. "We've got county health and the State Environmental Health departments reviewing medical reports for the last six months. The hospitals are reviewing their admissions, too. We're checking out anyone who's had a Staph infection, but there are going to be hundreds. Maybe thousands, depending on how far back we go."

Danny cleared his throat. "Did he call?"

Murphy looked surprised. "Who?"

"Gabriel. The note said to expect a call from him. It seems like he'd call if he wants his gold."

"Didn't call me." Murphy turned to the Mayor. "Ed?"

"I haven't heard anything."

"Would you?" Danny asked. "Rosa told me she has trouble getting through when your private line is busy. Did you tell your staff you expected a call from Gabriel? Would they know to put him through?"

Baca cursed and grabbed his cell phone.

Meanwhile, Foreman had questions about the death toll. "It's thirty-five now? How does that break down?"

"That's thirty-six as of ten this morning. Twenty-nine died after direct exposure at the concert and there were seven secondaries. Three of those died Monday night or Tuesday. The others went last night or this morning."

"This morning?" Foreman looked surprised. "Were they poisoned recently?"

"That's what the docs say, but they don't have any idea how."

"That doesn't make sense unless the cleanup failed somehow." Foreman shook his head slowly. "What about the Center for Disease Control in Atlanta? Did you send them a sample of the toxin?"

"The lab was supposed to."

"The CDC might not do anything if they believe the

outbreak is well-understood and under control." Foreman frowned. "I'd like to talk to the man at the State lab who examined your sample."

"Ask Brenda." Murphy pointed at his door. "She has all the numbers."

"Dad?" Danny took the opportunity to speak while the scientist hurried from the room. "If people are still getting exposed, maybe it's coming from their cars." He explained how Mike was afraid to open Tony's car because of the colored chalk on the seat.

"Right." The chief leaned heavily on his desk and scrubbed at his face with both hands. "Okay. I'll get somebody to impound the vehicle. Hell, we'll impound the vehicles of every patient in the hospital. All three hundred of them. God knows where we'll put them. I don't even know if they can be decontaminated."

"What about buses? And taxis?"

"You're making my day, son." He sighed. "These are good ideas. If you have any that will make my job easier, feel free to speak up."

Danny didn't know what to say. He smiled uncertainly.

Baca got off the phone. "Gabriel did call. He left a message. We answer the phone tomorrow at noon or else. He didn't say or else what."

The chief nodded. "We'll take it in your office?"

"My office, and I'll want everyone there." His voice was loud, angry. "Everyone!"

"We'll be there, Ed." Foreman re-entered the room. Murphy asked the scientist, "What did the state lab say?"

"He sent a sample to the Center for Disease Control in Atlanta, but he didn't expedite it because he recognized the symptoms and the sample tested positive for botulism. The sample also tested positive for Staph. He started a culture, but he said it looked just a little funny. Maybe a new strain."

"When will we know?"

"Friday morning."

"Is that our first contact with the CDC?"

Foreman shook his head. "The CDC supplies the antitoxin the hospitals have been treating the victims with. They know about the problem and they're getting duplicates of every swab, every specimen the doctors and health inspectors take."

"Okay." Murphy pulled himself together. "We're going to be busy before that noon call. Ed needs to get in front of this thing before it hits social media, not to mention the real news. I'll start some men looking for other sources of this toxin. Maybe Gabriel stole it. We also need to know how people are still getting exposed. Cars, buses, maybe even laundromats. Who knows? And we have to follow up on the possibility that Gabriel is a carrier for this Staph bug, and if he isn't, did he put it in the sample on purpose, and if he did, where did he get it. And why." He looked around the room. "Anything else?"

Danny raised his hand.

"What is it, son?" The Chief did not look happy.

"Shouldn't somebody buy some gold? I mean, unless you already have a bunch."

"Right." Murphy looked to the Mayor. "What about it, Ed? You have 5 K of gold in your desk?"

"I don't even know how much that is." Baca smiled tightly. "But I'm pretty sure it isn't in the budget, and if I pay this ransom, or extortion, or whatever Gabriel has in mind, my chances of reelection go way down."

"There is that." Murphy turned to his son. "Go home, Danny. I can't be there to take care of your Mom and Emma, so you'll have to do it for me. You know enough about what's happening to keep them safe."

Danny pushed a little. "What about the FBI? Did anyone tell them about the ransom?"

The chief frowned. "It's not ransom, Danny. No one was kidnapped. It's extortion. But, yeah, we'll send the note to the Feds as soon as it comes back from Forensics, and then they'll send us a note asking why they should care about a bunch of kids who ate some bad potato salad, or whatever. If we want their undivided attention, we're going to have to show them a terrorist or a bomb." He sharpened his voice. "We're doing this by the book, son. We'll catch the son of a bitch, maybe even before the Feds decide enough people have died to justify their interest. Just go home."

Danny was about to object when the mayor spoke up. "Stop at my house on your way. Tell Grace and Rosa what's going on, but try not to scare them."

"Okay." Danny knew when to give up. "One last question, though. What should I tell them about the water? Can we drink it?"

Both of the officials looked shaken. Foreman spoke up. "The water supply is chlorinated. It should be safe. Besides, if he poisoned the water, everyone would be sick."

As he walked to the door, Danny heard his father muttering, "The water? I didn't even think . . . damn it, Ed, I don't have enough men."

Chapter 5

Grace and Rosa Baca had an hour's worth of questions to his ten minute's worth of answers, but Danny embellished the facts with a few conservative guesses and left them more or less satisfied. He spent two hours with them before Grace, a thin, elegant woman with dark eyes and a bun of black hair, dismissed him with a handshake and a worried smile. Rosa walked him to his car and left him with a warm hug and a casual question. "Are you going to see Mike tomorrow?"

He nodded and made it home in time to run to the bank with his mother's ATM card and instructions not to come home with less than two thousand dollars and everything on her grocery list. He made it back in time for supper, then spent an hour watching his mother scrub the dishes before putting them in the dishwasher on the Sterilize cycle. While she cleaned, he answered questions. They were mostly the same questions he'd heard at the Baca's house, so he recycled the same answers. Once he'd satisfied his mother, he went upstairs and gave Emmie watered down versions of the same answers. Janis listened, somewhat skeptically, and then asked her question. He had to tell her he didn't know if the people who worked at the hospital were safe. She nodded like that was what she expected to hear.

His father still hadn't made it home when Danny finally gave in to exhaustion. He found his mother curled up under an old blanket on the living room couch and said goodnight, then collapsed into a fitful sleep in his bed. When he saw the time on his phone and realized that he'd overslept, he dashed to the kitchen and was relieved to find his mother setting the breakfast table.

She looked up, alarmed. "What? Has something happened?"

"No." He took a deep breath. "I was just afraid you went to work. Dad asked me to keep everyone home."

"Your father worries too much." She cracked an egg and asked, "Doesn't he?"

"Not about this." He poured himself the last inch of coffee. "Gabriel is supposed to call around noon. Maybe after that we can relax a little, but it won't be over until we catch him."

"Tomorrow is the Fourth of July. They called an in-service day today to extend the vacation." Work was obviously on his mother's mind. "It's not right to give this monster so much power over our lives."

"Dad's just trying to keep everyone alive."

"I know it."

"He's worried that Emmie will decide to go to the mall or something. She'll stay home if you're watching her."

"She's more responsible than you think, Danny."

He nodded. "She's a great kid. She just doesn't know how dangerous—"

"Are you sure you do?"

"Maybe not." He thought about the last four days. "I'm learning though."

After a moment, his mom cleared her throat. "Pam called to see how Janis is doing. She said they lost two more at Mercy and another at University Hospital, but the feeling is that they've finally turned a corner. She said, 'if they aren't getting better, at least most of them aren't getting worse.'"

"Could they be having a delayed reaction from what happened at the concert?"

"She said that's not likely. Some of them didn't start showing botulism symptoms until after they came in. One was an EMT who had a mild fever with diarrhea. She was only admitted because she'd transported victims. Pam said she was given something to bring down the fever and stuck in a corner until things calmed down. Four hours later her temperature

41

was up and she was in respiratory distress."

"Doesn't anyone know how she was exposed?"

"Not even a guess. She hadn't transported a victim for almost two days. Her unit was sterilized between transports. She received a preventive dose of antitoxin daily. And she still died."

"What did she do before she got sick? Where did she go?"

"Maybe Pam knows." Anne Murphy drained her coffee and made a face. "What are you going to do while I keep the girls from killing themselves?"

"Meet Dad. Tell him about Pam. Try to help Doctor Foreman."

She glanced at him and asked casually, "Is he making any progress?"

"Not really. Tony and his folks died from the chalk at the concert, but we don't know how people are still getting the poison. We don't know where Gabriel got the poison or why he's using it. He's supposed to call at noon. Maybe we'll learn something." He stood and stretched. "I've got to get going, Mom."

She said, "Let me know what happens."

"No problem." He took a quick shower and looked in on Emmie before he left. When he cracked her bedroom door, both girls opened their eyes. Only Emmie smiled at him. He asked softly, "Feeling better, twerp?"

She whispered, "I wish this was over. I wish Daddy would come home."

"He'll get the guy doing this. It'll be over pretty soon." He looked at Janis and added, "Your mom called from the hospital this morning. She's fine. She is just worrying about you."

Janis nodded. "I'm worried about her too." She blinked rapidly. "I miss her. It's lonely at home."

"You were staying alone?"

"Mom has responsibilities." She lifted her chin and added, "She's a doctor in the ER. She's very responsible."

Danny didn't know what else to say so he nodded. "That's really important work. She's saving lots of lives." Then he closed Emmie's door and slipped quietly out of the house.

Mike's place was not exactly on his way downtown but he

drove by anyway, maybe hoping for some tidbit he could contribute to the investigation. When he arrived, Mike was standing in his driveway, watching a pair of mechanics in hazmat gear load Tony's car onto a flatbed. They'd winched it up already and one man ran around the bed, fixing chocks and tightening chains, while the other tried to convince Mike to sign something on a notepad. He shook his head angrily and waved the man away, then saw Danny slowing by the curb, waved a finger at him, and stomped back into the house.

Danny sped away, feeling hurt or angry or both. By the time he reached his father's office, he was only confused. He walked in on a political argument disguised as a disagreement on a matter of public safety. Tomorrow was July Fourth and plans had been made. The Chief wanted to cancel the parade, picnic, and fireworks scheduled for tomorrow afternoon and evening. The Mayor also wanted to cancel them, but he didn't want to be blamed for it and he didn't think it could be done safely.

They faced each other in the center of the office, almost nose to nose. Murphy, an inch shorter than the Mayor, looked up at his boss. He repeated his point while jabbing a finger, not at Baca, but off to the side, toward a darker corner of the room. "It's not that goddamn hard! We announce everything is canceled. I'll put some uniforms on the street. We confiscate the fireworks and run off anybody who looks ready to march or open a bucket of potato salad. Damn it, Ed, people are dying! Taxpayers!"

Baca was equally adamant. "This is America, Ben. It's our national holiday and you want to keep people from celebrating? It's not going to work! There will be fireworks going up all over the city no matter what we do. If we cancel there will be drunks shooting off fireworks and probably burning ammo just for the noise. You think the fire department can handle that? Can you?" He took a moment to calm himself, then continued, "Cancel, and we risk turning this town into a tinderbox on the one night when every damn fool's got a match. There's a chance good people, voters, will die. It could be worse than anything Gabriel's planning, and we don't know if he's still planning anything." He turned away from Murphy, shaking his head, and his tone became somber, anxious. "How are you going to protect people from themselves, Ben?"

Murphy was also calmer. He suggested, "We haven't mentioned martial law."

"I've considered that." Baca said. "I ran it by the governor."

"And?"

"He's willing to think about it, but not yet. He says we're over-reacting. This is just food poisoning and a crazy guy trying to take advantage. Even if Gabriel is real, it's just another case of home-grown terrorism. An isolated individual. Good police work will take care of the problem, but he stands ready to help any way he can with the full resources of his office. And so forth."

"Christ." Murphy walked to his window and looked out at the city. He lowered his voice. "Does he know about the others?"

Baca nodded and repeated, "We're over-reacting. We have no proof. He said, 'Bring me something tangible.' Then he's willing to reconsider."

Danny had listened to the exchange carefully. He felt more and more sick. He also felt confused. He walked to his father and stood beside him. Outside the window the city looked normal. A bright warm summer morning. A few clouds in a blue sky. A few cars on the street below. Maybe too few, but no one would notice that if they hadn't just listened to talk of rioting and martial law. He lowered his voice. "What did you mean about the others?"

"Mmmm?"

"You asked if the governor knows about the others. What others?"

"Don't worry about it, Danny."

"Tell him." Simon Foreman said loudly. "He deserves to know."

Danny turned, surprised. He'd been too involved by the disagreement to notice the scientist. He found him sitting at his father's desk, working on his laptop.

"It isn't necessary," Murphy said. "Besides, we're just guessing. You're just guessing."

"He can't contribute anything if you keep secrets from

him."

Murphy lifted his voice. "You're just guessing. Speculating, damn it! Wait until we're sure!"

"Ben." Baca approached and put a hand on his shoulder. "Listen to him."

"We do know," Foreman said. "We know what's happening. We just don't know why, or how."

Murphy glared around the room.

Foreman said, "You tell him or I do, Murphy."

The Chief turned on his son. Danny backed away from his eyes and the harshness in his voice. "This is secret, Danny. Top secret. You understand?"

He nodded. When that didn't look like enough, he added, "I swear, Dad. I won't tell anyone."

"Okay." Murphy gave in. He sagged, and turned away. "Tell him, Ed."

The Mayor sighed. He said, "Here's the thing, Danny. The fatality count was thirty-six an hour ago, but at least seven and maybe as many as nine were not original victims. I mean, they weren't poisoned at the concert. They got the botulism later."

"That's it? The big secret?" Danny was incredulous. "Everyone knows that. They're getting it from peoples' clothes or cars or something. Maybe Gabriel is still walking around shaking his dust—"

"No." Foreman broke in. "The hospitals are in full quarantine, Danny. They're secure. Gabriel isn't spreading his poison there, but the toxin is still spreading among the patients."

"The bacteria? Maybe it got into the hospital?"

"They've swabbed everything, tested everything, and they still lost almost ten people."

"The food?"

"The kitchen has been tested. Besides, the cafeteria food comes out of the same kitchen."

Bewildered, Danny looked from one man to another. He thought the Mayor and his father looked as lost as he felt. Foreman didn't look lost. He looked frightened. Maybe apprehensive was a better word.

Baca checked his watch. He said, "Gentlemen, it's time to

go upstairs."

The Mayor's offices took up about a third of the top floor. Baca led them past his office to a small conference room. Three technicians clustered around a long table that held a black triangular device with a panel covered with buttons and some recording equipment. In the corner, another tech, an older woman, tended a workstation. She wore a headset, whispered into the mic, and pressed the earphone to her head. Murphy glanced quickly around the room, then spoke to Danny and Foreman. "The call will come in on the conference call station—" he pointed at the black triangle "—and we'll record it. Not just the voice. The data and metadata. Nancy will trace the call. If he's using a cell phone, she can triangulate for his location. I've got patrol cars all over the city ready to move on him."

Foreman snorted.

Danny checked his phone for the time. Eleven minutes to twelve.

Baca said, "When he calls, I'll do the talking. There's paper on the table. If you've got something I absolutely have to know, write a message. If I want anyone else to talk, I'll introduce him to Gabriel. If I point at you, write me a note. Don't talk unless you're introduced. I want absolute silence from the rest of you. Understood?"

Once everyone nodded, he asked, "Any questions?"

The Chief asked, "You've got the talking points?"

Baca nodded.

"The goal is to keep him talking, right?"

"The goal is to stop the killing, Ben. Catching him is secondary."

It took a few seconds, but Murphy eventually nodded. Reluctantly.

Danny checked his phone again. Three minutes to go. He edged over to Foreman and whispered, "You think this will work?"

"No."

Danny nodded.

His father glared at him and zipped his lips.

He checked his phone again. One minute.

Everyone in the room stared tensely at the conference

46

phone.

Twelve o'clock passed. Seconds started climbing up. Murphy stretched his arms out and cracked his knuckles.

Seventeen seconds after noon, the speaker phone rang.

Mayor Baca touched the control panel to accept the call and got dead silence. After a few seconds, he said, "Hello? Gabriel?"

"Mister Baca. Finally concerned enough to listen to me?"

Danny shivered. The voice sounded inhuman. Half robot and half wolf man at first, but it was all over the place. It growled and then it almost cackled. He thought, voice distorter. Of course.

Baca was looking around the table wildly.

Foreman slid a notepad in front of him. *Voice Morphing. Disguise.*

Baca nodded and took a deep breath. "I'm very concerned, Mr...what shall I call you? Mr. Gabriel?"

"Don't waste my time, Mayor. You have my demand."

"You mean your note? I didn't understand it. Could you tell me exactly what you want?"

"I want exactly what you are giving me, Baca. I just want it sooner."

"I haven't given you anything." Baca looked around the table, confused. Murphy scribbled hastily on a pad: *Gold?*

"Didn't your note say gold? You want gold?"

Gabriel laughed. The sound screeched from the speaker. "Oh, that. Of course. I want five thousand pounds of gold, by midnight, or else." He laughed again.

Danny felt like his stomach was crawling up his throat. He looked around. Baca seemed shocked, his father angry, and Foreman lost. The Mayor said, "Pounds? You want two and a half tons of gold? Tons?"

"You're right." Gabriel was still laughing. "That is way too much for a few thousand lives. Besides, it wouldn't fit in my pocket. Tell you what, Mister Baca, let's make it ounces. Give me five thousand golden Krugerrands by midnight, or else."

"I don't have . . . did you say Krugerrands? I need time to get them."

"Take as long as you like, Mister Public Servant, but we are on my clock, not yours, and every minute is costing you."

"What do you mean? Costing how?"

Gabriel stopped laughing. "You're working from the wrong script. I sent you a new note with some sample notes. They should give you a faint idea of your price."

Baca was shaking his head. Lost. He tried changing the subject. "Can you at least give us an antidote? Tell us how to stop the deaths? You'll get your gold. I promise—"

The call ended.

The room was silent. The technicians packed up, then gathered near the door. Nancy, the woman tracing the call, shook her head at the Chief before joining the others. Baca, meanwhile, pulled out a chair and sat heavily. Murphy muttered, "Crazy. Crazy."

Foreman had a quick conference with the techies and reported, "They got nothing, of course."

Murphy slammed a fist on the table and demanded, "Of course? What the hell does *of course* mean? You expected this?"

Foreman ignored the Chief's anger. "Gabriel won't be caught this easily. He used a Virtual Private Network and routed his call through an anonymizer running on an offshore server. What Nancy got was a throw-away telephone number. It can't be traced."

Murphy cursed angrily.

Baca said, "That doesn't sound crazy."

The Chief turned on him. "Damn it, Ed, the scumbag didn't know the difference between an ounce and a pound of gold! You call that sane?"

"I guess not."

"This makes our decision easier, anyway. I'm not canceling the Fourth of July celebration for a damned lunatic."

"Dad!" Danny was getting scared. "You have to cancel it! Don't you see? He isn't crazy. You just don't know what he's really after."

"And you do?" Murphy turned on his son, eyes flashing and lips tight. "Go home, Danny. Take care of your mother and sister."

"But—"

"Just go! Get the hell out of here!"

Foreman slipped an arm around Danny and pulled him

toward the door. He spoke softly. "Give him a few hours to calm down. I'll talk to you later."

Chapter 6

"Pancakes, Danny." Emma shook him awake after ten on the Fourth. When he failed to respond, she shook him again, more roughly. "Come on, Bro. The potato salad is made and the hot dogs are boiling."

"God. What's got into you?" He rolled over and slapped at her with one of the extra pillows his mother kept piling on his bed.

She ducked easily. "First time out of the house in three days, Danny. Jannie and I have a bad case of cabin fever, and Mom said Daddy might be at the parade. I'm gonna make him tell us what's going on."

"Good luck with that." He pushed her toward the door. "Get out of here, twerp. You're coming between a man and his pancakes."

She laughed and ran to the door before turning. "You were texting all night, Danny. What's up?"

"Out!" He threw another pillow.

Once Emma left, he locked his door and checked his messages. Most of his texting had been with Rosa. He was desperate to learn what happened after he was kicked out of the conference yesterday. She seemed willing to tell him what she knew but the mayor hadn't shared much with his family. The Fourth of July celebrations were going forward with an extremely heavy police presence. Her father wasn't happy with the decision, but he had no choice. Both radio and television reports suggested that the poison was spreading somehow and callers to his office asked about rumors of a 'ghost dust' that killed anyone who went to a hospital. People were frightened and canceling the parade, picnic, and fireworks might trigger a full-blown panic.

Rosa had even more questions for Danny. She knew nothing of Gabriel's demand for gold and seemed inclined to agree with his father that Gabriel was crazy. A man who didn't care about the difference between a pound of gold and an ounce? Crazy. And even after Danny confided his concern that Gabriel could have some motive they hadn't thought of yet, she agreed with her father. The risk of a panic was too great. The show had to go on.

She did have one suggestion, though: he should talk to Tony's brother. Mike was determined to find the man who killed his family by any means possible, and he seemed to have contacts all over the community. He might have an insight that had eluded the police chief, the mayor, and even the professor.

Danny took her advice and texted Mike with what he knew or feared. He described Gabriel's disturbing phone call and his own banishment from the mayor's conference room. Then he stared at his phone until he fell asleep. Mike's response came in after 3 a.m., about the same time his father rumbled quietly through the house. The text had been simple: *Daniel—still no Parker—left his bowl under the den window—check!—call if he came home.*

Daniel. Not Danny?

By the time Danny reached the kitchen, he'd lost his appetite for breakfast. Nobody noticed. Emma spent the meal whispering with Janis and his mother spent it on her phone conspiring with Grace Baca. After the dishes were cleared she informed him that he would drive everyone to the parade at noon, sit with her and the girls and the mayor's family in the reviewing stand, attend the picnic, listen to a concert by a group that didn't throw colored chalk at each other, enjoy the fireworks and, if his father was still at work, drive everyone home. Almost an afterthought: he'd better get to bed early because the girls had to be on the bus for their soccer camp at eight a.m. They had to be in the mall parking lot at 7:30, and he was driving everyone to that, too.

He stared at her incredulously. "Really?"

She nodded angrily.

"Okay, mom." He examined her carefully. "What's this about? Dad?"

She sighed. "He asked me to keep you close. He's afraid you might get up to something."

"Something? What does he think I'll do, Mom?"

"He's afraid you'll talk about Gabriel."

"What the hell?" Danny was angry. "Every cop in town is looking for the guy who passed out the colored chalk at the *Hue and Chrome* concert. Does he think that isn't raising flags?"

"He's worried, Danny."

"He should be." He shot a sharp look at her. "Does he even have a description?"

"Four." She shook her head. "All different. He's average height with long dark hair or a long dark wig, black or navy or blue hoodie, dark glasses, and jeans. Or dark slacks. Oh, and he wears cheap tennis shoes."

"Race?"

"Either a dark Anglo or Hispanic or light African, unless he was wearing make-up."

"Great. I don't suppose the police artist came up with anything."

She shrugged. "He left a couple sketches here. He said we need to keep our eyes open today. He said just in case."

"Right."

She reached for her purse. "We need to leave in an hour. If the girls have finished packing, bring their suitcases down. We can load the car when we get back."

"Suitcases?"

"Your father decided Emma is going straight to my sister's place in Denver after camp. Janis will go with her." She gave him a bleak look. "He said I may have to meet them there, depending."

Danny nodded. He didn't have to ask what her trip to Denver would depend on.

When he reached Emmie, the girls were repacking their bags, nervously comparing the contents against a printed list.

Hurrying them proved impossible, so the family left for the parade about twenty minutes late. It didn't matter. The cop directing traffic recognized their car and pointed to a privileged parking lot. They weaved through thin last-minute crowds. Every fifty feet a heavily armed officer nodded at the Chief's family. None of them smiled.

They joined Eddie and Grace Baca in the reviewing stand just before the first band marched into view. After saying hello to the mayor and has wife, Danny sat next to Rosa.

Baca immediately pulled his phone and hit a speed dial number.

Danny asked Rosa how her summer was going. She looked puzzled until he glanced pointedly over her shoulder. Then she started talking about a party she'd attended last month and her class schedule for the coming year. The noise level went up as the first band approached. Danny leaned toward her and cupped his ear. He pointed off to the side with his eyes. She nodded and turned to her mother. "Mom, we can't hear a thing. We're going to get a coffee from the concession stand."

Grace Baca nodded, her attention divided between the parade and her husband's conversation. Danny's mother frowned when they slipped into the crowd. The girls noticed none of that. Danny thought Janis looked sad and Emmie seemed to be trying to comfort her. He would have stopped to help but Rosa was almost out of sight.

She waited for him in the gap between the press stand and the bleachers reserved for dignitaries and pulled him out of the traffic flow with a tight grip on his upper arm. She demanded, "What? What have you heard?"

"Heard?" He was alarmed. "About what? Gabriel?"

She searched his face. "Your father didn't say anything?"

"I haven't even seen him since yesterday." He sounded defensive, and maybe a little bit angry. "What the hell are you talking about, Rosa?"

She sagged. "I thought you'd know. I overheard—"

"Wait." Danny was suddenly conscious of their location below the press box. He pulled her behind the bleachers and asked, "What did you hear? Did they find Gabriel?"

"It's not him." She looked around carefully. They were

almost alone. The crowds, not very large even before the parade started, had pushed to the curb in front of the viewing stands. She whispered, "It's the hospitals."

"What about them?"

"People are dying. Again." When he didn't look like he understood, she added, "More people. The people they sent home because they weren't too sick. Some of them died at home. Some made it back to a hospital, but they're worse. A lot worse."

"Oh, god." Danny felt weak. He leaned back against the wall. "How many?"

"Dad was talking to Mr. Johnson from the Health Department. He asked if he heard right, if the number was really seventy-two now."

"Dead?' Danny asked softly.

She nodded.

He shivered. She put an arm around him and suddenly they were hugging each other desperately. After thirty or forty seconds, Danny relaxed and pulled back a bit. He pretended not to notice that Rosa's cheeks were wet. He said, "I have to go."

"Where?"

"Mike needs to know this."

"I'm coming." When he looked ready to protest, she squeezed his arms and said, "You need me, Danny."

He shook his head.

"Think about it. If you disappear alone, they'll wonder what you are up to. If we disappear together, they'll know what we were doing."

She was right of course. When he nodded reluctantly, she grinned and kissed him. "Just smearing some lipstick," she said, "to give the old folks the wrong idea."

He leaned forward. "Maybe they need more evidence?"

She pushed him away. "I'm trying to give our moms the wrong idea, not you."

"Right." He grinned nervously and they walked to the lot while a high school band worked its way through *America The Beautiful*. The music faded about the time they reached Danny's car and a second band started, very faintly, with *Stars and Stripes Forever*.

The car was baking in the early July heat. They rolled their windows down and caught a faint breeze but there was no music and no traffic at all as they left the lot. The cop doing traffic control looked surprised to see them drive off. Rosa stared out the rear window at the officer and muttered. Danny said, "What now?"

"It was the same man who waved us in. He recognized me."

"So?"

"So now we need an explanation for leaving the parade."

"Oh." He frowned. "Got any ideas?"

"I will have." She set her chin and stared out the window. "Just drive."

Maybe the holiday had emptied the streets. Maybe the rumors emptied them. It didn't matter. They were empty and, Danny suddenly realized, silent except for the occasional call of a bird. He couldn't remember the last time he heard a bird while driving. He rolled his window up and they sped through empty streets to the Massini house.

Mike did not answer the door, even when Danny knocked and then pounded on it. Rosa finally grabbed his arm. "Let's go, Danny."

"Wait." He walked around the house to see if he could find Parker in the back yard. He didn't, but he found a throw away telephone in Parker's bowl. The phone was unmarked. When he turned it on, it asked for a passcode. He thought a moment, then entered 8533. The phone vibrated and told him he had nine tries left. He stared at it, shaking his head.

Rosa nudged his arm and asked. "8533?"

"His street number. I couldn't think of anything else."

She nodded, then said, "Try 6453." When he hesitated, she explained, "His name. The keys spell Mike."

He nodded and entered the number. The phone vibrated and told him he had eight tries left.

He tried to think. What four-letter word was on Mike's mind. He took a deep breath and keyed in 8669. Tony.

Wrong.

Seven tries left before the phone wiped it's memory. Who else did he care about? His mother's name was too long and he was named after his father, so.... He glanced at Rosa, then quickly keyed in 7672. When she saw the number, she shook her head and snorted.

The phone vibrated.

He had only six chances left and no clue where to go with them. He put the phone in his pocket, and stuck one of the artist sketches under Parker's dish. It might help Mike.

Back in the car, Danny sat behind the wheel with no idea where to go. Rosa said, "Take me home."

"What?"

"Our explanation for leaving the parade. I'll tell Mom I needed something for cramps. She'll tell your mom, they'll mention it to our dads, and no questions will be asked."

Danny nodded his head and drove to the mayor's house. He stayed in the car and played with the phone while Rosa ran in. He didn't try a passcode. He'd already failed four times and he had no idea what was on the phone. It might not even be important, but Mike was trying to find Gabriel, and if he could help, he would.

When Rosa returned, she grabbed the phone and said, "Okay, let's get back to the party."

Danny held out has hand and said, "My phone."

She gave him a neutral look. "Are you going to use it in front of your dad?"

He shook his head.

"Where are you going to keep it? Does your mom clean your room? Do your laundry? What about Emma? Will she say anything if she figures out you have a private phone?"

"Okay."

She put the phone in her purse and said, "Call or text me if you need it."

"And say what?"

"I don't know. Ask me for a date, Danny. Jeez, you're a big boy. Figure something out."

"Right." He put the car in gear.

By the time they reached the parking lot, Danny's phone was ringing and Rosa had three texts from her mother demanding to know where they were. He let her handle the mothers and concentrated on navigating through a stream of cars leaving the grandstand area. Rosa dropped her phone back in her purse and said, "We need to pick them up behind the concessions."

"What? Why?"

"I don't know. They'll tell us when we get there."

"But why your mom? Isn't your dad there?"

"Apparently not any more."

"But—"

"Damn it, Danny! I don't know!" She threw herself back in the passenger seat and glared out the window while he inched the car through the mob trying to escape. She repeated softly, "I just don't know."

Traffic eased up toward the back of the lot. Danny thought he'd probably spent only ten minutes or so getting to the concession stand, but it seemed to take that long again to get everyone seated. His mother wanted Grace Baca to take the front seat. Grace insisted that the spot belonged to Anne Murphy. Both Emma and Janis were willing to take it, or even share it, but they'd somehow acquired a double order of Nachos and two cokes which they offered around. They got no takers for the nachos and were forced to throw the leftovers away on the grounds that they'd stink up the car and smear cheese and chips over everything. Rosa finally solved the logistical problem by sitting between the mothers and giving the girls free rein next to Danny.

Once the last door slammed, he looked over his shoulder and asked, "Where to now? The picnic?"

Both women shook their heads. Grace Baca said, "Our house."

He shrugged and got in line for the exit. "What's going on?"

"Your father canceled everything." His mother looked angry. "He sent a patrolman to give us a heads up so we could beat the crowd, but we couldn't find you and then the girls disappeared. We looked everywhere. We found the girls pigging out at the concession stand—"

"We were hungry," Emma interjected.

Her mother ignored her and focused on Danny. "And where were you, exactly?"

Rosa whispered something. His mother said, "Oh," and bit her lip.

Emma asked, "What?"

57

Danny ran out of patience. "What the hell is going on? Why is everything canceled?"

"We don't know."

"What happened to Mr. Baca?"

"He got a call. Then he said there was an emergency and he had to run. He just took the car and left."

"An emergency." Danny's stomach was churning. Then he saw Professor Foreman standing by the exit gate. He waved and started to pull over but Foreman caught his eye and shook his head slowly. He lifted a hand and tilted an imaginary cup against his lips, then turned and disappeared into the crowd.

Once they cleared the downtown area, traffic was light. Danny made the drive back to the mayor's house in a quarter of an hour and opened the door for Grace. To his surprise, his mother climbed out of the car with her. She told Danny, "Grace doesn't want to be alone right now and neither do I. We'll wait here until we hear from Eddie or your father."

Danny shook his head. "I can't stay, Mom. I have something to do."

His mother frowned and said, "No, Danny." Emma and Janis climbed out of the car as he got behind the wheel. "I said no! I need you here!"

"I've got something I have to do, Mom."

"I'll go with him." Rosa tried to open the passenger side door. Her mother grabbed her arm. She tried to pull free.

Anne Murphy shouted, "Danny! I said—"

He gunned the engine and sped away.

There was no one at Mike's place. He took the spare key from its hiding place and looked indoors too, but the house was empty. When he checked the yard, his flyer was missing from under Parker's bowl. He tried Mike's number, but there was no answer. He called Foreman's number. That failed too.

He called his father's office. Brenda told him his father had left instructions in case he called: Take his mother home and stay with her. She refused to put him through to his father or even take a message. He heard shouting in the background. Brenda hung up without saying another word.

Danny was beyond angry. Go home. Sit around with the women and girls. Forget Tony. Forget the crazy terrorist with a sack full of the most deadly poison in the world. Just go home. He pounded on the steering wheel, but that didn't help much. He took a few deep breaths and decided to stop for coffee on his way home.

The Campus Corner Cafe was less than a block from the university. Danny had never gotten a table there without waiting, but he saw Foreman in a booth with a couple of students from their class. Foreman waved him over and made room on the bench beside him.

Danny took the seat and waited while Foreman dealt with a few general questions about the class, test schedule, and how the tests could be taken if no one was allowed to meet for class. Then he asked if Danny was ready for his private conference, and the other students politely cleared the table. He opened a notebook between them, pointed at a blank page, and asked in a low voice, "Have you heard from your father?"

Danny shook his head. "What happened after he chased me out yesterday?"

"Not much. They talked themselves into letting the parade go on." Foreman cleared his throat and added, "You made a good point, Danny. They couldn't get past that demand for gold. It seemed so stupid."

"So the parade went on, but everything else was suddenly canceled." Danny pointed his finger at nothing on the empty page. "What happened?"

"Two things," Foreman said grimly. "First, Gabriel sent us another present: a box with a note and a baggie full of money. Ones, fives and tens."

"He sent money? Money?" Danny was shocked. "What did the note say?"

"It said, 'Pay me or I whisper my little secret to the world.'"

"That's it?"

Foreman nodded.

"How are we supposed to pay him?"

"He didn't say."

"It isn't the gold. He wants something else." Danny stared at the table, trying to think. One of the students had abandoned half a cup of coffee when he left the table. He picked up the Styrofoam cup and took a sip. It was cold and bitter. "You said two things happened. What's the second? The ghost dust?"

Foreman frowned. "Where did you hear about that?"

"Rosa said people were calling her dad's office about some rumors. Apparently people are dying again and no one knows why."

"Rosa?"

"The mayor's daughter," Danny explained.

"Good connection." Foreman leaned forward and lowered his voice. "The only thing ghostly about it is that we can't see how the toxin is being spread. It's definitely botulism, but we can't find the toxin and we can't find the bacteria."

"And seventy people are dead?"

"Eighty-one at last count. It's driving the doctors crazy."

"Didn't Gabriel send a tube with bacteria in it?"

"The test results came back this morning, Danny. Staphylococcus aureus and E. coli. That's it. Absolutely no Clostridium botulinum. No botulism. None. And they've swabbed every surface in the hospitals. Nothing. It's impossible, and yet people are dying."

Danny felt cold. He began slowly. "You remember that quote from Sherlock Holmes? 'Once you've eliminated the impossible, whatever's left—"

"Must be the truth." Foreman said impatiently. "So? What's your point, Danny?"

"Remember the girl who did her report on genetic selection? One of the things she mentioned was gene editing."

"CRISPR?" Foreman paled. He shoved the table away. Coffee ran over it in a wave as cups tumbled. He pushed Danny out of the booth, shouting, "Move, damn it!"

Chapter 7

Danny woke up when his mattress sagged but he didn't regain full consciousness until he felt a heavy hand shaking him slowly. He opened his eyes. The red dial on the radio alarm his father gave him when he started high school told him the night was barely half over. A dim glow from the night light in the hallway outlined the shape on his bed. He asked, "Dad?"

"It's me, Danny." After a pause, "Sorry to wake you."

"No problem." He pushed himself up. "Is everyone okay? Mom? Emmie?"

"I haven't seen them yet." His father turned uncomfortably on the mattress so Danny saw only a half-silhouette against his doorway. "I just got in," he said. "I wanted to talk to you first. Before I see your mother."

"What about?" He twisted on the bed and dropped his feet to the floor. He sat beside his father and stared with him at the dim wall. "What's wrong? Is it Gabriel?"

"I need to apologize. Simon Foreman came charging into my office this afternoon. He said that you figured out how people are getting poisoned in the hospitals. He said you were smarter than I thought and I should stop blowing you off." He sighed. "I never meant to blow you off, son."

"It felt like you did."

"Yeah, Well...," Murphy took a deep breath. "I'm used to robbers and killers and dope dealers and whores. Old

61

fashioned crimes. This . . . it's beyond me. Outside my experience. I'm a cop, not a scientist. Hell, I still don't understand what this crispy gene thing is, and Foreman tried to explain it twice."

"What did he say?"

"A bunch of stuff about DNA and genes and mutations. I kind of spaced out after awhile." He swallowed. "I guess after he talked to you he called the lab that cultured Gabriel's sample and asked them to test the culture for botulism. They said that was stupid at first, because it didn't have right kind of bacteria, but they did the test and called him back all excited. They said the sample was making toxin at some crazy rate." The mattress shifted when he turned to look at Danny. "You understand this stuff don't you?"

"Some of it."

Murphy didn't say anything. He just waited.

After a while, Danny said, "Think of a bacteria cell like a tractor. It's got a lot of parts that do different things. Most of them just keep the cell alive, eating and moving and reproducing, but some of them interact with the its environment in other ways. CRISPR is like a tool set that can be used to swap out parts, like you could have a plow on the back of a tractor and then swap it out for a backhoe, or a grader, or whatever you need. All that matters is having the right tools and parts."

The Chief was listening intently. He asked, "So that's what Gabriel did? He swapped out a plow part for a grader part?"

"More like he swapped it for a poison sprayer. He changed a bacteria that wasn't too bad into something that will poison anybody who catches it, and the bacteria he used are pretty common. They live on our skin and in our noses and mouths. Even in our lungs."

"Jesus!" Murphy shook his head. "What about the germs we've already have? Will only the ones Gabriel is spreading kill people?"

"Except for a couple of things," Danny said softly. "When Gabriel's bugs get together with the ones we've already got on us, they might take over. But there's something called transduction. They can trade parts with each other."

The Chief groaned. "Well, I guess I understand a little

better but I'm not feeling real happy about it." He stood up. "Try to get back to sleep, Danny. Your mom is getting the girls up at six-thirty and you're going to drive them to their bus. I won't be here much until we've got this asshole behind bars, or better yet in the morgue."

"Don't do that!" Danny spoke loudly, sharply.

"Why the hell not?"

"Gabriel isn't the main problem, Dad. Technology is the problem. You need to find everyone he's talked to, every paper he's written, every tweet, every post, every file he's tucked away in the cloud."

"He killed almost ninety people, son." The chief was getting antsy. He stood and turned toward the door. "I've got a medal for any cop that puts him down. We'll clean up his mess after he's in the ground."

"Wait." When he stopped, frowning, Danny took a deep breath and said, "I spent an hour on the internet today. I wanted to know how many people could use CRISPR to edit bacteria to make botulism. I didn't get an exact number, but it is well over twenty thousand, and that is just in this country."

Stunned, his father sagged against the wall. "You mean—"

"If Gabriel 'whispers his little secret to the world,' how many people are unhappy enough to take advantage of it?"

He got no answer for several long minutes. Then the Chief pulled himself together, took a deep breath, squared his shoulders, and said, "Go to sleep, Danny. I can't protect your mom without your help."

His father disappeared before Danny could protest. He wound up wrapping a blanket around himself and staring at the wall until it disappeared. When he woke the next morning, it hadn't moved.

The Murphy kitchen was a somber place. Janis had her back to the wall at the far end of the table. She held her phone pressed tightly to her ear. Her cheeks were wet and the pancake on her plate hadn't been touched. Next to her, Emma had speared a bite of pancake and used it to stir a pond of syrup while she listened to Janis sniffle. Danny's mother had an empty plate and cup in front of her. She looked up when Danny walked in the room.

He asked, "Where's Dad?"

"At work."

"He just got home a couple hours ago."

"He's gone again." She stood. "You want pancakes?"

"Just coffee." He shot a glance at the girls and raised his eyebrows.

His mother shrugged and started pouring a cup. She spoke over her shoulder. "The girls' bags are ready. Can you take them out?"

"Right."

He had the trunk open when she walked out carrying his coffee and wiping her eyes. He took the cup and asked, "Janis?"

"It's just so sad." She leaned her head against his cheek and sniffled. "She's saying goodbye to her mom."

Danny put his arm around her shoulders. "They wouldn't let her mother out to see Jan off?"

"No."

He made a quick decision. "Get her mother—"

"Pam. Her name is Pam, Danny."

"Right. Call Pam. See if she can get to the emergency room entrance."

"What are you thinking?" she asked hopefully.

"Maybe we can do a drive-by." He began tossing suitcases and backpacks into the trunk while his mother hurried back in the house.

The girls sat in the back seat for the trip. They paid no attention to anything outside the windows until the cop doing traffic control by the hospital's emergency lot tried to wave them off. Danny rolled his window down far enough to say, "I'm making a delivery for Chief Murphy. We aren't going in and we'll be gone in sixty seconds, officer."

He peered into the car and looked like he might have recognized the Chief's wife, but Danny didn't wait to find out. He rolled into the lot while his mother thumbed her phone.

The girls sat up and looked around wildly as they neared the entrance. The masked and gowned orderly guarding it started toward the car when he saw Danny braking, but then the door slid open and a woman in protective gear stepped out and grabbed his elbow. Danny opened the window nearest the building.

Janis was on her knees at that point, leaning over Emma and pushing down on the glass. "Mom?"

The figure waved at her. "Jannie!"

"Momma!"

Janis grabbed for the door handle. Danny beat her to the lock. She looked over her shoulder and screamed at him. "Open the door, Danny! Open my damn door!"

"You can't get out, Janis. Look at your Mom."

She turned back to the window. He mother was backing toward the Emergency doors and waving her hand frantically. No. Don't.

Janis sobbed and cried, "I love you, Mommy!"

Pam answered, "Love you more, Jannie. Have fun at soccer camp. I'll see you in two weeks!"

"Love you the most, Mom!" Janis was crying again, harder than she had at breakfast. Danny eased the car forward slowly. Janis spun toward the back window, waving furiously. Her mother slowly turned away. The patrolman shook his head when Danny drove out, but he didn't say anything and Danny didn't stop.

The bus for soccer camp left from a mall parking lot some twenty-five minutes from Mercy hospital. Janis spent the first few minutes sobbing, but between Emma's comfort and the excitement of her first trip away from home she'd calmed down by the time Danny parked near the cluster of cars surrounding the huge yellow school bus.

The girls popped out the second the car stopped. They disappeared into the mob of girls by the bus. His mother followed them slowly, looking around for any adult with a clipboard. Danny joined the rest of the men pulling luggage from trunks and stacking it by the back of the bus. Then he wandered into the mob of fathers saying goodbye to daughters who were totally focused on saying hello to friends they hadn't seen in days and may not have texted for hours and mothers struggling futilely to rope the tornado swirling around the camp counselor's magic clipboard.

The mood changed as the departure neared. The girls sought out their parents. Their hugs lingered and their goodbyes came mixed with be carefuls. Toward the end, no one said goodbye. See you soon became the mantra of choice, and it sounded like a prayer as often as a promise. Emma, when she hugged Danny, whispered, "Take care of Mom."

He squeezed her tightly. "I will, Emmie."

"I'm not coming back."

"I know."

"They're sending me to Aunt Mary's, in Denver."

"I know."

"I don't want to go to Denver, Danny."

"I know."

"Mom said maybe Janis could come too. I'd like that, but I don't want to go." She held him as tightly as he held her. She said, "Help Daddy find that man so I can come home, okay?"

He promised and then he released her.

She was reluctant to let go, but the counselor kept blowing a whistle and Janis waited awkwardly behind her. As soon as Emma broke free, Janis sidled up and gave him a one-armed hug, the sideways kind that spoke loudly of shyness. Then she surprised him by crumpling something soft into his free hand and whispering, "If you can, I mean if you see Mom, could you give her this? She'll know it."

Danny made another promise. He shoved whatever it was into his pocket and went to his mother so they could stand and wave together until the bus twisted through the clutter of cars and turned onto the access road that led to the Mall exit and the Freeway north.

Once they reached the car, Danny looked at his mother and asked, "Home?"

"I suppose. It's as good a place as any." She leaned back and closed her eyes. "That was hard. I didn't think it would be so hard."

"It was hardest on Janis. Maybe I shouldn't have taken her by the hospital."

She looked at him. "No, that was kind. You gave her something to remember, Danny. A sight to remember."

"I don't know." He found himself squeezing the steering wheel like he could strangle it. "Do you think she's going to be okay?"

"Janis? She'll be fine once they get to—"

"I meant her mother. Pam."

"Oh...." She looked out the window and spoke tiredly.

66

"She'll be fine. She thinks they have a handle on the outbreak. Situation. I don't even know what to call it, Danny."

"Dad said it's getting worse. Almost ninety people are dead now."

"Yes, but they have a treatment that seems to be working. Heavy doses of antibiotics and start treating the botulism symptoms immediately. She said that will stop the progression."

"What?" He couldn't believe it. He pulled off the street and parked. His chest felt swollen, like his heart could explode, and an astonished grin spread his cheeks. It was over? How could that be? Why did his mother feel no elation? No joy? Why did she just lean against the door? He couldn't take it. He demanded, "What's wrong?"

"Gabriel. He's out there. He's planning something, Danny. We don't know what, and we don't even know why. Nobody who died ever did anything to him. He probably doesn't even know their names, but he killed them. Why? Who's next?"

That let a lot of air out of his balloon. He put the car back in gear and drove. After a few minutes, his mother said quietly, "Ben gave me a ticket to Denver last night. I leave in the morning. He wants me to be there when Emma and Janis arrive."

"I didn't know." This was too sudden. Danny began to feel dizzy.

"He gave me two tickets. He wants you to come with me." She finally looked at him. "I said he'd wasted his money. I said you wouldn't come."

He swallowed with difficulty. "You were right."

"I didn't want you to come." He'd lost her attention again. She'd gone back to staring out the window. Her voice was almost a whisper. She wiped her cheeks and added, "I want you to stay here. Look after Ben for me. Keep him from doing anything too crazy."

That sounded a bit like an impossible mission, but he nodded anyway. "I'll try, Mom."

"I know you will." She nodded and then she sat up straighter and shook herself. "Take me to Grace's. I packed last night, so there's no reason to go home right away. Eddie wants Grace to leave too. She hasn't made up her mind. I want to talk to her."

Danny took a deep breath and tried to come to terms with what was happening. It didn't work so he asked cautiously, "Are you going to talk her into leaving, or staying?"

"I don't know yet. That will be up to Grace." She thought a moment and added, "And Rosa. She hasn't told Rosa yet. Do you think Rosa will go?"

That required no thought. "No."

"Even if Eddie told her to?"

"No."

"Why? Does she have someone here she cares about?"

"I don't know, Mom." He let a little exasperation creep into his voice. "That's just what I think."

They made the rest of the drive in silence.

Grace Baca did not seem surprised to see them. She led his mother into her formal dining room where, Danny noticed, she had an open bottle of wine and two glasses, one half full, hours before noon. Rosa appeared just then and waved him toward the kitchen where he found two bottles of beer opened. He looked at her, surprised. "What's going on, Rosa?"

"You tell me."

He picked up a beer and took a long swig, looking at her over the bottle. "Cut the crap. You know something and want to know if I know it too. I repeat, what's going on, Rosa?"

She took a tentative sip from the other bottle and watched him carefully. "My father is buying gold."

She caught him in mid-swallow. He choked, then cursed. "Damn! Why?"

"That's obvious. Gabriel. The question is why did he start now? Do you know?"

He shook his head, leaned back, and changed the subject. "Dad is sending Mom to visit my aunt in Denver. Emma will join her there after camp. Her friend, Janis, is probably going, too."

"And her mother is okay with that?" Rosa looked incredulous.

"Mom wouldn't go along with it if she wasn't, but there's something funny there. Her mom is a doctor and she told my mom that they finally have the botulism under control. If that is true, why is she letting her daughter go?" Danny shook his head. "There's something else going on. Has to be something else."

"Maybe something he needs gold for."

"Maybe." He smiled grimly. "Or it could be a reason to get his family out of town as quickly as possible."

"It could be." She looked him in the eye and pushed her bottle away. "Why don't you offer to buy me a nice lunch, Danny?"

That surprised him. "Lunch? Where do you want to eat?"

"I've been in a bit of a rut lately," she dead-panned. "Maybe we could try something different. Maybe down town."

Danny stared at her for a moment. "Different works for me, Rosa. Here's a thought: there are dozens of nice places around City Hall. We could just drive down and take our pick."

"If we're going to be in the neighborhood, we could see what our dads are up to. Maybe even invite them for lunch."

Danny pushed his beer away and stood. He held out his hand and grinned. "It's a date."

Chapter 8

The Mayor's office was open when Rosa and Danny arrived shortly before noon. It was also empty. Even his secretary had apparently deserted her desk. They peered through the door to his inner office. The visitor chairs scattered around the wood-paneled room faced a white board on an easel standing in the far corner. A mix of ceramic and cardboard coffee cups littered the tables and his desk.

Rosa stepped into the office and wrinkled her nose. Danny, immediately behind her, looked over the dark smudges on the white board. Behind him, a harsh voice demanded, "What are you doing? Who are you?"

Rosa spun around. She said, "Where's Dad, Patty? We want to invite him for lunch."

The middle-aged woman confronting them frowned. "The Mayor is in conference. Does your mother know you're here?" She pointed at Danny. "Who's he?"

"You remember Danny Murphy. The Chief's son? I know you were introduced at the awards dinner last May. Do you think Papa will be done with his conference in time for lunch?"

"I'm sure he won't." She walked into the inner office and stood aside, holding the door. "You have to leave now, Miss Baca. Does your mother know you are here? With Mr. Murphy?"

"She knows we're together. Why don't you call her if you're

worried about me? What's going on, Patty?. You never acted like this before."

The woman closed the door firmly, then strode to her desk. She picked up her phone and started to dial, but she suddenly ran out of steam. "I'm sorry, Rosa. Things are happening. Everyone is nervous." She sighed. "I shouldn't take it out on you."

"But what is going on? Mom is jumpy and Dad has hardly been home all week."

"Ask the Mayor. I can't talk about this, but I'm sure you'll see him tonight. He has something to give you and your mom."

Danny couldn't help himself. "Airplane tickets?"

Patty didn't look surprised by the suggestion. She bit her lips and spoke directly to the girl. "Whatever it is, you should listen to your father." She hesitated, then added softly, "My Jim is taking the kids on a little vacation tomorrow. Just a short one. Just to get out of town. For a break, you know?"

"My God!" Rosa backed away from her, staring. She glanced at Danny and saw that he wasn't surprised. She turned and walked quickly out of the office.

Patty turned to him. "It's just that they miss their grandparents. That's all."

"Of course."

He found Rosa in the hall, leaning against the wall opposite the mayor's door. She wiped her cheeks when he leaned beside her. She said, "They're sneaking us to safety and leaving everyone else here!"

"If you had a baby, wouldn't you try to keep it safe?" He sighed. "Maybe they think they can't do their job if they're worrying about us."

She looked at him expressionlessly. "So you're going?"

"No. I told him I wouldn't leave. He's still pushing, but I won't go." He looked at Rosa. "I told Mom that you wouldn't go either."

"You told her," she said flatly. "Just when did you make this decision for me?"

"She asked after we dropped the girls at the bus, on the drive to your place. That was when I found out about your Dad buying tickets. I haven't had a chance to talk about this

71

before, Rosa. I wasn't hiding anything, and I didn't make the decision for you. Mom asked what I thought you'd do and I gave her my opinion of you, that's all."

"What did she say about you? I imagine she wants you to go with her?"

"She wants me to stay here and take care of Dad."

Rosa looked surprised. "He can't take care of himself?"

"I don't think she meant it like that. She wants me to keep him from thinking too much like a cop."

"Can you do that?"

"I can try."

"Okay." Her cheeks were mostly dry, but she wiped them again for good measure and pushed away from the wall. "We should get going."

"Where?"

"Your Dad's office," she said firmly.

"Do you think we'll have better luck there?" But he shrugged and pressed the button for the third floor when the elevator doors closed. They reopened on a man in a suit behind a folding table who took one look at them and asked what they were doing in the building.

Surprised, Danny asked, "Who are you?"

He flashed a badge, said, "Federal Bureau of Investigation," and repeated his question.

Danny introduced himself and Rosa, adding, "We're here to see my father."

The agent pushed a clipboard across the table. "Sign in, please, and let me see your identification." He glanced at Rosa. "Both of you."

While they sorted out their driver's licenses and signed the first two lines on the visitors list, Danny said, "I've never seen you guys here before. What's this all about?"

"The mayor will be making an announcement later."

Rosa started to ask a question. She got as far as, "Is it—"

Danny accidentally stepped on her toe.

The agent looked at her curiously. "Is it what, miss?"

She looked flustered. "The chief? Can we see him now?"

He stared at her without answering, waiting to see what she'd do next, but she recovered and repeated her question. "Is it possible to see Chief Murphy?"

He shook his head slowly. "I'm sorry, Miss Baca. The chief is unavailable today."

Danny said, "Then I'll talk to Brenda. His—"

"Mrs. Gander is also unavailable."

"Then I'll talk to—"

"Unavailable, Mr. Murphy. Everyone is unavailable."

"Then why the hell did you make us sign in?" Danny was angry. He shrugged Rosa's hand off his shoulder, leaned over the table, and took a deep breath.

She stepped on his toe. Hard. "Let's go, Danny. We'll talk to them tonight."

Right. He took a moment, then turned and jabbed repeatedly at the down button on the elevator. It hadn't left the third floor, so the doors opened quickly enough, and he still had a good glare left for the agent as they slid shut. It might have been more gratifying if the agent had even noticed, but he was busy talking into his lapel.

By the time they reached the parking garage, Danny had himself more or less under control. He asked, "Where do you want to go next?"

"Well, so far this has been the worst lunch date ever. Don't you ever feed a girl?"

"When I must. What's your pleasure, girl?"

"Burgers and beer or pizza and beer?"

He snorted. "No beer."

She stopped walking. "Do you have a better idea?"

"I'd like to swing by the hospital first and get back to our lunch date later."

"The hospital? What on Earth . . . I mean, why?"

So he explained about the drive to the soccer bus and the stop in the hospital parking lot and Janis and the message she'd given him for her mom. He pulled it from his pocket, as much to see what it was himself as to show Rosa, and found a fluffy little pink bunny with long droopy ears and huge eyes nestled in his palm. Rosa looked from it to his face and back and bit her lips to keep from smiling. He looked at the bunny and blushed. He said, "There's another reason."

"There would have to be."

He stuffed the bunny back in his pocket and focused on getting to Mercy. Rosa kept mostly silent on the drive, although Danny did have to ignore an occasional quiet giggle. They faded quickly once they found parking and started over the nearly empty lot.

A small group of reporters and cameramen blocked the emergency entrance when they arrived. A masked and gowned woman stood in front of the automatic door, flanked by an orderly and two cops. If their job was to hold the press back, they were not necessary. No one seemed eager to approach the door too closely.

Rosa started to push into the crowd. Danny held her back. He whispered, "We don't want to be recognized."

The woman finished answering a question. "...so while the fatality count has increased, the most recent casualties have been people who went to the concert and either didn't seek medical help or were discharged with non-life threatening symptoms and never returned when their botulism symptoms reappeared. The patients in the hospital are all either stable or improving, so it is important that anyone who might have symptoms of botulism should seek medical attention immediately. On your other question, we don't have an accurate mortality rate. We don't know exactly how many people were exposed, so we can't say what percentage of them died."

A woman near the front called, "You know about how many people came for help after the concert, don't you?"

The doctor nodded. "Over three hundred."

"So would it be safe to say that the mortality rate is around thirty percent? Approximately?"

This time, the nod came more slowly, reluctantly.

The crowd went wild. Everyone tried to shout a louder question.

In the rear, Danny raised his hand. He opened it. The doctor, scanning the crowd for a friendly face, froze when she saw the small pink bunny. She pulled one of the officers to her and spoke in his ear. He looked at Danny, nodded and spoke into a mic clipped to his collar. Danny turned away from the crowd and stepped back a few feet.

Rosa followed him, demanding, "What's wrong? Where are you going?"

"We lucked out," he told her. "I didn't know how to get to

Janis' mom, but that was her talking. I saw her when we drove Janis by on the way to camp. I think she'll get to us."

"I think you're right." Rosa faced him, her back to the hospital wall, and her eyes on the empty lot. She slowly raised her hands and said, "Don't make any sudden moves, Danny."

"What?" He started to turn. She kicked his shin and hissed, "I said slowly!"

He saw the alarm in her eyes and moved his hands away from his body as he turned. The two men approaching him didn't wear uniforms, but they carried very large pistols. Glocks, like his father carried sometimes. He took a deep breath and asked, "Police?"

"Put your hands behind your head."

They did. Slowly. Rosa identified herself, adding, "My father is Mayor Baca."

"You have ID?"

"In my purse."

"Okay. Step away from your friend."

"You mean Danny Murphy? The Chief of Police's son?"

"Shit." The gun barrel focused on Danny dropped an inch. "You have ID too?"

He nodded.

"What have you got in your pocket?"

"A pink bunny."

One of the plainclothes cops laughed. The other said, "Take the bunny out of your pocket. Slowly."

Danny nodded and said, "It isn't loaded."

Rosa snorted. The cop with the gun still pointed at Danny said, "What about it, Jim? You worked the parade yesterday. You remember him?"

"Yeah. I think he was in the stand with the mayor. Her too."

"Well, hell." He holstered his firearm. "What are you doing here?"

"Can we lower our arms?"

"Just keep your hands out of your pocket. I don't care if that bunny isn't loaded. I don't want you going for it."

Danny laughed. Rosa lowered her hands and rubbed her upper arms. She said, "We need to see the doctor."

"Are you sick?" The one named Jim took a step back.

Danny answered. "No, her daughter asked me to give her the bunny when I took her to the bus this morning. They didn't really get a chance to say goodbye and I promised the little girl."

The cops glanced at each other. One asked, "Does your father know you're here?"

"I tried to tell him but I couldn't get past the FBI agent at the elevator."

Jim asked his partner, "You want to call this in?"

"I don't want any part of it." He looked around. "We can't take them in the hospital."

Rosa asked, "Why not?"

The cop ignored her. "How about we find an orderly and send the bunny to the ER with him? That way the doctor will make the call?"

Jim nodded and gestured toward the main lobby entrance. Ten minutes later, they both wore green hospital gowns and face masks. The bunny sat on a glass table in the hotel lobby, and Pam sat opposite them, buried under even thicker protective garments. She spent more time looking at the bunny than at them. She said, "It was so sweet of Jannie to send Hopalong to me, but it wasn't really necessary."

"She's worried about you."

"I'm safe here."

"Are things really getting better?"

"Of course. Some of the original patients started showing worse symptoms and they all require more antitoxin than we expected, but we're holding our own."

"What about you? Are the staff safe?"

"We're taking precautions." Pam thought a moment, hesitated, and then pulled a handful of plastic rectangles out of her pocket. She picked up the bunny and left the rectangles in its place. "We can't find any sign of the botulism bacteria, but a combination of methicillin and cipro seems to keep the patients from getting worse. We started taking a tablet of each every day as a prophylactic and so far we've all been safe." She stood abruptly. "You shouldn't stay here any longer than you have to."

Danny stood with her. "Can I give her a message? I'll call Emmie tonight. Maybe I can talk to Janis too."

76

"Thank her for sending me Mr. Hopalong. Tell her he'll keep me safe, so she shouldn't worry. Tell her to go to Denver if she has to. Tell her to be a good girl." She swallowed and added, "Tell her Mommy loves her."

Pam walked quickly back into the hospital corridor.

When Danny looked at Rosa, she was closing her purse and the table was empty. He started back to the car. When Rosa asked where they were going now, he said that they were officially back on their lunch date.

"Lunch? It's almost four o'clock," she said. "Time for burgers and beer."

He shook his head. "I'm a cheap date. You'll be lucky to score a sandwich and a coffee."

Traffic was noticeably light for a Saturday afternoon near campus. They found parking directly in front of the Corner Cafe. Half the tables inside were empty. Simon Foreman had one of the others to himself. He stood when they approached, nodded at Danny, and held out his hand. "You must be Rosa Baca."

"How did you know?"

"I know Mr. Murphy."

Danny left them to finish their introductions and walked to the counter. He returned with a tray loaded with coffee, sandwiches, and chips. Rosa quickly snagged a bag of chips. She ripped it open and started wolfing them down. Danny sipped a coffee and asked casually, "Any news from my father's office?"

"I was going to ask you the same question."

"All Dad tells me is, 'Take care of your mom and sister.' Then he sends my sister out of town and buys my mother a ticket to Denver. He won't talk about Gabriel."

"He sent his family out of town?" Foreman whistled. "Why not you?"

"I refused to go."

"Okay." Foreman took a deep breath and said, "At eight thirty this morning, I got a call from the chief telling me my job as an unpaid voluntary consultant was no longer covered by the city budget and cautioning me not to come to City Hall for our scheduled meeting. He said that my position had been filled by professionals from the federal government who had a good handle on the situation."

Danny set his coffee down and stared. "I don't know what that means."

"Sure you do. It means something got their attention."

"But what? Dad was going to send them that first note when the forensics department was done with it. Did he do that?"

"They got it Thursday."

"When we saw you after the parade, you said Gabriel's second message included a note and a baggie full of money. The note threatened to 'whisper his little secret' to the world."

Foreman nodded. "That's always been the real threat. You know that."

"Did the Feds got involved before or after they received that note?"

"I was fired today." Foreman shrugged. "They had time to look at yesterday's note, but not much time."

"So something in one of the notes got their attention."

"That's the logical inference." The professor smiled. "It was either the chalk or one of the notes, probably the first. They had it longest."

Danny frowned. "Was there anything special about the money?"

"They counted it and then sent the baggie to forensics. I imagine the Feds took charge of it when they took over this morning. In any case, they decided to take over before they had the baggie of money, so something else pushed their button."

Rosa, meanwhile, had finished her chips and opened one of the sandwiches. She opened her purse and felt around for her phone. "I can probably get an answer out of Dad. I'll see if he came home."

"What can we do in the meantime?" Danny looked hopefully at Foreman. "Did you hear anything from the state lab about our gene editing idea?"

He shook his head. "They'd have to sequence the genome of both strains of bacteria in Gabriel's sample to prove that Gabriel edited them and they don't have the resources for that. I know they expedited the sample to the CDC, but it will take time and the answer will go to the feds, not to you and me."

Danny frowned. "But there is still the culture result. The toxin."

"Right." Foreman looked carefully around the cafe. It was mostly empty and no one was paying them any attention. Still, he spoke softly. "A sample that we know contained nothing but staph and E. coli bacteria is producing botulism toxin."

"How can we explain that without gene editing?"

"We can't."

Rosa suddenly tossed her phone on the table. She said angrily, "We have to go, Danny. Our moms are pissed. Apparently we're too young to be out alone."

Danny groaned and started to stand. Rosa crossed her arms and said, "I told Mom we'd be back when we got back. She asked me where we were and what we were doing that was so important. I told her we were looking for condoms and a sleazy motel."

Danny stared at her. "You know your chances of a second date with me are going way down?"

"I don't care. She makes me so mad." She ripped open the second sandwich wrapper and took a bite, then looked at the wrapper, chewing thoughtfully. She asked, "How did you pay for this, Danny?"

He looked confused. "I paid cash. Why?"

"When Gabriel sent that colored chalk the first time, he was telling us that he was spreading the poison with chalk."

"Yes?" Danny couldn't take his eyes off her. He felt a chill. "So?"

Foreman had the same problem. "Say it, Rosa."

"This time he sent money. What if he poisoned the money?"

She left the question on the table. Danny could think of no way to answer it. He imagined the bills he'd handed the cashier. If they'd been infected, the bacteria would spread to every piece of paper they brushed against. And not just paper: the cashier's hands. The money she touched. The plates. The food. Anyone who got change from that register. Anyone.

He felt like throwing up.

Simon Foreman apparently had the same vision. He asked, "Do you both carry credit cards?"

Rosa lifted her purse from the floor by her feet and opened it. Danny thought she was looking for plastic until she pulled out the stack of cards Pam gave them at the hospital and dealt one to Foreman and two to Danny. Methicillin and Cipro.

Foreman said, "The mayor needs to know about this. Can either of you get into City Hall?"

Danny shook his head. Rosa said, "Our mothers can at least get a call through."

Foreman abruptly scraped his card off the table popped it open. He swallowed the tablet and stood. "Let's go."

Chapter 9

Danny Murphy managed less than three hours of sleep Saturday night. The day had ended when he and Rosa walked into her house and their mothers opened up on them. The screaming match ended when Rosa tossed a handful of drug packs on the coffee table. Both mothers stared at the pile of plastic-sealed tablets. Grace looked horrified. Anne looked puzzled. She raised her eyes to her son and demanded, "What are those, Danny?"

He said, "Rosa will tell you," and went to search for their phones.

He found them where the ladies abandoned them when they heard the front door open, side by side on the kitchen table. On the way back, he stopped and filled two glasses with water. He carried everything back to the living room in time to hear his mother whisper, "Oh, my God," over and over.

Grace Baca said nothing until he handed her her phone. She took it reluctantly but dialed with increasing urgency. It took her almost an hour to reach the mayor. Anne Murphy never did get through to the Chief of Police, but Anne told her the mayor would give him the word. Grace and Anne each took two pills. Then they sat and waited as dusk seeped into the room. Every now and again one said, "what if—," but no one ever finished the thought. Once Anne said, "At least Emma is safe," and added an afterthought, "and Janis, of course."

Around eight, Danny's stomach growled. Grace looked up and suggested calling for pizza. Danny asked how she would pay and if she wanted change. Then Rosa said she thought there were leftovers in the refrigerator, but before she made it to the kitchen their phones started ringing.

The mayor and chief left identical instructions: pack lightly, take all valuables and important papers, be at the airport when it opened and buy tickets on the first flight out. If none were available, use the tickets they already had. Don't stop on the way to the airport. Try not to alarm anyone, but get out.

The instructions were simple and clear. Neither woman wanted to follow them. They refused to leave without their husbands. Eddie Baca only convinced Grace by pointing out that Rosa wouldn't leave without her. Ben Murphy pointed out that Anne needed to be in Denver when Emma arrived and that she had to convince Danny to accompany her. Both emphasized that the trip was only temporary. The FBI would have things straightened out in a few days. Gabriel couldn't hide forever.

Danny gave up listening to his mother's arguments and drove her home where, despite serious misgivings, she packed. Then she repacked, tossing aside dresses and jackets and even favorite shoes when she saw the pile of deeds and titles and bank books and tax records and jewelry still waiting for bag space.

While his mother agonized over how many bags she could check, Danny stuffed some underwear and two days worth of socks, shirts, and pants into his backpack. Then he built three sandwiches and carried them to her bedroom with a cup of tea. She barely noticed when he slipped out of the house and texted Rosa from the back yard: *Call me.*

When his phone rang ten minutes later, she whispered, "What is it?"

"Can you talk?"

"I'm in the bathroom. I have to be quiet."

"Do you still have my thing? The thing you took from me?"

"The . . . oh, yes. Of course."

"With you?"

She hesitated. "I can get it."

"Try 4676. Call me back."

"4676?"

"Horn. Like Gabriel's horn."

"Oh. I'll try." She hung up. A few minutes crept by while Danny stood in the dark and waited. His phone rang again and she said, "Five tries left."

"Okay." He sighed. "Do you have any ideas?"

After a long silence, she said, "4653? Gold?"

It didn't feel right, but he had nothing better. "Do it."

Someone's breath was heavy on the line. He couldn't tell if it was hers or his. Then she said, "Four."

"Damn."

"Danny?"

"I know, but I don't know what else to do." He waited for what felt like too long, then asked softly, "What are you going to do?"

She knew immediately what he meant. "I'm not leaving."

"Neither am I." He asked, "How are you going to get your mom on the plane without you?"

"I have a couple of ideas. You?"

"I won't have a problem. She has to take care of Emmie."

"Lucky you."

"Yes." He hung up.

His mother finished packing well after midnight. He carried their bags to the car and lay down for a few hours, but sleep came slowly. Hours passed before the tightness in his chest faded away. He found himself jerking awake over and over. When he could finally get up and dress, he went to wake his mother, but her room was empty. He found her in the kitchen cleaning the sink. When he appeared, she said, "We need to leave soon, Daniel. We're stopping for Grace and Rosa. We'll give them a ride." She sipped her coffee. "There's no point in leaving two cars at the airport for God knows how long."

He nodded. "Have you been up long?"

"I haven't slept."

"You need rest, Mom."

"I'll rest when I know Emma is safe. And you, and your father." She threw her sponge in the sink. "I'll rest when Gabriel is dead. When this nightmare is finally over."

Danny pushed himself to his feet and stepped behind her. He put his hands on her shoulders and kneaded the stiff muscles there. He said softly, "I was up most of the night too, Mom. You know what kept me up? Thinking what would happen when someone kills Gabriel, the FBI or a cop or even me. What kept me up was wondering if things could go back to normal, and I don't see how. I can't see a way back, Mom."

"We'll damn well make a way back, Daniel," she snapped. "We have to!"

Grace and Rosa waited beside a small mound of suitcases and overnight bags at the foot of their driveway. Danny quickly packed the trunk and they walked their bags into the airport after an unexpectedly quick drive. The only difficulty they encountered came when they tried to find parking. The long term lots were completely full. He parked in short term and assured his mother that his father would have the car picked up to stop her from fretting over the expense.

The Baca's flight departed at eight-ten. Danny and his mother left for Denver half an hour later. They cleared security at six-thirty and bought coffee and breakfast sandwiches. Grace insisted on paying, but Danny beat her to the register with a credit card in hand. Rosa quickly stepped in front of him and pushed two twenties at the clerk, then told the woman to keep the change. It was a tip.

When he started to complain, she gave him a bland look, muttered, "Idiot," and carried the tray back to the mothers. It took a few seconds for the light to dawn. Then he followed her back and announced that he wanted to buy some snacks for the flight before they boarded.

No one had much appetite, but the clutter of paper sacks on the table gave everyone something to look at while they weren't talking about poison. Eventually Anne asked Grace if she'd been able to talk to Eddie last night.

"He called," she shook her head, "but he's under so much pressure! The reporters. The council. The health department. All those people who lost someone, or have someone in the hospital. And he can't find the gold. Anne, he doesn't even know what is expected of him. Every day he goes to his office and he looks like he's walking into a lion's den. I feel so bad for him."

84

Danny had been half-listening while she spoke, but something changed at the table. He looked around. Grace had fallen silent. She seemed focused inward. His mother watched her with sympathy, but that was expected. Rosa, though: Rosa had forgotten her mother. She stared intently at Danny, as though willing him to wake up, to pay attention.

She kicked him and nodded down the concourse.

He looked at her, confused. She kicked him again, then pushed away from the table and announced, "I'm going to look for a newspaper."

"I'll go with you. I want to get those snacks."

Both mothers looked suspicious. Anne said, "Don't get lost, Danny. We have to board in an hour."

He mumbled something reassuring and hurried after Rosa.

She was waiting for him behind a magazine rack in the nearest souvenir shop. When he approached, she threw an arm around him and pulled him to her. She stood on her toes and whispered in his ear, "Are you stupid or just asleep? Idiot!"

"What do you mean? What happened?"

"What did Mike call you in his last text?"

He thought a moment. "Daniel?"

"And what did he ask you to do?"

"Look for Parker?" He had no idea what set her off. She was making no sense at all.

She slapped his head and demanded, "Where did he tell you to look for Parker?"

"Under the den window?"

Rosa dropped back onto her heels. She put a hand on each of his cheeks, pointed his face directly at her, and spoke slowly. "Listen carefully, Danny. There might be a clue here. Daniel. Look. Den. What did Daniel find in the den?"

"A lion?" It hit him. "A lion!"

She pulled Mike's phone from her purse and opened the pass code screen. She said, "We have only four tries left. Do you want to use 'lion' for one of them?"

He nodded.

She carefully keyed in 5466, waited a second, and squealed, "Got it!"

85

She opened the phone. It had a bare-bones installation: only the camera, messenger, and contacts held any data. The only photo was an old picture of Parker standing beside his bowl and looking up into the camera. Danny grabbed her hand when Rosa started to close the photo. He stared at it for a long time before he finally let go and wiped his cheek.

When Rosa started to say something, he growled, "Don't call me an idiot."

"I wasn't going to, Danny." She sounded almost tender. "Are you ready?"

He nodded. She gave him a few more seconds before switching over to the messenger. The only text was from Parker to Parker. It asked a simple question: Who are we?"

She opened the contacts list. It had only one entry, Peter, with a number neither of them recognized. Danny shook his head. "Mike's off the deep end. What's he so paranoid about?"

"He must have a reason." Rosa bit her lips. "Call him."

He clicked on the entry and waited for the ringing to stop. "It's about time."

The voice was familiar. Danny said, "Hi, M—"

"No names!"

"What the hell is going on, M—"

The phone died. Danny and Rosa looked at each other, puzzled. She suggested, "Call him back. Go along with him."

He shrugged and dialed again.

"Who's calling?"

Danny took a deep breath. "Spidey."

"Better. Delete the picture and text and call back from somewhere you can talk." The connection dropped.

Rosa pulled Danny from the store and led him to an unused gate. He dialed again and when Mike answered, he asked, "What's with the name game? You recognize my voice."

"I won't always answer the phone, Parker. Always identify yourself as Spidey. If you miss one time, both phones are trashed. Understand?"

"Right." Danny was about out of patience. He said, "I might not always be the person calling, Peter."

"I don't like that." After a pause, "Who else knows about the phone?"

"Mary Jane."

86

Mike waited longer this time before saying, "Okay. Make sure she knows about Spidey."

"She's right here. Do you want to talk to her?"

"No, just tell me what the hell is going on, Parker."

Parker? Now he was a dog? Danny asked, "What do you mean?"

"There are uniforms and plainclothes crawling all over the city looking for bags of money. If they find one, they disinfect the hell out of it. If they find someone who found a baggie, the confiscate it and the guy."

"Oh, God." Danny held the phone tightly to his ear, but Rosa had her ear jammed next to his and snaked her arm around his neck so tightly that he couldn't pull away. He asked, "They confiscate the guy? What does that mean?"

"He disappears. They tell his buddies he's going to a hospital, but they don't say which one and if someone calls around, none of the local hospitals have admitted him."

"This happened a lot?"

"I repeat, what's going on?"

So he explained about Gabriel's last message, the packet of money, and the bacteria with edited genomes that Simon Foreman had discovered. Mike listened carefully before asking, "He hasn't demanded the gold again?"

"Not that I know, but Dad kicked me out last Thursday and the FBI took over yesterday morning. There's no telling what's going on now."

"Okay." Mike said nothing for a few seconds, then continued, "Look, Parker, you've got to get back in with your father. We need to know what Gabriel is doing."

"Not happening, Pete. I told you, Dad isn't running the show any more. The feds took over."

"They will keep him informed. Besides, you've made good suggestions in the past. Show them you can be useful."

"How the hell am I supposed to do that? I've got nothing to bring to the table."

"Think of something. Maybe we can give you something. Let me work on it." He hesitated, then asked, "We done for now?"

Rosa squeezed Danny's arm and whispered in his ear. He nodded and relayed her question. "One last thing. Who is we?"

"People who want Gabriel stopped. People who lost someone. People who want their world back. There are more of us every day. I'll text you when I need a call or you can call me when you have something. Okay?"

"Another last thing, Pete. Pick a name. Am I a dog or a bug?"

Mike laughed. "Bye."

Danny closed the phone and asked Rosa, "Are you staying here? For sure?" When she nodded, he handed her the phone and said, "We better get back. Your mom needs to board pretty soon."

When they reached the table, the women were sitting side by side. Anne had been crying and Grace had a hand on her arm. Rosa took a chair silently, but Danny couldn't help himself. He asked, "What's wrong? Did something happen?"

His mother shook her head. "I'm being silly. That's all."

"Okay, but what's wrong?"

She took a napkin and inspected it for ketchup or smears of egg, then blew her nose. "I was thinking about Emma, that's all. I know she's only been gone one day but it's her first trip away from home and I miss her. She's so sweet. And cute. I yelled at her for wasting her trip money on those nachos at the parade Friday, but I wasn't really mad. I just didn't want her to run out of money."

Danny asked, casually, "What did she say?"

"She said Janis bought the nachos, but I know she doesn't have any money either. Pam gave me enough for her, but I was waiting until we got to the bus."

Danny nodded. He felt cold. He glanced at Rosa and found her staring, looking frightened. He said, "Well, it's almost boarding time. We should get to the gates."

They gathered their carry-ons and started down the concourse. It was more crowded than Danny expected. He told himself that he wasn't used to traveling at that hour. It was probably normal.

The flight board at the Baca's gate notified passengers that their flight was delayed. Danny and Rosa got their mothers seated with the bags and pushed into the crowd to see what was going on, but the airline counter was unmanned. He worked his way back out of the crowd and walked over to the nearest departures board. Most of the flights later that day were marked as delayed. He asked Rosa to call the airline and walked back toward the security gate. He stopped the first TSA agent he ran into, a woman walking around the gates searching the floor, along the walls, and under the chairs, and asked if she knew what was going on with all the flight delays.

She answered with a smile that didn't reach her eyes and a suggestion that he call his carrier. He explained that his mother needed to get to Denver to see his little sister who'd be stranded in a strange city if they missed their flight. The woman didn't have an ounce of sympathy in her body. He tried charm. That didn't work either, but he wasn't very good at it. Finally he gave up and walked back toward the gate only to meet all three of them coming toward him. When he asked what happened, his mother pointed at the nearest departure board. All flights out were canceled.

The farther they walked the more crowded the concourse became. The crowd grew with every gate they passed as the airport emptied. Eventually Danny was jostled one time too many. He pulled his mother out of the traffic stream. He asked for her phone and dialed his father. When Brenda answered he told her to get the Chief on the line.

Maybe he wasn't busy. Maybe his wife's number got his attention. Maybe Brenda heard the urgency in Danny's voice. Whatever the reason, Ben Murphy answered the call sounding worried. "What's wrong, Danny?"

"The airport's closed. Nobody's getting out today."

Murphy cursed, then said, "Okay, get your mother back to the house and stay with her."

"That's not going to happen. I'm leaving as soon as she's settled."

"I don't have time for this, Danny. Just do as you're told."

"What's happening at the hospitals, Dad? Are they filling up again?"

His father hesitated, then asked, "What do you mean?"

"I heard cops all over town are looking for plastic baggies with money in them. Homeless guys who find money are disappearing. TSA agents are searching the airport. You know what I haven't heard? I haven't heard a single damned public service announcement warning people about poisoned money."

After a longer pause, Murphy said, "That wasn't my decision."

"Well, this is my decision. I'm driving up to the soccer camp and I'm going to bring Emma and Janis back. You know why I'm doing that? Because you didn't make a decision and Emma and Janis bought themselves a double order of nachos and coke at the parade Friday. They didn't have enough money, and they bought nachos and coke. Where do you think they got the money, Dad?"

He hung up and found his mother and Grace and Rosa all staring at him. He didn't care. He grabbed a couple of bags and pushed blindly back into the mob shuffling toward the exit.

Chapter 10

Somewhere on the walk out of the airport, Anne decided that Danny was not going to rescue Emma without her and she spent the drive to the Baca's explaining why her presence was vital. Her baby needed her. If the girls were sick, they'd need a woman to help them. The camp wouldn't let the girls go without their legal guardian present, and that was her. And finally, her baby needed her. While she pressed her arguments, Grace made soft, comforting noises, Danny drove, and Rosa quietly dialed her phone.

His phone rang while his mother was saying goodbye to Grace Baca. He'd just finished carrying Grace's bag into her house. He recognized his father's office number and stepped into the kitchen to answer the call. His father got down to business quickly. "Have you left yet, Danny?"

"We're dropping off Grace now. I'll leave as soon as I get Mom home."

"I made a mistake, Danny."

"What?"

"Rosa called me. She's a smart girl. You don't know how smart."

"What did she say?"

"She said we were both being stupid. She said I should talk to that professor of yours about Emma. Well, about the whole situation, but about Emma too."

"You talked to Doctor Foreman?"

"I told him everything that's been going on. He estimated at least half our girls would need to come home, and he said that we couldn't wait to get Emma help while you played hero. And he's right."

"I'm not playing hero, Dad!"

"You're not thinking about Emma." Murphy sighed. "I called the camp director and confirmed that a lot of our girls aren't feeling well. The kids from other towns are okay, but not ours. She was thinking about calling a doctor. I told her I'd have someone there ASAP and then we'd need to get the girls home. I called the state health department and arranged for them to bring a local doc up to speed and get him to the camp. Then I arranged for a school bus to make a run up there and pick up the girls."

"So you've handled it?" Danny felt both angry and relieved and he felt ashamed of both feelings. "I'm out of it? That's what you're saying?"

"Listen to me, Danny! This isn't for general release. The state police set up check points this morning. All roads out of the city are closed. They—"

"They can't do that!" Danny exploded. "How can they do that?"

"The governor mobilized the national guard. The freeways will be completely barricaded sometime this afternoon. In the meantime, they have APCs and troops stationed at the checkpoints. The state cops are in charge, for now, but—"

"Why, Dad?" Danny's mind was reeling. "This doesn't make sense!"

"Listen!"

"Okay." Danny shut up.

"Apparently we didn't understand Gabriel's message quickly enough. He must have left some of his little presents at the airport and train and bus terminals. There have been outbreaks of botulism in Kansas City, Los Angeles, and San Francisco. The Feds think they are contained for now, but they won't take any chances. Nothing and nobody is getting in or out of town until this situation is handled."

"In or out?" He abruptly sat down on the tile floor. Rosa came into the kitchen and stood quietly, watching him and trying to figure out what was happening. He asked, "How will people eat? Where will they get fuel? What about the commuters?"

"We have enough food in the city to last a couple days. After that, truckers will have to drop their trailers at the check points and trucks from the city will pick them up. As for the rest, we're on our own until we catch Gabriel."

Danny whispered, "Is it really that bad?"

"Over two hundred are dead now. About fifty of them were homeless. My cops are poking everybody sleeping on the streets to make sure they're really asleep. We're trying to keep it low-key. We can't afford a panic."

"Can't afford? Jesus! Don't people deserve some warning?"

"Suppose people decide to run? Suppose the state guard has orders to shoot?"

"Shoot? They'd shoot?"

Rosa knelt beside him. Danny put his phone on speaker so she could hear.

". . . can't allow this thing to spread, Danny. The whole damned country could go under."

"Okay. I get it, so just how in hell are you going to get a bus past the barricades?"

"I got the bus, Danny, but I couldn't find a driver. Nobody wanted to spend three hours in a bus full of botulism toxin, so I called Eddie and he authorized the city to lease the bus and provide a city driver. That's you."

"Okay." He closed his eyes a moment and rephrased his question. "How the hell am I going to get a school bus past the barricades?"

"Easy," the Chief said. "The state police will escort you from the checkpoint to the soccer camp. They will ensure that no one leaves the bus at the camp and that everyone who boards it there stays on board. The state escort will drop off when you get back to the check point. My officers will take you the rest of the way to the hospital."

"Is the hospital expecting Emma and Janis?"

"It's been told to expect about thirty patients."

"Do they have room for so many?"

"They're making room." He changed the subject. "Just get to the city yard. A bus will be gassed up and stocked up. Drive

93

carefully, but make as good time as you can. Your escort will be running full lights and sirens, but you'll set the pace. Get our kids and bring them home safe."

"Right." He hesitated, then added softly, "Thanks, Dad."

"Thanks?"

"For letting me do this. For trusting me."

His father's answer didn't come immediately. Then he said, "I love you, son. Be careful. Get your sister."

When Danny tried to collect his mother for the trip home, she was still determined to accompany him. He told her about the bus and that every seat was needed for a girl. She said she'd stand in the aisle. He finally just refused to take her and she countered by grabbing the car keys. Rosa offered to drive him to pick up the bus. That only worked because Grace Baca distracted his mother.

Once Rosa had the car moving, Danny picked up her purse and opened it. She raised her eyebrows but didn't say anything until he pulled out Mike's throw-away phone. Then she nodded and slowed slightly while he dialed and waited. A woman answered with, "Who's calling, please?"

"Spidey. Is Peter there?"

"No. What have you got for him?"

Danny felt funny about talking to someone he didn't know, so he started by asking, "Did he leave a message for me?"

"He said if you're nervous to tell you that Parker is still missing."

"Okay." He took a deep breath, then said, "Tell him that the governor closed all the roads in and out of the city. Tell him all flights in or out are canceled. I'm pretty sure that's true for buses and I don't think any trains will be stopping here."

"We heard most of that."

"Tell him the National Guard is activated. They're going to have troops at all the state police barricades by this afternoon."

"Okay." The woman was silent for a moment. She asked, "Are they armed?"

"They will be."

"This is crazy."

"I know. I heard the death toll is over two hundred now."

"Two hundred sixty-three an hour ago. The good news is that they aren't dying in the hospitals, so whatever treatment they're using works."

"Where are they dying?"

"Most are homeless or isolated. They have no family or close friends and they die in a sleeping bag or a cardboard box or an empty building. No one misses them. They generally aren't found until they make themselves known."

"Make themselves known?"

"Stink."

"Oh."

"Have you been watching the news?"

"Not really."

"You should." She hung up.

Danny stared at the phone thoughtfully, then dropped it back in Rosa's purse. He used his own phone to search on Botulism in their zip code. He got hits from dermatologists looking to remove wrinkles from their wallets and several dozen bloggers about the botulism outbreak after a concert by *Hue and Chroma*. The consensus was that the specific source of the botulism had never been identified and that the loss of the lead guitar, drummer, and sitarist was a tragedy. No one mentioned hundreds of deaths. No one mentioned extortion. The only references to Gabriel referred to an archangel.

He abandoned the search when Rosa pulled into the city transportation yard and parked between an ambulance and a yellow school bus parked by itself. Rosa stared at the ambulance. She said, "Danny? What's going on?"

An EMT backed out of the ambulance with a load of blue bundles and carried them into the bus. He walked them all the way to the back and handed them to another figure, one Danny recognized. He dashed to the bus and peered down the aisle. "Pam?"

She gave him an exhausted smile. She seemed thinner than yesterday morning. Almost gaunt. The EMT pushed by Danny and Rosa, who had followed him onto the bus, and hurried to the ambulance for another load.

Pam said, "You're here. Good. We're almost ready to go."

"What are you doing here? What's all this stuff?"

"The girls will need some of this. I won't know until we get there."

"We?"

"I'm going with you." She didn't sound like it was an option. "Are you ready?"

Rosa broke in. "I'm coming too."

She didn't sound nearly as sure as Pam had. The older woman looked her over carefully and asked, "Can you change diapers? Wipe up vomit? Urine? Feces? Do you know CPR?"

"If I can't," Rosa said firmly, "I can learn."

Danny glanced from one of them to the other. He'd been thinking of this as a heroic dash to rescue his sister. This new dimension alarmed him. He swallowed nervously and asked, "Are they that sick?"

Pam gave Rosa a slow nod before answering him. "We don't know. If this toxin came from botulism bacteria, the girls would have symptoms within three days, but it didn't. It came from modified Staph or E. coli. We don't know how fast the modified bacteria produce the toxin. We don't know if environmental factors affect the rate. We don't know what other changes were made to the bacteria. All we know is how the recent admissions responded."

The EMT came down the aisle again. He pushed past Danny with a cold pack and a medical bag, then smiled tiredly and said, "That's all of it, doc. Good luck."

Danny didn't take his eyes off the doctor while the man made his way off the bus. He asked, "Based on those recent admissions, what do you expect?"

"Jannie and Emma were exposed at least 48 hours ago. Even if none of the other girls were exposed before the trip, we have to assume some were exposed on the bus or in their dorm. Some of the original concert goers died from secondary exposure within two to three days. Others are still recovering." She leaned heavily on the back of a seat and then collapsed slowly. "I'm hoping for the best and I will not, will not, ever accept the worst. I won't!"

Rosa turned to him and said, "Drive."

He started the engine and spun the wheels on his way to the exit. When he turned onto the street, a patrol car pulled in front of him. Its emergency lights flashed on and it led him toward the freeway. A second car slipped in front of it and pulled ahead, clearing traffic. Danny stepped hard on the throttle. He only let up a little when the bus began to tilt too far on an interchange. As soon as the lane straightened, he hit it again.

The city seemed to be slowing down. Very little traffic blocked them, but the Chief's officers did a great job with the little they faced. The lead cars slowed as they approached the exit onto the freeway north. Their sirens kicked on. Two officers began kicking traffic cones blocking the exit out of the way. All three vehicles weaved through the gap and the cops repositioned the cones behind the bus.

Even fewer cars dotted the freeway north.

Rosa made her way forward and took the seat behind Danny. He asked, "How is Pam?"

"Exhausted. Terrified. I don't know if she's passed out or asleep."

"Terrified?"

"For her daughter." Rosa leaned forward and whispered. "I was looking at the supplies in the back, Danny. She has body bags there."

He groaned and stood on the gas pedal. The cop in front of him sped up until they were doing eighty-five, but after ten minutes or so, he began slowing. When Danny tried to go around him, he cut over, blocking the lane, and continued slowing. Danny slammed his fist on the steering wheel. Rosa squeezed his shoulder and said, "Look!"

He looked and then braked. Flashing red, blue, and white lights blocked all three lanes of the highway ahead. Behind the cars, two armored personnel carriers blocked the northbound lanes. The southbound lanes were also blocked, but only by the state police patrol cars.

The escort cars pulled to the side. The city cars blocking the road backed out of his way. Danny inched the bus forward. As he neared the APCs, a state patrolman wearing a surgical mask held up his hand. When Danny stopped the bus and opened the door, he stepped cautiously into the bus and looked down the aisle. "Three of you? I was told to expect two. A doctor and a driver."

"The doctor is asleep in the back," Rosa told him. "I'm the nurse."

"No nurse is authorized."

"Someone has to change the diapers and mop up the puke." Rosa smiled at him. "If you want to take my place, I'm happy to get off the bus."

"No one gets off the bus," the officer said hastily. He turned to Danny. "You'll be escorted to the camp by two cars, one leading and one following. Stay between them and park when they stop. Do not exit your vehicle under any circumstances. Camp and medical personnel will help your passengers board. Any luggage and cargo will be placed in the under floor compartments, so you don't have to worry about that. As soon as loading is complete, you will be escorted back to this checkpoint. Any questions?"

Just for the hell of it, Danny asked, "What if I need gas?"

"Don't let that happen." He nodded politely, stepped off the bus, and waved. One of the APCs backed away and Danny crept through the space between them. As he pulled away, a state patrol car pulled into the lead slot. A second bracketed him. They stayed close to him and kept his speed to a steady seventy-five for rest of the drive north.

Pam kept her eyes closed for the next hour, but every time Danny checked the overhead mirror she'd twisted herself into a new position. She finally gave up and joined Rosa on the seat behind him. "Where are we?"

"I'm not sure," Danny confessed, "but based on the timing, we have about twenty minutes to go."

"They've probably got the girls lined up, ready for us." She turned to Rosa. "Honey, would you grab two of those bundles of blankets on the back bench seat? Put them on the seat by the door."

Rosa slipped into the aisle and made her way toward the back. Pam leaned forward. "How are you doing?" she asked softly.

"Okay. A little worried."

She reached forward and rested her hand on his shoulder. "Don't feel bad. I'm right there with you."

"How bad will it be?"

"Be ready for anything."

He tried to take a deep breath but his chest was too tight. "How can you do it?" he asked. "I mean, I thought doctors didn't treat their own family."

"I can't not be here," she said. "Could you ask someone else to come for Emma?"

"No." He thought a moment. The steering wheel vibrated steadily in his hands. He said softly, "Mom wanted to come. I was afraid seeing Emma might be too hard on her. Now I think maybe I took the easy job. Waiting would be worse."

"We'll see. We never know what what's coming until we're in the middle of it and then we just have to deal with it."

He lifted a hand from the wheel and patted her hand. He said, "Are you trying to prepare me for something?"

"No." She took her hand away. "I'm telling you not to worry about yourself. You will be strong enough."

He nodded even though he didn't believe her. Then he had to slow down because the lead escort pulled off the freeway and Pam hurried to the back of the bus. She returned with Rosa. They were both wearing scrubs, hair nets, face masks, and latex gloves. She tossed him a bundle and said, "Change as soon as we park."

"Here?" He was surprised. "In front of you?"

"We'll try to resist the temptation to look," Pam said drily, "but hurry. You won't have much time before the girls start boarding."

The lead escort vehicle pulled into a parking lot shaded by giant cottonwood trees and stopped in front of a two story red brick building, immediately behind another patrol car and an APC. A man wearing scrubs and a surgical mask approached.

Danny opened the door and tried to change quickly while Pam and Rosa focused on the doctor. By the time he had his mask hooked behind his ears, the doctor was gone. Pam looked him over carefully, adjusted his mask, told him to put on his gloves, and then abandoned him to Rosa, who adjusted his mask again and tried to put his gloves on for him. He was saved by Pam's soft cry. "Oh my God."

He had to stand up to see them. A line of 13 and 14 year-old girls wearing surgical masks and clutching blankets around themselves shuffled toward the bus. The first eight looked weak but managed on their own. The next thirteen supported each other, but they managed the walk with only a bit of help on the steps, where Pam handed them off to Rosa for the trip down the aisle.

Danny scanned each face as it passed. He didn't see either Emmie or Janis but he did see that every forehead had letters scrawled on it in black marker: 'A,' 'C,' and 'M.' Another two were helped from the building. They walked bent forward and holding their bellies. Pam started to step out of the bus to help them, but a uniformed officer shouted her back in. Their transfer to the bus was awkward.

The last three came out on stretchers. The bearers handed the front end to Pam while Danny maneuvered around and grabbed the back. They rested the stretchers on the seat backs near the front of the bus and hung the bag of saline drip that came with each stretcher on the rack over the seats.

When Pam saw the pale face on the second stretcher, she released a little cry of joy. When he didn't recognize the face on the third, Danny almost lost it. He wrestled the stretcher into place and made it back to the door in two steps.

He stood on the bottom step and leaned through the door. The baggage compartment was still open. Three officers wheeled a dolly loaded with small wooden chests up to the door and heaved them into the compartment. Danny leaned out farther to see what was going on.

One of the officers put a hand on his holster and yelled at Danny to step back in the bus. Another began to close the baggage compartment when a voice from the building door stopped him and the bearers appeared with another stretcher. A small gray body bag rested on it. They slid their burden into the luggage compartment and slammed the door. One of the cops waved at Danny and another shouted, "That's it."

He returned to his seat and turned the ignition. When the engine caught, he rested his head on the steering wheel until the blaring horns made him lift it. The bus jerked when he put it in gear. Two state cars pulled away first, lights flashing. Danny followed them and the APC trailed everyone.

He drove mechanically, mindlessly. At one point, Rosa shook him and handed him her phone. His father asked, "How is she, Danny? You didn't call. I'm dying here."

"Go home, Dad. Mom's going to need you."

The chief's answer, when it finally came, was a groan and a broken connection.

PART TWO

Cauldron

Chapter 11

Eddie Baca found his daughter and Danny Murphy sleeping together when he entered her bedroom early Monday morning. Finding Danny's car parked in his driveway had caused him to enter without knocking. The two heads on her pillow stopped him in the doorway. He stood there long enough to realize that he didn't feel angry or even disappointed. Hollow came closer. Even emptier than he felt half an hour earlier, when he sat in his car in his reserved parking spot in the city garage and tried to work up enough enthusiasm to drive home. But he couldn't allow a hollow feeling to cripple him. He had to deal with this situation too, so he lifted his hand and banged on the door, loudly.

When their eyes opened, he tried to be firm but calm. "I want to talk to you downstairs. Both of you. As soon as possible." Then he closed the door and went to make a pot of coffee and try to think of what he could say.

A heavy pounding jerked Danny from a deep sleep into a fog of dread. At first he confused it with the headache that had troubled him ever since he stepped off the school bus yesterday afternoon. Then he realized the soft breast in his left hand belonged to Rosa. When he opened his eyes and saw the mayor's back through her closing door, he realized his headache would get worse shortly.

Rosa threw the bedspread back and pulled the breast from his grip, muttering a few words that sounded like the beginning of a prayer but weren't. She stormed out of the room after her father. Danny shook his head and sat on the edge of the bed while he tried to remember where he was and why he felt so bad. Then he remembered and tried to forget. That didn't work either, so he went down to face the music.

He located Rosa and her father by following the shouting to the kitchen, where he found her making loud points about lack of trust and fully clothed and nothing happened and it was her body and her business anyway and her father had no right. Baca ignored her and stared into an empty coffee cup until he noticed Danny. He pointed to an empty chair and said, "Sit down."

Danny took the chair silently. He didn't feel much like talking. Anyway, Rosa had pretty much covered all the points that needed making at least once. When she began repeating herself, her father silenced her by confessing, "You're right, Rosa, but I didn't yell at you. I didn't accuse you of anything. I wanted to ask if you knew where Danny was. Your mom called me when he didn't come home."

"Mom is at the Murphy's?"

"She was there when Ben came home and told her about Emma. Ben asked her to stay with Anne until Danny got home."

"He didn't stay with his wife? He told her that her daughter was dead and then he just left her alone?"

"He asked Grace to sit with her," Baca said roughly. "He had to go back to work. Things are happening."

"That's horrible! Could you do that? If it was me?"

When the mayor failed to answer, Danny blurted, "It was the gold."

They both looked at him. Baca spoke carefully. "What do you mean?"

He felt numb. He stared at the wall behind the mayor. "When I didn't see Emma at the camp, I stuck my head out of the bus. I was anxious. Scared. I saw a bunch of cops loading boxes, small heavy boxes, in the luggage and then two guys brought out . . . it had to be Emmie. She didn't get on the bus so it had to be her." He closed his eyes. "They put her in with the boxes and the suitcases and dirty clothes. Only two cars escorted us to the camp. On the way home we had two cars in front and an armored car behind us and I think another cop behind him, all the way to the checkpoint, and then there were four cars with us to the hospital. At the hospital they unloaded the boxes and all the cops disappeared." He looked around. The coffee was ready. He started to get up but Rosa beat him to the coffee maker, so he finished, "Then they unloaded the girls. Then they took Emmie out. After they got the gold, they let my sister out of the baggage compartment."

The mayor had been watching him carefully. He said, "You know we are all sorry, Danny. There are no words."

"I know." Rosa put a cup in front of him. Danny picked it up but didn't drink. "You're going to pay the son of a bitch, aren't you?"

"I don't have any choice."

"You're protecting your job."

"That's not fair. My job is gone no matter what. Even if nobody else dies, the voters will remember that this happened on my watch." He slammed his cup on the table. "I don't see any way to keep more people from dying."

"Paying the ransom won't help. Gabriel isn't after gold."

That got the mayor's attention. "What do you mean?"

"He sent two threats, but he had already carried out the threat before he sent the notes. You can't stop him, Mayor."

"We have to try. What else can we do?"

"You could warn people about the poisoned money. Maybe Emmie would still be alive."

"Have you thought that through, Danny?" Baca sighed. "You won't listen to me. Talk it over with that professor of yours, but go home first. Your mom is hurting worse than you are."

"Right." He left his cup on the table and got as far as the front door before Rosa stopped him. She handed him his shoes and hugged him, murmuring, "I'm so sorry."

"Thanks." Danny wrapped his arms around her. He felt angry at her father, but angrier at himself. He said, "About last night...."

"Don't." She spoke softly. "There's nothing to apologize for."

"I couldn't stop thinking about Emmie."

"I couldn't stop smelling the bus. I guess that makes us

even."

"Maybe we can try again after I kill Gabriel."

"Maybe." She released him quickly. "Put your shoes on. Go show your mom you're still alive."

Grace was waiting in the living room when Danny stepped quietly through the front door. She glanced toward the back of the house and held a finger to her lips, then collected her purse and met him at the door. She whispered, "She's asleep. She cried all night but she dropped off about an hour ago."

"Has she eaten?"

Grace shook her head. "She's too upset."

She gave Danny a quick hug and slipped out. He thought about making coffee or looking for a bottle of aspirin but he decided to check on his mother first. Grace had left the door to his parents' bedroom open a few inches. He stood outside it, listening. When he didn't hear anything, he pushed it open far enough to stick his head in.

His mother asked, "Has she gone?"

"Yes."

"Come here." She wore a loose house dress and lay in the darkened room on her comforter under a light blanket. He sat beside her and she grabbed his hand. She squeezed it tightly and stared at him with red eyes. "Are you okay, honey?"

He didn't feel okay but he said, "Sure. I guess."

"You're all I've got now, Danny."

"You've got Dad."

"He isn't here." She licked her lips. "I tried to get him to take me to see Emmie. He said they wouldn't let me see my baby. Is that true?"

"I think so, Mom. I'm pretty sure. She isn't in the hospital."

"Where is she then? Why can't I see her? Can you explain that?"

He didn't want to. How could he explain that when he climbed out of the bus, when the orderlies and nurses pushed him aside and began carrying stretchers through the electric doors into emergency, he'd stood in the parking lot wondering why it seemed so much smaller. And louder. And realized half the lot was taken up by large refrigerated trailers parked with their coolers roaring in the July heat. He hadn't understood until two men carried a stretcher with an improbably small bag on it toward steps on the nearest truck, until they rested it on two very convenient sawhorses and unzipped it, and reached in with carefully gloved hands and pulled out a sheaf of papers and ripped off the top sheet and put the rest back and zipped up the bag again, but not before he recognized the still white face. How could he explain that?

"They have a special place for her, Mom. They probably have to do some tests and they're very busy. We'll be able to see her in a few days, when the emergency is over."

"Is there something you aren't telling me?" Her eyes searched his face. "You wouldn't lie to momma would you?"

He patted her hand reassuringly and said, "Of course not, Mom. Never."

She sighed and closed her eyes. After a few minutes, she began breathing deeply. He sat with her for another hour before releasing her hand and pulling the blanket over it. Then he tip-toed from the room and dialed Rosa. When she didn't answer, he texted her to call him and waited in the kitchen with a fresh pot of coffee.

She responded over an hour later. "What do you need, Danny? I'm really busy here."

"Where is here?"

"I'm at Mercy, and I'm busy," she snapped. "Now, what do you want?"

"I'm worried about Tony's dog, Parker. He must really miss Mike."

"Parker?" She lowered her voice. "What would Parker say to . . . Mike?"

"He'd talk about his trip. He'd talk about how many exciting things he's learned and how much he misses his family."

She thought about that for a moment. "How desperate do you think he would be to see his family?"

"Very."

She gave him a few seconds to continue, then asked, "How are you doing, Danny?"

"I'm home. Mom is sleeping. I've been better. Thinking, you know? I keep thinking I'm going to wake up and . . ." His voice broke. He took awhile before continuing, "It was a difficult trip for you too. Is that why you're at the hospital?"

"I asked Pam how I could help. She said she'd put me to work if I was serious."

"So you're a nurse now?"

"Of course not. I'm unloading helicopters."

"Come again?"

"There are two helicopters with antibiotics and antitoxin every day. I'm going to help unload this morning's shipment."

He remembered the bus, the stink, the girls who could barely speak and whimpered softly for ninety miles. "Is it helping? Do you feel better?"

"Not much. Some. Maybe." She sighed and asked, "Anything else, Danny?"

There wasn't. He apologized. "I shouldn't have called you. I just needed to talk to someone."

"What are you going to do?"

"If Mom is okay, I'm going to grab coffee this afternoon. Maybe Doctor Foreman will be at the Corner Cafe after two. I have a few questions about his class and some other things. It would be nice to get back to normal."

With that, Rosa wished him good luck and hung up. He went back to his mother's room and watched her sleep until noon. Then he opened a can of soup and fed her. They talked for another hour and she didn't cry, except once, and that didn't last too long. She understood when he said he had to go out.

He saw very little traffic on the streets. Even after he reached the university neighborhood, he rarely met more than two cars on a block. Sidewalks normally crowded with students were nearly deserted. Everyone he saw wore a mask of some sort and they all walked quickly, as though eager to escape from the dangers of open space. On the up side, parking was easy.

A sign taped to the glass door of the Cafe stopped Danny in his tracks: *No Cash No Cards! Apple Pay Only!* He shrugged and pushed in anyway, only to bump into a small table holding several open packets of sanitary wipes and another hand-printed sign. *Wipe often or wipe out.*

He used two sheets. When he looked around for a place to drop them, he found a waitress standing four feet away and holding a mask at arm's length. He took it with a smile and the girl seemed much more comfortable after he covered his face.

The cafe was almost empty. Two tables had single customers. Both of those looked directly at him, but the masks threw him off. He didn't recognize either immediately until the nearer one lowered his mask for a second. He smiled and told Foreman he'd just be a minute before sitting at the second table. "Hey, Mike."

"Who's your friend?" Mike glanced casually at the table where Foreman watched them with a puzzled expression.

"My Science and Society teacher," Danny told him. "He's also been advising the mayor about this thing with Gabriel. He's the one who confirmed the gene editing."

"That's confirmed?"

"The CDC hasn't mapped the genome yet, but we ruled out everything else."

Mike said, "We've been assuming that Gabriel has a biology background."

Danny eyed him carefully. "We?"

"I'm not the only one who wants the bastard."

"Tony was your brother, but he was my best friend, and now Gabriel killed Emmie. My sister, Emma. She died yesterday, Mike. She just turned fourteen."

"So you still want a piece of him?"

Danny shook his head. "I want him all."

"Don't be greedy." Mike looked past Danny and said, "Why don't you invite the professor over? I'd like to meet him."

Danny nodded, but leaned across the table. "Before we do that, you should know that the gold arrived yesterday."

Mike didn't look surprised. "When is the payoff?"

"I don't think he's told us yet."

"As soon as you find out— "

"Wait for a call from the spider." He stood and waved at the other table. "Doctor Foreman? Can I introduce someone? This is Mike, Tony's brother."

Foreman joined them quickly and asked, "You're the man running TonysWay, aren't you?"

When Mike nodded, he added, "Tony was in my class. You know that, of course, but he was one of my best students. We

109

miss him. You have our sympathy."

"TonysWay?" Danny was lost. He looked from Foreman to Mike for an answer.

"It's a blog," the professor told him, "and I guess you'd call it a social activist group?"

"People need news they can trust," Mike said. "The government isn't telling us shit, but one of my readers heard from a cop that the guy who poisoned everyone at the club calls himself Gabriel and he's also passing out poison money. Nobody knows why he's doing it, but we're keeping our eyes out for anyone suspicious, and in the meantime we try to help each other. We check on shut-ins or anyone who lives alone to make sure they're okay. We deliver food and medicine. You know that one in four people doesn't have a bank account? They have to use cash, but nobody is willing to take cash any more so they're getting desperate. We help them get accounts or teach them how to use Apple Pay. We also teach people about alternative currencies and we launder money for the ones who can't get off the dollar."

Danny stared at him, stunned. "I had no idea."

"We were on the news yesterday. I thought you knew."

"I was bringing my sister home. I didn't have time for news."

"Your sister?" Foreman clearly hadn't heard, so Danny started to tell him. He got choked up and Mike had to finish the story. Foreman patted his shoulder awkwardly and apologized. "I had no idea, Danny."

While Danny recovered his composure, Foreman asked Mike how he was laundering money. It turned out that he was literally laundering it and then cooking it. He had a group who collected cash for people who had nothing else and washed it in an antiseptic solution, then baked it for half an hour at a temperature that would kill any remaining bacteria and break down any toxin. "The problem isn't making it safe," he added, "The problem is getting someone to trust it. We can deposit small amounts in a few banks here, but they can't take much because eventually they're going to have to get rid of it too. We wind up smuggling most of it out of the city."

"I imagine you have to discount it?" Foreman asked.

Mike nodded. "We wind up paying about ten cents on the

dollar. We feel bad about it, but that's barely enough to keep us in business."

"What's that doing to the economy?"

"What economy? Nobody has any money to spend, but there isn't anything to buy except booze and guns and ammo. There's a market for those because people are looking down the road a week or two and don't like what they see, but other than that?" Mike spread his hands and shrugged. "A little bird told me the city was going to start distributing food in a couple of days. If it isn't free, a lot of people will go hungry."

"I figured things would get bad," Danny finally broke in, "but I never imagined it would be so fast."

"Civilization is only about two weeks deep." Mike stood up. "And on that depressing note, I'll be on my way." He nodded at Foreman and said, "Nice meeting you, doctor, and Danny, stay in touch. If you're sticking around, have a cup of coffee on me. I told the cashier your money's no good." He chuckled. "That's a joke. Get it?"

Chapter 12

Tuesday morning, Danny woke up to a dream of killing Gabriel. Tony and Emmie appeared in it. Their faces flickered in and out of the chase whenever he tired and the angel slipped too far ahead of him and they each brought a dose of rage. That helped catch Gabriel but killing him was a different matter. Just as he wrapped his hands around the bastard's throat, Mike jumped him from behind, screamed, 'He's mine!", and dragged him down, smothering him, binding him, crying, "Daniel . . . Dan . . . Danny! Wake up, Danny!"

Of course, when he opened his eyes, Mike turned into his father shaking his shoulder with a hard hand until Danny jerked upright and spent long seconds staring wildly around the room while gasping for breath. Eventually he shivered and asked, "Dad?"

"That must have been some dream."

"It was." He scrubbed his face to clear the fog of sleep. "What's up? Is Mom okay?"

"She's asleep." He paused, obviously looking for a way to start. "Look, son, we've been crosswise of each other the last few days. We need to get past that."

"We?" Danny's anger ballooned. "I did everything to help you right up until you kicked me out of the mayor's office and then I babysat the mayor's wife and daughter. Then I drove that damned bus and brought Emmie home and smuggled in a bunch of gold with her. For you. And I held Mom's hand all day yesterday, for you, Dad. While you and the mayor hid in City Hall. Where the hell does this 'we' come from?"

The chief sagged as Danny grew more upset. He sat on the bed and talked softly while Danny jumped up and strode around the room. "Do you know how many officer involved shootings I had while Eddie and I were hiding in city hall? Three. Three separate incidents, three citizens down, eight citizens detained. You know what their crimes were? Evading a quarantine. Trying to get their families out of town. And why were we trying to stop them? Because just outside our lines, the National Guard has another line and it has orders to shoot. And that's just one of the things I was hiding from, Danny. We had a near riot at the North Park gym when a medical team ran out of antibiotics and masks. Two ambulances have been hijacked. No one was hurt, thank God, but they were stripped. What else? I've got officers doing crowd control at both hospitals and every supermarket in town. Eddie ordered all retail gun shops to close and I have to enforce that. If it weren't for Tony's brother—"

"Tony's brother? Mike?"

Murphy nodded. "He started some sort of organization. They are collecting food and feeding the homeless. I don't understand how, but they're also helping people who only have paper money buy things they need, and they've been helping keep the lines orderly at distribution points."

"Good for him."

"Yeah." But he didn't sound happy about it. "Protecting the public order and safety is my job, Danny, but I don't have the manpower to do it. My men are exhausted and I'm asking them to do things they never signed up for. Arresting a guy for selling drugs is one thing, but it's something else when the drugs are antibiotics and the buyer is scared silly for his kids' lives."

"Okay." Danny sat beside his father. His anger had evaporated. He asked, "How can I help? And don't tell me to hold Mom's hand. That isn't enough."

"I know. It wouldn't have been for me either at your age. I was desperate. I still am, and I feel guilty. Not just about Emma. I should be protecting Anne and comforting her. I tell myself what I'm doing is to protect her, but it isn't what she

113

needs. I know that too, but there isn't enough of me. I—"

"Just tell me what to do, Dad."

"Yeah. Okay." Murphy took a deep breath. "The mayor has a meeting at eleven. Can you find your professor? My guys can't seem to catch up with him and we'd like his input on Gabriel. The FBI has a profiler, she calls herself a forensic psychologist, on the case, but I don't trust her. I'd like his input."

"I might be able to find him. What's wrong with the profiler?"

"She's thinking about this Gabriel like he's just a criminal, an ordinary man, you know? I'm afraid she is making the same mistake I've made since this whole thing started. I didn't see it until Foreman pointed it out, but something is going on that I don't understand." He shook his head. "I hope Foreman will have a different perspective. An insight."

"I'll try. Does Mayor Baca know about this?"

"It was mostly his idea." Murphy forced a humorless chuckle. "I think he realized an old cop isn't going to cut it anymore."

"Okay, Dad, but I want to be part of your investigation. No more babysitting." Danny stood abruptly and opened his dresser. "Anything else?"

"One thing. How close are you to Mike?"

"What?" He froze with a pair of socks in his hand. "Why?"

"The FBI has agents looking for Gabriel. My men are looking for him. They all keep hearing about people asking questions, people wearing green armbands." He looked directly at Danny. "TonysWay wears green armbands. You know anything about that, Danny?"

"Not a thing, but I'll ask Mike. He'll tell me if he's up to anything."

"Okay." The chief grunted and stood up. "I've got to check on your mom and try to catch a couple hours of sleep. I'll see you downtown."

"Dad?" Danny stopped him at the door. "There's nothing wrong with looking for Gabriel."

"There are two problems with looking," Murphy said gravely. "The first is what you do if you catch him. We need him alive. We have to find out what he did and how he did it

114

and who else knows about it. And the second is that these amateurs are confusing our investigation. They are contaminating the crime scene."

That made no sense. "What crime scene?"

"My whole damned city is a crime scene, Danny, and these guys are mucking it up. That is going to stop, one way or another. If Mike is trying to find Gabriel on his own, he needs to stop before he gets caught. If his people are doing it behind his back, he needs to stop them or report them." With that, Murphy left to check on his wife and close his eyes until his phone rang again.

Danny was a little surprised to find Corner Cafe open when he arrived just after seven. All classes and nonessential services had been canceled after the first poisoning at the *Hue and Chroma* concert, but over a thousand students were stuck on campus by the quarantine. Danny thought that might explain the crowd on the sidewalk in front of the building, but he realized he was wrong when he approached the crowd.

It had an equal mix of males and females. Most were student age. They clustered in small groups around individuals with a clipboard or a handful of printed sheets. No one was laughing or even speaking loudly. They spoke quietly and seriously when they spoke at all. They had only two things in common: everyone wore a green armband and everyone wore a surgical mask.

Danny was conscious that the crowd was aware of him, but no one stopped him until he threaded his way through the mob and reached the door. Then two of the larger males got in his way. One told him the cafe was closed for cleaning until ten. The other nodded like it was true.

Danny smiled at them and said, "Tell Mike that Spidey wants to talk."

They looked at each other. One shrugged and said, "Wait." He cracked the shop door and slipped inside. Three minutes later he reappeared, nodded at his partner, and held the door. Danny ducked under his arm and found the cafe busy. Every table but one was occupied by two to four silent people wearing bright green armbands so focused on the white ceramic cups in front of them that not one looked in his direction. When he stopped to look around, Mike stood and pulled his mask down enough to be recognized, then waved him over to a corner booth.

"What's up, Parker?"

Danny shook his head. The comic book was getting old. "Nothing new yet on the angel," he said, "but I've been drafted to spy on you."

"Really?" Mike didn't sound surprised. "What started that?"

"A bunch of guys with armbands asking around about Gabriel."

"And this is a problem how?"

Danny leaned closer and lowered his voice. "First, they want him alive, and second, you're screwing up their crime scene, which I guess means they want to get people's first impressions and they don't want anybody else getting second impressions."

"In other words, they don't trust anyone without a badge." Mike smiled. "Okay, I got the message. Now, what about you? Do you want Gabriel alive?"

"Until I get my hands on him."

"So you can kill him yourself?"

Danny nodded.

"Are you willing to help catch him?"

"Of course."

"Do you know how many people in this room want to kill Gabriel?"

Danny took a slow look around. He estimated there were forty or fifty men and women in the room. Maybe half were students, but some of the others were well above fifty. All were anonymous, hidden behind the ubiquitous masks. "Most of them?"

"Everyone here lost somebody. Friends, lovers, sons, daughters, parents." He lowered his voice even more and whispered, "Brothers. Sisters."

"Okay. I believe you, but it doesn't change a thing. I still want him."

"So do I, bro, but meeting these people — starting TonysWay — changed things. Gabriel is still going to die, but he'll die for what he did to all of us. Not just me. Not just you. Can you live with that?"

116

"No problem. I'll kill him for all of us."

Mike stared at him for a few seconds. Then he sighed and said, "Well, it took me a while to get it. You'll come around. In the meantime, you can help us find the SOB." He caught someone's attention and pointed to his arm. An older woman appeared immediately with a green scarf. He tossed it to Danny and said, "We meet here every morning. If that changes, I'll get word to you through Mary Jane. When you've got something I need to know, come on down or have her call me. Wear the armband and a mask. You'll fit right in."

Danny looked around the cafe, then tied the scarf around his right arm and said, "Okay, Yesterday I told you that when I brought Emmie . . . Emma's body home, the mayor had a separate cargo on the bus. The gold."

Mike nodded. "How much?"

"He asked for five thousand Krugerrands."

"That's about...how much?"

"Eight or nine million dollars. Almost four hundred pounds."

"That's. . . ." Mike couldn't think of anything to say.

Danny suggested, "Crazy?"

"What's he going to do? Push a wheelbarrow full of gold down the street?"

"I don't think he's even told them how he wants it delivered."

Mike snorted. "They could truck it directly to the loony bin."

"That might be funny if it weren't for Emma."

"Yes." Mike turned deadly serious in an instant. "Look, if you're going to spy on me, you will have to give them something. I scheduled a spontaneous rally for six tomorrow at the university stadium. A couple of people will give speeches about how the mayor isn't doing enough, there'll be some talks on how to protect ourselves from the plague, and I'll talk about how we all have to stick together and help each other to get through this. It'll be all the stuff the mayor should be saying if he weren't hiding in city hall. I won't call for armed rebellion or anything like that. Tell your father about the rally. Tell him you're going to join TonysWay to keep an eye on us, but we're suspicious of you, so you have to let us know how the search for Gabriel is going and what the city's up to. Sort of provide some credibility, right?"

"Okay." Danny pushed his chair back. "You know you're going to have to change my secret identity to Bond."

"I'll take that under advisement, but remember, you don't have a license to kill."

"Then I'll forge one." He started to stand.

Mike asked, "Did you get everything you came to see me for?"

"I didn't come to see you. I was looking for Doctor Foreman. I just stumbled onto you."

"The professor? He shows up around ten. You want to leave a message for him?"

Danny shook his head. "I'll be back."

He left the cafe shortly after eight. He had two hours to spare, so he drove to Mercy hospital. The emergency entrance was blocked, as usual, but he managed to get in the main entrance by dropping Pam and Rosa's names and asked an orderly to let them know he was waiting.

Twenty minutes later, Rosa flopped into the chair beside him. He looked over at her and wondered how she'd made it to the lobby. She looked dead on her feet. He asked, "Pam?"

"The doctor in charge put her down an hour ago. She could barely walk from bed to bed."

"Is she going to be alright?"

"We hope so." The way she said it reminded Danny that not all outcomes were good. "She's been taking stimulants to keep going."

"Things are that bad?"

"We have a full house here, and a lot of the staff moved to the gym at Central High. All the new patients go directly there if they aren't critical. Last I heard, they had over three hundred beds, most of them occupied."

"New patients? I thought the antibiotics stopped it from spreading."

"It slowed way down, but people are still getting sick. They come in with a staph infection or maybe E. Coli, and we get that under control and suddenly they're full of botulism toxin. It's a nightmare." She closed her eyes and asked, "What do you want, Danny? Why are you here?"

118

"Do you ever see Janis? How is she?"

"She is responding to the antibiotics. The diarrhea and fever are under control and she's regaining muscle control. The antitoxin doesn't cure anything. It just keeps the poison from doing any more damage. Did you know that?"

"I read up on it after— Anyway, it takes time for her nerves to regenerate."

"That's right. Why are you here, Danny?"

"I want to see Emmie."

"That isn't possible." She shook her head. "You know that."

"I think she's in one of those freezer trailers out front, Rosa. She's all alone."

"Nobody is alone out there."

"You could get me in. Just for a minute. Please?"

"I've been in those trailers, Danny. Believe me, you don't want to go there."

"But. . . . " He took a deep breath and changed direction. "What are you doing here? You aren't a nurse."

"I'm doing the same thing I did on the bus. Changing diapers, wiping up puke, changing sheets, picking up blankets."

"I could do those things. Do you need help?"

"You're still trying to get into the trailers." She forced herself up and patted his hand. "Go home. Take care of your Mom. Or my Mom. Help your Dad or help Mike. He's doing good work, saving lives with his volunteers."

"Look." He pulled the armband from his pocket. "I am working with Mike. I just want to see Emmie one last time."

"You will," she assured him. "When this is all over, we will release the . . . the dead, and we'll have a nice funeral. Until then, let us take care of her. She's safe here."

Danny looked at her like she was crazy. She realized what she'd just said and started to apologize, but he nodded and said, "Take care of Janis, Rosa. If I can do anything, call me." He hurried out of the hospital. It was almost ten o'clock and he still had to find Professor Foreman.

119

Chapter 13

When Danny reached the mayor's office with Foreman in tow, Baca's office manager led them directly to a large conference room. She ignored the agent guarding the door and pushed them inside. A large oval table, easily capable of seating twenty people, occupied the center of the long room. Chairs lined three walls, far enough back from the table for the crowd of less important invitees to make their way to the refrigerator and coffee pot on the fourth wall.

Foreman took in the power structure around the table in one glance. He led Danny to empty seats directly behind Baca. Only one spot at the main table, the chair beside the mayor, was empty. Everyone in the room wore a surgical mask. A few had supplemented their masks with latex gloves.

The men and women at the table represented the major players in the crisis. The chairs pushed back against the walls held the not-so-major players, the assistants, bag carriers, gofers, and warm bodies required to cement the right of the majors to a seat at the table. Danny wondered if his spot on the wall represented a promotion. He was about to ask his professor when his father entered the room. He smiled at Foreman and gave Danny a quick nod before sitting beside Baca.

The best dressed agent at the FBI end of the table, the end nearest the coffee pot, immediately tried to open the meeting. Baca cut him off. "If you don't mind, Agent Bakey, the search for Gabriel is going to occupy most of our time. I don't want to miss the reports from the other people here so I'd like to start by going around the table quickly and getting a short update from everyone. We can take up Gabriel last and stay with him for as long as it takes."

Bakey hesitated, then nodded reluctantly, adding, "I have a telecon with Washington at one."

"Not a problem, Frank. We've all got things to do." Baca smiled, looking around the table. "We all introduced ourselves at the last meeting, so let's skip the formality. Just like yesterday, we have the governor's office on a conference call." He pointed at a triangular black box centered on the table, then continued, "The only new faces are Simon Foreman, who teaches Science and Society, among other things, at the university and one of his students, Daniel Murphy. Danny is the son of Chief Murphy and is present because he had some good insights when this terrorism or plague or whatever the hell it is first started. Oh, and because Doctor Foreman insisted. Any questions?"

There were none, so he continued, "I'll start with a quick review. First, the overall situation in the community isn't as bad as it could be. We've had no real riots. There were some fights at the food and medicine distribution points, but those stopped when Chief Murphy assigned patrols to keep an eye on things. Also, that new community service group, TonysWay, is helping keep things orderly. We've had a rash of residential fires, probably arson, in homes of the plague victims. Crime is up in a few categories, but in general it is down. The chief blames that mostly on the fact that nobody wants to steal cash, but he did say that there have been a few hijackings of food trucks—"

Someone interrupted. "What crimes are up?"

"Public intoxication. Assault, mostly between drunks. Prostitution." Baca shook his head. "Amateurs are entering the profession. The ladies aren't taking cash, though. Frozen meat and canned food are apparently high value items, but . . . well, that leads me to the next problem. Our economy. The problem is we don't have one. We can't export goods and services because we can't get any raw materials in or finished goods out past the quarantine and the only services we can export are through the internet. I heard a new call center started up. I don't know how it's making payroll or paying rent, but it's not my problem. The city stopped writing pay checks after we heard that the mail might be contaminated, but almost all our employees are on direct deposit and we're paying the ones who don't have bank accounts with food, clothes, things like that. So we're muddling along. We've have firemen at the stations, cops on the street, and clerks in city hall, at least for another week. If we don't have Gabriel in jail before then, we're going to need more help from the state to pay for the free food we're handing out."

A thin-faced blond woman down the table growled, "Why free? Why not make them pay for it? They can work for a living like everyone else."

"I'm sure they can, Carley," Baca said, "and I'm sure you'd be happy to count their cash if I had someone collect it from them."

"You could demand payment by credit cards," she wasn't giving an inch, "or ATM cards, for that matter. The point is that we shouldn't let freeloaders ride on our hard work."

A short, chubby man sitting on the other side of the mayor spoke quietly. "Has anyone else heard rumors of people catching the botulism from credit cards?"

"What? No!" The woman looked horrified. "From credit cards?"

Danny had the chair directly behind his father. The sudden tension in his back and shoulders was obvious. The Mayor felt it too. He leaned over the table and asked a black man behind a CDC place card, "Is that possible, Doctor Marchand? Does the CDC know anything about this?"

"We've have unconfirmed reports."

"It's possible?"

"Of course. All it would take is a small spray bottle with the bacteria in a nutrient solution. Walk around squirting a bit into any convenient ATM and the next twenty or thirty people who swiped a card would be contaminated. For that matter, your terrorist could just spray a bit on his card and go shopping. Every time he bought something, the next customers would be contaminated."

"Can we find out which machines are poisoned?"

"No. You could swab the machines and grow cultures to see if they have bacteria, but the cultures would take days. Anyway, those machines are filthy. Every one of them would grow a jungle of bacteria." He thought a moment. "I suppose you could send somebody around to spray some bleach or maybe hydrogen peroxide in every card reader in town, but that wouldn't stop it from being recontaminated the next time a customer with a dirty card used it. And who knows what it would do to the card readers."

"God." Mayor Baca sat down slowly. He looked around the table. No one had a comment, but the FBI agents were all scribbling furiously. He turned back to the doctor. "Do you have any good news at all? Gabriel's message yesterday said he was emailing proof of what he did and how he did it to your office. Did you examine that?"

Marchand shook his head. "Either Mr. Gabriel was lying or his email went directly into our trash folder. I'm sorry."

Murphy snapped, "Didn't you look in the damned trash?"

"It would do no good. All contents of the trash folders are deleted automatically every morning. It helps us keep the memory from filling up."

"So there is no hope?"

"I looked everywhere on my office machine and even on my laptop. If he sent anything, it's gone now. I'm sorry."

"Sorry!" The chief slammed his fist on the table. The report echoed in the room. The blond accountant flinched. Bakey kept scribbling.

Danny raised his hand. "Excuse me?"

The chief turned and glared over his shoulder. He looked ready to explode. He somehow calmed himself, but his tone remained harsh, impatient. "What is it, Danny?"

"I just...," he really felt intimidated.

Beside him, Foreman murmured, "Just spit it out."

"Well, I mean, just because the email isn't on your server today doesn't mean it's not still on your server yesterday."

"What the hell does that mean?"

Baca looked confused too. The agent looked interested.

"Well, the server is probably backed up every day. Did you check the backup before the trash directory got emptied? You ask your IT guys to restore it and...."

"Of course!" Marchand hurried from the room, biting his lips.

Murphy stared at his son. His face slowly cleared. He turned to Baca and said, "That's why I invited him."

The mayor nodded and got back to business. "We'll table the CDC report until Andre gets back, so FEMA is up next. Paul?"

A stocky man wearing a light jacket and facing away from Danny cleared his throat. "Well, we're still doing advance planning in case we have to evacuate, but that can't happen unless the president declares a disaster. As far as planning goes, Option A is the evacuation of all the people who never had any exposure to the bugs. We move them out of the city as quickly as they can be identified. We'll put them into camps until we're sure they're clean. The docs say 7 days should be enough, but we're planning on ten, just to be sure. Then we release them with some kind of papers saying they are safe to be around and they're free to go."

"Go where?" That was the mayor.

"Well, they'll probably have family somewhere, out of state, preferably, and they'll have work experience, so they can get a job. We might be able to give them a little help, financially, if congress passes a bill, but it won't be much."

"What if they don't have family or work experience?"

"Then they shouldn't be considered for evacuation."

"They will be trapped in the city?"

"Yes, well, that brings us to Option B. We clear people in place and gradually shrink the quarantine perimeter. Anybody cleared stays outside and is free to leave, or whatever he wants —"

"Or *she* wants." The accountant lady's voice almost dripped acid.

"Sure." The FEMA agent sounded confused. "Sure. I mean, she is free to do whatever they want. If they are a woman. Or if they are a guy, then he, I guess, but—"

This time the mayor interrupted him. "Never mind that. What happens to the people who can't be cleared right away?"

"Well, she would move back inside the quarantine line if they might have been exposed, or if he had a lot of cash or worked around the sick people, or if someone in his, I mean her, family was sick. We'd have to decide what the conditions were."

"What if this person—," Baca glared at the blond, "—worked inside the perimeter?"

"Then she'd either have to quit or move inside the line, whatever they chose to do, but these decisions haven't been made yet. Option A would obviously be safer and healthier. The only reason I mentioned Option B is because somebody at headquarters said it might be cheaper. We're running short of trailers for the camps in Option A, because of the hurricanes, you see?"

"Okay. Enough." Baca pinched his nose and asked, "Do you know how many people would have to be quarantined in the city?"

"Well, some of our medical experts think it would be only about two percent of the population."

"That's about fifteen thousand people, Paul."

"And some said it might be five percent."

"Almost forty thousand."

"But still, it's a very small percentage."

Baca looked angry. "They are not a percentage, damn it! They are—"

Brenda interrupted him before he could finish. She opened the door and stepped into the room and waved at her boss. She looked frightened. She had a manila folder in one hand and a large plastic baggie in the other. Murphy looked at her and cursed. He rose and started for the door.

Mayor Baca glanced from the chief to Brenda and announced, "This meeting is adjourned. We will resume tomorrow unless you hear different." He hurried after his chief of police. The crowd at the FBI end of the table rose as one and followed them. After a short period of confusion, the others began trickling out.

Danny looked at Foreman and raised an eyebrow. "Follow them?"

"Let's steal a cup of coffee. I think we'll get an invitation in a few minutes."

"Then why wait?"

Foreman grinned. "Makes it harder for them to kick us out."

"I'll remember that." Danny smiled. "You learn a lot hanging out with a physicist."

"Philosopher."

"Really? I thought your doctorate was in physics."

"Oh, I've got one of those too, but my true love is philosophy."

"What's the difference?"

"I think of it this way. If the universe was a car, a physicist would try to figure out the engine, transmission, gear ratios, and so forth. A philosopher would try to map the highway system."

"Is that really true?"

"What is truth?" Foreman shrugged. "I'm not sure, but I have a piece of paper that qualifies me to ask the question."

"Does it help?"

"Not when it comes to the important things, like catching girls and winning Oscars." He looked past Danny and said, "I think it's show time."

The mayor's admin, Patty, waved urgently at them from the door.

The Gabriel conference resumed in Baca's inner sanctum with the Mayor, the Chief of Police, two FBI agents, three uniformed cops, one Doctor of Philosophy, and one double agent named Danny. Everyone except Danny and Simon Foreman had stiff shoulders and red faces. One of the uniforms had a hand near his service automatic and eyed the two agents nervously. Mayor Baca, Agent Bakey, and Chief Murphy shouted at each other from three sides of the mayor's desk. The objects of contention, a small plastic bag holding a credit card, a letter-size manila envelope, and a flat sheet of paper, lay on the desk between them. Bakey was making loud and passionate points about national security and the rights of the federal government. Baca felt that if the government did a better job of protecting the citizens, there wouldn't be an issue. Murphy's only point was that his job was protecting his people and he was by god going to do that and do it his way whether a bunch of federal prima donnas liked it or not. His men seemed to agree with him.

Foreman walked over to the fourth side of the desk and said, very quietly, "Gentlemen, could we elevate this discussion beyond the high school level?"

They turned on him as one, but before anyone could attack, he picked up the manila envelope and asked the chief, "Do you expect your labs to get any more out of this than they did the first four?"

Murphy shook his head angrily.

"Then let's let the Feds play with it."

He tossed it in front of Bakey, who made an angry comment about contaminating evidence. Foreman said, mildly, "My prints are on file. If you find more than one set, then you can probably identify several postmen, a kid in the mail room, the Chief's secretary, and maybe even Gabriel if he was exceptionally careless this time."

Bakey glared and told him he was a pain in the ass.

Foreman nodded agreeably and lifted the baggie. He held it up so everyone could see the plastic credit card inside. He squinted through the plastic and said, "This might be more useful. The name on the card is Gabriel, and I suppose his street address, account number, zip code, and maybe his birthday could be encoded on the magnetic stripe on the back. Does anyone here think that we could dash over to that address and arrest him?"

"It's at least a place to start," the chief growled. "That's more than we have now."

"Good point," Foreman said. "I also notice that the card seems to be wet, as if the inside of the bag was sprayed with something. Would you like to open it and run the card through a reader?"

"I'll have the card disinfected, sterilized, and then read it," the chief said grimly.

"Will you have the fluid in the bag analyzed? Cultured? Maybe get the genome read? Can you get all that done as quickly as the feds?"

"No, but—"

"But you don't trust them to share their findings. Is that it?"

"In a nutshell." He glared at Bakey.

"What do you want, Murphy? A personal guarantee?" Bakey was just as angry as the police chief. He pointed a thumb over his shoulder. "You want a hostage? You want me to leave Dexter here until I give you the results?"

Foreman sighed. "I don't suppose either of you has considered trying to swipe the card through the plastic." He looked at them in turn. "No? Cashiers do it all the time."

Murphy looked at one of his officers and grated, "Card reader. Now."

"And that leaves only this." Foreman looked at the sheet of plain white printer paper. Three sentences in a typewriter font and large black type. He read it aloud.

`The CDC has my file.`

`The gold buys silence.`

`Instructions tomorrow.`

The note had captured every eye in the room. Danny had edged up beside Foreman. He couldn't take his eyes off it. He felt sick and started to say something until the scientist elbowed him quietly and shook his head.

Bakey cleared his throat and said, "Get Marchand. The CDC guy."

"Yes, sir." Dexter hurried out of the room.

Murphy asked, "The file?"

"If Gabriel sent it, we need to know how dangerous it is."

Baca said softly, "We have to pay. He already showed what he can do."

Again, Danny took a deep breath and opened his mouth. Again, Foreman elbowed him. This time he nodded firmly at Agent Bakey. Danny closed his mouth and waited. Again.

Dexter popped back into the room. "He wouldn't come. He has to get back to Atlanta. He said it's an emergency."

Bakey cursed.

Foreman asked, "Did he find the file?"

"He said it was everything he hoped it wasn't."

"Okay." Bakey scooped the note, envelope, and baggie into an evidence bag. He looked at the Chief. "You okay with this?"

Murphy started to object. Foreman told him it didn't matter. He looked at the scientist for a moment, obviously thinking hard, then said. "Yeah. Okay. Just tell me what you find."

As soon as the two agents cleared the room, he demanded, "All right. What the hell is going on?"

Foreman gestured at the two remaining uniforms.

Murphy ordered them to guard the door.

They left.

Foreman took a deep breath, then said, "Danny's been dying to tell you, so I'll let him say it."

Murphy and Baca both focused on Danny.

The Mayor said, "What?"

Murphy said, "Speak up, son."

"It's just that Gabriel sent three different threats. The chalk, the money, and the credit card." Danny cleared his throat. He felt self-conscious. "He already poisoned the chalk at the concert before he sent the first note. He spread the poisoned money around before we got the second note. If that rumor is right, he already poisoned some card machines before we got the card. And now he's threatening to tell everyone how to make poisoned bacteria. Or at least that's what it sounds like to me."

Baca leaned back in his chair. He seemed to deflate slowly. He glanced at Foreman. "Is this what you wanted to say? What you didn't want the FBI to hear?"

Foreman nodded. "We don't want them to think they have to use a shotgun to kill our fly."

Chief Murphy growled, "What the hell does that mean?"

"How much of the city would they sacrifice to keep Gabriel's secret?"

Chapter 14

The rest of the meeting accomplished nothing at all. Frantic movement in every direction led nowhere. The chief asked what the card reader found on the magnetic stripe. It said, SHOW ME THE MONEY.

Baca started to giggle when he heard that. Within seconds his head was on desk, on his arms, and his shoulders began to shake. He stayed like that until he could look up with dry eyes, but his sleeves were damp. He suggested arresting the university, or at least the biology department. Foreman said the FBI already interviewed everyone in the department who might know the difference between DNA and RNA. They were making a list of all current and past biology students who looked suspicious.

Chief Murphy asked if it could be useful to identify which labs had equipment that could be used to modify genes. Foreman said it wouldn't hurt and asked to see the file Gabriel sent. He said the biology department faculty could be more helpful if they knew what kind of equipment and supplies Gabriel used, so Murphy called Bakey back and asked for a copy of the file. Bakey said it was classified and even the FBI wasn't allowed to see it. Foreman tried calling Dr. Marchand at the CDC directly. It took hours to get through and all he learned was that the CDC only had access to the file on a need to know basis. That didn't include Dr. Marchand, but Gabriel had used CRISPR editing tools and the note included a number of long gene sequences and instructions on how to insert them into the bacterial nucleoids.

When Foreman reported that conversation, the mayor and the chief just stared at him blankly. Danny didn't feel much more knowledgeable, but he did feel confident enough to ask, "You mean the chromosomes, right?"

Foreman told him that bacteria were prokaryotes and didn't have chromosomes because, obviously, they didn't have a nucleus. Danny blushed and decided to keep his mouth shut until he knew what he was talking about. When he shut up, his father asked Foreman to write down as much as he knew and sent a pair of detectives to the department head with the note. He also had instructions to identify and seal any laboratory at the university that could be used to do the work.

That opened the meeting to a number of other detectives as well as some medical personnel from the health department. Within an hour, suggestions were flying around the room at a furious pace. Most were immediately shot down, but occasionally one would send a team of detectives or doctors on an urgent mission. Danny felt more and more isolated, and he finally ducked out. The sun floated only an inch above the horizon by the time he reached his car. He drove home through deepening shadows and found the house empty. He called his mother from the kitchen and bedroom wings and even checked the garage.

Her car was missing.

He went through the house again, then started dialing. When she didn't answer her phone, he tried Grace Baca. He thought she might go there. He couldn't think of any other friend she'd want to see during this crisis. Grace didn't answer, so he took a chance on Rosa. She didn't answer either, but that didn't really surprise him. He eventually tried texting his mother, though as far as he knew the only texts she'd ever answered were from Emma, who didn't know you could actually talk on a phone. Emmie.

When his mother didn't answer his text, Danny drove to Mercy hospital to find Rosa. He needed to talk. He didn't know what he needed to talk about but he felt full of words. Sunset faded into deep dusk by the time he parked, and he changed his mind about Rosa while crossing the lot toward the hospital's main entrance.

He walked past the entrance and circled the lot until he neared the Emergency doors and the three refrigerated trailers sitting in the lot. A generator roared on each trailer. There had only been two trailers when he delivered Emmie. Which one was she in? He thought maybe the second. He crouched by it. The heavy bulk of the box cast a dark shadow on the side away from the parking lot's overhead lights. The exhaust from the generators burned his eyes a little. They stung anyway. Burned just enough that they'd begun to water. That annoyed him so he sat on the pavement in the deeper darkness under a double wheel and tried to breath deeply so his eyes would stop watering. Didn't work of course.

He sat there, waiting to dry up, pretty sure the exhaust was his only problem because he wasn't sobbing or anything stupid like that, and then he suddenly realized that Tony was here too. Probably in the same trailer. Maybe even together. He thought they might be able to take care of each other, but deep down he thought they would be better if he could be with them too. But he couldn't, not while Gabriel lived.

That gave him a reason to stand up. That and the realization that someone was approaching the trailer with a flashlight. So he stood up, not paying any attention, and banged the hell out of his forehead on the edge of the wheel well. He fell on his hands and knees and stayed there, dripping on the pavement, until the flashlight spotted him and he saw the drops puddling in the yellow pool of light.

"Are you all right, sir?"

Woman's voice. Not friendly, but not hostile. He nodded and more drops fell and the puddle spread, mostly clear but a lot of red too. Red and wet black asphalt.

"What are you doing here? Have you been drinking?"

"No."

"What happened? Been in a fight?"

He shook his head. "No fight. No drink. Came to see Emmie. And Tony."

"Can you stand up?"

"Don't want to." If he stood up, he'd have to start doing things.

A hand slid into his armpit and lifted, so he went ahead

and stood up. Path of least resistance and all that.

"You look familiar. Have we met?"

He glanced at her. Uniform. Badge. He said, "Danny Murphy."

"The chief's son?"

He nodded.

"What are you doing here, Danny?"

"Came to see my sister. And my friend."

"Where are...?"

He pointed at the trailer. She said, oh. Then she said, "You're bleeding pretty bad. What happened?"

"Bumped head when I stood up. Stupid."

"You need a bandage. Maybe some stitches."

"Okay." He started walking toward the emergency exit.

She said he couldn't go in there. He said he had friends there. Doctor Pam and Rosa the nurse. She said okay, we'll see, and helped him as far as the door where the orderly guarding it took one look and the names and went inside.

Later, Rosa came out and gave a little cry when she saw him. She put a mask on him and took him just inside the door, where the light was better, and called someone to look at his head. It wasn't bad. They put five staples in it and wrapped it and gave him a bunch of antibiotics, then told Rosa to get him outside. She led him back through the doors and asked if he could get home by himself.

He said, "I need that phone, Rosa."

She looked confused for a moment, then nodded and went inside. He waited beside the orderly and the lady cop until she came back and put it in his pocket. He asked her how Janis was doing. She said better, but it would be a week before she could go and they had to find a place for her to go.

That confused him. "Why can't she go home? How long can Pam keep working like this? Gabriel can't last forever."

Rosa stared past him at the trailers. She said, "Pam didn't make it."

"Didn't . . . ?" He reached out for the wall and started to sag. She ducked under his arm and took his weight. The exhaust must have gotten pretty bad again. He was having trouble seeing.

Rosa told the orderly that she would walk him to his car.

He tried to tell her that wasn't necessary but by the time he got the words out she had already done it. She put him in the back seat and got in beside him. She just held his hand and after a while he looked over and realized the exhaust was bothering her too.

He said, "I couldn't find our moms."

She nodded. "They came down to volunteer. They're working at the gym."

"Gym?"

"At the high school. They have cots set up. We send the patients who aren't critical there. They have a doctor and four nurses and a bunch of volunteers."

"I don't understand." Danny shook his head. "What are they doing there?"

"The same thing I did on the bus. Changing sheets and helping. You know, cleaning up. We have three hundred beds there. The doctor and nurses take care of medical emergencies, but the volunteers do all the rest. Feed them and wash them and other things. Whatever has to be done."

"Will they be okay?"

"They are safer than at home, Danny." She wiped her cheeks. "They get antibiotics and there is antitoxin if they have any symptom at all."

"But what about Pam?"

"Pam worked herself to exhaustion. Her immune system failed. They said she caught pneumonia and hid it. She didn't take care of herself and I think she missed Janis terribly on top of everything else. She died, but she didn't have Gabriel's plague."

"Okay." If the doctors said that, it must be true. "It sucks for Janis though. Does she know?"

"Not yet. They have to tell her pretty soon."

"I'd like to see her."

"You can't. Not until she's discharged. They'll probably send her to the gym soon. Maybe you can see her there. Your mom might be able to get you in. Or mine."

"I want to help her if I can, Rosa. I have to."

"Why?" She stared at him.

"Because of Emmie. She was Emmie's friend."

Rosa nodded slowly. She reached over and took his hand

and squeezed it. "She's a sweet girl. She's going to need help, though. We all are."

"Yeah."

Danny leaned over and tried to kiss Rosa's cheek. It didn't feel right through two surgical masks so he took his off and threw it out the window. It was heavy with blood. He tried again. It still wasn't much of a kiss, but he did catch a corner of her temple above her mask.

She laughed, said, "Goodbye, Danny," and ran for the ER.

For long minutes, Danny watched the brightly lit entrance with the red emergency sign glowing in two-foot high letters on the wall above it and the well-lit parking lot, the humming refrigerated trailers, and the stiff orderly guarding the door, armored by his surgical mask, hair net, green robe and latex gloves. Then he took the throw-away phone Rosa had slipped into his pocket and dialed the entry for Peter.

When Mike answered, he said, "Spidey."

"Yes?"

"It looks like the payoff will be tomorrow."

"Do you know how?"

"They're still waiting for instructions."

"I need details."

Danny needed to calm himself. His hand was sweating on the phone. He took a deep breath and said, "I want something too."

"Parker. . . ." A sigh, dead silence, and then: "What?"

"A gun." He swallowed and added, "Bullets."

"I can't do that."

"Yes you can."

"Think about what you're asking."

"You don't care who kills him."

The response was sharp and instant. "I lost my whole family!"

"And now you want justice. Justice!"

"Don't you?"

"I want him to look at me while he dies."

"Jesus."

"You know where I am? I'm sitting in my car in the lot at Mercy and I'm looking at the trailers. My sister is in one of them. My best friend. Your mom and dad." He lowered his voice to a near whisper. "Give me it, Mike."

He listened to silence until he almost gave up. Then he heard, "Tomorrow. Come to my meeting."

The connection went dead.

Danny's hand trembled when he shoved the phone under the seat and started the car, but he had it under control before he parked in front of the high school gymnasium. He dug a mask out of the glove compartment and pulled it on before going in.

A cop met him just inside the doors. He sat at a folding table in the lobby area just in front of the double doors that accessed the gym floor and he stood the moment Danny entered. He wore the uniform with one addition: a bright green band around his left bicep. He held up his hand and said, "Sorry, sir. This area is off limits."

"I just need to talk to my mother for a minute. She's volunteering here."

"It's not going to happen. There are sick people here. You can't disturb them."

"I am going to see her if I have to call—" He stopped a moment, then pulled the green band Mike gave him yesterday from his pocket and slipped it over his right arm.

The cop took in the armband and nodded. "There are fresh gowns on the table to the right of the doors. You'll need to wear one of those, a hair net, gloves, and shoe covers. The docs say you can't catch anything here but it's best to be careful."

"Right. Thanks."

He dressed and stepped into the gym.

The bleachers had been folded back against the walls. Six rows of cots ran the length of the polished wood floor. Almost every cot was occupied by a body, male or female. Most lay curled on one side or another. Some lay flat but they all stared blankly into the dim shadows that filled the room. The place smelled faintly of antiseptic, urine, feces, and sweat. It looked like one volunteer drifted around the floor for every twenty cots delivering water, soda, or clean sheets. None of them wore name tags, though, so he had to walk around, peering into each face, trying to recognize the eyes between the paper masks and the head coverings.

136

He never found his mother. She found him and tapped his shoulder. "Danny?"

"Mom!" He opened his arms and stepped toward her, but of course she backed away and he remembered where he was and froze. He started to ask if she was okay but found he couldn't speak. He just stood there searching what little he could see of her face.

She asked, "Is something wrong? Is your father okay?"

"He's fine, Mom. What are you doing here?"

"Where should I be? Sitting alone in my empty house? Waiting for Ben's three hours with me? Or yours?"

Stung, Danny said, "We're trying to stop Gabriel."

"And now I'm trying to save these people."

"I know, but. . . ."

"I wanted to be more than a piece of furniture sitting alone and waiting for someone to talk to me. I called Grace and she told me what Rosa was doing. We talked it over and came down to volunteer. A lady from TonysWay put us to work right away."

"From TonysWay? You aren't working for the hospital?"

"We're working for the future."

"Oh." He didn't know what to say to that. "Does Dad know you're doing this?"

"Feel free to tell him if he notices I'm missing and bothers to ask."

"Okay." He hesitated. "Are you coming home tonight?"

"They have a dorm set up for us here. We can leave, but after we've been exposed they say it's better not to. I'll be fine, Danny. I'm sure you can make your own supper."

"Right." He felt defeated and turned away from her, then spun around and called, "Mom?"

She looked at him and waited.

He said, "I love you. I'm proud of you. This is important work."

After a moment, she nodded and the mask over her face wrinkled a little, like she might have smiled. Then she turned to the nearest bed and said, "Just go, Danny. "

Dusk had long since settled into night when he reached his car. He called his father's office to see if Foreman needed a ride home. Brenda answered and said the Chief had arranged for a patrol car to take him home later. He'd also left a message for Danny: go home, take care of your mother, and try to attend the eleven a.m. conference in the morning. And don't worry about collecting Doctor Foreman for the meeting. One of the patrols would handle that.

Danny allowed himself five minutes to feel abandoned before he turned the key in his car and started home to see if he could find any leftovers. He almost made it before deciding that he couldn't face the empty house any more than his mother could.

Very few businesses wasted money on electricity for signage any more, but a green neon shamrock, *Paddy's Pub*, blinked on his left a block ahead. It looked like a good place to hide for a couple of hours and might even have an open kitchen, so he parked and walked across three empty lanes. No traffic in either direction for at least a quarter mile. When he opened the door and held up a credit card, the bartender shook his head. Then he noticed the green arm band Danny'd forgotten to remove and smiled. "They're in the back."

Puzzled, Danny walked the length of the bar and found a private room behind a beaded doorway. Eight tables, pushed into one long column, filled the center of the room. It was full of men and women, all of whom sported green armbands. Another table partially blocked the entrance. The man sitting there looked at him suspiciously. "You're a new face. You sure this is the right meeting?"

"Not really." He shook his head and looked around, wondering what the hell he'd walked into. "I'm hungry. I came in for a burger and a beer and the bartender sent me back here. What's going on?"

"Whose team are you on?" When Danny looked confused, the guard repeated his question more firmly. "Who gave you the arm band, guy?"

"Oh!" The question suddenly made sense. "Mike. Mike Massini. Do you know him?"

"Just a minute." He lifted a cell phone and speed-dialed. He spoke quietly into the phone for a few seconds, then pushed his chair back slightly. Two men at the near end of the table shifted slightly. The guard looked up at Danny. "What did you say your name was again?"

"I didn't." He was beginning to rethink how badly he wanted that beer. "If that's Mike, tell him Spidey is here."

The guard nodded and said a few words into the phone, then looked back at Danny and described him. Another wait and then, "Is there another name he might know you by?"

"Oh, hell!" He was angry. "Just forget it, okay? I'm not that hungry!"

He started to turn, but the bartender was suddenly behind him and the two men from the table were approaching. The guard was on his feet too. He said, "I think we need that other name, buddy."

"Damn it. Parker. Tell him Parker." He held out his hand. "If that's really Mike on the phone, let me talk to him."

The guard held onto his phone and repeated the name. Then his eyes widened and he relaxed. He waved the two men back to the table and apologized. "I'm sorry about the confusion here, friend, but you walked in on a private meeting. You can't attend, but you're welcome to eat at the bar. Anything you want. As much as you want. On Mike."

"Christ!" Danny stamped back to the bar and ordered a cheeseburger and fries with a tall beer. He sipped the beer and thought about the meeting he wasn't welcome at until he noticed a talking head moving her mouth on the television over the bar. He caught the bartender's attention and pointed at his ear, then watched television while he waited for his food.

The news wasn't bad. A list of free food and drug distribution sites. The name of the supermarket chain designated to sell food people might actually want to eat for the rest of the week. The application process for permission to leave the city, along with requirements and documentation to present at the civic auditorium tomorrow. The number of new infections reported. The number of new suspicious house fires reported. Parking and ticket information for the big TonysWay rally tomorrow evening. And then his cheeseburger arrived. He wolfed it down, stuffed as many fries as he could into his belly, washed them down with the last of his beer, and set out for home.

He didn't make it that time either. He drove right past his turnoff and ten minutes later found himself at the Massini's house. He sat in the driveway wondering why the hell he couldn't get home. Then he walked around the house and looked in the back yard. Parker's bowl was empty and the dog was nowhere to be found. He looked around for him, but shadows concealed most of the yard. He called him a couple of times. Parker! Parker! Lights came on in the neighbors window, but the dog did not come. So he got back in his car and drove around the neighborhood, calling for Parker whenever he saw a suspicious shadow under a tree or beside a house. The shadows remained shadows. When he passed Tony's place the second time, he turned toward home.

Chapter 15

The house still felt empty when Danny woke up Wednesday. The bandage stuck to his forehead when he showered so he ignored it. The kitchen table and stove were spotless. The dishwasher was empty. He checked the garbage pail under the sink hoping for a hint that someone, anyone, had been in the house. He wanted coffee, but the thought of dumping grounds in the untouched garbage seemed wrong somehow.

As a last resort, he checked his parents' bedroom. His father lay on the bedspread. He had most of a bottle of Jameson's on the bedside table next to a pad of post-it notes. He walked close enough to check the top note. His father had scrawled, in a very shaky hand, *Danny, when you get up, please—*

He started to wake him, but his father's sleep was so deep that he hadn't the heart. Instead, he went out for breakfast and couldn't find a single restaurant open. Even the Campus Cafe was closed and the streets seemed strangely empty. He decided to take his chances on finding a cup and a donut at his father's office and headed for the city admin complex. That's where he discovered the reason for the closed shops and the empty streets.

To reach the admin building, he had to pass the civic auditorium. He couldn't. A half mile away, the streets were jammed. Bumper to bumper traffic inched along. Even the sidewalks were full. A parade of families, couples, groups of friends, all pushed toward the auditorium. Every face was covered by a surgical mask, scarf or bandanna. Blankets covered baby carriages. Blankets draped infants in their mothers' arms. Every mouth seemed to be moving, but Danny couldn't make out a single word. He rolled his window down and immediately rolled it back up when he heard nothing but desperation and anger fueled by fear.

The only pockets of order on the street surrounded men and women wearing green armbands and armed with whistles. They cleared traffic jams, moved jaywalkers out of the street, and halted traffic so the mobs piling up at every intersection could cross.

Danny decided to try another route and turned right at the next cross street. A woman with an armband waved him back into line, blowing her whistle furiously. He kept turning. She stepped in front of his car and blew her whistle. Her face was red. She looked like her next move would be to craw up on the hood and bash in his windshield. He dug his armband from his pocket and held it up. She nodded angrily and cleared a path for him through the milling horde. As he inched by her, she pounded on his window and shouted, "Next time wear the damned thing! How the hell am I supposed to know you're a friend if you don't wear the colors? Asshole!"

He looked as apologetic as he could, pulled the band over his arm, and crept on down the block. Traffic eased considerably. Still, he didn't get to the admin building until almost eight. His father's office was full of uniformed cops shouting into telephones. Worse, Brenda was nowhere to be found and the coffee pot was missing. He stepped out of the confusion and leaned against the wall to decide on his next move.

"Danny Murphy?"

He needed a few seconds to recognize the man in front of him. Bakey, Special Agent in Charge. He nodded.

"You look like you could use a cup of coffee. You mind if I call you Danny?"

Danny laughed tiredly. "Throw in a donut or a Danish and you can call me Waldo."

The agent offered a hand.

Danny shook it and followed him down the hall to a small conference room. A sheet of paper with 'FBI' hand printed on it in black marker was taped to the door. Inside, steel desks with a computer and one or two flat screens occupied three walls. A long folding table against the fourth wall held a large metal coffee urn, a column of paper cups, a stack of napkins, and three boxes of mixed pastries. Fresh! Danny started salivating the moment he smelled them.

Bakey waved at the table. "Help yourself."

He did. One full cup of black coffee and two Danishes balanced on a napkin. He mumbled his thanks around a mouthful of sweet bread and raspberry jam.

"We get a shipment every morning." Bakey said. "Feel free to drop in again before the eleven o'clock meeting."

"Every morning?"

"They come on the morning chopper." Bakey nodded at his arm. "When did you join TonysWay, Danny?"

"I didn't, really." It occurred to him that the pastries might not be free. "Mike gave it to me, probably because I was his best friend."

"You are Mike's best friend?"

Danny shook his head. "Tony's. Mike is . . . was his brother. I met Tony when we were just kids. We started first grade together. I've always known him. Why?"

"I'm curious. Mike is becoming an important man. He's got a lot of supporters. People do what he tells them."

"He's just trying to help, that's all. Did you see the mess around the civic auditorium? His people are directing traffic and they distribute food and medicine."

"I realized that. They also check on their neighbors and take folks to the hospital if they get sick. They're doing a great job."

"But?"

"Some people would say those are the mayor's jobs," Bakey said softly. "Or your father's."

"They don't have the people, or the money."

"That doesn't seem to be a problem for Massini." Bakey said. "Do you know where he gets his money?"

"No." Danny felt a chill. "Probably donations. That's just a guess."

"He must be a great fund raiser," the agent said mildly, "working in a city without a banking infrastructure, a city where no one uses cash. I'd really like to know how he manages that."

"You could ask him."

"I'm asking you, Danny. His brother's best friend."

"I told you, I'm not part of his group. He just gave me the armband."

"And yet you attended a meeting of the planning committee last night."

"What?"

"Paddy's Pub? Remember?"

"I don't believe this!" Danny began pacing. "I stopped in for a sandwich. It was the first place I saw open. I didn't know there was a meeting and I damn near got thrown out. The meeting was in the back room. I wasn't allowed to attend it. I had a quick burger at the bar and got the hell out of there. If you were watching the place, you know that, and if you weren't watching, you know it now."

"Calm down, Danny. Nobody accused you of anything."

"It sure as hell feels like it."

"Listen, we have no evidence that Mike is doing anything wrong. He might be exactly what he seems: a good citizen doing his best for his community, but the bureau has three obligations here. The first is catching the poisoner, naturally, but the others are just as important. We have to minimize the damage and do everything we can to see that this never happens again. That means that when this is all over, our democracy is strong and the government that protects it is strong. Don't you want those things too?"

"Mostly I want Gabriel stopped."

"Spoken like your father's son." Bakey nodded approvingly. "That's what the bureau wants too, but the rest of it matters just as much. If we can't keep our country safe, then Gabriel has won, no matter how many times we hang him."

Danny tried to act casual. "How close are you to hanging him?"

"We're making a little progress. We have a lead on a possible lab and our profiler has a good handle on—"

He started to say more, but a commotion in the hall

interrupted him. A uniformed officer threw open the door and shouted, "Mayor's conference room, now!"

"What the...?" Bakey jumped and ran.

Danny filled his cup and grabbed another pastry before following them. The elevator was full, so he took the stairs. The climb gave him an opportunity to think about exactly how many people the bureau had watching Mike. They obviously had some sort of surveillance on the pub last night. That could mean an insider at the meeting or something as simple as a bug, and if Bakey really thought Danny had attended the meeting, then he probably didn't have either an agent or a bug in the bar. That implied a man, or at least a camera, watching the front door of the pub. In any case, Mike needed to know about it, and Danny did not need to be seen telling him.

The top floor was crowded and way beyond tense. Danny got as far as the door to the conference room before he came to a complete stop. He couldn't see anything and he heard only voices loudly demanding updates before first the mayor and then his father shouted, "QUIET!"

It didn't get quiet, but the volume in the room dropped enough for him to hear a television announcer: "—peating, first reports have one officer down and two more possibly injured. Exclusive video from our sky-cam shows at least eight bodies on the steps of the civic auditorium and— Wait, that video may be too disturbing to some of our viewers so we won't— What? It's already on air? Right, our exclusive video on— Just a moment. We have a report from our own Rachel Birmstat who is on the scene— Rachel, could you tell us exactly what . . . Rachel?"

Five or six seconds of silence followed before a woman's voice cut in. "Yes, John. This is Rachel Birmstat reporting for — wait — twelve? Is that right? Twelve? Okay, this is Rachel Birmstat reporting exclusively from the civic center. We now have reports of at least twelve casualties after mob violence broke out when FEMA abruptly closed the applications for exit permits— What? Oh *beep*!" A volley of gunfire followed her last transmission and it became impossible to hear more as the men and women in the room shouted, "Did you see that? What happened? Oh my God!"

At that point, Danny decided he could do without the

shared experience and walked down to the mayor's office, where he found Patty watching the same program with only a box of tissues for company. He joined her and watched while the the count of dead went up and down and the injured count went up. When they settled, an hour later, one policeman had been killed and two others injured, one critically. The seventeen dead civilians included one family of three— mother, father, and eleven year old daughter—and a mixed bag of adult men and women. Various numbers of injured bystanders had been taken to emergency clinics and an outlying hospital since the two main hospitals were inundated by the botulism plague. That was the first time he'd heard it called a plague rather than a poisoning.

When the anchors started repeating themselves, Danny asked the secretary, Patty, if she'd try another channel. She shook her head. "Don't you watch TV? This is the only local news channel."

"You're kidding." He hadn't turned on a television in over a week. He'd seen them on frequently, but always tuned to the local channel, and usually to the same two talking heads. "You mean none of the nationals are covering the poisoning?"

She shook her head. "I guess it's not that important."

"I can't believe that." Danny felt a little numb and a lot apprehensive. He'd been too focused on his own dead to see how much was dying around him. He needed to discover the true scope of this thing and he didn't know how to do that. He asked, "What are people saying on the social media, Patty? They must be going crazy."

She looked at him like he'd suddenly grown a second head. "What social media? The internet is up and down all the time. Sometimes I can read posts and email, but mostly—" She leaned toward him and whispered, "People say it's the government, but I don't believe that. It must be Gabriel doing it somehow."

Before Danny could form another question, the mail room delivered a heavy tube, about eight inches long, tightly wrapped in a re-purposed manila folder and carefully taped at both ends. The guy pushing the cart tossed it on Patty's desk with a pile of envelopes and inter-office folders.

Danny watched as he wheeled his cart out the door and

then turned to find Patty's chair pushed back from her desk and Patty backing away from the desk and breathing heavily. She also seemed to be whimpering as she stared at the tube. He said, "Do you mind if I put it on the mayor's desk?"

She shook her head, so he picked it up and carried it to the inner office. He stopped on his way back and told her not to notify anyone until he got the mayor up here. She nodded and told him she was going to the restroom. He asked her to wait until he returned with the mayor and then ran for the conference room.

The crowd there had shrunk, but he still had to push his way through the door. He waved to get the mayor's attention, then mouthed, "Excuse me, sir. It's Rosa!"

Baca snapped, "Later, Danny! I'm in the middle of a crisis here!"

"So is she, sir. You really need to take this!"

Baca hesitated, then announced he'd be back in a minute and made his way toward the door. Danny stopped him with a hard grip on his arm when he tried to push by. He leaned into the mayor's ear and whispered, "Ask Bakey to take the meeting."

Baca looked surprised, then very worried. He made the request, which left Bakey looking surprised, but pleased, and then followed Danny out. Once they were in the hall, he demanded, "What is this? What's going on? Is Rosa...?"

Danny waited until they were well out of earshot before he whispered, "Your office. Another message."

The mayor ran.

When they pushed through his outer door, Baca looked around. "Where's Patty?"

"Toilet probably. She's scared. First the shootings and now this." Danny pulled him into his private office and pointed to the tube. "It might be instructions for the gold. I thought you should see it before Bakey."

The Mayor nodded. "You have a pocket knife?"

"Yes." He swallowed nervously before asking, "You want me to open it?"

"You might get in trouble with Bakey. Anyway, it's addressed to me. See if you can get your father down here without getting Bakey too excited."

147

"Right." He pulled a used print-out from the trash beside Patty's desk and scrawled a quick note, in large letters. "MOM." Back in the conference room, he waved it at his father. Bakey looked annoyed. Murphy looked even more annoyed, but he came to the door, listened a second, and beat Danny to Baca's office.

Danny locked the outer door before joining them at the Mayor's desk. One end of the tube had been cut open and both men were looking into it. Finally, Baca said,"What the hell," and shook the tube over his desk. Another tube slid out: pages of white copier paper wrapped around a water bottle and held together by a small strip of tape.

Baca stared at it uncertainly. "Now what?"

Danny picked up the knife.

The Chief said, "Don't touch it!"

"If the FBI get a hold of it, we may never see what he wants," Baca said. "We have to know."

"Okay."

Danny cut carefully through the tape and the tube opened when the paper began to uncurl. A bottle of drinking water rolled across the desk. When the paper had completely flattened, a second piece of tape stopped the bottle and left them face to face with Gabriel's final message:

IF Payment delivered and
　　　　exactly 20:00 9 July and
　　　　exact locations and
　　　　equal parts and
　　　　green sacks;
THEN
　　　　Delete Gabriel and
　　　　Delete 2001:0db8:85a3:123F::9d0F:8a2e:0370;

That was all.

The Mayor and Chief of Police looked confounded. Danny looked sick.

His father demanded, "What the hell is this?"

"Pseudocode." When they showed no sign of under-standing, he added, "It's a logic statement. It says that if we pay the gold at exactly eight o'clock and make the drops in certain places and green sacks, then Gabriel and something else will go away."

"What locations?"

Danny used the blade of the knife to flip over the next two pages. "There are fifty addresses here. Fifty! This is stupid!" He shook his head. "There's no way he can drive around collecting fifty different payments."

"Maybe he doesn't want them all," Baca said. "We can't watch fifty separate drops."

"After the shootings this morning, we'll be lucky to watch any," the chief sounded grim. "That TonysWay meeting starts at eight and I have to give it priority. Another incident like the one at the auditorium—"

Baca pointed at the last line. "What is this gibberish?"

"It looks like an internet address."

"Like google? Bullshit. That doesn't look anything like a web site."

"It does to a computer," Danny told him. "We can check it out later. What do you want to do now?"

"I want a copy of this," the Chief said, "before Bakey shows up with his experts."

"Okay." Danny pulled out his phone and took a picture of each page, then asked, "Is Brenda downstairs?"

"She better be."

Danny nodded and emailed the pictures to his father's work address. Then he held the camera so both men could see it and deleted the photos. They nodded and Murphy said, "I'm going to have Brenda print them. You want to come along, Danny?"

"Just call her," Baca suggested.

"There's another matter, too. Let's go, Danny." He led his son into the hallway. They started for the elevator just as Bakey came out of the conference room looking around suspiciously. Murphy waved to him and called, "Frank! We just got another message from Gabriel. Baca's office!"

"You didn't open it, did you?" Bakey started running.

"Opened it but didn't touch it." He waved at the Mayor's door and called, "Eddie will explain. I'll be right with you."

He changed direction and pushed into the stairwell, then stopped with his hand on Danny's shoulder. He looked worried. "Do you know where your mother is? She wasn't home last night and I didn't see her this morning."

"Rosa told me Mom and Grace went to the gym to volunteer so I went down there to see what was going on. She said she was tired of being alone and needed something important to do."

"The gym?" Murphy searched his son's eyes. "When is she coming home?"

"She didn't say, Dad."

"You couldn't tell me? At least leave a note?"

"You weren't home and I thought Mom probably told you."

"She asked me to call her yesterday. I didn't have time." He rubbed his scalp and sighed. "Okay, get Brenda to print Gabriel's message. The addresses for drops too, of course. Have her lock them up, her desk, not mine, and delete those emails. Then check out that web address thing."

"No problem." He started for the stairs.

"Danny?" His father stopped him. "After that, I want you to find your mom. Tell her . . . tell her I'm sorry. I'll be back home as soon as this is over."

"Okay."

"I want you to go to the meeting tonight. Listen to Mike and the others. Talk to people. Find out what's going on. Will you do that for me?"

"I'll do what I can."

Chapter 16

The Chief's outer office was only half full when Danny walked in. One lieutenant and two sergeants conferred in the corner by the coffee pot. Three uniforms huddled just inside the door. They managed to look simultaneously alert, bored, and thirsty. All six of them looked up with varying degrees of suspicion as he entered the room, but Danny recognized the lieutenant from earlier visits. He waved and they all lost interest.

He gave Brenda a look, nodded at the inner office, and just walked in. She followed him, looking wary. "What is it, Danny?"

"Dad said you have the password to his computer."

She nodded.

"I just emailed him three pictures. He wants you to print them and lock the prints up safely in your desk. Make sure no extra copies come out of the printer. I have to make sure no extra copies are left on his computer."

"My desk? Not his? Is this about the—," Brenda looked grave, "—situation?"

"Yes."

She nodded grimly. A few seconds later she sent a document to the printer.

When she started for the door, he opened a private window on the browser and carefully typed in the IP address from the open picture of Gabriel's note. When he got a "connection timed out" error, he verified that he'd typed the address correctly and tried again. He got the same error, so he closed the private window and deleted the browsing history and trash folders, then opened a command window and pinged the address. That earned him four "request timed out" errors. At that point, he gave up.

He spent a few minutes trying to remember everything he'd ever heard about Windows security, then started deleting every file he could find with a TMP extension and every temp directory he could find.

Brenda returned just as he began emptying the windows recycle bin. She looked nervous about something so he asked what was bothering her, beside the obvious.

"I couldn't help seeing the note," she said.

"Don't worry about that. Just don't talk about it." When she looked even more upset, he asked, "What is it, Brenda?"

"Well, I was thinking, green sacks aren't easy to find on short notice."

"Right! I'd better—" He jumped up and made it halfway to the door before he came to his senses and said, "You have an idea, don't you?"

Relieved, she grinned and told him about it.

Danny didn't stop smiling until one of Bakey's junior agents put a hand on his chest in the Mayor's outer office and told him to go away. A very loud discussion was going on in the inner office between Agent Bakey and the Mayor. He decided it might be interesting to interrupt it, so he said, very loudly, "I need to see my father! It'll just take a minute."

The noise level in the other room dropped appreciably and Murphy opened the door. Behind him, Baca and Bakey stood over the mayor's desk with its note and water bottle. They both looked angry. Foreman sat to one side looking upset.

Murphy waved at him. "What's the matter, Danny?"

"Do you still want me to hang around. I was going to look up Annette, but I can't find her address anywhere—"

"Who?" His father looked confused.

"Annette." He emphasized the second syllable. "I can't find the address."

"Oh." Murphy smiled. "Did you ask your mother?"

"Haven't seen her yet. If you don't need me, I'll go by the

gym now." He shrugged. "It's a little boring here, you know?"

"I imagine." Murphy's expression turned sour. "Nothing going on here but a riot and a bunch of shootings, right? Get out of here, Danny. Go to the gym, but don't forget your other chores. And stay away from crowds. And guns."

"Right." Danny snapped his fingers like he'd just remembered something. "Mom wanted me to find some of those environmentally friendly bags for her. You want me to do that before I start my chores?"

"What does she want with...?"

"For those angels. Her sewing club?"

Murphy recovered quickly. "How long would that take?"

"A couple hours. No more."

"Okay, help your mother out, son. Just don't forget—"

"My chores. Don't worry."

Foreman stood up then. "Are you going anywhere near the university, Danny?"

"It's on my way, Doc."

They left only after Agent Bakey took Foreman aside for a serious discussion of secrecy oaths and consequences. Once they were in the car, he started laughing.

Danny said, "What?"

"Annette address? Environmentally friendly bags?"

"I didn't think I was that obvious."

"No offense, Danny." Foreman kept chuckling. "I doubt even Mayor Baca got it, and Bakey was way too focused on his problem to hear you."

"Oh?" That sounded interesting. "What's Bakey's problem?"

"He doesn't want Gabriel paid. He doesn't think it will silence him."

"I agree with him on that."

"You do?" Foreman looked surprised. "So do I, but what's your reason?"

"The gold won't change anything. Gabriel always does something before he threatens to do it. Every time. I thought everybody would have noticed that by now."

"I think they know it."

"Then why deliver the gold? Assuming they are delivering it."

"Baca's desperate," Foreman spoke softly. "He's finished as mayor, no matter how this turns out, but he sees this as his only chance to save the people who elected him. Your father, on the other hand, sees this as his last best chance to catch Gabriel."

Danny raised his eyebrows. "Tracking chips?"

"He has something like that. He'll put one in each sack and follow any sack that moves."

"That's going to be tough tonight."

"Because of the TonysWay meeting? You know it, but he has a plan. He just won't say what it is."

Danny thought that over. He asked, "What's Bakey's game then? Is he worried about the money?"

"I think he's afraid Gabriel might really disappear if he gets paid, and his superiors want Gabriel more than anything," Foreman said, "even if it means he stays in town spreading his poison."

Danny had nothing to say to that. Just hearing it gave him chills. He drove a few blocks, then asked, "What's your take on Gabriel, Doctor Foreman? Is he going to keep poisoning people?"

"Probably not. If I knew why he started, I could make a better guess."

"It wasn't the gold."

"No, Danny. If he gave a damn about the gold, he wouldn't be playing that farce with the bags. Speaking of which, where in hell are you going to get fifty green sacks in a couple of hours."

"Dad once said that when he needed something impossible done, he asked a secretary. I asked Brenda." Danny parked in front of a fabric store was in a strip mall on the next corner and said, "Be right back."

Ten minutes later he walked out with two yards of heavy green cotton cloth and twenty five feet of cording. An older red Toyota had parked beside him. He handed his package to the woman in the driver's seat, then slid into his car. Foreman grinned and said, "Very efficient. Do you have to come back for the bags?"

"She'll get them to Brenda somehow." Danny cleared his throat. Curiosity was eating at him. "I heard a lot of arguing when I got back. What was that about?"

"The gold, of course, but it started with the shootings. Everything was reasonably quiet at the auditorium at first. The crowd was huge, but people lined up with their IDs and other documents. Some of the adults even brought vaccination records all the way back to grade school. They sat down with the interviewers and answered questions about how often they took the free antibiotics, their family physicians, whether they'd found any cash or bought bottled water, any symptoms of staph or E. coli infections, and their credit ratings."

"Their what?"

"Exactly. Credit ratings. It didn't take long to sink in that there are two ways out of the zone."

Danny said. "People who can pay their own way get out first. Everyone else who passes the interviews has to wait."

Foreman nodded. "And no one ever exposed to the plague will pass the interviews, Danny. That includes caregivers as well as patients."

"My mother? Rosa? Her mother?"

"And you."

"Right." That was obvious. "What started the shooting this morning?"

"Word spread about the options. Nobody liked their odds and when they started complaining, FEMA just canceled the registration. Somebody started a fight and things went downhill from there. At least that's the official line."

"What do you think?"

"Someone made a bad decision. People died." Foreman shrugged. "Does it really matter? Just add this body count in with the rest."

Did it matter? How could Foreman ask that? Danny held his temper as well as he could, but he could almost hear his teeth grinding. He said, "The little girl they shot was only eleven."

"How old was your sister?"

Danny slammed his hand into the steering wheel and shouted, "Gabriel killed Emmie, damn it! Gabriel!"

"Gabriel killed them both, or they both died because they were in the wrong place at the wrong time."

Danny stamped on the brake. His car squealed to a stop near the curb. "Get out!"

"Thanks for the ride." Foreman sighed and opened his door, but before leaving the car he said, "I know you're hurting, Danny, but before you surrender to revenge, ask yourself who you will hurt and who you will help."

He stepped out and closed the car door gently, then walked away.

Danny squeezed the steering wheel and trembled until he calmed down enough to drive to the high school gym. He made sure his arm band was in place before he entered the building. The guard in the lobby smiled when he saw the green band and said, "Hello, friend. Go right in."

Danny thanked him and started looking for his mother. When he couldn't find her, he asked one of the other volunteers and was told to check the boys' dressing room. That sounded strange, but he found her sitting on a cot beside Grace. They each had a cup of tea and they both looked exhausted. They smiled when he walked directly up to them. His mother said, "Hello, friend."

It took him a moment to realize she didn't recognize him. He lifted his mask and said, "Mom?"

"Danny!" She stood and hugged him, then pushed him back where she could see him easily. "How are you? How's your father?"

Grace rose, saying, "I should get back to work."

"Don't be silly, dear. We have another twenty minutes on break and you're just as interested in how your Eddie is doing as I am in Ben."

"Well, yes." She sank back onto the cot. They both stared at Danny, and waited.

"Okay. They're both okay." He stammered a bit. "Uh, Mr. Baca didn't know I was coming. Dad misses you, Mom. He told me to ask when you're coming home." When they said nothing, he continued, "They're both busy. Stressed. There was a big shooting this morning. They're evacuating the city. And Gabriel is still poisoning people."

His mother said, "We heard about the shooting."

Grace added, "We had Friends there, of course."

"Friends?" Danny was confused. "Who was there?"

156

Anne Murphy squeezed her son's shoulders and explained. "Everyone in TonysWay is a Friend, Danny. It's what we call each other."

"The only way we will get through this horrible time is by relying on our Friends," Grace said gently. "We have to trust our Friends and help our Friends. That is Tony's Way. That's what Mike Massini realized after he lost his family."

"I see. I guess." Danny felt more than a little uncomfortable. He asked Grace, "Does Rosa know about this? I mean about the Friends?"

"Of course." Grace smiled. "Rosa told us about the Way when she asked us to help here. I'm not sure how, but she got in touch with Mike and then she showed us what needs to be done. She showed us the Way."

Anne nodded. "You wear the colors, Danny, but you don't seem to know much about the Way. You should ask Mike to explain when you see him."

"I will." He swallowed nervously. "I'll probably see him tonight. I'll ask him then. I have to go now."

They nodded together and spoke as one. "Goodbye, Danny."

He muttered a quick 'see you,' and got as far as the door before remembering. He turned and asked, "What should I tell Dad? When are you coming home?"

"When he needs Friends more than he needs Gabriel."

At that, Danny got the hell out of there. He sat in his car and tried to figure out what was happening for a long time. Then he dug out the throw-away, dialed Peter, and told the woman who answered that Spidey was calling. After a minute or two of silence, she came back and invited him to stop by the Corner Cafe for a cup.

He worried all the way and by the time he parked, he felt sick. The sidewalk seemed more crowded than he remembered from his last visit. He had to push through groups of subdued friends, and the two men at the guard table stopped him despite his armband. He protested, "Hey, Mike invited me!"

"Fine, but leave your keys here. You'll get them back when you leave."

"Does he know about this?"

"He knows everything he needs to know, Friend. Just give me the car keys and have a cup of coffee. You won't wait long."

Danny gave up. He left his keys on the table and entered the cafe.

Rosa met him just inside the door. He started to smile when he recognized the eyes above her mask and stopped when the implication hit him. His gaze dropped to the green band on her left arm, then rose again. "How long?" he asked.

She took his elbow and guided him to a table with a single chair near the window. On the way, she murmured, "You mean TonysWay?"

He pulled his arm from her grasp and said, in a low, angry voice, "I mean Mike, Rosa. When you took that phone, I thought it was to help me. Not to—"

"I am helping, Danny." She kept her voice low, too, but she was obviously trying to soothe him. That angered him more, but he kept listening. "Not just you. Everyone. We're all trapped and Mike says the only way we'll get through this is by helping each other."

"I already heard that line from our mothers."

"Does that mean it isn't true? Or is it simply not what you want to hear?"

"It means I'm sick of all this 'Friend' bullshit," he snapped. "What matters now is Gabriel. Finding him and killing him. What you do with Mike is your business."

"I told you I was with Mike last year. You knew that. You're jumping to conclusions now and you've got no right. Focus on what matters. We have almost five hundred people infected with some kind of killer bacteria that's already killed almost three hundred. Our city is quarantined and we'd be starving if the government didn't ship in food we can't pay for. People are afraid to shake hands with their neighbors or go outdoors. We're hiding behind masks and wondering what's next on the poison list. Medicine? Baby formula? Water? Air? And now we've started shooting at each other."

She pushed him weakly and he slowly sank into a chair. She took a deep breath and told him, "We need to find a way out of this nightmare. We need Friends, Danny. We don't need more enemies."

She disappeared.

Danny sat alone, shaking. Someone put a cup of coffee on his table. He lifted his mask and sipped it, looking around.

Rosa was nowhere in sight. Mike sat at a large round table in the far corner of the cafe. Almost every chair at the other tables was full. In fact, the only empty chair in the room was on the wall to the left of the entrance, opposite . . . Foreman? Watching him?

He couldn't make up his mind what to do. He probably owed the man an apology, but on the other hand, he was still pissed at him for writing Emmie off as just another casualty. And he couldn't help wondering what Foreman was doing with TonysWay.

Mike took the decision out of his hands. When the crowd at his table abruptly left, Mike waved him over. He set Danny's keys on the table and pushed them a few inches toward him, then asked, "Do you have something for me?"

Danny felt more than a little hostility at the moment. He said, "We agreed on a trade, Mike."

"I'm trading. I asked a friend to clean your car. He said it was too dirty to do a good job. You'll need to clean under the driver's seat."

"Okay." Danny relaxed. He opened his cell phone and asked. "Is the cafe printer still on Wifi?"

When Mike nodded, Danny located his most recent email and sent the attachments to the cafe printer. "You've got them."

Mike pointed a finger at the counter. A moment later, Rosa hurried over with the printouts. She handed them to Mike and left without looking at Danny. Mike beckoned at another table and handed the two sheets that listed the drop locations to the man who appeared. "Scout these. See who else is watching. Be ready to tag a pickup after eight tonight."

The man and the paper disappeared. Danny said, "I want to go."

Mike ignored that. He pushed the picture of Gabriel's message toward him and asked, "What do you make of the water bottle?"

Danny glanced at it without much interest. "He's saying the water bottles are poisoned."

"Maybe." Mike pulled the picture back and studied it

159

pensively. "There's another way to think about it though. That bottle came from a local plant. We used to export water, produce, and a lot of other stuff, to most of the region. Suppose people starting thinking everything we export could be poisoned? What would that do to the city?"

Danny stared, horrified. "The city?"

"Precisely. We wouldn't have one."

Danny grabbed his keys and pushed away from the table.

Mike grabbed his arm. "You're going to our meeting, Danny. You and Doctor Foreman will be my guests. You can kill Gabriel tomorrow if you can find him."

"I'll be back. I have to see my father and the mayor about the deliveries, but I'll be here by five."

"Okay." Mike released him. "You and Foreman can walk over together."

Chapter 17

Rosa was leaning against Danny's car when he reached it. He shook his head and sighed. "What are you doing here?"

"You're going to city hall aren't you?"

"So?"

"I need to see Papa."

That pretty much trumped any objection he might have made. He said, "Get in."

Traffic was a bit heavier than yesterday, but it ran to bicycles and pedestrians. Danny wondered idly if gasoline deliveries had stopped. He wondered how hard it would be to pedal a bike while wearing a surgical mask. He wondered how many sacks of gold coins it took to make killing three hundred people worthwhile. He wondered if the gun was really under his seat. He wondered why Rosa had to visit her father.

When he couldn't take the silence any more, he asked, "Did Mike tell you to keep an eye on me?"

She shook her head. "He told me to explain TonysWay. He said it's important that you understand. We are the only solution to what's happening. The only solution. The feds won't solve our problem. Neither will the police. Neither will a gun."

Danny's grip on the wheel tightened. "You know about that?"

"I put it under your seat."

He asked quickly, "With ammunition?"

161

She smiled. "How good a shot are you?"

"It doesn't matter. I'm going to shove the barrel up his ass and pull the trigger until it stops banging. That should solve our problem."

"Your problem maybe." She shook her head and sighed. "It won't solve my problem, or your mother's, or the city's, or the country's."

He didn't say anything for a long time. Then he nodded. "I know that, Rosa. I'm not stupid."

"Just selfish?"

"Probably." A block later he whispered, "When I dropped Emmie and Janis at the bus, she told me she wasn't coming back. She meant because she was going to Denver, to our aunt's, and that's what I meant when I told her I knew that, but damn it, she said she wasn't coming back and then she didn't." He had to blink to keep driving. "And I just let her get on the bus and then a day and a half later I drove a bus to that damned camp and I brought her home in the fucking baggage compartment!"

Rosa stared through the windshield. Her jaw was tight and she said nothing.

Eventually Danny wiped his cheeks and said, "You know the real problem? Science is a tiger. That's the problem. We're riding a tiger and we can't get off."

"You mean gene editing?"

"And drones, and nukes, and chemical weapons, and ICBMs, and tanks, and everything, all the way back to machine guns and gun powder and steel and fire. Hell, maybe even sharp rocks. Some genius stuck a sharp rock on a stick ten thousand generations ago and now Gabriel killed Emmie and a couple of hundred other people." He felt his rant running down and added softly, "Maybe it isn't science. Maybe it's brains. Maybe Gabriel became inevitable when our first ancestor evolved a bigger brain."

"Maybe you're over-thinking it," Rosa said softly. "Suppose it is just the way we divide people into us and them. Friends and enemies. We can disagree with our friends without killing them. That's what TonysWay is about. We can share the world with anyone willing to share it with us."

Danny smiled grimly. "What does Mike say about

Gabriel?"

"Well, he did give you the gun."

"He doesn't expect me to use it."

"He wants you to attack the problem, not the symptom."

"The technology?" He snorted. "Lots of luck on that, Mikey."

Rosa gave him a moment before changing subject. "The message included an internet address. Did you check it out?"

"I tried, but there's no way to tell if it exists without internet access, and it looks like the FBI or Homeland Security has that blocked."

"Are you sure it is blocked for everyone?"

That was a thought. "Who do you have in mind?"

"Well, the FBI has an office right down the hall from your father. I don't think those guys would be out of contact with their headquarters."

"Right." He remembered Bakey's office from his cautious interrogation that morning. Three desks, each with a desktop computer. "We might manage that."

Danny casually slipped a hand under his seat after he parked, just to reassure himself. When he closed the car door, he found Rosa smirking at him over the roof. He shrugged and tried to beat her to the mayor's office.

Guards in the outer office patted them down, checked IDs, and sent their names in to make sure they were welcome. The Mayor opened his door almost immediately and waved them in, then closed and locked it behind them. The Chief barely looked up when they joined him at the desk. He was totally focused on an open box half full of gleaming golden coins.

On the other side of the desk, Brenda carefully counted Krugerrands into stacks of ten and arranged the stacks into two rows of five stacks. One hundred coins, total weight seven pounds, give or take. A hundred and seventy thousand dollars, give or take. Then she pushed each pile to a police lieutenant standing on her left. He recounted it, added a small white disk, and passed it to a uniformed officer who scooped the coins into a small green sack and wired it shut, then handed the sack to the mayor's secretary. She attached a numbered label to the sack, logged it on a clipboard, and glued a label to the sack. Another officer added the sack to the growing mound in a wheelbarrow near the door. A very serious-looking man wearing a suit and tie held a video camera on the operation.

Danny and Rosa joined the Chief. Danny whispered, "You're really doing it?"

Murphy nodded. "The governor's having a shit-fit. He's on the phone with Eddie every five minutes, screaming about this law or that procedure. We'd all be in jail right now if he could find anyone willing to enter the quarantine zone to arrest us."

Rosa snorted. "Saved by the plague?"

"That's one way to put it." Murphy made a sour face, then asked Danny, "You talk to your mother yet?"

"She joined TonysWay with Mrs. Baca. She said she'd be home when you needed a friend more than you need Gabriel."

"Crazy." His father shook his head and shot a glance at Danny's arm. "I guess you joined her?"

"No, Mike just gave me the band so I could get in to see him. They're recruiting me pretty hard though."

The Chief snorted at that. "Just don't forget where your loyalties lie, son."

"No chance of that." Danny changed the subject. "Rosa had an idea how we could check that internet address. We just need—"

"Don't bother. Bakey had his wizards in Washington check it out. He said the page doesn't exist but the address is good. A '404 error', whatever that means. Anyway, it sounds like we don't have to worry about the gene editing secret getting out."

"Don't be too sure." Danny looked nervous. "If the address is good, the web site could just be hidden. Gabriel could create it just by changing a file name."

"Really?"

Danny nodded. "And there's another thing. Gabriel gave us one address, one he promised to shut down, but he could have hidden his little secret on servers around the world. He could shut one site and open another in less than a second, if he even intends to keep his promise. And Dad? So far everything he's said was a lie."

The Chief took a long time to digest that. Then he rubbed his eyes and muttered, "We need to know exactly what is on that server. Can Bakey find out?"

"I hope so."

"Okay. I'll tell him." Murphy sighed. "You have anything else for us?"

"Not unless you'd like me to deliver three or four of those bags for you."

"Smartass."

They turned to Rosa, who'd been explaining the TonysWay philosophy to her father. ". . . so when he says our power is growing too rapidly, he doesn't mean things like the plague. As long as we divide the human race into friends and enemies, we'll always be racing our enemies for more power and more possessions. Mike says our only hope is to redefine ourselves, to choose what we become, and we have to choose friends, not enemies."

"Sounds wonderful." Baca smiled tolerantly at his daughter. "It's a shame he couldn't sell Gabriel on his vision of paradise."

"There will always be Gabriels," she said, "and we'll have to deal with them. You should really come to the meeting tonight, Papa. He's got a really big announcement to make and it's going to—"

"What announcement?" Murphy interrupted her.

"You're invited too, Chief. Come and find out."

"Right after I catch Gabriel and end the plague," he told her. "Meantime, I've got some gold to throw away and Danny has an errand to run."

Danny took that as an invitation to leave. He jumped on it. He had two hours before the meeting and things to do. He suggested dropping Rosa at the Campus Cafe or even at the stadium, but she stuck with him. She didn't ask a single question as he drove, seemingly at random, through the neighborhoods surrounding the university, but when he parked near the cafe a few minutes after five, she asked, "Did you make up your mind?"

"What do you mean?"

"I copied Gabriel's list for Mike, Danny. There were only three sites near the university and you drove by each of them at least twice." She spoke matter-of-factly. "You aren't as clever as you think."

Danny rubbed his forehead. "Why did Mike want copies of

the list?"

"He wants Gabriel as much as you do. The difference is, you want to kill him. Mike wants to neutralize him."

"Killing him will pretty much neutralize him, Rosa."

"It won't stop the spread of his gene editing technology."

"That ship has sailed, and it wasn't even Gabriel's boat, damn it. The minute it became possible to rewrite life, it became inevitable. Doesn't Mike know that?"

"He knows that you can't neutralize an idea with a bullet." She pushed her car door open, but before stepping out, she said, "You neutralize an idea with a better idea."

Danny hopped out and called after her, "Then what the hell does he need Gabriel for?"

"It isn't enough to have a better idea, Danny. You have to sell it, too. Gabriel's head will be the proof of concept for TonysWay."

Well, Hell.

The idea of using Gabriel's head to defeat him made sense. It was even an attractive option in an unsatisfying, nonviolent way. Whatever Mike had in mind, Danny doubted that it involved the bastard's eyes clouding over while Danny whispered Emma's name in his ear. Or pounded his skull into a red sack of bone shards and scrambled brains with the butt of Mike's gun. Those, Danny felt, would be truly satisfying options.

He frowned his way into the cafe and met Foreman by to the door. When he tried to sidestep, Foreman grabbed his elbow and said, "Walk with me, Mr. Murphy."

"Why?"

"Think of it as your mid-term."

Danny's expression didn't soften, but he turned on his heels and followed his professor toward University Drive and the football stadium. Couples and families strolled along as they walked. Not as many as a football game would attract, but the meeting wouldn't start for almost an hour. Friends directed traffic here, too, along with frequent police patrols. The two groups eyed each other cautiously, but they did not seem antagonistic. Danny was surprised to see that a small percentage of the police officers wore a green armband, and some of those without armbands had a green ribbon tied around their right arms.

The crowd thickened once they crossed onto campus. Danny instinctively turned right, toward the stadium, but Foreman led him left, to a seat at one of the concrete picnic tables that lined the Greenway. He asked, "What do you see happening here, Mr. Murphy?"

Danny looked around but he didn't see anything remarkable. "People going to a meeting? What are you looking for, sir?"

"Think bigger. Think of the whole city, the whole country. Maybe bigger than that. Think of our city in the world. What do you see?" When Danny looked puzzled, he added, almost as if he were talking to himself, "I see a pressure cooker. Hundreds of thousands of people trapped in the quarantine zone and Gabriel is turning up the heat a little more every day." He shook his head violently. "Gabriel started the fire and the plague keeps it going, but the fire is everywhere. That's what my class is about. I just didn't see it until this started."

Danny watched Foreman carefully until he continued, "I brought you here to talk about TonysWay. It reminds me of a political movement, maybe a religious movement. At first I thought Mike's philosophy was just the golden rule, re-hashed. Instead of that simple-minded 'do unto others' pablum, he was feeding the crowd an even simpler line: 'be humanity's best friend.' But it's tougher than that. Have you noticed most of the friends wear their armband on the left arm, but some wear it on the right?"

"I didn't notice." Danny instinctively looked down. He'd put the band on his right arm without thinking. "What's the difference?"

"Most Friends share the Way. Some enforce it."

"Against Gabriel?"

"At the moment. The question is who comes after Gabriel. Think about that." He stood abruptly. "We'd better go. I'm not sure when I'm scheduled to go on stage."

"You're talking?" Astonished, Danny jumped up and hurried after him. "You don't believe in TonysWay."

"I haven't enlisted yet," Foreman spoke as he walked. "This feels like a crusade and when everyone else picks up a sword, only a fool reaches for a book."

"So you're going to join." He sounded disappointed, even to himself.

"I'm a fool, Mr. Murphy. Always have been." Foreman sighed. "But in this case, I lack options. It won't take long after Gabriel dies for Mike to see that men like me are also his enemy."

"You mean scientists?"

"I mean everyone who isn't a true believer, Mr. Murphy."

Danny paced him in silence for a few moments, then asked, "Doctor Foreman? Do you think I could go back to being Danny? Instead of Mr. Murphy?"

Foreman grinned and nodded.

Rosa met them just outside the main gate. She looked anxious until she saw them together. She walked the professor to Mike's table before taking Danny to a chair in the reserved section set up on the grass in front of the stage. She sat beside him and grabbed his hand and squeezed, but her focus was on the stage. She whispered, "It'll just be a few more minutes."

"What's on the agenda?"

"Mike will speak in a few minutes. Doctor Foreman will talk about the problems we're facing. Some of the Friends will tell how TonysWay is organized and how people can help, what we need and what people can do. There may be other speakers. That was still up in the air an hour ago. And then Mike will wrap up the event with his announcement."

"Sounds wonderful." He sat back, concentrating on the play between Rosa's fingers and his, and prepared himself for a few hours of boredom.

Mike disappointed him. He devoted first part of the presentation to a description of Tony's death, followed immediately by the loss of both his parents in the same emergency room. Maybe even on the same bed. He talked about his anger and his grief and how he reached out to others suffering the same emotions. The difficulty of changing his focus from revenge to healing. The realization that while Gabriel might be a symptom of a wider problem, symptoms had to be treated. And so he started TonysWay with two goals: help people survive the plague and stop its spread. The first was easiest. Tony's army of Friends fed people, gave them medicine, and helped them survive the broken economy, and even find a bit of hope. The second goal seemed easy at first. Identify Gabriel and destroy him. But there was a difficulty. His secret needed to be destroyed too, and that was where Mike introduced Simon Foreman, who held PHDs in Philosophy, Physics, Sociology, and probably a couple of other disciplines Mike wouldn't try to pronounce.

That brought a sympathetic chuckle from the audience and a modest round of applause for Foreman. He opened his talk with Gabriel, gene editing, and an estimate that everything used to kill three hundred people, put six hundred others in the hospital, destroy the city's economy, and force the federal government to quarantine half a million citizens, give or take a hundred thousand, had probably cost less than two thousand dollars. That drew a gasp of surprise. Then he revealed that better, cheaper, simpler technologies were already available and that gene editing would soon be done by robots. Another gasp. Soon it would be possible to tailor diseases to target specific ethnic or racial groups. Another gasp. Drugs that treat mental disorders can also control political and even religious beliefs and bacteria can be modified to make those drugs. Gasp. Artificial intelligence that controls cars, trains, and refrigerators can just as easily control tanks, bombers, hand guns, and the machines that edit bacteria. Gasp. Then he spoke for a few minutes about the destruction of reality itself. What began generations ago as propaganda and rapidly became fake news was on the verge of becoming universal. A man or woman's face or even body can be pasted into anything from a pornographic video to a confession of treason. Your voice, your exact, recognizable voice, can whisper hate or love or lust or lies to anyone. Anyone. When your identity can be stolen, when your face and voice and signature can be taken with it, what is left?

Gasp. Gasp. Gasp.

By the time Foreman handed the mic back, even Danny was appalled.

Two very earnest Friends, a man and woman, finished the evening by talking about TonysWay and how it enabled people to trust each other. They revealed that the movement was spreading. Branches now existed in all major cities and many foreign countries. It offered hope.

Mike took the microphone back. To prove that hope was real, he announced that TonysWay was taking over the evacuation process from FEMA. Friends would complete registration forms in safe, comfortable locations. No one had to worry about being shot by the police or the national guard, and there would be no charge for the service. It was, after all, being done by Friends for friends.

Danny decided the time had come to leave.

Rosa had long since dropped his hand to applaud more easily and she didn't notice when he slipped from his seat. Mike may have, but he was in the middle of another revelation at the time: the mayor had decided to pay Gabriel's extortion money, in gold, and the Friends would put any coins found to good use caring for the poisoner's victims.

Danny's first stop was the car. He left it wearing a loose pullover and a loaded .38 Special.

Eight o'clock had come and gone while Mike spoke. The street lights cast deeper shadows under the cars parked near campus. Danny thought most of them belonged to people at the meeting. He wondered, briefly, at how Mike ended it with a plea for stolen gold. That thought got him moving.

Danny wanted Gabriel and he knew that if Gabriel intended to collect any of the gold, he'd be in at least one of fifty locations within the next few hours. Three of the designated drops were in walking distance from campus. If Gabriel had some association with the university, he'd probably go for one of those. So would Danny.

He started at the farthest, a fifteen minute walk from the car, intending to work his way back. He moved quickly from one pool of light to the next. All the shops, used book stores, restaurants, bars and smoke shops were shuttered. No cars and no pedestrians shared the street as he approached the first drop, an alley on his right halfway down the block. The green sack should have been left on the sill of a door ten feet in. He slowed as he approached the entrance, but then he saw, or thought he saw, a shadow move in the cab of a truck further up the street. He kept walking and kept an eye on the truck as he passed it. He turned left at the next corner and walked on. About fifty feet ahead of him a sedan flashed its headlights. He thought the light might cover a camera flash. He ignored it and kept walking.

Two blocks later, he turned left again. The detour had taken him out of his way, but he felt the precaution was worth it. He saw no sign that he was being followed. The walk to the second drop took almost twenty minutes.

This close to the university, the stadium lights made the sky a little brighter. The meeting must have been over, though. Small groups on the sidewalks hurried away from the university. They spoke quietly among themselves and generally stopped speaking as he approached, at least until he was close enough for his arm band to show.

The second drop should have been under a blue mail deposit box on the next corner. Danny thought he saw something there as he drew closer. A small dark irregularity in the shadow. He stopped in the doorway of a closed comix store and watched the mailbox reflected in the glass. Three couples and a group of friends walked by the box without slowing. Then two men approached it, walking purposefully. They stopped beside the box. One of them looked like he was dropping an envelope into the slot while the other stooped and reached under the box. He stood with a dark sack in one hand and something that flashed in the other. Then he swung the sack violently along the sidewalk. A shower of gold flew in every direction. Coins clinked together, then rolled toward the shops and into the gutter.

Headlights flared up and down the street.

Danny yelled, "Hey! Stop!" He ran toward the two men, trying to fish the revolver from his belt as he ran.

Tires squealed behind him. The men were running toward him. One veered into an alley. The other darted across the street.

Danny finally had the gun in his hand. He heard a loud pop behind him and looked over his shoulder. Then something slammed into him and he went down, scraping his forehead, nose, and cheek into the concrete. Something else hit his head. He blacked out.

171

Chapter 18

Danny woke with half his head bandaged, his hands cuffed to the rails of a hospital bed, and a uniformed cop in a plastic chair leaning against the wall a few feet from the foot of his bed. His head was splitting and his face felt like he'd run it though a meat grinder. He didn't realize he'd been cuffed until he tried to raise his hands to his temples. The handcuffs rattled as they slid down the rail and jerked to a stop. He groaned.

"How you feeling?"

He groaned again. "What happened?"

"Your buddies beat you to the gold."

"What?" He tried to sit up. The cuffs held him back. The cop pushed himself upright and left the room, leaving Danny shouting after him, "What? What's going on?"

He twisted back and forth on the bed until he realized that the commotion was just making his headache worse. He closed his eyes and tried taking deep breaths to calm himself. It didn't help. He was close to panic when a woman carried a clip board into the room. She moved the chair closer to his shoulder and stared expressionlessly. He stared back, trying to get a sense of her features behind the mask. It occurred to him that she was having the same problem and decided that, given the handcuffs, the mask might be an advantage. Then there was her silence. He knew that she wanted to make him uncomfortable, but awkward conversational pauses didn't

172

bother him, so he just smiled until he realized that smiling is a wasted effort when your face is covered.

He said, "You obviously know who I am. Who are you?"

"Detective Gonzales."

"Sheila Gonzales?"

Her eyes widened. "Have we met?"

"Sometimes I have to go to awards banquets with my family. I think you got a plaque a couple of months ago."

"And you remembered me?"

"The mask doesn't help." He shook his head. "You're with internal affairs, aren't you?"

She nodded cautiously.

"So why you? And why the handcuffs?"

"Why do you think?"

"No idea." He rattled the cuff nearest her. "Am I under arrest?"

She nodded.

"Care to hint at the charge?"

'We haven't decided yet, Mr. Murphy. We have plenty of options. Disturbing the peace. Riot. Conspiracy."

Danny thought about that list. His first reaction was relief that she hadn't mentioned the gun. Possession of a concealed firearm would have aggravated the other charges, but he quickly realized that she could be holding that back for later use, and in fact she had no obligation to be truthful about anything until charges were actually filed. On the other hand, if he hadn't been charged with anything yet, maybe he still had some wiggle room. On the other other hand, he had no idea what he needed to wriggle around. He said, "I deny everything, of course, and I want a lawyer as soon as the friendly part of our conversation is over. Speaking of which, why Internal Affairs?"

"Good question." Gonzales pulled her mask down and said, "It's supposed to be sterile in here. We can probably do without the coverings, as long as we're being friendly."

"I'd like that." He couldn't reach his own mask, so she tugged it off. Bandages still hid half his face. He waited.

She said, "It's been suggested that a man seen casing two different locations identified for payment of extortion money might have had knowledge of exactly where to find the gold.

It's also been suggested that if such a man had a relative in the police force who possessed such knowledge, it would be prudent to investigate the possibility of a conspiracy to misappropriate some of the gold."

"I see." Danny felt cold to the bone. He'd compromised his father. He clenched his jaw but doubted that helped hide his burst of anger. He drew a slow breath, then asked, "Where are these suggestions coming from? Not the department."

"They probably originate with a source outside the department, but working closely with it." Her tone remained flat. "That doesn't mean they were automatically rejected by all members of the department. It also doesn't mean that they won't be investigated carefully and dispassionately."

"Okay." Danny took his time before continuing. "An investigation should consider a few facts," he said slowly. "First, any man intending to misappropriate gold would not walk past a sack left unattended in an alley and then try to retrieve coins scattered all over a crowded sidewalk. Second, the fact that the scattered coins were scattered by a third party indicates that knowledge of the gold was not limited to members of the force and might have been fairly wide spread. And third," his voice rose sharply, "the person casing the gold might have been looking for the son of a bitch who killed his friend and his sister and might not give a flying fuck about the god damned gold!"

Gonzales was watching him intently. She asked, "Is that what you were doing on the street, Danny?"

He rubbed his mask against his shoulder until it halfway covered his face. "I think I need to talk to that lawyer now, detective."

She sighed. "You might have a long wait, Mr. Murphy. Good lawyers have been reluctant to visit the hospital recently."

He lay back and waited for something else to happen. When he opened his eye again, his headache had matured into a throbbing explosion behind his left eye and a new face occupied the chair at the foot of his bed. An aspirin might have been available, but someone had thoughtfully clipped the nurse's call button well below the range of his handcuffs and he was damned if he'd ask his guard to push it for him.

The pain eased enough by midmorning for Danny to think seriously about his situation. Then it came back in spades. The worst part, worse than being handcuffed to a hospital bed with a face he probably didn't want to see anytime soon, was his father's absence. The Chief's face should have been the first thing Danny saw when he woke up and his mother's the second, although she might not be able to get away from the patients in the gym. It was even possible that she didn't know what happened, but his father certainly knew. And he hadn't come. Was he in custody too? Did he see Danny's actions as a betrayal? Or just unforgivable stupidity?

The handcuffs kept him from wiping his cheek, but he could twist far enough to his right to half bury it in the thin hospital pillow. The bandage covered the rest of his face. He was hiding, but that was okay.

After an hour of this, he began to feel stupid. Not better. Just stupider. He gave his face a final wipe on the pillow and opened his eye just as a woman entered the room with a tray. He didn't recognize Rosa until she told the guard to wait outside while she changed his bandages. The guard said she could do whatever she had to do while he watched. Then something really surprising happened. Rosa pulled up the sleeve of her gown and showed him the green band on her left arm and the guard just nodded and walked to the door. He stopped long enough to say, "You know I have to report this?"

Rosa replied, "Of course. Do your duty, Friend."

And then they were alone.

She approached the bed, pulling a key from her pocket, and unlocked his handcuffs. Then she lowered her mask and told him to sit up.

He discovered a new pain in his ribs when he pushed himself up.

She nodded when she saw him wince. "You have fractured ribs. They will hurt for a week or so."

"My face?"

"Staples in your eyebrow and seven stitches over your cheekbone. You lost some skin on the concrete. You'll have a scar, not as impressive as the one on your forehead, but enough to give you a bit more character."

He glanced at the door and lowered his voice. "My dad?"

"He's angry. I'm pretty sure he'll get over it."

"So. Nothing to worry about?"

"I wouldn't say that." She smiled briefly and lifted scissors from her tray. She began cutting the gauze away from his face.

He watched her eyes as she peeled away layer after layer. When the final layer came off and her expression didn't change, he felt a little better. His left eye was stuck shut but it was still there. The exposed skin burned in the cool air. His headache hadn't changed. He asked, "Is he in trouble because of me?"

"He has enemies, but he also has friends. He'll be okay." Her tone remained businesslike. She smeared an ointment over his face and added, "You have friends too, Danny. Just be patient."

He swallowed nervously. "Do you know what I'm charged with, Rosa?"

She gave a tiny nod.

He whispered, "Was it the gun?"

She applied a gauze pad to his face and began wrapping him up before she answered. "What gun? You didn't have a gun when you were arrested. I'm sure I would have heard about that." Then she said, "I have to put the handcuffs back on. Do you need to use the bathroom first?"

He did and then he lay quietly while she fastened him back to the bed. Just before she left, he thought to ask for an aspirin. She told him she'd send a nurse with one. The last thing she did in the room was cover his mouth with a new mask, lay her hand on his chest, and repeat softly, "Don't worry too much. Trust your friends."

The guard entered as Rosa left. A few minutes later, an orderly carried in a tray with small dishes of jello, cottage cheese, something mashed, something gray and flat, and a nice cup of lukewarm tea. The excitement of lunch passed quickly. Danny spent the afternoon waiting for a nurse to bring his aspirin and wishing he'd thought to ask Rosa to move his call button closer to his handcuff. The aspirin appeared and his headache disappeared about the same time, so he sent the aspirin back with the nurse.

Then Special Agent Bakey showed up and chased the guard out. He waited a few minutes, eying Danny curiously, before asking with a tiny smile, "You ready to confess yet?"

Danny tried to look like he was thinking it over, then said, "I didn't do it."

The agent snorted. "Prove it."

"What's the charge?"

"Corruption. Conspiracy to commit corruption. Mayhem and anarchy. Maybe piracy. I haven't decided yet."

"Piracy?"

"Gold coins? Stolen treasure?" Bakey shrugged. "Sounds like piracy to me."

"Did you come here to talk to me, Agent Bakey, or just to joke around?" Danny shook his arms. The handcuffs rattled against the aluminum rails on his bed. "Because I'm really not enjoying this as much as you are."

"I'm here to talk." He moved the chair closer to Danny and took a seat. "I need some answers. How did the son of the Chief of Police know where seven million dollars in gold coins would be hidden? Did he tell anyone else about the gold? Why did he ruin an opportunity to capture a mass murderer? Why was he involved in a riot that involved the theft of over a hundred and forty thousand dollars in gold? What does he know about the disappearance of the rest of the gold? Was he waging some sort of private vendetta against the killer, as his father suggests?" He leaned into Danny's face. "Or is he just incredibly stupid?"

Danny shook his head slowly. He didn't like the smell of Bakey's breath. He wanted him to go away and leave him to his misery. That wasn't likely to happen, but Bakey had said something— "The gold was stolen? All of it?"

"Goddamn it, answer my question!"

"You weren't guarding it?"

"Your father was guarding it, Murphy!"

"Without the FBI? That doesn't sound right."

"How did you know about the gold?"

"Tell me something, Bakey. Gabriel has always acted first and threatened later. Did he do that this time, too? Have you been monitoring that website in his note?"

"How do you know about the website?"

"I was there when the note arrived, remember? Tell me about the website and then we can talk about your other questions."

"I don't have to tell you a damned thing, kid. I'm asking the questions here."

"And the clock is ticking, Bakey." Danny started feeling more confident. "We can always wait until my lawyer shows up and I start remembering things. Of course Gabriel will be doing whatever the hell he's planning while you pretend you actually think I'm guilty of something and the clock ticks on."

Bakey leaned back in his chair and stared. Then he said, "Your old man is a pain in my ass, Murphy. So are you, but you aren't the chief of police. You've got no badge protecting you."

Danny nodded. "Tick, tock."

"Damn it!" Bakey sighed. "Okay. Yes, the gold is gone. All of it. There were fifty drops. At forty-eight of them the bags were cut open and the coins scattered. In the riot that followed, all the gold disappeared. In the other two cases, the bags just disappeared. We think Gabriel got one or both of them."

"Weren't those two being guarded?"

"The men watching them got called to assist in crowd control when the riots broke out. When we got back to the sites, the bags were gone."

Danny thought a moment, then asked, "How bad were the riots? Was anyone hurt?"

"They were the most orderly riots I ever heard of. Lots of commotion. People running around shoving gold coins in their pockets and yelling at each other, then running away while other people ran in. Everything was staged, but we didn't put it together until later." Bakey cursed, then added, "You were the only injury. We stopped a lot of people, but we couldn't find any reason to hold any of them. We interrogated them and released them."

"Why was I so lucky?"

"You attracted a little attention on your walk, and when you were injured, we just kept you after picking you up. You're officially a person of interest. Now, let's get back to how you knew about the gold drops."

"You haven't answered my question. What happened with the web address?"

"The site suddenly appeared around seven o'clock last night. It took us until midnight to shut it down but it keeps coming back."

"So you found the server?"

Bakey shook his head. "It's off shore. We're trying to pressure the locals to close it down, but we haven't had much luck yet. Meanwhile, we're trying direct attacks."

Danny whistled. Direct attacks on a server on foreign soil meant something on that site was a major threat. "Okay," he said, "I saw that some of the addresses on Gabriel's last message were near the university stadium. Dad asked me to let him know what happened at the TonysWay meeting, so after it ended, I walked around to see if Gabriel showed up. I wanted to kill him for what he did, but I never saw him, unless he was the guy who pounded me into the sidewalk."

"Not likely," Bakey told him. "We have some poor quality video of the location, but after you charged into the mob the camera focused on the coins. You didn't get back on screen until the crowd disbursed. By then you were down and bleeding."

"Right." Danny asked, "Lots of evidence against me there. Any jury in the country would convict me of walking down a street and getting beat up."

"The problem is that you knew which street to walk down."

"Maybe." He had another idea. "What was attendance like at the other forty-seven riots?"

"About the same. Does your father know you want to kill Gabriel?"

"He knows that son of a bitch killed Tony and Emma." Danny took a deep breath and grated, "He should thank me for killing the bastard."

"Uh huh. Right after he arrests you for murder. Maybe he'll have the pleasure of strapping his son down for a lethal injection. Maybe your mom would thank him for that." Bakey shook his head. "Idiot!"

"Yeah." Danny knew he wasn't thinking clearly. He shook his head violently, trying to get his focus back. "Did you say Gabriel escaped with two sacks of gold?"

"I said two are missing. That's not quite the same thing."

"So he's still on the loose?"

"He is. You aren't, and it's going to stay that way until we bag him."

"Okay." He stared at the ceiling. "You're no closer to getting him. He's going to get away with everything. Tony. Emma. Pam. All those hundreds of people in the trucks. And Gabriel is going to walk away. I feel sick."

"We're getting closer," Bakey told him. "We found the lab he used to edit the bacteria, and we found some of his equipment suppliers. We'll get him."

"I hope so," Danny whispered. "I hope so."

"That leads me to the other matter I wanted to talk to you about."

"Anything."

Bakey nodded at his response and asked carefully, "Just how well do you know Simon Foreman?"

Chapter 19

One week after Emmie and Janis bought themselves a plate of nachos with a handful of poisoned dollars during the city's Fourth of July celebration, his guard's broken snoring woke Danny Murphy from a nightmare. He had no memory of the dream itself but a sense of horror lingered. He felt pretty sure it would disappear when he opened his good eye. He was equally sure that the coming day would be worse than the dream, so he lay motionless under the thin hospital blanket. Even with his eye closed, the room was obviously still dark. Noise drifted through the open door, conversation and clatter. Smells. Breakfast? The headache hadn't abandoned him. His arms remained immobile. His left shoulder and both knees felt bruised today. New pains. What else? Right. No father. Special Agent Frank Bakey of the FBI stood in for him yesterday. A lot of accusations that made no sense, a few answers that made less, and a hasty departure after dropping an ugly suspicion on the bed.

Professor Foreman?

And then Bakey slipped away. He left no evidence against Foreman, only a hint that the man had more biochemistry on his résumé than he'd admitted and a veiled suggestion that keeping an eye on the scientist might earn favorable consideration down the road. Ridiculous.

Danny's anger eventually inspired him to discover the reason the door to his room was open. Rosa stood in the half-gloom watching him sleep. He glanced at the guard, still snoring in the chair at the foot of his bed, then back at the mayor's daughter and raised his eyebrow. She asked, "Are you ready for an aspirin?"

"Thanks."

The guard jerked awake, looked at them for a moment, and left the room.

Danny asked, "What's going on today?"

"You're resting here. Healing."

"I could do that better at home."

"Except for the handcuffs."

"Right. Except for these." He rattled them for effect, then lowered his voice. "What's going on, Rosa? Out there?"

"Nobody died yesterday. We're still getting an occasional case of the plague, but the friends have been catching them before they need hospitalization. Most of them go straight to one of the care centers for a few days and then they are released."

"Care centers?"

"Like the high school gym."

"Oh." He looked at the ceiling and asked carefully, "Is my mother still there?"

"Yes. So is mine."

"Does she know I . . . what happened?"

"I told her you are okay."

"Does she know about these?" He shook the cuffs again.

Rosa nodded.

He felt sick. "I guess that's good."

She waited a moment, then said, "I have to go soon. Do you need anything else?"

"Can I have my phone?"

"No."

"I'm lost here, Rosa. It's like I'm trapped. I need to know what's happening. Did Gabriel really escape with two bags of gold? What is Mike doing? What about the evacuation? Does Bakey have any leads on Gabriel? How is the city? Is Mom really okay? What about—?"

She stopped him by laying a hand on his chest. "I'll see Mike in a few hours, Danny. I'll talk to him. In the meantime, your mother is fine. She's working hard, but it is good work.

She's happy. Janis is moving to the gym later today. I'll try to let you see her if you want. Maybe you can give her a message for your mother."

"I'd like that."

"Okay." She smiled and started to leave, then said, "You may have some visitors this afternoon. Friends."

Before she got out the door, he stopped her again. "Rosa...?"

She turned. When she saw the pain on his face, she swallowed and said, "He came last night, Danny. You were asleep and he didn't wake you, but he came."

He nodded and closed his eyes. He didn't open them again until an orderly woke him with a breakfast tray. Oatmeal, dry toast, cool juice, lukewarm coffee. He would have turned on the TV but the controller was out of reach. He dozed until a nurse woke him with another aspirin. Then he tried to find shapes in the pattern of holes in the acoustic tiles on the ceiling. He found an angel, a dragon, a spaceman, and two that he was glad his mother couldn't see. The angel bothered him. He devoted most of the morning to it, although the dragon ran a close second. Only part of the spaceman's helmet really looked right and he couldn't devote much time to the other two, not with a cop in the room.

Right after lunch, Rosa pushed a wheelchair into the room and asked the guard to transfer the handcuffs to the armrests on the chair. She told him that she'd have his prisoner back in a couple of hours and wheeled Danny toward X-Ray, but changed directions at the elevator. She pushed the up button, removed the handcuffs, and adjusted his mask. "Be careful here," she said. "It is important on this floor."

"Where are you taking me?"

She ignored the question. Two minutes later she rolled him into a dark room. It took him a few seconds to recognize the thin shape under the blanket. "Hello, Janis."

"D-Danny?" She had a harder time of it, probably because of his bandaged face. "Is that you?"

"Sure is."

He didn't expect her to turn her face away, or to start weeping. He didn't expect her to try to apologize or to break down completely or lose her breath and start gasping for air.

He abruptly reached for her hand and squeezed it at the same time that Rosa said, "Don't—!", and then, "Oh, hell!"

He said, "Don't say you're sorry, Janis. You have nothing to apologize for."

Rosa snapped, "Damn it, Danny, she could still be contagious."

Janis wailed, "I killed Emmie, Danny. I didn't know about the money, but I took it and split it with her and then we bought the nachos and I killed her."

"No!" Danny felt like his day just broke in half and he'd lost touch with both pieces. He jumped out of the chair and leaned over the bed. He lay his cheek, the unbandaged right one, along hers and whispered, "It was Gabriel, sweetie. He killed Emmie and almost killed you. You are innocent. It was Gabriel."

Rosa said, "Idiot."

"If I didn't do anything wrong, why did mom have to die?" Janis shook her head. "You don't understand. It's all because of me."

"No," Danny answered angrily. "That was Gabriel too. Pam was a good person and she had to help the people he poisoned. She had to try anyway, and that's why she died. That's the only reason."

He lowered his voice and thought a moment. Rosa took the opportunity to pull him back into his wheelchair. He asked, "Did Rosa tell you we brought your bunny, Hoppy—"

"Mr. Hopalong."

"Yes, Hopalong. We brought him to your Mom. She was really happy. I think she kissed him, and I bet he was with her when she . . . went."

"Really?"

Danny nodded. Rosa said, "He was. She asked for him when she got really sick and I brought him to her. He was with her. He still is."

Janis sat up. "He's with her?"

She searched Rosa's face, then pulled her hand from Danny's. "You shouldn't touch me," she told him. "I might be contagious."

"I'm an idiot."

"I know. Rosa told me." She smiled. "Will you come again

before I go?"

"She's being transferred to the gym this afternoon," Rosa explained. Then she said, "He can't, Janis, but Emmie's mom will be there and she'll take good care of you. You will have lots of friends there."

"And I'll see you as soon as I get out of here," Danny added. "You're going to be like my sister now."

That must have helped. Janis asked Rosa to open her blinds, just a little, before she wheeled Danny out. Rosa stopped at the nurses' station long enough to feed him an extra dose of Cipro and Methicillin and then pushed him to the cafeteria for the only item on the menu, a baloney and cheese sandwich with a cup of warm tea. She apologized. "You'd get better food in your room, but we'd have less privacy."

"Privacy is good." The room was nearly empty. He took off his face mask and asked, "What's up, Rosa?"

She leaned closer. "I asked Dad what you are charged with. He said you aren't charged with anything, Danny. You're being held on something called 'preventive detention.'"

"What?" He dropped his sandwich and stared at her. "What the hell is that?"

"It means they are holding you so you won't do something. They are afraid of what you might do."

"Who? Who is afraid?"

"The police, I guess. Maybe the FBI. You told everybody you want to kill Gabriel. You were walking around with a loaded gun."

"Which you gave me." Danny hesitated before asking, "Does my father know?"

"He doesn't want you getting in trouble. He's trying to save you."

"Oh, god. I don't believe this." He covered his face. "My mother? Did he tell her?"

"I did."

Danny's gaze jerked to her face. "You? Why?"

"So she would know you are safe. She was worried."

"I suppose she feels better knowing I'm locked up," he said bitterly. "They have to let me go after three days, right? They can't just keep me here forever."

"That's if you are detained on suspicion of something."
Rosa spoke softly. "It's different with preventive detention.
They can keep you until it's safe to release you."

"Forever?"

She nodded reluctantly.

"What about Mike?" Danny's mind was spinning. "He gave
me the armband. I'm his friend. Does he know I'm here? Can
he help?"

"He has the whole city to think of," Rosa said. "More, after
Las Vegas and Atlanta, and the evacuation registrations, and
the shrinking quarantine, and the food shortage, and the
medical distributions and the clinics. He simply doesn't have
time."

"Can you ask him? At least ask him?"

She shook her head.

"Then ask him to see me? He should say no to my face,
Rosa. He owes me that."

She shook her head again. "He owes thousands of people.
Tens of thousands, and some of them aren't just
inconvenienced. They are dying."

"But—"

"No, Danny." She stood. "I have a few errands. Do you
want to go back to your room now or would you like to stay
here a few minutes longer?"

"Not my room, please."

"Okay, Danny." She checked a pocket on her nurses' gown
to verify she still had the key, then very carefully recuffed his
left wrist to the wheelchair. "I'll be back for you in about an
hour. In the meantime, enjoy your tea and try to be patient.
Mike says that things happen in their proper time. It doesn't
help to push them. You understand?"

He nodded. A tiny weight dropped into his lap. He gave it
a quick glance. Her handcuff key. He closed his legs over it,
then watched Rosa walk out of the cafeteria. Less than a
minute passed before Simon Foreman walked in through the
same door. They must have passed each other in the hall.
Danny thought that was interesting.

Foreman came directly to his table and sat. After a
moment, he sighed and said, "I suppose you're going to want
an extension on your term paper."

186

It took Danny awhile to process that. He said, "I might need to take an incomplete in Science and Society this semester, Doctor."

Foreman snorted. "You're too late, Mr. Murphy. I've already turned in the grades."

"Really?" He'd meant it as a joke. "What about the final exam?"

"Anyone who survives this," he waved vaguely at the hospital and the city outside it, "deserves an A."

"I guess you're right." Danny sat quietly for a moment, then decided he had to speak. He lowered his voice. "You know that Agent Bakey is suspicious of you. He asked me to watch you."

"Of course." Foreman did not seem concerned. "Do you know who he asked to watch you? The guard in your room? Rosa? Your father, maybe? It isn't just me they are watching. Nuclear physicists have been under the microscope since 1945 and they aren't as dangerous as biochemists or programmers or even philosophers, for that matter."

"What do you mean?"

"A single man can't build an atomic bomb. That takes huge factories and test facilities. A government. But a single man can edit a few genes or hack into a power grid or water supply or the control system for a gas pipeline and destroy a nation, maybe even a civilization. When you think about it, Gabriel has been very kind to us."

"What?" Danny was speechless.

"He told us what he was doing and how he was doing it. What do you think would have happened if he'd just gone on a trip around the country dropping his poison bacteria into corn silos and bottling plants and stock yards? He could have poisoned our country and everyone we do business with. Even if we discovered the bacteria, we couldn't treat half our population. Our economy would collapse and so would—"

"Okay, okay!" Danny felt numb. "I get the picture."

"Do you really?" Foreman forced a tight grin, more like a rictus. "Because that was Gabriel's promise on his web site. 'Here is a weapon,' he said, 'and this is how to build it.' Then he provided the genetic code that makes any organism produce the botulism toxin and described how to insert it into bacteria using CRISPR. And finally, he explained his goal. He wants the weak and powerless equal to the strong and powerful. After today, we are all truly equal. His words. Or hers, if Gabriel turns out to be female. That is the true target of the quarantine, Mr. Murphy. Not the bacteria and not even the gene-splicing technology. The idea that one individual can defeat a nation is the real threat, as they see it. The reality is that one man can now destroy a civilization. Or a species."

"My god." After awhile, Danny asked, "What can we do?"

"Well, Agent Bakey and your father are installing cameras everywhere, and of course they will restrict access to education or any kind of sensitive information. Your friend Mike is going the other way. He'll have just as many eyes looking over our shoulders, but they will belong to our friends and family." Foreman shook his head regretfully. "In the end, there will be no difference between the two approaches, and of course neither will work."

"Why?"

"Who could you trust not to abuse the power? And more important, this genetic coding is just the first patch of ice on a very steep slope. We may stay on our feet for a few more years, but we're sliding downhill and the trail doesn't end in a green pasture. It ends at a cliff."

Danny felt sick. "You don't see any hope?"

"The problem isn't with science or technology. It's with our nature, our character. We are monkeys, Danny, and as long as we devote ourselves to monkey business we will be stuck in the monkey cage. The cage has a door and the lock isn't complicated, but we have to stop fighting over bananas to open it, and we are sure that if we ever stop fighting, some other monkey will steal our banana."

Foreman looked over Danny's shoulder and said, "I should be going. It looks like your keeper is back."

He nodded to Rosa on his way out.

Rosa looked like she was in a hurry. She started to cuff his right hand the moment she reached him.

"Tell me something before we go, Rosa."

"What?"

"You said Mike was busy, especially after Las Vegas and Atlanta. What happened in Las Vegas?"

She sat. "There was an outbreak at the airport in Las Vegas. Nobody has said what caused it, though it obviously couldn't have come directly from here. The governor immediately quarantined the airport. That cut off the flow of tourists and pissed off some important men. They put pressure on the mayor and she made some poor decisions. There was a confrontation between the guard and the police. Shots were fired. The governor declared martial law. About a hundred and fifty people died. We hear different numbers."

"From botulism?"

"From one thing or another. We have a lot of Friends there, but the situation is unsettled. That's what Mike says."

"And Atlanta?"

"We aren't sure. Something very bad started there and it isn't over yet." Her neck must have been stiff. She rubbed it. "I really need to go. Do you have anything else?"

"Two things. First, leaving me here with Doctor Foreman was obviously a set up. Why?"

"Mike wanted you to hear what he has to say." She met his eyes squarely. "What else, Danny?"

"You." He watched what little he could see of her face carefully. "When this all started and we got together downtown, I thought we were friends. Like on the same side. But now it seems like you're working for Mike, or TonysWay, and you might be working against me. Which is it, Rosa? Whose side are you on?"

"I'm your friend." She began pushing him toward his room and his guard. "We all are your friends."

Chapter 20

Back in his room, or hospital cell, Danny had one small victory before his day ended. An orderly set the tray with his evening meal on his bedside table and pushed it over his legs. The tray held a paper plate with a scoop of reconstituted potatoes, a microwaved hamburger patty, and half a cup of canned carrots. A cup of lime jello and a small tea finished the meal.

He had no complaint abut the food. Supplies were tight, and from the interest the guard showed in his tray, Danny suspected he was eating better than a majority of the citizens. The handcuffs were the problem. In order to eat, he had to get food onto the fork in his left hand, stretch his right arm out behind him, and lean close enough to the fork to get it in his mouth. The third time he dropped a bite of mashed potatoes and carrots onto his sheet, he tossed the fork against the wall and pushed the table aside. He threw his head back against the thin pillow and swallowed a curse along with his anger and humiliation.

"You need a little help there?"

Danny looked at the guard, surprised. He nodded.

The guard stepped out and returned almost immediately with a set of leg irons. He looped them around the bed rail, then moved Danny's handcuff from the rail to the irons. "That better?"

"Thanks." The longer chain allowed Danny to finish the

potatoes and carrots easily. He didn't have the stomach for the patty and he sure didn't want the cup of green jello. He pulled up his blanket, wriggled into a more comfortable position and, in case the guard took the leg irons back, slipped the key Rosa had dropped to a spot just inside his pillow case.

The guard eyed the hamburger patty. "You done with dinner?"

"Sure. Get rid of it."

He grabbed the tray and stepped out of sight. A moment later, he reappeared licking his fingers. They said nothing more to each other, but Danny kept the leg irons and the freedom allowed him to roll onto his side. Sleep came a bit easier.

Shortly after midnight, Saturday morning exploded. His eyes jerked open and he sat, breathing heavily, as tall as the chains let him. He stared wildly around the room

"What's wrong?" The guard sounded alarmed.

"What time is it!"

"Just after one. What's wrong?"

"I thought I was late." He fell back onto his pillow. "I have to take Emmy to the bus."

"What?"

He'd regained control of his breath. "My sister. She's leaving for soccer camp this morning. I have to drive her to the bus."

"You're not—"

"Janis too. I'll take her to see Pam first."

"Listen. . . ."

"Oh, God." His eyes began to flood. "She's dead isn't she? Pam's dead."

The guard didn't say anything.

Danny rolled back on his side and stared at a dark wall. After awhile, he whimpered. "Janis too. Just not Emmie. Please not Emmie."

An hour or so later, he realized his pillow would be changed. He moved the key to a new hiding place and spent the rest of the night blinking and reliving his last ride with his sister, drafting all the things he'd say to her the next time. It was a long night. He had a lot to say.

He didn't notice light creeping into the room, but he could

suddenly see the off-white wall, the blond Formica of his bedside table, the red skin under the cuff on his wrist. Breakfast noises grew louder in the hallway. When a gowned figure put a tray on his table, he pushed it away.

The guard looked a question at him, then smiled at his answer and made the tray disappear. Danny went back to mapping the pattern of holes in his ceiling tiles. Two of yesterday's figures had disappeared completely. The dragon had flown away leaving a vaguely dog-like shape, and spaceman looked more like a skull. The biggest change was to the angel. Gabriel looked a lot like Emmie. He hadn't noticed that before.

The guard changed mid-morning. The new one didn't notice the longer chain on Danny's left arm. He just settled into his chair and stared into space. After a bit, his eyes closed and didn't reopen until a nurse appeared with an aspirin and a pair of scissors. She ignored the guard and attacked Danny's bandage.

The first few layers of gauze came off easily. The last stuck a bit, cemented in place by dried blood or some other gunk. When she had the last of the gauze off, she threw tenderness to the wind and attacked Danny's eye with a scouring pad and a spray bottle. He bore the assault in silence until she broke through the gummy seal and his eyelid popped open.

He immediately closed it.

"Open it." She was having none of his nonsense and pried his lids apart with a thumb and forefinger. "Let's see how we're doing."

She sprayed his exposed eyeball with whatever liquid she'd loaded in her bottle that morning. He flinched and tried to defend himself, but the handcuff and leg iron jerked him to a stop before he could get his fingers around her throat. The moment he accepted defeat and relaxed, she leaned so close they were almost sharing the same mask and peered into his socket. She said, "Not bad, Mr. Murphy."

"Do you know me?"

She said, "I worked with Pam until she collapsed. Then I worked on her."

"I'm sorry."

"We all are." She backed off a little and examined his face

critically, turning it from side to side with a hand on his chin. She sprayed his eyebrow, the tight area on his cheek, and the staples from his collision with the refrigerated trailer. Then she patted them dry with gauze. Finally satisfied, she applied ointment and covered everything with smaller dressings. "They closed up nice. I don't think you need the full mummy treatment anymore. Do you want a mirror?"

He shook his head and asked, "How is Janis? Did she get out yesterday?"

She gave her head a tiny shake and glanced quickly toward the guard. "We decided to keep her for an extra day, just to be safe."

That alarmed Danny. "She isn't worse?"

"No. Partly it's because we loved Pam and partly because she doesn't have anywhere to go."

"She could stay with us," he suggested. "I mean with Mom and me."

"Your mother is pretty much living at the gym annex," she smiled, "and you're tied up for the foreseeable future. But it's a kind offer."

"Right." Danny rattled his chain and groaned, then asked, "How are things in the city? Is the plague under control?"

"I wish." She sighed. "We're treating the botulism symptoms pretty well, but the infections keep popping up in new places. The CDC sent out a memo telling us to look for carriers, people who spread the Staph and E coli without actually having any symptoms."

"How do you do that?"

"We don't, not without a lot more resources." She smiled tiredly. "It's not all bad news though. The Friends are registering people pretty quickly. The cards and chips are helping with the evacuation. I heard they got twenty thousand out of the city so far."

"Cards and chips?"

"ID cards. When you are registered, your information goes in a database and you get a card with everything on it. If the health department clears your info, your name shows up on a list at the border and you can show your card and go outside."

"You're kidding."

She shook her head. "It's the same with the chips, except

those go under the skin behind your wrist and they can wave a wand over you and know who you are."

"Where do they get all these chips?"

"From the vets, mostly. The government is giving them out free."

Danny couldn't believe it. "Doesn't anyone complain?"

"Complain? They get you out of the city. People are fighting for them."

"Okay." Different world, he supposed. "What about Gabriel? Has he—"

The guard, who had been conspicuously not listening, cleared his throat and shook his head. The nurse quickly gathered up her scissors, spray bottle, ointment, and bloody rags. She made a hasty retreat and Danny went back to studying the ceiling. The hour he dropped the girls at their bus came and slipped away without an earthquake or thunder or any sign at all, and that seemed so damned wrong that he screamed inside. Then the hour came when she waved goodbye for the last time.

He wanted to kill something. Hurt something worse than he was hurting.

Hours later, the food cart began rumbling down the hall. They rumbled right by his door without stopping. The guard's phone played a short riff. He read a text, then shrugged and left the room, closing the door carefully behind himself.

Five minutes later, Mike walked in with a hot pepperoni pizza. He set the box on the bedside table. Danny started salivating even before he opened it. He said, "Okay, Mike. Now I'm a believer."

"In TonysWay?"

"In you." He accepted a slice of paradise on a torn paper towel. "I'm still agnostic on the green armband thing."

"Then let me convert you, my friend." Mike pulled two cans of beer, still wet with condensation, from under his surgical gown and popped their tabs. Danny's chain rattled against the bed rail as he grabbed for the nearest can. He took a sip while Mike folded a slice of pizza in half and held it for him.

Mike had one slice. Danny finished the rest. Then he sat back, sipped the last of his beer, and examined Mike curiously. "Why?"

"For Tony." Mike shrugged. "And you're a friend."

"Not like the guard."

"Him?" He glanced at the door. "A few of the cops are Friends and a few more are sympathetic, but most of them are lining up behind the chief and the mayor. Your guard is sympathetic, but mostly he's hungry." When Danny looked confused, Mike explained, "I brought two pizzas."

"Oh." He studied his handcuffs for a moment, the repeated, "Why?"

"Why am I here?" When Danny nodded, he went on, "You need a friend. Not an arm band, but a friend, like Tony. You need someone who cares that you're stuck here for as long as Bakey and your father keep you sidelined. You need someone who recognizes that you have a legitimate role to play in this thing that's happening to us. You've paid, Danny. You paid with your sister and my brother and the rest of your family. Hell, you paid with your future."

Danny thought that over. "And you're it? You're my friend?"

Mike shrugged and waved at the empty room. He said, "I'm here. How many other friends do you see?"

"Right. Good point, I guess." He reached a decision and leaned forward. "Tell me about Gabriel. Start with the gold."

"What about it?"

"How much did he get?"

"There were five thousand coins. Around forty-three hundred were donated to TonysWay. About five hundred disappeared from known drops. Two sacks vanished completely. Both of those were from drops located on the edge of the commercial district northwest of the airport. Gabriel may have one or both of them."

"Or neither."

"That's possible too."

"What about the tracking chips?"

"Both showed up in that vacant stretch east of town, about halfway from Painter Heights to the Stone Mountain casino."

Danny was surprised. "Together? In the same place?"

Mike nodded. "Stacked, one on the other."

"So one person got both bags. That doesn't mean it was

Gabriel."

Mike agreed, but added, "Still, the odds against someone else lucking into two sacks of gold are pretty high."

"Unless that someone had access to Gabriel's list and knew exactly where to look."

"There is always that." Mike smiled. "Of course, only two groups had that list: TonysWay and the city government. We've already admitted to receiving donations from the citizens who found gold on the street that totaled over forty-three hundred coins. We would have no reason not to claim an extra couple of hundred coins if we had them. That leaves your father and his cops. You think they have the gold?"

Danny shook his head.

"I didn't think you'd like that possibility," Mike said dryly. "Now we're overlooking one other party. The guy apprehended skulking from one hiding place to another immediately after the drops were made."

"Skulking?"

"Walking, if you prefer."

"I prefer strolling. You know I didn't have anything to do with it."

Mike nodded. "But the knowledge is based on knowledge of your character, not on knowledge of what happened to the gold."

"Cut the crap, Mike. I didn't have time to get to the airport and back after your little tent show."

"Yeah. Sorry." He sighed. "I'm just at a loss here. Your professor thinks the cops, or maybe the FBI, already have Gabriel."

"Foreman thinks that? Why?"

"His colleagues in the biochemistry department were suspicious of one of their students. Foreman wanted to talk to her, but the FBI beat him to her. She apparently had a private lab near the university. When Foreman showed up, they had the whole building wrapped in crime scene tape and the girl was nowhere to be found."

"Gabriel is a girl?" Danny shook his head. It sounded so wrong. A girl killed Emmy? "That's ridiculous."

"Is it?" Mike rubbed his eyes tiredly. "You're probably right, but three weeks ago I would have said this whole thing is ridiculous. Now my family is dead. The city is dying. People I don't know treat me like some kind of prophet."

"I noticed." As soon as he spoke, Danny realized how he sounded. He looked down and apologized. "Sorry. I didn't mean it like that."

Mike looked distant, as though he'd backed away somehow. "I'd rather have Tony than TonysWay, damn it."

"I know." He cast around for a way to change the subject. "How is the rest of the country reacting to all this?"

"There isn't a lot of publicity, but money is pouring into Homeland Security. Cameras are going up everywhere, especially around the universities, and a huge effort is underway to give security agencies access to private databases. Manufacturing and sales records for medical and biological materials have highest priority, along with social media and private messaging channels."

Danny looked shaken. "Isn't that over-reacting?"

"You didn't see Gabriel's web site. Anyone with a little education who accessed it could modify most bacteria to produce botulism, but it included a path to generate other poisons too. Cocaine. Heroine." Mike stood and started taking off the surgical scrubs he wore into the room. He had street clothes under them. The scrubs went into Danny's locker. "Think about it. Every lake and river in the country is full of bacteria. Any of them could be modified."

"How long was the site up?"

"It's still up. As soon as they shut down one server, the site pops up on another. It's mirrored all over the world, and not just by our enemies."

Danny couldn't think of anything to say to that.

"The good old days are finally gone, Danny. From now on, we're all guilty until proven innocent, and the only way we're going to survive in this world is if we have the right kind of friends. Trusted friends." Mike stopped on his way to the door and said, "It's time for you to pick a side and act, my friend. You've been patient long enough."

After Mike's departure, Danny stared at the door until the guard returned, wiping his lips and looking very pleased with himself. He checked the handcuffs and lock on Danny's irons. Then he settled in for the night. Danny turned his attention to the constellations on his ceiling. He no longer had to search. They were old friends now.

He closed his eyes even before the lights dimmed, but sleep eluded him. An hour passed. Another. Danny became aware that his guard was in trouble. He gasped and seemed to be trembling.

He sat up and squinted, trying to see what was going on in the chair, but it was too dark. Still, the man's breathing did not sound good. He shouted, "Nurse! NURSE!"

He kept calling until a woman strode angrily through the door and demanded his problem. When he pointed at the guard sliding slowly out of his chair, she cursed and ran. Sirens blared. People swarmed in with a gurney and needles and vials and aspirators and saline bags. Then they swarmed out, shouting terse commands at each other, and left Danny alone in his room, thinking about what had just happened. The visit. The guard's pizza. Mike's last words. "You've been patient long enough." Very true, he thought. He'd been a patient long enough. He didn't know what else he could be, but it was time to find out, so he took the key from its hiding place and opened his cuffs. Then he dressed in the scrubs Mike left in his locker and walked out of the hospital in the shoes the nurse pulled off the guard.

PART THREE

New World

Chapter 21

Danny slept on Mrs. Massini's couch because he had nowhere else to go. The cops would search his home as soon as someone noticed the empty handcuffs hanging from the rails of his hospital bed. Of all the friends he'd made growing up, none would welcome the kind of trouble he'd bring. Only Tony had been close enough for that, so he went to Tony's house. The walk took two hours. He felt self-conscious walking in scrubs so late at night, but the city shut down earlier in this newly poisoned world. Mike wasn't be there, Mr. and Mrs. Massini wouldn't mind, and Tony would have welcomed him. Also, he knew where the key was. That helped.

He let himself in and stood in the dark, feeling the emptiness of the place. He started to turn on a light but thought better of it. He didn't need to alarm the neighbors. Besides, he didn't need light here. Tony and he had spent endless hours watching cartoons or playing video games on that couch. He skirted carefully around the coffee table, mindful of the times he'd bruised his shins on it, and collapsed. He stared at the dark living room ceiling, happy not to see any figures waiting there, especially not an angel. Eventually he kicked off his shoes, curled up around his taped ribs, and closed his eyes.

When the afternoon sun woke him, he told himself that Sunday was a day of rest. In truth he simply couldn't move. He just lay on the couch, vaguely aware of passing time, hunger, thirst, motes of dust floating in the stale air stirred by his breath. Someone knocked and then pounded on the door. He ignored it and the knocking stopped. He closed his eyes again.

The next time he woke, the room was darker. He made a trip to the bathroom and stopped for a glass of water on his way back to the couch. The kitchen counter was cleaner than when he visited Mike. Mr. Massini's tequila still sat next to the shot glass, but the coffee cup had disappeared and the counter had been scrubbed clean.

Danny spent a long time standing in front of the refrigerator. He thought of opening it, but he didn't want the light and food had no connection to the pain in his belly. Eventually he felt his way back to the couch. He didn't sleep right away. He spent some time thinking about Tony. Wondering where he was. Probably in the refrigerator with Emmy. His mother, of course, was busy saving lives. Saving strangers. He had no idea where his father was. At work or asleep, probably. Hunting Gabriel. Maybe he'd found him already; the angel had abandoned his post on the ceiling.

Danny's eyes popped open after midnight. He'd dreamed he was back in his hospital room, staring at the ceiling there, and an insight startled him awake. The figure he'd taken for spaceman, later a skull, was the mouth of Gabriel's horn, the trumpet that announces the end of the world. He lay awake, trying to work out if the horn had sounded, if the end had passed unnoticed while he slept, until dawn finally worked it's magic and the room slipped quietly back into a gray on gray existence around him. He watched the materialization as color began to blossom. Then he closed his eyes until the world resurrected itself with an aggressive pounding.

He pushed himself erect and stumbled to the front door. A quick glance through the peephole showed Rosa standing stiffly and hammering on the door with a shoe. He turned the lock and returned to the couch. He wasn't particularly surprised when she followed him.

"What the hell, Danny? Are you hiding? What are you doing here?"

He probably could have answered one of the three questions, but that would require thought. He closed his eyes.

She swept his feet off the couch and told him to stand up. When he left his feet where they landed and settled deeper into the cushions, she tried to slap him. She had a bad angle and barely connected, so he ignored her. She didn't seem to like being ignored and slapped him again.

"Cut it out, Rosa."

"What's wrong with you? You're finally out of the hospital and you aren't doing a damned thing."

"What do you want me to do, Rosa?"

"Something! Find Tony's dog. Ask your father why he locked you up. Kill Gabriel! That's what you've been whining about ever since Tony died. If you don't want to do that, help your mother carry bed pans. Just for god's sake quit hiding here."

"If I were hiding, at least I wouldn't be listening to you. For the last time, what do you want? Why are you here? Did Mike send you?"

She stood beside the coffee table, looking at him and shaking her head.

When he tired of her judgment, he rolled to a sitting position. "What does he want from me, Rosa?"

"He wants you to rejoin the human race, Danny. Come back to life. Do something."

"What about you? What do you want?"

"I want— ," she shook her head. "What do you want? What are you hiding from?"

"I'm not hiding." He sighed, rubbed his face, started to stretch, and winced when his ribs issued a sharp warning. "I don't know what I want, Rosa. I want my mother home. I want Emmie back. I want Tony back. I want to know what I did wrong. I didn't shoot anyone. I didn't steal any gold. I tried to help my father. Your father. Hell, I helped Mike as much as I could."

"He helped you too."

"He gave me a gun," Danny said sharply. "I'm not sure that was a big favor."

"He took it back when you dropped it. That was a favor."

"Right." He had to concede the point. "But I still spent three days chained to a bed."

"You'd be in a cell if he hadn't interfered."

"Maybe." He wasn't sure. "You think dad would have put me in jail?"

"I don't know." She sank onto the couch beside him and squeezed his hand. "Papa says he didn't have a choice. If the police showed any favoritism, the whole city could explode. There were several riots anyway—"

"Wait a minute!" Danny interrupted her. "Are you saying the mayor told my father to chain me to that hospital bed?"

"It was a mutual decision. They both wanted you off the streets, Danny. You kept telling Mike what Gabriel was up to, even after you were warned, and your father was afraid of what you'd do. He wanted you safe. That's probably the biggest reason he put you there."

Danny sighed. He felt a little better, but only a little. "What about you?" he asked. "You passed everything you heard to Mike."

"I wasn't stupid about it!" Rosa snapped. "I didn't run around town with a gun in my belt."

"You didn't lose your best friend, either. You didn't lose your sister."

"I lost enough," she replied softly. She stood suddenly. "Are you ready to end this pity party? Have you eaten?"

"I'm not hungry."

She took that as a 'no' and headed for the kitchen. She stopped on her way long enough to throw a suggestion over her shoulder. "Those scrubs could use a heavy duty cycle in the washer."

Right. He lifted an arm and verified the truth of that, but Mike's scrubs were his only option, unless.... Tony kept a robe on a hook behind the hall bathroom door. Danny ducked in there, and turned on the hot water in the shower. He felt fully prepared until he dropped the scrubs, pulled off his mask, and saw his face in the mirror. The bandages over his left eyebrow and cheek had crusty brown centers framed by dingy white gauze and tape. The wide scabs on his forehead and jaw made the bandages look good. On the up side, his right cheek was merely dirty and unshaven.

He found a fresh razor in Tony's drawer and unwound the compression wrap over his ribs, then stepped gingerly into the shower. Warm water quickly soaked the bandages and loosened the tape holding them in place so that they dangled loosely from the dry blood in their centers. He splashed a bit of shampoo in his hair and worked the suds, then eased a handful down over his face and patted gently at the gauze until the scabs released it. Then he grabbed a bar of soap and finished everything below his chin as quickly as possible. He'd planned to shave in the shower, but by the time he'd rinsed off, his forehead and chin had begun to sting. He was pretty sure a single swipe of the razor would leave them bleeding again. He decided scruffy would probably be a better look for the day than hamburger face, so he called it a job.

When Rosa saw him, her eyes dilated, but she said only, "I like the zombie look, but you're a couple months early."

"Huh?"

"For Halloween? Get with it, Danny." She pointed at the table. "I made coffee. The eggs were still good, so I scrambled them all. The bacon wasn't too gray, so I fried it in case you want to take a chance. No toast, though. The bread was moldy. I trashed it."

"Okay." He sat and loaded a plate, then looked up. "Aren't you eating?"

"I ate at the cafe." But she took a seat and eyed him speculatively. "What are your plans? Are you still going after Gabriel?"

He considered the question while working on the eggs. "Is that what Mike wants?"

"I'm asking what you want."

"Bullshit!" His angry flare surprised them both. "I call bullshit, Rosa. You're here because Mike sent you, and he sent you because he wants something. What?"

She focused on her hands where they lay on the table, obviously thinking. Finally she whispered softly, "Gabriel."

"Dead?" Danny was surprised. "He always tried to talk me out of it."

"Things are different. That web site—"

"Didn't the government take that down?"

She nodded. "They had it down the next day, but somebody scraped it or something. It popped up immediately on a Swiss server. They took that down and a server in the Philippines had it. Then one in the middle east. Then Africa.

Then Argentina. Then Missouri. The big powers hit the sites they can reach legally and the ones they can't reach have mysterious explosions, but it doesn't stop the spread, and there is more. . . ."

"What?"

"Doctor Foreman said there hasn't been time for anybody to modify their own bacteria, but there have been new outbreaks. Minneapolis and a little one in Miami. We hear rumors from Rio and from Shanghai. Foreman thinks the website has been up for weeks but just not publicized." She met his eyes. "The thing is, before they moved out of Atlanta, the CDC tested samples from Miami and they found a different strain of Staph, one called epidermitis. They are afraid that the edited genes migrated from the Staph Gabriel made to the new strain. It isn't common, but it happens."

"My god." Danny pushed his plate away. His appetite was gone.

"And there are new threats from Iran and Korea. This is the weapon of the future and they want it. They think it is the only way to protect themselves."

Her voice trailed off. They sat on opposite sides of the table and watched her fingers knot around each other in silence. When the silence became uncomfortable, Danny asked, "How is killing Gabriel going to fix this?"

"TonysWay is spreading," Rosa said earnestly. "Everywhere there has been an outbreak, green armbands appear. Death breeds Friends, Danny, and people need friends. As long as the usual governments are in charge, they will compete for more and better biological weapons. Botulism is just one toxin. There are worse now, and if the governments put their labs to work, they will invent worse and worse poisons. The only hope is to change the way people think about war and killing each other. They need to look around the world and see friends, not enemies."

Danny took a moment to digest that. "So that is Mike's plan? He wants to take over the world? How will killing Gabriel help?"

Rosa began shaking her head even before he finished speaking. "He doesn't want to take over anything. He wants people to take back their lives from the governments, and he says the only way people will accept TonysWay is if Gabriel is dealt with by Friends, not by armies or police states. He says they will still have their religions and their countries and everything. They just have to get rid of the hatred that drives them apart. He says—"

"Stop!"

She quit talking, but she looked hurt. She'd obviously just gotten warmed up. He couldn't take any more. "Get out of here, Rosa. Tell Mike I'll think about it. Tell him to leave me the hell alone. Tell him I knew Tony a lot better than he did and if I kill Gabriel I'll do it for Tony and Emmie, not for him."

Rosa nodded and edged toward the door. She said, "I'll tell him you're making up your mind."

"Tell him— Damn it, Foreman said Gabriel might be a woman. Does Mike know that? Does he actually care if Gabriel dies, or does he just want a body he can point at and say, 'See? Only we can save you?'"

"He wants—"

"Never mind." Danny was pretty sure he knew what Mike wanted. "Just get out of here."

Naturally she had the final word on her way out. "He said to keep an eye out for Parker. He still hasn't shown up."

He stared at the door long after Rosa closed it. Then he threw the rest of the eggs and the bacon in a trash bag. He rooted around in Mrs. Massini's knife drawer for her sharpest paring knife and took it to the bathroom.

The knife wasn't quite up to the job. It cut the sutures on his cheekbone, but he had to find tweezers to pull the thread out of his face and he had trouble getting the point of the knife under the staples. He worked at it for a few minutes, then cursed and left them when he started bleeding. A hat would hide them completely, and if he left the house, a surgical mask would cover both the thin scab over his scrapes and the angry jagged red lines over his cheekbone and forehead. But he had no intention of leaving the house. Mike could kill his own damned angel.

Danny returned to the couch and curled up on it. He tossed and turned, trying to find a comfortable position. For some reason, his ribs bothered him more lying down. He gave it a few minutes before giving up. He collected the dirty scrubs and stuck them in the washer with a healthy squirt of detergent and started the machine. When the agitator started, he slipped off the robe and tossed it in with the scrubs. Then he walked into the kitchen and refilled his coffee cup. He had a decision to make. To kill or not to kill; that was the question.

Well, not really.

Before you can kill an angel, you have to catch him. Her. It. And he had no idea how to find Gabriel. His father had been searching for Gabriel for weeks now. The FBI was also in hot pursuit. What about Homeland Security? Other agencies? Now that the secret was out, they might decide to squeeze the perimeter until they squeezed the angel out. No point in sending healthy agents into the city.

And that left TonysWay. Mike had as many Friends as he needed, and every one of them could be relied on to bag the bird.

Danny shook his head. Bag the bird? What the hell was he thinking? If Mike led him to Gabriel, pointed out the man or woman, and told him to take his time, line up a good clean shot, and enjoy his revenge, Danny was no longer sure he could pull the trigger. He wanted the hunt, the chase, the hot blood, the anger, the rage. He wanted to feel the jerk of the weapon in his hand or against his shoulder and he wanted to feel the images of Emmie, of Tony, even the exhausted face of Pam, all lift away from him, released by the twitching body at his feet.

That was what he wanted. He knew he was a fool to even hope for it. He didn't live in that kind of world. He didn't know what kind of world this was.

He started to pour another coffee, then suddenly imagined what Mrs. Massini would think if she found him drinking coffee, naked, in her kitchen. He left the cup on her counter and checked the washing machine. It had finished, but of course everything was damp. He moved the load to the dryer and decided that Tony wouldn't mind loaning him a pair of pants.

He loaned Danny more than that. He loaned him a full set of clothes, a pair of shoes, and his bed, which looked too inviting to pass up and which did not bother his ribs when he lay down for a quick nap and woke late in the day from a

208

dream involving his father and handcuffs.

So little remained of the day that Danny decided to use the night to make his decision. He still didn't want to alert the neighbors by turning on lights, so he went to the kitchen to prepare an early dinner. He got a can of beans open and a spoon in the can, but he couldn't take it any further. He thought maybe Parker would eat the beans, if he ever came home, so he went out back to put them in his bowl. The bowl, of course, was not empty. It was full of a green arm band and, under that, a loaded revolver.

Chapter 22

Danny drifted into a muffled wakefulness. He only learned sleep had slipped away from him when he tried to lift his head and found his cheek stuck to Tony's pillow. He'd kicked off his shoes sometime during the night and pulled the cover over himself without undressing further. He lay on his side and the pillow stuck to his left cheek. He pulled his right hand from under the pillow to push it away from his face and bounced the gun in his hand against his nose. That popped his eyes fully open. He stared at the revolver like a thing he needed to make sense of, an unexpected intrusion that required explanation or integration. It came to him that the explanation was Gabriel. He dropped the gun and pushed away from the mattress to start his day.

He stepped out back and discovered Parker had not visited over night. His bowl was still full of the beans Danny left last night. The air was cool. The sun had barely risen above the neighboring roofs and the yard still lay mostly in shadow.

The yard wasn't big. Three weeks ago it had been beautiful. The huge sycamore Mr. Massini had been talking about taking down for at least ten years dominated the yard, but enough sun reached the far left corner to support his garden: four tomato plants, a row of string beans against the back wall, two healthy zucchini plants, an eggplant. Onions. Carrots. And along the other walls, Mrs. Massini's roses and iris. She loved her iris. But the lawn was overgrown and looked dry. The vegetables weren't too bad, but without care, the weeds were taking over.

He found a hoe in the shed and spent an hour weeding the garden and roses before deciding that the iris were on their own. He also gave the lawn mower a long look, but the argument that kept the lights off at night also applied to it. He pulled a trash bag off the roll in the shed and raked the weeds into it, then carried it to the garbage container beside the house.

He noticed the sour-sweet gagging smell of decaying meat even before he lifted the lid on the bin. He almost tossed the bag of yard clippings in and slammed the lid without looking, but he'd never smelled anything quite that bad. It just didn't belong. He knew that, and so he stepped away, dropped the bag, took a deep breathe, and peeked into the bin. That's when he found Parker.

He turned away and vomited. After he wiped his lips he went back into the house and rinsed his mouth over and over. When he could finally swallow without gagging, he sat at the table. Staring at the wall, trying to think. Did he need to tell Mike? Would anyone else care?

Probably not, to both questions.

He dug a grave between the squash and the tomatoes. He dug it deep. As he tipped Parker into it, he wondered how long he'd had been dead. There were lots of very active maggots, but Danny didn't know what they meant.

After he filled the grave, he rinsed the container twice and poured a gallon of bleach into the water. Then he ran the washing machine again to get the stink out of Tony's clothes. That helped, but the odor was trapped in his nose. He thought a cup of strong coffee might clear it, might even help him make a decision.

He sat at the kitchen table, sipped his coffee and stared at the revolver and armband. He wondered if Rosa knew they were in Parker's bowl when she came yesterday, if she'd put them there herself. He also wondered if she'd known where Parker rested when she asked him to keep an eye out. And that brought him to Parker.

Tony got him on his eleventh birthday, after the party. The other boys had all gone home, but Danny was spending the night. He and Tony had been excited all day, but couldn't wind down, even after a late supper of left-over hot dogs and cake, because Mr. and Mrs. Massini so obviously had one more card up their collective sleeve, and judging by the smug and superior looks Mike had thrown around all day, it was a doozy. And then Mr. Massini disappeared after dinner, claiming he needed to 'get comfortable' and Mrs. Massini insisted that everyone move to the living room and then, very casually, began rearranging furniture while pretending to straighten up the room. She sat both boys on the couch and told Mike to move the coffee table so they'd be more comfortable, which made no sense at all, and had them searching each other's faces for clues, or even guesses, at what was coming. And then they heard a yap and a tiny ball of black and white fur pulled Mr. Massini into the room on a thick checkered leash.

Parker.

He spotted the two boys and instantly abandoned Mr. Massini by ducking his head and slipping the collar over his nose. The next thing they knew, the boys each had a lap full of wriggle and a face full of tongue. All of which ended eight years later in a freezer trailer in the emergency parking lot at Mercy, a hole in the garden, and a .38 Special wrapped in a green arm band on Mrs. Massini's kitchen table.

The doorbell rang. Danny ignored it. When the ringing became too insistent, he answered the door more to escape his thoughts than to silence the bell, and led Simon Foreman back to the kitchen.

Foreman declined Danny's offer of a coffee. He fingered the revolver briefly then picked up the arm band and sent him a sharp look. "Are you a convert now, Mr. Murphy?"

"I'm not sure. More like a draftee, I guess."

"You're not sure." Foreman shook his head, as though wondering how anyone could be unsure of the answer to such a simple question. "TonysWay is an organization of volunteers. How does one get drafted into a voluntary group?"

"Well, there's the gun—"

"Which I think you requested," Foreman interjected quickly, "with the aim of killing Gabriel."

"But I lost it when I was arrested, and now it's back. I

didn't ask for it back."

"So it just appeared, magically, on the table?"

"No. It was in . . . I found it in. . . ."

"Where did you find it?"

"In P-P-Parker's bowl." He closed his eyes to concentrate on getting the words out without embarrassing himself. "I f-found it."

"What else did you find, Danny?" His voice sounded surprisingly gentle. "The arm band?"

"No." He had his voice in check again but didn't want to open his eyes. "Parker. Tony's dog."

"I see."

"He was in the garbage all along." Closed eyes couldn't hold the memory in. Danny had to wipe his cheeks. "All the time we were looking for him."

"We? Do you mean you and Mike?"

Danny nodded.

"And you think Mike knew and just pretended to look for this Parker?"

Danny nodded again. "I'm afraid Mike killed Parker." His voice was hoarse. "I can't think why anyone else would do that. I think he did it a long time ago, when he came home after his Mom died and his father died and Tony died."

"He killed the dog because he was in pain? He just lost his family and wanted to hurt someone?"

"No!" Danny's eyes flew open. He felt angry, misunderstood. "Mike loved Parker too, but he was Tony's dog. Mike wouldn't know how to explain to him that Tony was gone. I think he wanted to save Parker from what he was feeling."

"I see."

"Really, it was Gabriel. Gabriel killed Parker when he killed Tony."

"And that's why you want to kill Gabriel."

Danny nodded, then corrected himself. "No. That's why I don't want to kill him any more. If I kill him, then I'm responsible for everything that falls out of his death. I guess I could live with that, but I learned something when I was digging the grave for Parker. I'm worse than Gabriel. I don't want him dead. I want him hurting. Suffering worse than any soul in hell. I want him to feel all the pain he's caused a thousand times."

"If you can do that, you will feel better?"

"I don't think I'll ever feel better."

Foreman sat back in his chair and watched Danny carefully. He asked, "What do you think Mike wants?"

"Gabriel dead." That was easy. "He wants TonysWay to get credit so more people will become Friends."

"You think he wants power?"

"Not exactly. I think he wants to make the world safe from the next Gabriel and he thinks the only way to do that is to change the way people treat each other."

Foreman nodded thoughtfully. "And what about your father? Does he want credit for killing Gabriel?"

"Dad is a cop, all the way through. He wants Gabriel alive to face a judge and jury, and then he'll be happy to put a noose around his neck with his own hands, but he knows that's not going to happen. Not for a long time anyway."

"Why not?"

"The FBI and Homeland Security and probably a dozen other outfits want to squeeze every once of information they can get out of Gabriel." Danny's voice cleared as though he'd just realized something. "I don't think they'll ever allow him to be killed. They'll always be afraid that he has one more answer they need if they can just find the right question. They'll lock him up, sure, but they might even trade him a decent life for cooperation."

Foreman poured himself a coffee and freshened Danny's cup. When he sat back down, he asked, "Do they have anything in common?"

"What do you mean?"

"I think you know what I mean. How are their goals different from yours?"

Danny shook his head stubbornly. He picked up the gun and spun the cylinder, then replaced it. "Maybe I care more."

"More than Mike, who lost his whole family? More than your father, who lost his daughter and his city? Maybe his whole family?"

"No." He wouldn't meet the professor's eyes.

Foreman sighed. His attention drifted around the kitchen

214

before fixing on the counter. He asked, "Are you taking anything for this unbearable pain?"

"What do you mean?" Danny looked over his shoulder and saw Mr. Massini's bottle of tequila. "That belongs to Mike. He's saving it for the celebration."

"Okay." Foreman changed the subject. "You know I was a physicist first. Did I ever tell you why I got into philosophy?"

"No." Danny looked confused and not very interested.

"I worked for one of the secret labs. We designed triggers for the really big bombs. You know what I mean?"

"Atomic bombs?"

"Fusion weapons in the megaton range. Large enough to kill the biggest city, but that isn't the point. The man I worked for came from overseas. He worked for our worst enemy during the cold war, and he worked on their version of the doomsday device."

"The what?"

"This happened during the MAD years, the time when reasonable men all over the world firmly believed in Mutually Assured Destruction. MAD was the idea that suicide is the only perfect defense. To be secure, you had to be willing to destroy the world. Everything. Your enemy and his friends and his children, all the children's children, and yourself and your children, and your dogs and horses and even the flowers. Only by being demonstrably insane, by building the device and putting the trigger in the hands of men who would follow orders, only in that way could a nation be free to do anything it wanted, anything at all, secure in the knowledge that no one would dare stop it."

Danny was incredulous. "These doomsday machines were really built?"

"As far as I know, we both failed. The technology was too complicated."

"So. . . ?"

"Think about Gabriel."

"You think he built a doomsday bomb?"

"I think he detonated one," Foreman said gravely. "I think he changed the world. I think he ended one world and left us to invent a new one."

"That seems a little . . . ," Danny searched for a word, ". . .

215

extreme."

"Really? He modified two very common bacteria to kill anyone they infect, and his change has already spread to a third, even more common bacteria. In addition, he published instructions that will allow anyone on Earth to do the same thing. Other men have already begun making even more deadly diseases." Foreman hesitated a moment, then changed tack. "Those doomsday machines didn't fail because men came to their senses, Danny. They failed because the bombs were too complicated and too expensive. Gabriel's little surprise is simple and cheap. It is also irreversible."

"Irreversible?"

"Men changed bacteria. Now bacteria are changing bacteria. What comes next?"

Danny shook his head.

"The bacteria will begin to change men. They will even change the delicately balanced network of living organisms that make our world sustainable." Foreman pulled an envelope from his pocket and set it on the table. "I will never be allowed out of the city, Danny. Nobody wants me to talk about this, and I can't keep quiet. I'm stuck here until the perimeter squeezes me into the hands of the government. Mike might protect me, but he would just offer me a different kind of cell." He pushed the envelope across the table. "This is a thumb drive with everything I know or suspect about where the gene mods are taking us. There are other things on it. My will. A few personal letters. The envelope is addressed to an old friend, a man I trust."

"You want me to deliver it?"

Foreman nodded. "I can't. I'm a scientist. All my friends and acquaintances here are scientists or with the university. We're already being watched." He swallowed nervously. "Your father is a policeman. You have a good chance of getting past the quarantine line, and you were Tony's best friend. You have a good relationship with Mike and his Friends."

"I don't—"

"I have no one else to ask, Danny."

He stared at the envelope like it was poisoned. "What about Gabriel?"

"Chase him. Mike will give you any assistance you need if

he thinks you are hunting him, and your father will also help if you promise to turn him over to the authorities."

Danny looked sharply at the old scientist. "Which should I do? Kill him or save him?"

"It doesn't matter. The bomb has already gone off. Do what is right for yourself." He watched as Danny slowly reached over the table, then he stood, looking a little less stressed. Danny followed him to the front door where he turned awkwardly and said, "We probably won't see each other again. If we do, we won't be able to talk. I enjoyed having you in my class, Danny. Your friend too, of course, but your . . . insights. It was a pleasure knowing you and I wish you good luck in the coming months. Years."

He opened his arms very hesitantly. Danny stepped in for a quick hug, then backed away feeling a little uncomfortable. He muttered an abrupt thank you before asking, "You once told me that Gabriel might be a woman, but you keep referring to him as a man. Why?"

"Habit, maybe. Killing thousands of people seems more like something a man would do. I'm probably biased."

"But where did you hear it could be a woman?"

"Your father was discussing Gabriel before my appointment with the mayor last week. It seems the FBI found a record of shipments of lab equipment to an address near the university. The address was abandoned months ago, but it had been leased by a woman named Julia Pinker. There's no record of her anywhere and their search didn't turn up anyone, so it isn't certain, but it is possible."

"Julia Pinker?"

"Even if she was involved, it's probably a false name, and there is no evidence that the bacteria were actually created at the address. For that matter, she could have been working for someone else. Male or female."

"Was there a description?"

"Do you remember that drawing of the man who handed out the colored chalk? Imagine it was a woman dressed as a man."

"Thanks."

"Of course." Foreman left with a smile on his face that didn't reach his eyes.

Danny walked back into the kitchen wondering how he could find anyone with no more information than he'd been given. He picked up the revolver and spun the cylinder. He pointed it at the refrigerator and said, "Bang." The stove. "Bang." Mr. Massini's bottle of Patron tequila. He didn't say anything. He walked to the counter and picked up the bottle. It was half full.

Chapter 23

Danny spent the last half of that Tuesday cleaning Mrs. Massini's house. He did her floors, emptied the dishwasher and then hand washed everything he'd touched over the last few days. He scrubbed the hall bath—tub, toilet, counter, and everything in between. He washed the sheets on Tony's bed, dusted his desk and the top of his dresser. He washed a few windows, inside and out, raked the mound in the garden smooth, and emptied the bleach and soapy water from the garbage container. He even tried to dry beads of water that clung to the inside and bottom, though he couldn't finish that job. The only things he didn't touch, indoors or out, were Mike's possessions, the master bedroom, and the bottle on the kitchen counter.

When the light failed, he wrapped himself in a blanket and settled on the couch. He'd worked hard all day. He ached and he wanted to sleep, but he couldn't get comfortable and he couldn't close his eyes without seeing Parker in the garbage can. He listened to the house, seeing nothing, feeling its emptiness. For the first time since he let himself in, he felt unwelcome, but not like the house wanted him to go. More like he'd never belonged there. His memories, even those from before Tony's birthday party, felt like stories from a different book.

The night eventually won. He had too much to do tomorrow and decided that if he couldn't sleep, he could at least pass out. He made his way into the kitchen and felt around in Mrs. Massini's tool drawer for the flashlight she kept there. Then he carried the bottle into the hall bath, where a light could never be seen. He set the bottle beside the sink and looked at it for a minute. It looked exactly half full. Then he took the flashlight and a hand towel and went hunting.

He didn't waste any time in Tony's room. Mike's was a different matter. He poked in every drawer, searched every shelf. He even dug to the bottom of his laundry bin without luck. When he found nothing, he fought back the sense that he was invading the Massini's privacy and searched their bed and bath. Again, he found nothing. Back in the bathroom, he pulled the cork from the tequila and took a long swallow. He coughed a few times and drank from the sink faucet. He stood, leaning on the counter and staring at his face in the mirror. The long red wound over his cheek looked a little swollen, but it didn't need attention. He could make out some of the staples in his eyebrow and forehead. He managed to hook one with a finger nail and popped it out. It fell into the sink and he started to wash it down the drain, then thought better of that and pocketed it. He ran the water a long time and decided not to bother with bleach. He'd left too many other traces to hope he could clean the house completely.

He resumed his examination of the mirror. It didn't help, but a second long pull at the tequila gave him an idea. Mr. Massini's car was parked in the garage. Mike had locked it, but his mother's set of keys was in her key drawer, and when Danny unlocked the car, he found three plastic bags in the trunk, one each with the personal possessions of Mike's mother, father, and brother. He carried them back to the bathroom. He opened Tony's bag and pocketed his driver's license, then resealed it. He needed another shot of tequila for nerve before he placed the bags with the Massini's possessions carefully on their pillows. He left Tony's bag on Mike's pillow.

Danny turned his attention back to the mirror without seeing a damned thing in it. No present, no past, and no future. He started to take another hit of the tequila and changed his mind. Instead, he used the towel to wipe everything he might have touched again. Then he retrieved the revolver. He flipped the cylinder open to examine the cartridges. Two had been fired. He closed the cylinder and wiped it carefully before pushing it deep in the laundry basket in Mike's room. He collected the scrubs and shoes he'd worn for his escape. Finally, he used one of Mrs. Massini's plastic baggies to seal Doctor Foreman's letter and bury it. When he stepped out the front door and looked up and down the dark street, he felt alone in the night. Safe.

He pulled the car out of the garage and returned the spare house key to its hiding place. He sat in the drive, lights off and engine idling, and remembered Tony, Parker, Mrs. Massini's dinners, all long hours of his childhood. Then he drove through empty streets to the high school gym. He drove very carefully, parked in the gym lot, closed his eyes, and finally slept.

A large white van with a green flag flying from a window post woke him shortly after dawn. It parked on the sidewalk by the main entrance. A couple, both wearing the arm bands, hopped out and opened the back doors. Two men climbed out of the cargo area with a dolly and began unloading insulated plastic boxes. While they worked, the couple looked Danny over suspiciously. When he turned and lifted his right shoulder enough to show his arm band, they relaxed.

When they had a full dolly, he pulled Danny's baseball cap down far enough to hide his eyebrow, hooked the mask over his ears, made sure it covered his cheek, and joined the Friends wheeling boxes into the gym. From the smell, they were breakfast boxes. His mouth watered.

Nobody questioned him when he trailed the group onto the floor. A third of the cots were empty. A few Friends and helpers tended the remaining patients, but most surrounded the Friends with the food. He wanted to catch his mother alone, so he ignored the food and wandered through the beds peering into the faces of the orderlies and their helpers.

"Danny?"

The voice came from one of the cots. A girl. He didn't recognize her right away, but then he sat on the cot and lifted his mask slightly to show her his smile. "Hello, Jannie."

"I knew you'd come." She covered his hand where it rested on her bed. "I knew you'd find me."

"I promised, didn't I? You're my sister now." He squeezed

her hand and hoped she couldn't see his surprise and embarrassment. "How are you doing, twerp?"

She suddenly sat up and wrapped her free arm around him, sobbing. He started to pull back, then leaned in and hugged her to his chest. He said, "Jannie? What's wrong? I came as soon as I could, but—"

"You called me twerp." She was blubbering. "That's what you called Emmie."

"Oh." He pulled her closer, blinking rapidly. He took a deep breath and said, "Well, I told you you're going to be my sister now."

"Like Emmie?" She was getting herself under control too.

"Emmie will always be my sister," Danny told her, "but I need someone I can hug now, so you're my sister too."

She leaned back and searched his eyes. "For always?"

"Yes. Always." He realized how deeply he meant it. He pulled her back into a tight hug. "So, how are you doing, sis?"

"Better now." She lay back. "They're going to let me go as soon as they find a place for me. I can't go home. Did you know my mom is dead?"

"They told me the same day I saw you in the hospital."

"So I won't have anywhere to go."

"What about our house, Jan? I'm sure my mom and dad would welcome you."

She gave him a strange look and shook her head.

"What? Did you ask?"

She teared up again. "I'm sorry, Danny."

"What? Why?"

A figure approached with two breakfast boxes. "Excuse me? What are you—"

Danny looked up, stood, and said, "Hello, Mom."

"Danny!" She dropped the boxes on the mattress and hugged him. "I missed you! Are you okay? I was so worried."

He reassured her as well as he could, then asked, "You heard what happened?"

"Rosa said your father had you arrested," she said vaguely. "I'm glad he let you go right away."

"He didn't. I was handcuffed to a hospital bed for three days."

"She said you weren't hurt very bad."

"Not too bad." He released her and stepped back. Her tone puzzled him. "What's wrong, Mom?"

"Nothing, now that you're free." She began opening a box for Janis who had been watching them silently. "Thank god your father came to his senses."

"He didn't. I escaped." He had to ask. "Did you ask him to let me go?"

"I didn't know right away." She focused on opening a breakfast box for Janis. It looked like a croissant with scrambled eggs and melted cheese and it smelled wonderful. She added, "Rosa told me not to worry. She said your friends would take care of you."

"Really. So you haven't called him?"

"I've been very busy, Danny."

"I see that." He glanced around the gymnasium. "Is Mrs. Baca here too?"

"She's working with Eddie. The mayor is a Friend now." She picked up the other box. "I've got to deliver this. I'll be right back."

She left him standing there. He looked after her, then down at Janis, who repeated, "I'm sorry."

"I don't understand what happened."

"Neither do I. She talks about the Friends all the time. When I ask about Mr. Murphy, she just shrugs. I asked when you were coming and she said you were busy."

"And Dad hasn't been here?"

"I haven't seen him."

"Right." Danny swallowed, still watching his mother opening a breakfast for a patient three rows over. "We might be in the same boat, Jannie."

"Nowhere to go?"

"No." He shook himself and smiled at her. "I'll find a place. Somehow."

"For me too?"

"For us." He stood abruptly. "I've got things to do. If she asks, tell her I'll be back as soon as I can. It might be tomorrow."

"But you're coming for me too? You won't forget me?"

"Never, twerp."

On his way out, he grabbed a handful of unused masks

from the guard table by the main door. He stopped at the van and borrowed two breakfast croissants on his way to the parking lot. The couple guarding it smiled cheerfully when they saw the band on his arm and offered him a hot coffee. He wolfed the sandwiches down before he reached the car, then sat a moment, sipping the coffee appreciatively. It felt good to have friends, so good that he stopped at the van for a refill before leaving. The man smiled at his thanks when he handed the full cup back to Danny, then pointed at his dash and said, "Don't forget your colors, Friend."

Danny drew a blank for a few seconds, then nodded. "Of course." He pulled his arm band off and draped it over the dashboard, remembering the nasty look he'd received from the woman directing traffic just before the auditorium shooting.

The flags had grown more important in the week since. He passed only seven vehicles on the drive to the university. Five of those either flew the flag or had a green cloth draped on the dash or rolled into a window. The other two were police vehicles. They seemed to be keeping a sharp eye on the bicycle and foot traffic while carefully ignoring anything green.

The city had changed since Danny went looking for Gabriel after the TonysWay rally. Motor vehicles were very rare, but bikers and pedestrians crowded the streets. Nobody paid much attention to traffic laws though. Of course the bikes slowed the progress of anything without a siren and the jaywalkers slowed the bicycles, so maybe traffic laws mattered less now. Other changes: the men and women on the street looked thinner. Not starving, but thinner. Very few teenagers on the street. No children, but it was still early. No cars in the metered parking along the street. He assumed gas was either rationed or unavailable.

The windows made the greatest impression on him. Many stores were closed, and the windows of those remaining open were spartan. Not many items on display, and the things available looked utilitarian. Like the people.

He noticed a crowd on a corner near the university and pulled to the curb to see what drew it. Pedestrians kept well clear of his car as he parked, and after he transferred the green band from the dash to his right arm, the men and women in the crowd edged out of his way, gave him a clear path to the front row of a semicircle around a bulletin board screwed to the brick wall of a closed grocery. A large map of the city covered half the board. Cork board covered with private and public notices, some of them looking very official, made up the remainder.

A clear layer of thin mylar overlaid the map and two friends were drawing on it with colored markers. One looked around when Danny stepped up behind him and nodded at his armband. Then he went back to his artwork. The other never looked around at all. She was completely intent on completing the web she was constructing.

She'd drawn an incomplete spider web over the city. Only the outer third was covered by irregular concentric lines in black ink. Each roughly traced a series of streets around the city until it met itself at one of the three lines leading from the city to the world.

Danny felt a chill as he studied the map. He checked the legend. The black lines marked the current location of the quarantine line. The outer circle was dated July 6, the day he'd driven to soccer camp to rescue Emmie. The line the friend worked on so intently carried a neat July 16 label. Eleven lines, and the city's area had shrunk by well over half.

The outgoing lines were marked by a red circle where they met the quarantine line. He checked the legend. A red circle was a checkpoint, the only way in or out of the city. With a sigh, he turned to the other half of the bulletin board. The notices there included small cards offering services, some more personal than others, and larger cards identifying meeting times for TonysWay circles of trust or distribution points for medical supplies or food.

Two sheets the size of copy paper at the far edge of the board drew most of the crowd's attention. Danny edged closer to them. The top sheet looked like a standard wanted poster. It had a badge on red bar that read 'Wanted by the FBI' across the top and under that a line drawing of a thin-faced woman with short dark hair and high cheekbones. She had heavy eyebrows, dark eyes with darker circles, and an anxious look. Below the drawing, he read, 'Gabriel, AKA Julia Pinker,' and below that he read a long list of speculations that included

225

hundreds of homicides. And below that, he saw another wanted poster, this one posted by Homeland Security. The name under the picture was Daniel Murphy and the charge was Murder.

Murder. Danny eased back into the crowd, away from the accusation on the bulletin board. He wanted to be angry, but mostly he felt ashamed. *Murder.* He'd never killed anyone. He wanted to kill Gabriel, but that didn't feel like murder. Justice, or maybe revenge. And he failed at that. Was he ashamed of his failure?

The crowd filled the vacancy left by his slow retreat. *Murder.* The word created a space around him. He felt trapped in a bubble even as strangers jostled him from all sides. He had no doubt who he stood accused of killing, but the confirmation came when the friend updating the board ripped Julia Pinker's wanted poster off.

Danny studied the board while he fought to regain his composure. He eventually pushed out of the crowd and drove with no destination in mind. He needed to be alone and at the same time he needed a connection of some sort. He'd lost too much, almost too much to bear. He'd alienated his father. His mother just sort of walked away from her life. He'd lost his sister and the only close friend he'd ever made. Tony. He felt like Gabriel had hooked a giant pump to his life and sucked everything out. Even the dog.

When he found himself near Tony's house, he thought maybe he'd sit with Parker for a few minutes. He almost turned onto the block, but the cops in the front yard stopped him. He slowed enough to count two patrol cars and a Crime Scene van. Three uniforms lounged around the yard inside the yellow police tape. At least two of them sported a flash of green on their right arms.

He drove up the cross street and parked. He had no plan B. None of his friends or acquaintances would welcome a wanted murderer. Foreman couldn't risk drawing attention to their relationship. Mike had fingered him for the murder. Rosa probably planted the murder weapon. Danny needed to think. He had been trapped, neatly trapped. He needed a way out and he had no confidence that an escape existed.

He wanted a refuge, a place to think. He decided he'd have

to settle for a safe place to park for a few hours. The high school gym lot might work, but the hospital drew him. He'd be closer to Emmie there. He could close his eyes there and feel safe. Safer, anyway. He stopped just long enough to secure his arm band on the scrub jacket he'd worn for his escape. Tony's cap went on the floorboard. That was about the best he could do for a disguise, so he crossed his fingers and drove.

He knew something was terribly wrong even before he parked. The emergency parking lot was empty. Danny dashed onto the lot, looking around wildly. The lot was silent. The trailers were gone. Emmie was gone.

Chapter 24

Both the police officer at the entrance and the orderly guarding the door were watching him. The cop began approaching him. He ran up to the orderly and demanded, "Where's my sister?"

"What are you talking about?"

"The trailers! Emmie was in . . . what happened to the trailers?"

"Calm down, sir." He glanced at Danny's armband and waved the cop off. "The bodies have been released. Did you say your sister was in . . . waiting for release?"

"Yes." Danny felt dizzy. He leaned on the wall and tried to breath slowly. "What— Where are they?"

"The families were all notified, friend. Did she have anyone else?"

"My mom." He closed his eyes. "Dad."

"Talk to them," the orderly said gently. "They'll tell you about the arrangements."

Danny nodded. He slid slowly down the wall until he sat on his heels.

The orderly volunteered, "They have to be cremated. The health department insisted."

"When?"

"The truck pulled them out two days ago. I heard the families were invited to a ceremony, but I don't know any more than that. Why don't you check the board?" When

Danny looked at him blankly, he added, "The bulletin board in the lobby?"

"Oh." It took a few seconds for the meaning to sink in. He struggled to his feet and started slowly toward the lobby. By the time he reached it, he was running.

The board provided some information. Family inquiries were referred to a designated grief counseling team. Threats, however vague, must be reported to the Friends in the security office. Four members of the Mercy Hospital family had succumbed to the plague: Doctors Pamela Oliver and Jason Kemp, RN Roger Arnault, and Orderly Alan Pasco. Anyone wishing to attend the memorial and interment ceremony Friday afternoon should request time off from their supervisor. Transportation would be provided.

Other than an updated telephone list that included a number for the Admissions desk at the gym annex, that was it. There wasn't even a wanted poster for the notorious murderer, Danny Murphy.

Danny needed answers desperately enough to take a few chances. He decided to start with a phone call and dialed his father's office from a courtesy phone near the closed gift shop.

"Homeland Security. How can I direct your call?" Brenda's greeting was so unexpected that Danny went blank. He took a breath and asked, hesitantly, "Is the Chief in, Brenda?"

He must have caught her by surprise too. It took her a long time to respond. Then she said, "I'm sorry. We have no one here by that name. You must have misdialed. Please check your number very carefully and try again." She repeated, "Very carefully." Then she hung up.

Danny stared at the screen. He felt completely lost. Finally he shook his head and dialed the number for admissions at the Gym annex. He asked, "Is Anne Murphy working today?"

"Just a sec." Papers rustled in the background. "Sorry. She's not scheduled back until Saturday. Can I take a message?"

"Do you know if she's gone home?"

"No idea, friend. You wanna leave a message or not?"

Danny refused. As soon as he hung up, he realized he should have asked about Janis. He didn't call back, though. He didn't want to give the guy on the other end any more reason to remember him. He hurried back to the car and started the engine before he realized he had nowhere to go. He rested his forehead on the steering wheel. Eventually he began beating his head against the wheel. Not too hard. Just enough to focus his thoughts.

Brenda had identified her office as Homeland Security before she heard his voice. Danny had no way of knowing what that meant. Did his father move to another office? Did he take orders from Homeland now? Had he been fired? And why did Brenda hang up? She always seemed to like him, and her suggestion sounded like a warning. 'Check your number very carefully,' she'd said, but was she waving him off or did his father's new position, whatever that was, need to be protected from the embarrassment of a murderous son? Or maybe she simply wanted to avoid turning him in herself?

Wrestling with those questions got him no farther than beating his head on the steering wheel, so he eventually quit both. He thought perhaps his mother could tell him what was going on if he could find her. At least she might not call the cops on him. Or Homeland Security, or whoever ran the city at the moment.

As soon as his hands stopped shaking, he drove home. He didn't stop there. Two nondescript cars with city plates on the street scared him off. In any case, he had no way of knowing if his mother was even home. He passed the house without slowing and circled the block.

The house behind his had been listed for sale for months and the sign was still up, so he stopped there. He glanced in a few windows to verify that it was still vacant, then walked around the side and studied the back of his house over the wall. He learned nothing. Blinds were open. No one moved behind the glass. He heard nothing except a neighbor's dog. The hummingbird feeder was dry. Either his mother hadn't been home for several days or she had more important things on her mind than hungry birds. He turned away from the wall.

"Hey! What ya doing?"

Danny jumped and spun around. The boy hanging over the cinder block side wall stared at him curiously. He swallowed nervously and asked, "Billy?"

"Yeah. What's up?"

"Just checking out the house, that's all. Why are you home?"

"Everybody's grounded because of the bottle-ism. You grounded too? You're too old for that."

"I guess I'm reverse grounded. Instead of staying home, I'm supposed to stay out."

Billy thought that over for a minute, then commented, "That'd suck. What happened to your face? You get in a fight?"

Danny touched it. "Lost one, I guess. Your folks home?"

"Nah. Mom's working and Dad's out with the Friends. Why?"

"They'd probably tell my folks I sneaked in the house is all."

"How are they gonna find out?"

"You won't say anything?"

Billy grinned. "My Frisbee went in your yard last week. Dad says I can't go in after it without permission."

"You got it."

"Great!" He climbed onto the wall, stood up, and began walking.

Danny snapped. "Be careful, damn it! If you kill yourself, I'm taking the permission back."

"No worries. I do this all the time."

"Not when your mom's home, I bet."

Billy snorted and hopped into Danny's back yard. "You coming?" When Danny hesitated, he added, "Nobody's been home all week."

"You sure?"

"I been watching." He walked around the yard while Danny hopped the wall. He paused once to scoop his Frisbee from under a scraggly bougainvillea, then walked to the back door. "How are we going to get in?"

"You're not. You'd be in more trouble than you ever dreamed."

"I could help."

"I just need to get some stuff. I'll be right out."

"But—"

"If you want to help, you can keep watch from your yard. If you see anything, throw your Frisbee against my bedroom window. You know which one?"

Billy nodded. "But it'd be faster if I helped."

"Listen, there's two carloads of Friends out front and some of them might know your dad. You want to take a chance on him finding out you helped me?"

Billy changed his mind and pointed. "That's your window, right?"

When Danny nodded, he dashed for the wall and shouted, "Can't miss it!"

Danny grinned and shook his head. The sliding window in the utility room was unlocked, as always, and a patio chair got him in the house. His first stop was upstairs. He slipped off his shoes and moved quietly, listening for any hint that his parents had slipped in unnoticed, but he heard only the hum of the refrigerator in the kitchen and the soft grinding of the motor in his father's old-fashioned radio alarm clock.

The hallway and master bedroom were both dim and stuffy. The bed was made, but the spread on his father's side was wrinkled like someone often slept there without getting under the covers.

His father carried a work phone on duty. His personal phone was on the bedside table, along with some pocket change, a small knife, and a comb. Danny took the phone and checked the drawer. He found miscellaneous junk and an automatic pistol, one of his father's personal weapons. He closed the drawer. The last thing he needed was another gun.

His bedroom felt even emptier than his parents'. He opened the door and immediately wanted to collapse on the bed, but it wasn't his anymore. A fugitive didn't belong any-where near it, so he pulled his gym bag from his closet and loaded it with shoes, jeans, underwear, and a few shirts. Then he stood, looking around in case this was his last goodbye. He no longer needed his text books. Papers? No. Maybe his passport. He found that and his health records, added them to the bag, and left. He made it as far as the hallway and could go no further. He walked slowly, step by hard step, toward Emmie's room. Her door was closed. He stood in the hall with his hand on the knob, but he couldn't make himself turn it.

Emmie was not home. The room was empty. Nothing scary in there. Nothing at all. The room held too much nothing. That explained why he couldn't open the door. It didn't explain why he couldn't take his hand off the knob, why he couldn't turn the knob and push into the room or open his hand and walk away.

Emmie was not home but the room held the five thousand days of Emma. They started a month after his father became Chief of Police, the day he moved the family to the new house, the day Danny sat, cross-legged on brand new carpet in the brand new room, and worried about losing his friend, starting first grade, and keeping the screw drivers straight while his dad reassembled his old baby crib. They ended two Saturdays ago when he carried the bags out for the girl's trip to soccer camp. Between the two days: more than five thousand memories. Rubbing her back through the bars on the crib to help her sleep. Dashing into the room when she fell out of the crib on her first escape attempt. His astonishment the time he watched mom change her diapers and realized that girls were built nothing like boys. The day he helped dad bolt her first real bed together. All the days she conned him into helping her pick up her stuffed bears.

That finally broke his paralysis. He couldn't walk away without something of hers, and he knew exactly what he wanted. Her first dog, Goofy, from their first trip to Disneyland. He pushed into the room and stopped in his tracks, surprised by the sleeping bag and an open suitcase. He'd forgotten Janis.

He quickly grabbed Goofy from his position of honor under her dresser mirror and opened her bedside drawer, looking for a small, easily carried photo. He didn't see one, but her passport was there.

Danny heard a loud bang as something hit his bedroom window.

He stuffed the passport in his pocket, picked up his bag, and snatched Janis' case on his way out. He ran out the back door, tossed both bags over the back wall, and scrambled after them. He landed on his back, staring up at Billy standing on top of the cinder block wall. He pushed up to his knees, ready to run, and demanded, "What? What's happening?"

Billy grinned at him. "Told you I could hit that window, no problem."

Danny peeked over the back wall. Absolutely nothing was

going on in the yard. "Why'd you throw the Frisbee, damn it?"

"What took so long?"

"I was busy. Why'd you throw it?"

"I needed practice, to be sure I'd hit your window if the friends started nosing around." He acted like that was obvious.

"Right." Danny's heart rate felt closer to normal and any more questions would probably push it back up, so he let it go and picked up the two bags.

"Where you going?"

"I need to talk to a woman about why I'm in trouble and I don't know how to get to her."

"This about you being wanted for killing that Gabriel?"

"You know about that?" Danny felt faint.

"Sure. Dad and those friends been warning everybody about it, but kind of like bragging, like you should get a reward, except for it's against the law and everything."

"I didn't do it, Billy."

"I know that. They said Gabriel turned out to be a girl. Nobody kills girls."

Danny couldn't argue that without creating doubt about his innocence. He smiled and said, "Well, thanks for believing me, Billy, and thanks for your help."

"Why don't you just call her?"

"What?"

"Why don't you just call that woman you need to meet?" He pointed at the cell phone laying on the grass. It had obviously popped out of Danny's pocket when he fell.

"Thanks." Danny scooped the phone up and carried the bags away from the conversation as quickly as he could. He didn't relax until he reached the university area and could lose himself in the crowd of Friends on campus. He located a lunch wagon far from the Campus Corner Cafe that still had a few picked-over cheese sandwiches and a bottle of water available.

He carried two sandwiches to a bench near the library and tried to make some decisions. He'd obviously been set up, if not by Mike then with his sanction. But who was he kidding? TonysWay was Mike, and Mike was why the gun had reappeared in Parker's dish. It had been used at least twice, presumably on the same person Danny had been threatening

234

to kill for the last two weeks. The police couldn't have had the gun when the wanted poster was printed; the crime scene van hadn't been at the Massini's house until later. And he couldn't see any reason for the police to search that house except, he suddenly remembered, there were a lot of green armbands wandering around the yard when he drove by the street. Green seemed to be the color of betrayal today. Mike arranged for the gun to appear in Parker's bowl. Maybe he sent it with Rosa when he sent Danny the message: *Keep an eye out for Parker.*

Did she know the gun was in Parker's bowl? Did she put it there? He didn't want to believe that, but then he didn't want to believe a lot of things that could put him in prison or leave him waiting for a needle. For instance, he didn't want to believe his father let him be him charged with murder. He must have evidence, but what? Who else could have killed Gabriel? Rosa had the gun more than once. Mike had it and that meant pretty much anyone with a green armband could have pulled the trigger.

He dropped his trash and worried his way back to the car. Only Mike and his father could answer his questions and he didn't dare contact either of them. Brenda might be willing to talk to him, but he couldn't risk visiting city hall for the conversation. Billy suggested he call her. If he had her number, he'd be on his father's phone in a second.

He realized, at that moment, that he was an idiot.

He opened the cell phone, entered the pin number his father used for everything not work related, and checked the contact list. Brenda was there, of course. She had numbers for work, for home, and for her mobile phone. He dialed the last.

She obviously recognized the number he called from. She answered suspiciously, "Who is this?"

"You know me."

She lowered her voice. "How did you get his phone?"

"I went home." When she said nothing, he added, "I had to, Brenda. They released Emmie. Nobody told me. I don't even know where they're going to put her. I wanted to say goodbye, so I went home."

"You shouldn't have. It was dangerous."

"I don't understand why." He'd lost control. His voice

came out hoarsely. "Why are they doing this to me, Brenda?"

"Gabriel was turning into some kind of legend among the people who want to destroy everything. They needed to kill him publicly. They want to ruin his reputation and if he was killed by an amateur, a student . . . ."

That made some sort of sense. "But why me, Brenda? Why did Dad let them pin it on me?"

"You did that," she whispered, "walking around with that gun, telling everyone you were going to kill Gabriel. You pinned it on yourself. Your prints are on the gun that killed that woman."

"Who said my prints are on the gun?" Danny demanded. It wasn't possible. He'd wiped the gun before hiding it in Mike's room.

"The FBI. TonysWay. The mayor. Everybody." She hesitated. "They found the gun. They tested it. They found your fingerprints, Danny."

He took a deep, slow breath. "I didn't do it, Brenda. I'd never shoot a woman, even if she was Gabriel."

"She wasn't."

"What?" He was stunned. "She wasn't Gabriel?"

"I typed up your father's meeting notes. Pinker was just a woman. Gabriel hired her over the internet to rent some office space and accept a few equipment deliveries for him. That's all. The FBI found her dead when they tried to pick her up. She'd been shot and the bullets match the ones from your gun."

"It's not my gun, damn it!"

"It had your prints on it."

Danny was silent, trying to digest that. Then he said, "I don't know what to do."

"Turn yourself in. He will see you get a fair trial."

"Right."

After a long pause, Brenda said, "I have to tell him you called."

"I know." He took a deep breath. "Tell him I didn't do it."

Chapter 25

As soon as Brenda disconnected, Danny removed the battery from the cell phone and began driving. His destination was away from the university, away from wanted posters and dead sisters. When his jaw began to hurt he made an effort to relax, to breath slowly, but then his leg began to hurt because he couldn't stop pounding it with the fist he couldn't open, so he pulled off the street to park and calm himself, and when his eyes stopped burning and he could see again, he discovered himself in the parking lot in front of the emergency annex at the high school gym. He wanted to go in, but he felt too shaky, too finely balanced, and too likely to lose control. He moved the car to a far corner of the lot, close, but not too close, to some vans and older SUVs clustered around a port-a-potty. Heads appeared in most of their windows when he drove up, but when he parked a polite distance away and sat, staring at the gym entrance, the heads dropped back out of sight. A couple of kids chased each other between the vehicles and a small brown dog chased the kids.

Danny focused so tightly on the annex that he completely missed the sunset and didn't even notice its loss until he looked around and saw that all the parking lot lights were off except one over the portable toilet and one over the main entrance to the gym. He made a quick trip to the toilet, then resumed his watch over the annex.

His belly woke him when the sun popped above the gym

roof and lit his car. He woke almost instantly, but he had trouble making himself move. The sun slowly crept up the sky, the kids huddled up with their backpacks near the corner, women lined up by the port-a-potty, and men jumbled, scrubbing their faces and cursing, over by the coffee cart. That's right. They had a coffee cart, and a Friend passing out burritos from a stack mounded next to the coffee pot.

Danny ignored the rumbling from his belly and watched the show playing outside his windows. He had no desire to join it. The simple act of opening his door would break the spell protecting him from the passage of time and time would flood over him, a tsunami slamming him into a future he couldn't bear.

But time passed. Even in Mr. Massini's car, time passed. Danny's hunger grew and eventually he surrendered, cracked the door, and let the flood carry him to the only sister he had left. Janis. He wanted to know if she'd heard about the wanted poster, if she'd turn away when she saw him. She didn't. She wasn't even there, and no one could say where she'd been taken, or by whom.

Empty cots spread evenly over the basketball court. Only those nearest the exit were still in use. Their occupants seemed healthy enough. Most of them were grouped around one bed or another, talking or playing cards. One of the nurses, an older woman wearing green, caught him staring at the cots and stopped beside him. "Is something wrong?"

"I'm looking for Janis Oliver."

"The doctor's girl? She checked herself out yesterday."

He gave the woman a sharp glance. "Checked herself out? You mean no one came for her? She's all alone?"

"We're Friends, not cops." Her voice was as sharp as his look had been. "What did you want her for? Tony's business?"

He couldn't answer that. "We had some questions." He spoke vaguely. "I'll have to keep looking."

"You'll probably find her at the memorial tomorrow. She talked about that a lot. Her mom, you know."

"Right. Thanks." But he didn't leave immediately. There was something wrong with the remaining patients. He asked, "Who are they?"

"Holdovers. Is there a problem?"

He shook his head slowly. "They just look different."

"Really? They've been here all along."

"Are they still contagious?"

"No. They're being held over." She pulled him away from the beds and lowered her voice. "They were living on the street when they got sick. If we discharge them, they have to go back on the street."

"And they don't want that?"

"These folks don't. Some of the others couldn't wait to get out of here."

"They wanted to be homeless?"

"I think they just didn't like rules." She gave Danny a long look, expecting judgment. When she found none, she added, "Safety isn't for everyone."

"Sometimes it isn't even an option." Afraid he might sound bitter, he changed the subject. "How long will you keep them?"

The nurse looked surprised. "They will be welcome as long they need a friend." She hesitated and touched his armband before adding, "You should know that, Friend."

"Of course." He didn't know what to say. There was doubt in her gaze, doubt he had to intercept before it became suspicion. He said, "I've been away."

She nodded. "I should have known. You Right Arms can't always follow the Way. I apologize for saying anything."

Right Arms? Danny felt a momentary confusion, but then it hit him. Almost everyone wore the band on their left arm. He'd put his armband on his right arm when Mike gave it to him in the cafe, but he'd just been copying most of the people there. Apparently the band on his right arm meant something. He became aware he'd missed something. "Excuse me?"

The nurse lowered her voice even more. She was nearly whispering. "I just asked if you'd been outside. I understand if you can't say, but. . . ."

"Oh. Yes, outside." He wasn't sure exactly what that meant.

"Minneapolis?" There was urgency in her voice. "Or Las Vegas? I have family—"

That answered his question. Outside meant outside the perimeter. Danny shook his head. "No. I was back east."

"Oh my God! Atlanta? Was it as bad as everyone says?"

He had no idea what everyone said, so he just nodded.

"Is it true that they caught that strain from . . . Belgrade?" Her voice had dropped so much that he barely heard the name, *Belgrade*, but the horror in it was palpable.

He shook his head and looked around for any way to change the subject. He settled on the remaining patients. He asked, "Isn't there more we can do for them?"

"Oh." The change unsettled her. She stepped back and said, vaguely, "They will be resettled into a group home as soon as one is confiscated."

"Confiscated?"

"Some of the abandoned homes weren't burned. We're using them." She looked him up and down. "I just realized, if you were outside, you probably haven't been confirmed yet."

"Confirmed?"

"I thought not. Come with me." She pulled him to a table across the court where two friends were lounging in front of a laptop connected to a small box. She pulled his mask off and one of the friends snapped a digital photo before he could protest. Then she held out her hand. "Let me have your ID."

"My ID?" He froze. ID? Not Danny Murphy's ID. Danny was wanted for murder. He had Tony's license. He took it yesterday to remember his friend by. He said, "All I've got is a travel document. I'd better come back for this, ah, confirmation."

"You don't have time. The name is correct, right?"

"No." He tried not to sound as desperate as he felt. "They spelled it wrong, and the address—"

"Everybody's address is wrong." She gave him a sharp, no-nonsense look. "Just give me what you've got. You can give Robert the correct spelling while he's entering you in the database."

"But my picture—"

"I can see that you had a bad time in Atlanta. The scars should fade with time and those abrasions on your cheek will go away. You can redo your picture after you finish healing if it bothers you, but there really isn't any point. Nobody's going to see it."

"Then why...?

"Biometrics. It's for the facial recognition software. Your actual picture isn't stored anywhere, friend. Just a bunch of numbers for the computers. The same goes for your thumb print."

He had no real choice. He handed the woman Tony's license reluctantly, but he began to see some advantages to a new ID card. He walked around the table and leaned over Robert's shoulder while he typed. It took less than a minute to enter Anthony Messing in the database with an address near the university. When Robert leaned back and told him to grab a cup of coffee and a sandwich from the table in the lobby, Danny didn't hesitate. He was hungry.

The nurse showed up while he was finishing his third sandwich. He was too busy getting it down to pay much attention when she swabbed his inner arm, just above his wrist, but he definitely noticed when she stuck a needle under his skin and pressed the plunger. "Hey!"

"Don't be a baby. It only stings for a minute or two."

"What is it? Another vaccination?"

She snorted. "It's your chip. When you need to identify yourself, just wave your arm over the reader. You pay for food and a bed the same way."

"You mean everything is free?"

"Some things are. Things like food and medical care or a place to sleep, but that's just basic. Everything special is charged against your account."

"I have an account?" He felt a little dizzy.

"Everyone has an account, Anthony. That's where you keep your bennies."

When he looked blank, she said, "Look, the basic allotment for a Friend is five bennies a month. My apartment costs me one bennie. A nice meal is a point, maybe two if I have a couple of drinks. There are a hundred points in a bennie. Five a month is more than enough for me."

"What about money? Real dollars?"

"They're still the coin of the realm, backed by the full might and majesty of the government, but try finding somebody willing to touch one." She gave a short laugh, then turned serious. "Mostly dollars are used between businesses and for transfers between banks. I guess they are useful." She sighed and added, "Look, there are classes on this stuff. Check a bulletin board. Meanwhile, I have to organize lunch. Will you want a bed for the night?"

Danny shook his head and ignored her offer of a free sandwich on his way out. His stomach was bothering him again, and the sense of unreality had returned. He hated what he had to do next.

It took him three stops to find a board with an address for the crematorium. By the time he was a quarter-mile away, he thought he could have found it just by heading toward the bank of white smoke. He parked three blocks from the address and walked into the haze. It grew thicker for the first two blocks. He had the sidewalk to himself. The buildings on the far side of the road floated by as he walked, faint and ghostly in the haze. Those on his side seemed a bit more solid, at least until he passed them. Most were separated from the street by narrow parking lots: businesses and small commercial storefronts emptied by the plague. He ignored the smoke as much as possible, but he was glad of the surgical mask he still wore. The air smelled. His eyes burned.

Then the breeze shifted. The haze thinned abruptly and drifted off behind the buildings. The odor cleared and Danny found himself in front of a long red brick building surrounded by a wider parking lot. The sign above the door read *Smith and Thorne, Funeral Home*. The double doors in front were closed and there were no lights in the building, but the smoke seemed to hover over the back, so he walked on around. That's where he found the refrigerated trailers, parked beside a low white-brick building with a pitched slate roof and two very busy smoke stacks.

The compressors were roaring on all three trailers. Two men with heavy masks hanging under their chins smoked on the ramp behind one of the trucks. They didn't seem to have anything to say to each other. Neither did the thirty or so people scattered along the back wall of the funeral home. They just stood, mostly couples, and stared intently across the drive at the entrance to the white brick building. The couples stood close together, shoulders touching. Occasionally a woman would rest her head against her partner or a pair of hands would seek each other for a moment before separating, as locked in their shared solitude as the individuals were in their private grief.

"I thought you'd get here sooner."

Danny took a quick look at the figure beside him. "How'd you recognize me?"

"That's Tony's hat."

"I didn't think he'd mind."

"No." Mike waited a minute before asking, "You here for Emma?"

Danny nodded. "Tony too. Am I late?"

"They're working from the back of the trucks forward. They'll get to your sister before my family, but they have over two hundred to go."

"What?"

"They have two furnaces going, but it's taking about three hours, counting the cool-down, and . . . ah, shit, Danny. This sucks. They can only do about eight a day in each one. That's sixteen counting both furnaces. There was another crematorium, but they ran out of propane. This one uses natural gas, so fuel isn't a problem, but— Figure almost twenty days. Seventeen more. It would be easier if we could bury them, but the health department . . . they want everything gone. Burned up. Burned—" Mike abruptly walked away and leaned against the back wall of the funeral home.

Danny waited until he came back. They stood together until the door of the white building opened. A man stepped out and waved, then held up a finger. The two smokers stood hurriedly, pulled masks over their faces, and opened the back of a trailer. The shelves inside were stacked with long dark body bags. They shifted one to a rolling gurney and pushed it into the building. Then they pushed the empty gurney back. By the time they had the trailer door closed, the man who'd called for the body was back. He scrawled a name on a clipboard hanging beside the door and then looked over at the men and women waiting. He shrugged and called out, softly, "Angela Johnson, sixteen."

A shudder passed through the thin crowd, but Danny heard no particular cry of grief. He felt inexpressibly sad and at the same time relief that the name had not been Emma's. Or Tony's. He said, "I have to ask, Mike."

243

"Why?" Mike frowned. "The facts of life? Your dad hasn't given you the talk yet?"

"His version. I want your your take on crime and punishment." He forced a smile. "And guilt and innocence."

Mike nodded. He knew the question was coming. "After all the people who've died, the scales have to be balanced. When we convict you of killing Gabriel, there won't be any question that he's dead."

After a moment, Danny sighed. "Why me?"

"You volunteered for the role." Mike said. "It won't be that bad. Just don't let the Feds get you. Surrender to TonysWay. You're the man who killed Gabriel. You're a hero to every Friend in the country, maybe the world. We'll slap your wrist. Hell, we might even give you a medal in a couple years."

"Right." Danny tried to sound like he believed that. He asked, "You keep saying 'he' like Gabriel is a man, and you keep using the wrong sex. I need to know, who was Julia Pinker? Was she Gabriel?"

"As far as the world knows, Julia was Gabriel. When we catch the real Gabriel, he or she will just disappear into the ground. This is not about justice, Danny. It's about keeping the machine running. It's not what I wanted for my family or what you wanted for yours, but it gives people enough hope and confidence to stay on their feet, do their work, and live their lives, or what will pass for their lives from now on."

"You're saying she was innocent?"

"She accepted the wrong job. That's all."

"Who killed her?"

"Does it matter?"

"Yes!"

Mike said nothing. He just watched the white door.

Eventually Danny asked, "So what now? Are you going to call the cops on me? Or your Right Arms?"

"The feds and the police both want you badly, but they'd each prefer that the other actually catches you. There isn't any glory to be had by arresting the man who killed Gabriel. Personally, I hope you choose to come to us. We can take care of you."

"Better than the government?"

"In three months, we will be the government, Danny. This

was one city. Plague has already hit Minneapolis, Denver, Vegas, LA, Miami, and Boston. There have been close calls in Baltimore and Brooklyn, and those are just North America. Wherever the plague hits, we have new Friends. Belfast. London. Shanghai." Mike smiled. "You don't understand what has happened. Nobody does, really. Not even that professor of yours."

"Doctor Foreman?" The name took Danny by surprise. "What does he say?"

"He thinks science can cure what science created." Mike grimaced. "He doesn't understand that science just handed us more power than we have the wisdom to use."

"I'd like to see him."

"Turn yourself in. It might happen." He stepped away. "I'm taking off now, Danny. I'll be back when my family comes out of the truck."

"Wait."

"Yeah?"

"What is the memorial tomorrow about if the ashes aren't ready?"

"People need to grieve, and they need to move on." He hesitated. "Is that all?"

"One more question. What happened in Belgrade?"

"Where did you hear about Belgrade?"

"Just answer me."

Mike stared at him silently for a long time before answering. "Gabriel created this plague by editing some common bacteria to produce botulism toxin. That killed over three hundred people, put a thousand in intensive care, and that was one city." He swallowed a couple of times before continuing. "In Belgrade . . . imagine that one of the bacteria everyone has in their mouth or on their skin got modified. Imagine that whoever did it didn't add botulism toxin. Imagine they added genes from a really nasty flesh-eating bacteria. Imagine that just kissing or touching your girlfriend could turn her into a thing that would make a zombie puke. Imagine that."

Danny shivered. "How did they stop it?"

"The Friends did everything they could but the Russians ran out of patience when it started to spread. They cremated the city." He hesitated before adding, "I'm not sure they were wrong."

After a long time, Danny said, "I heard it spread to Atlanta."

Mike said softly, "We don't talk about Atlanta." After a pause for emphasis, he added, "You've had a short grace period, Danny, but I can't wait much longer. You need to come in after the memorial. If you don't, the police will get serious. All the police."

"You really have that much power?"

"When people get scared, they line up behind anyone who can help them." Mike shrugged. "They're scared now. After they learn about Belgrade and Atlanta, they will be beyond scared, and I can help them." He added, "I can help you, too, but you have to trust me. You have to get in line."

Chapter 26

Danny arrived at Veterans Memorial Park two hours before the scheduled service and discovered he was actually a week early. Bleachers fifty feet back from the platform stage looked ready for at least a thousand people. The grass on either side of the bleachers could accommodate another two thousand. Only five hundred or so were present when he arrived, not counting the small army of green armbands busily setting up tables and tents in a semicircle behind the bleachers. Some tents had been set aside for grief counseling, comfort, or just a shady break from the late July heat. Others held food coolers, coffee pots, or stacks of cold water bottles. A range of police and government vehicles were parked at a discreet distance behind the line of Friends. The sight of the patrol cars almost turned Danny away when he approached the gathering. Only the need to say goodbye kept him going, but he relaxed a bit when he noticed that a third of the uniformed officers also wore green on their right arms.

The mood of the mourners and the friends working the tables was subdued, almost listless. The heat, the lack of a breeze, and the fact that people had walked a long way to reach the ceremony contributed to the atmosphere.

Two nine- by twelve-foot screens flanked the stage. A wall of white canvas blocked the view behind it and shaded the screens. Danny wandered far enough to one side to see what the wall concealed and realized that the day's agenda had changed: the steel heart of a memorial, a three dimensional maze of interconnected beams and rods, looked incomplete. It rose from the hollow center of an unfinished concrete circle almost three feet high and sixty feet in diameter. Three wide steps surrounded the outer circle. A central depression left ten feet of the concrete ring for a walk or promenade, half polished to a smooth finish. A waist-high polishing machine sat on the boundary between the rough and smooth surfaces. He stared at the project for a long time. It looked nothing like a funeral monument. No statues, crosses, angels, headstones, or markers. Nothing Danny saw spoke to him of Emmie or Tony or the Massini's.

Nothing.

The speakers caught his attention. A Friend on the platform stage tapped a microphone while two others made final adjustments to a line of chairs behind him. His father and Mike Massini stood at the foot of the steps leading up to the stage, surrounded by men and women in uniform or wearing green on their right arms. Mike was busy speaking to his lieutenants. The Chief hung back a few paces, waiting. His head swung back and forth as he scanned the crowd.

Danny watched them for a few seconds. The sixty or so feet separating them felt like an unbridgeable gulf. He didn't want to be seen and at the same time he wanted to rush over, tackle them, shout, "Hey! I'm still alive!" And he wasn't even sure that was true. He wasn't alive in the same sense he'd been a month ago.

He eased deeper into the crowd, toward the rear where he could duck out easily. He wished he had somewhere to duck out to. He was pretty much surrounded by Friends in the tents behind him and by police and guards near the stage, but the crowd grew quickly and he soon felt invisible. He grew confident enough to visit one of the tables for water and a sandwich.

The Friend working the sound system ran another test of the mic and speakers. The projection screens flashed a series of random colors, then settled into an image of the woman working the mic. She tapped it a few more times before clearing her throat and calling for attention. When the crowd settled down, she introduced the Mayor.

Eddie Baca climbed onto the stage to unenthusiastic applause. He paused awkwardly before confirming that the memorial ceremony had been postponed. He found a gentler way to explain it, but the gist was simple: it takes time to burn three hundred bodies, and the health department insisted that nothing else would do. Gabriel's engineered bacteria had to be destroyed completely. Beyond that, the memorial to recognize the dead would be beautiful, worthy of their memory, but it would not be complete for another week. So: everyone was invited back a week from today, and in the meantime a representative of TonysWay had a few announcements to make on yesterday's incident.

Yesterday's incident? Danny had no idea what the mayor was talking about, but the crowd around him tensed and leaned forward. Mike walked onto the stage. After apologizing for hijacking the ceremony, he hesitated and then added, "You may have heard a rumor that Gabriel has been captured. That is almost true. Three days ago, your friends in TonysWay identified a woman named Julia Pinker as a probable suspect for the botulism poisonings. She has since been confirmed as the poisoner by our city police with the assistance of both the FBI and Homeland Security."

A sigh went through the crowd and a male voice high in the bleachers demanded, "You caught her yet?"

"Unfortunately, Pinker was killed before she could be taken into custody. Her identity was learned by Daniel Murphy, the son of our chief of police. Daniel was Tony's best friend, and his sister was a victim of the poisonings. He may have been overcome by grief, but for whatever reason, he appears to have taken justice into his own hands."

A voice shouted, "Good for him!"

Another began chanting, "Danny! Danny! Danny!"

Applause began to build. Danny tried to shrink into the crowd. He glanced around. Most of the shouting seemed to come from green arm bands, but the rest of the crowd slowly joined in and the chant built steam. He began to look for a way out. Then he saw a young blond girl half way up the bleachers: Janis, staring at him, looking uncertain.

Danny nodded at her and gave a tiny wave. She ignored him and focused on the crowd behind him. He looked around and discovered line of uniformed policemen moving slowly through the crowd. He backed deeper into the mob and searched the bleachers, trying to discover who was directing the police. He spotted his mother, several rows above Janis. She was focused on Mike, or maybe on one of the Friends sharing the stage with him. She hadn't seen Danny. She might not be looking for him. Janis, meanwhile, had begun making her way off the bleachers. The roar of the crowd was deafening.

"Danny! Danny! Danny!"

On stage, Mike tried to quiet the mob. "We all have mixed feelings. It's good that Gabriel is dead, but our problems aren't over." The chant began to subside. Mike helped it along by announcing, "Our investigation of Gabriel's lab suggests that she only intended to poison one strain of the E. coli bacteria. Our scientists think that she was herself infected with the Staph bacteria and that she somehow contaminated her samples. What this means is that it is easier than we thought to spread toxins, and that is a disaster. One madman could poison us all by accident, and at least two have already released new plagues. On purpose!"

He waited for the crowd to quiet down before continuing. "We have to protect ourselves from anyone who would use the CRISPR technology. This has to be decided on a national level, maybe even international, and we will have to lock down the biologists more than the physicists."

The green arms began clapping. The rest of the crowd joined them within seconds. Mike held up his hand for silence and eventually got it. Danny used the time to push toward the far side of the mob. He'd lost sight of Janis, but his mother had spotted him. She waved toward the stage and then pointed at him. He cursed and changed direction. Right, left, and straight ahead were all blocked. He edged back toward the bleachers and his mother. His father began speaking into his lapel mic.

When Mike regained the audience's attention, he continued, "Unfortunately, keeping an eye on the scientists won't guarantee our safety. There are those among us who want to harm us. Some are terrorists like Julia Pinker. Some are ordinary criminals. But in order to survive as a human society, we will have to be friends to each other and enemies to our enemies, all of our enemies." He took a deep breath and searched the crowd. His eyes never found a target, but Danny felt like their target and ducked deeper into the mob.

Mike said, "That brings me to the final matter demanding our attention today. You all know that at least three criminal gangs have been operating in the city throughout the emergency. These people not only break our laws, they threaten our continued existence as a civilized society." He paused for effect, then added, "Yesterday afternoon, two of the gangs started a war. They conducted two drive-by shootings. Several gang members were killed, along with one innocent man, a scientist who fought on the side of the Friends against Gabriel and other rogue scientists. We will miss Doctor Foreman's wisdom and knowledge greatly. The gang's criminal behavior puts every one of us at risk, and so a task force of Friends associated with the police and the federal agencies went to arrest all known members of the three gangs operating in our home town."

That generated a burst of enthusiastic applause from the Friends and most of the citizens.

Mike continued, "The news of their pending arrest leaked to the gangs and they resisted. Our friends did their duty for our city. They completed their mission to protect our homes and our families." He looked over the crowd somberly and added, "None of the gang members survived. None. Mayor Baca has signed an order disbanding all gangs, groups, or organizations engaged in any form of criminal activity. He directed the police to treat any assembly of two or more people for the purpose of conspiring to engage in criminal activity as gang activity and to respond firmly."

The brief silence that hung over the crowd when Mike quit speaking was broken by a slow flood of applause encouraged by the Friends. While that rose and fell, Danny climbed into the bleachers. He felt light-headed, unbalanced by the shock of learning his teacher was dead. He looked wildly around the crowd, searching for some sort of anchor, and settled on his mother. He climbed toward her.

She watched him approach with a smile and wrapped him in a warm hug the moment he came within reach. He didn't push her away, but he felt stiff. She lay her cheek against his and whispered, "I'm glad you came, dear. We weren't sure you would."

"I thought they were going to bury Emmie. I had to come." He pulled back from her, wondering, *We?* He asked, "Have you talked to Dad?"

"He's been busy, Danny." Her eyes searched his face, lingered on his scars. "What happened to you?"

"I don't know." He shook his head. "Dad. Mike. Tony's fucking Way."

"Don't talk about your friends that way. Look." She pointed to the foot of the bleachers. The steps were thick with green arm bands. "They're protecting you, Danny. All you have to do is go to them. They will see that no harm comes to you."

"They killed Doctor Foreman." He put his hands on her shoulder and shook her. Not hard, but tight. "What happened? How did they get to you?"

She shook her head. The accusation hadn't even registered on her. "Friends don't hurt anyone. We wouldn't."

"What about Dad?" He wasn't sure if he was asking about her feelings or his father's guilt.

His mother smiled gently. "The Friends give me what I need, Danny. They give me meaning. A purpose. You left and then Emma was . . . gone, and Ben barely came home after Emma. Then he stopped showing up. I needed a connection to life."

Danny took a deep breath. "I need something too, Mom."

"I know, Danny. Just trust our Friends. They will give you what you need."

"Will you do something for me? One last thing?"

"What?"

"Just close your eyes and don't say anything for two minutes. Will you do that?"

She hesitated. Her gaze jumped between his eyes. She gave a tiny nod and closed her eyes. She started counting slowly.

He dropped to the wooden walk by her feet and rolled under the bench, then climbed down the metal scaffolding under the bleachers. He reached the ground in seconds, reversed his cap, and strolled casually toward the circle of tables.

Before he'd gone twenty feet, someone took his arm. He jumped and jerked his head sharply. He expected to see a uniform or a badge or at best an armband, but it was Janis. She looked worried and pulled him to the right. He had no better direction in mind.

She skirted the crowd gathered around a refreshment stand and slipped between two tables. A few of the friends glanced at them curiously, but Janis' age and his arm band satisfied them. The grass between the tables and the police cruisers parked on the street was sparsely populated. Danny eyed the cops stationed there warily and hesitated.

Janis wrapped her left arm around his waist and pointed to a row of port-a-potties set up near the intersection. He nodded, took a deep breath, and tried to look desperate. It wasn't difficult. They blended in with scores of others on the same mission. By the time they reached the lines twisting from the toilets toward the back of the bleachers, Danny felt a little more confident. He led Janis between two lines and ducked around the white plastic toilets to the street. No one was paying attention to them so he started across the street.

Janis balked. "Where are we going?"

"I have a car."

She made a face. "But where are we *going*?"

"Oh." He had no idea. He stopped and stared at her until he realized that standing in the middle of the street would eventually attract attention, so he pulled her to a storefront away from the park and confessed. "I don't know. I just need to get away. Everyone is after me. Even the police."

She nodded. "Because you killed Gabriel."

That stunned Danny. He turned his back on her. After a moment, he started walking away from Janis, the park, and the question. He managed half a block before he realized she was following him. He stopped and waited for her to catch up, then demanded, "Who told you that?"

"Everybody knows." She spoke cautiously. "We're all proud of you."

"Proud?" He still wouldn't look at her. He knew he sounded bitter. "When did you hear about it?"

"After you came to see me. One of the patients saw a

poster on the bulletin board."

That sounded right. Danny said, "I didn't kill anyone, Janis. I don't even know that Gabriel is dead."

She looked shocked.

"I know Emma is dead. Tony is dead." He sounded shakey even to himself.

"My mom is dead." Janis grabbed his hand and pulled him down the street. "Come on, Danny."

"Where are we going?"

"My house."

"Right." Given a destination, Danny walked with more enthusiasm, at least until it occurred to him that he may not have escaped a trap at the memorial. He may have simply been herded into a different cage.

Chapter 27

When Pam Oliver accepted the ER position at Mercy, she rented a small townhouse halfway between the middle school and her work. It was a brisk half-hour walk from Memorial park through nearly empty streets. Automobile traffic was rare. A few food trucks and passenger buses competed with bicycles for the streets. There was only foot traffic and not much of that. Protective masks had begun going out of style when the reports of new infections slowed. Around half the peestrians still wore one, so Danny's mask didn't draw attention, but he felt self-conscious and imagined that everyone he met eyed him suspiciously.

He set a fast pace, like a man on an important mission, until he reached the end of a block and suddenly realized he had no idea whether to turn right, left, or push straight ahead. He looked around for Janis and found her a hundred yards back, walking very slowly. She looked despondent at that distance. He went back for her and, when he got close, saw that she was crying. He put an arm around her and asked, "What's wrong?"

"I'm suh-sorry, Danny." She wrapped her arms around his waist and hid her face against his breast. "I'm sorry!"

"For what?" He patted her back awkwardly. "What did you do?"

"I was just trying to be a good sister when I waved. I thought you'd want to see your mom." She hugged him tightly.

"I know you'd rather be with Emmie."

"No, Jannie. No."

"What?" She glanced up at his face. She looked as confused as he felt.

He took her hand and started walking slowly. After a block he said, "Emmie is gone. Gabriel killed my best friend. My mother has turned all weird about TonysWay. My father wants to arrest me for a murder I didn't commit. Doctor Foreman is dead. I only have you."

Janis had stopped crying and watched him with red and swollen eyes.

He hesitated, then said, "I'll be the best brother I can, Jannie. I won't walk away from you again. I didn't mean to do that today."

"You scared me, Danny. You just kept going farther and farther away. I don't understand why you did that."

He squeezed her hand and asked, "You've seen the posters?"

"The murder posters?"

He nodded.

"The picture doesn't look much like you."

"I feel like everyone is staring, like they know who I am. It's like the cops are waiting around every corner."

She stopped walking and faced him. "Would your dad really arrest you?"

"Yes." They had reached a small brick town home with an attached garage. Danny focused on the sidewalk and shrugged. "He wouldn't have any choice. The FBI has me on their list too. Homeland Security, for sure. Even Mike."

"TonysWay?" She sounded surprised.

"Yeah."

She thought a moment. "I guess that explains it." She led him to the doorway, fumbled a key from her bag, and unlocked the house. She didn't open the door. She didn't even turn the knob.

Danny asked, "Explains what?"

"You know Rosa is Mike's girlfriend?"

"I figured that out."

"You know she got her mom and dad to join TonysWay? Well, she's the one who got your mom to join too. She got both moms to volunteer at the hospital and then she was around a lot. She brought other Greenies around and they signed almost everyone up." She trailed off. "I don't know how she convinced them."

"She didn't." Danny spoke harshly. "Gabriel convinced them. Everyone started dying and money was poisoned and there wasn't enough food and you couldn't even trust bottled water. The politicians and the police couldn't do a thing, and then Mike came along and said we just have to trust our friends, and we all have to be friends to each other, and that started working. That was the only thing that beat Gabriel. Trust. That's what Dr. Foreman said, anyway. Gabriel destroyed our trust in each other. Mike gave it back."

"So he's our friend?"

"I don't think so." Danny shook his head and looked from Janis to the closed door. He asked, "This is your place, right? Are we going in? I understand if you don't want me—"

"No!" She grabbed his arm to hold him there. "I . . . last night was my first time back since. . . ." She bit her lip and finally turned the knob, pushed the door open, and waited.

Danny entered first. The house was warm, almost hot, and silent. No air moved. It smelled empty, dusty. She followed him in and closed the door softly. He gave her a puzzled look. She pointed at a knotted blanket on the couch. "I slept there. I couldn't go any farther."

"But you live here, Jannie. Your clothes, all your things—"

"I felt dead. They said I could stay at the gym and work with the volunteers, the Greensleeves, but I couldn't. I didn't belong. I had Mom's keys so I came here, but I can't get any farther than the couch."

Danny stared around the empty room. He imagined the little blond girl huddled on the couch, alone all night. He felt cold. "I don't understand."

"I looked in my room but I didn't recognize it. Everything there belonged to another girl. And I wanted to look in Mom's room, but I couldn't open the door." She lowered her eyes. "I was afraid."

"Of what you'd see?"

She shook her head. "Of what I wouldn't see. I slept on the couch so I could open the door for you when you came. But

257

you didn't come."

"I'm sorry."

"It's okay. Everything is confused. You too. I figured that out."

"I'm here now." Danny put an arm around her shoulders and then her arms were around his waist and she was sobbing. He let her cry until she ran out of tears, then sat with her for the rest of the day. She talked a little about the soccer camp and how excited she and Emma were before they left, even though they would miss their moms. She said that every girl who went to camp was sure to make the junior varsity team at least, and there might even be boys' teams at the camp. She said getting on the bus was hard. She and Emmie had tummy aches, but they thought it was excitement and worry. Emma was really worried about her dad and Janis was scared because her mom was trapped in the hospital with all those sick people, but they never thought anything bad could happen. Not to them. Not really. They were just excited, at least until they got to camp and started getting really sick. Then all those abstract concerns evaporated, replaced by more desperate questions: where is the nearest toilet? Why won't my arm move? How can I breath? Who is touching me? Is this dying?

She talked well after dark. Danny listened. He sat beside her and held her when she trembled or sobbed. He asked questions when she grew silent, when he feared she had fallen into a black memory she couldn't escape without help, but mostly he just sat beside her and listened, and each time she said "I," he heard "Emmie," and his heart broke a little more. When she finally ran out of words, or had at least released enough internal pressure to slow the flood of anguish, he gave Janis a final hug and searched the kitchen for canned goods.

When he returned with a small bowl of tomato soup and a plate of cheese and crackers, he had to wake her and coax half the food down her. Then he carried her into the bedroom with a new double bed littered with stuffed tigers and unicorns and got her shoes off before folding the comforter over her. She grabbed his hand when he smoothed the cover over her shoulders. She refused to release it until he promised to leave her door open, sleep on the couch, and come immediately if she called.

He found a news channel of sorts on the TV and turned the volume so low that he had to sit on the floor a foot from the screen. He finished the soup and crackers while a middle-aged housewife wearing a green armband read announcements from TonysWay. Most of them listed distribution center locations and schedules, but a few came close to news. For instance, the memorial service for Gabriel's victims was delayed again by the continuing shortage of propane. A disagreement over disposition of the cremains of Julia Pinker, AKA Gabriel, had been resolved by Michael Massini. Her ashes had been emptied into the city sewer. The time and place of disposal had not been recorded. Mister Massini had rejected a popular petition that would have given him the title of Chairman, President, or Leader of TonysWay. His only title would be First Friend, and he would serve without salary or other compensation. In other news, the latest estimate for lifting the quarantine was two weeks. The requirement that all citizens must wear protective masks in public was rescinded. Mayor Baca announced that friends of TonysWay would receive favorable consideration for all future hires by the city.

In regional news, the CDC confirmed that the outbreak of cholera in New Orleans is not, repeat not, associated with the Gabriel technology in any way. The rumored quarantine of Rio De Janeiro is confirmed, but no further information is available at the moment. The blackout of communications from Moscow continues. China remains dark. And finally, the search for Daniel Murphy, wanted for the murder of Julia Pinker, AKA Gabriel, now extends beyond the local quarantine zone. A recent photograph appeared on-screen, along with a telephone number to call with information. The reward for his capture is now one thousand Bennies.

When she began to repeat herself, Danny turned off the TV and tried to get comfortable on the couch. It wasn't easy. His mind kept spinning. That recent photograph came from his high school yearbook; it looked nothing like him. Someone was making it easy for him to hide. The more he thought about it the less sense it made. His father might not want him caught, but his allegiance was to the law, and in any case, the

FBI and Homeland Security had no reason to be merciful. Bringing the man who killed Gabriel to justice would boost their prestige no matter how a trial turned out.

TonysWay was another matter. In theory, the Friends had no say over who was charged with the crime. In practice . . . well, Mike had green armbands everywhere. Rosa wore one, her father wore one, and his mother wore one. The friends were so ubiquitous that they had nicknames. Greenies. Greensleeves. Right Arms.

Everyone trusted them. When Mike announced the massacre of gang members, no one raised a voice. The power was real and Mike held it. Was it enough to control who was charged with murder? Maybe. Mike as much as promised he could get Danny off. If he could do that, he could have kept him from being charged in the first place. Why hadn't he? Because Danny was running around town telling everyone he was going to kill the man who killed his sister? That would have been empty boasting without the gun, and the gun came from Mike. And Rosa.

Danny woke the next morning with no memory of falling asleep. He had no memory of waking up either. He was only aware of a rich, powerful scent that grew into an obsession: coffee. And when he opened his eyes, he found Janis sitting on the couch, her hip by his waist, with a cup in her hands and her eyes glued to his face. He smiled. "Is that for me?"

"Maybe."

"Maybe?" It wasn't the answer he expected. "What do you want for it?"

"You have to promise me, Danny. Wherever you go, you'll take me. You won't leave me alone."

"I'm not going anywhere." He grinned and reached for the cup.

She pulled it away. "Don't lie, Danny!"

"What do you mean?" He tried to sit up.

She put a hand on his forehead and pushed him back against the cushions. "I said, don't lie! And don't think I'm stupid either!"

It wasn't the hand on his head holding him down as much as the cup of coffee in her other hand, the one hovering over his face. He relaxed and looked at her seriously. "I don't know

260

what's going to happen, Jannie. I need to protect you, and I don't know what that is going to take. It seems like everybody is after me, and if you're with me, then they'll be after you, too."

She stared at him intently. "Will you talk to me? Take me seriously?"

"Over coffee?"

"Okay." She sealed the contract by handing over the cup and making room for him to sit beside her. Then she said, "I know you have to get out of the city. Your mom thinks Mike will help you escape if you let him, but your professor said he can't. He said you have to be captured and tried so Mike can start rebuilding the world."

"Doctor Foreman?" He hadn't expected that. "How did you meet him?"

"He came to see your mom. He talked to her first and then she introduced me and left us to talk. He wanted you to know not to trust Mike too much."

"Was that all he said?"

"Just what I told you about the trial. We didn't have long to talk before the Greenies came."

"What?"

"They took him away. Then they asked me what he wanted, what he talked about. They asked if he gave me anything."

"Gave you anything?" Danny was beginning to feel very stupid. He was also beginning to feel a little sick.

Janis nodded. "He didn't. I told them everything he said, except about wanting you to know about Mike, and I told them he didn't give me anything, but they searched me any way. They made me get up and stripped the bed. Then they called your mom. They made her search me again."

"Again?"

Janis nodded. She stared into his face. "She searched inside me." Her face showed nothing.

"Oh." He felt sicker. Ice cold. He asked, "They came right after—"

"After she introduced him and left us alone." She bit her lip. "I'm sorry."

"So am I. Very sorry, Janis." He hesitated, then said,

reluctantly, "When Mike was talking at the memorial yesterday, he said Doctor Foreman was killed—"

"I heard that. It must have happened right after the Greenies took him."

"If it happened that way." He had another thought. Maybe even more disturbing. "If it happened at all."

Janis swallowed and shook her head sharply. "That's sick!"

"Yes, but it means you'd be in danger with me, Jannie."

She slapped his face, rocking him, and leaned into him, forehead to forehead, nose to nose. "You promised," she hissed. "Would you leave Emmie alone?"

"You wouldn't be alone," he protested.

"Who would you leave me with, Danny?" she whispered. "Your mother?"

"No." He barely heard his own answer, so he repeated it, louder. "No."

"Maybe if Emmie didn't die things would be different. Your mom would still be at home and she'd take care of both of us. All of us."

"Not me." He forced a smile and pushed her back a little. "Tell me about the Greenies. Were they regular friends, or—"

"They were Right Arms," Janis said firmly. "They weren't nice."

"Did they say what they were looking for?"

"No, they just looked." After a moment, she added, "It must have been pretty small if they thought I could hide it, you know, down there." She blushed. "I think they searched your mom too. When they didn't find it on me, they took her away and when she came back she looked kind of mad. And maybe a little sad, too."

"Right." Danny rubbed his temples. "But whatever they did, it didn't change her mind about anything. She still pointed me out to the Right Arms."

"You don't know that," Janis said sharply. "Maybe she did it for your dad."

"Would that be any better?"

"At least he didn't give you the gun, Danny, and I don't think a policeman would have searched me like those Greenies."

"Don't kid yourself. If they knew about it, they'd want it

just as bad."

She leaned away. "You know what they were looking for?"

"How could I?" Danny shook his head. "Come on, Janis, let's get moving."

She glared at him a moment, then shrugged. "You wouldn't lie to Emmie."

"Sure I would." He forced a grin. "I'll use the hall bath. You take your mom's room. It will be faster."

"No!" She spun away from him. "I'll take the hall."

Danny stared at her. Her back was stiff and her shoulders trembled. He put his hands on her upper arms. "What's wrong Jannie?"

She was shaking. "The hall bath is mine."

He remembered that she made him enter the house first yesterday, that she'd slept on the couch before he arrived, that she didn't even enter the kitchen until she made coffee for him. He rubbed her arms gently. "Is it your mom?"

Janis covered her face.

Danny wrapped his arms around her. He didn't know what to say. Everything he thought of sounded stupid. She suddenly turned, threw her arms around his waist, and wiped her face on his chest. He patted her back awkwardly and whispered, "It'll get better. It's got to get better."

She shook her head and sniffled. He repeated himself. "It's got to get better." His cheeks were wet too, but he had nothing to wipe them on so he just held her until they dried and then he pulled her slowly toward the open door to her mother's bedroom. She followed, but with her eyes closed, her face hidden and her arms tight around him.

Every room has a unique presence, subtle patterns in the way sound, even labored breath, echoes from the walls, ceiling, furniture. Maybe Janis sensed that, though Danny doubted she heard much over the beating of their hearts. Or maybe it was a change it the light that jerked her eyes open. She froze and then she cried, "No! Danny, no!"

"It's okay, Jannie." He tightened his hold and pulled her on into the room, over to the bed, and sat her on it. Then he knelt in front of her and shook her, not hard, but enough to bring her eyes to his face. "It's okay. It happened to me too. It's okay."

263

"No." She twisted away from him and tried to stand.

He held her back and lowered his voice. "It happened when I went home. I went in Emmie's room. I wanted to get a picture so I could remember her alive, not like the last time, and I couldn't do it. I couldn't open her door, but then I did and it was okay. It will be okay for you, too. Just think about how much you loved her and how much she loved you." He swallowed, then whispered, "It worked for me, anyway."

She hiccuped, searched his face a moment, nodded, and stood up. She took a deep breath. Danny gave her room. She moved slowly around the bedroom, looking at pictures, a small ceramic plate on the dresser holding a few earrings, a scarf tossed on the chair under the window. When she stepped into the bathroom, he went to sit at the kitchen table. He stayed there for three cups of coffee, then went looking. He found her on Pam's bed, weeping softly, wearing a set of her scrubs and holding a hair brush against her cheek. He watched for a minute, then left her alone. When he returned, hours later, she was asleep. He sat beside her in the fading light.

Chapter 28

That evening, Janis woke for long enough to eat a plate of canned spaghetti and pretend to listen when the local newswoman read the notices from the daily bulletin board. Only two mattered: FEMA was sending a new high-volume portable crematorium to the city and plans to relax the quarantine were canceled. The Memorial service would be held a week from Wednesday unless something delayed the truck and no reason was given for the new quarantine restrictions.

She reported no progress in the hunt for Gabriel's killer, but the reward for information leading to his capture had been doubled. His picture appeared on screen again. This time it lingered a full thirty seconds. Danny stared, incredulous. He looked even younger in this photo.

He turned to Janis to ask her opinion, but she'd fallen asleep on the couch. He carried her to bed and sat with her for an hour. He wasn't really worried about her. She had every reason to be emotionally exhausted, and she hadn't recovered completely from the poisoning. He didn't know what else to do for her, so he rested a hand on her shoulder and waited until she began to breath deeply.

When he returned to the TV, he found two channels with reruns of sitcoms and the new government channel which alternated documentaries on personal hygiene and bioterrorism. They had him nodding in minutes. He tried to sleep in the master bedroom, but the scent lingering on Pam's perfumed sheets drove him back the couch.

Janis slept late and seemed listless when she finally appeared. Danny made a short stack of toaster waffles for her. She only ate one before drifting back to her bedroom. He waited an hour before checking and found her lying on the bed, fully clothed, listening to her heart with her mother's stethoscope.

He sat beside her and asked, "Are you okay, Jannie?"

"Of course." She gave him a quick look. "Why shouldn't I be?"

That didn't really need an answer. Danny rubbed her shoulder and waited. Eventually she said, "I have to be."

"Same here." He thought a moment. "Where do you want to live?"

"What do you mean?" She looked alarmed. "I finally went into her room. I haven't even said goodbye, Danny. I need to say goodbye."

"You have time. We both do. It's nine days until the Memorial. I don't even know how we'll get out of the city yet. I have things to do before we leave." He hesitated, then added, "If you want to stay—"

"No!"

"I didn't think so."

She tossed the stethoscope aside. "What do you have to do before we leave?"

When he didn't answer, she sat up and faced him squarely. "When I asked what the Right Arms were looking for when they searched me, you didn't answer. What were they looking for?"

Danny walked away from Janis after she asked that question. He felt like they needed a break from each other. She must have felt the same way. She hid in her room for the rest of the morning.

He gave her as much time as she needed, but he'd exhausted both the patience phase and the pacing phase of his wait before her door opened. He'd resorted to standing at the front window, counting traffic. Hundreds of pedestrians had passed, along with scores of bicyclists and five cars. Every car had a green cloth draped over the dash. She passed him

266

without a word. He bit his tongue and waited while she made noises in the kitchen.

Ten minutes later, she shoved a bowl full of gray paste into his hands. He examined it suspiciously. "Oatmeal?"

"Mom says it never goes bad. I mean, she said it—"

"I know what you meant." He forced a smile. "Your brother says it started out bad and can't get worse."

"You don't like it?" She sounded angry.

"Lighten up, twerp. I was just teasing." His smile faded. "Oatmeal is fine. It is my Mom's go-to breakfast."

"Oh." She blinked rapidly. "I guess teasing is allowed."

She stepped back, stared at him critically, and announced, "We've got to do something about your face."

"My face?" He touched it and ran his fingers along the scar. "What's wrong with my face?"

"It's not ugly enough. The scar helps, but it's fading. We need to change your looks more." She squinted at him, then said, "Maybe if we cut your hair. . . ?"

"No."

"Yes, and that reddish brown color stands out. I'll dye it. How do you feel about blond?"

"No."

"Yes." She grabbed his hand and pulled him toward the bathroom.

"Wait!" He resisted long enough to grab his oatmeal.

Two hours later, he sported a head of really short, chopped-up hair that varied from pale blond to pale green and his scars, outlined with some sort of makeup, looked a much angrier red. Janis had contributed to the overall effect by tweezing away the part of his eyebrow hiding the jagged tear over his eye, and she did something to exaggerate the splotchy pattern left by the scabs on his other cheek. Then she pronounced his new look almost perfect.

"Almost?" He examined his reflection in the bathroom mirror. "I'm ready for a bad production of Frankenstein."

"Pretty awesome, huh?"

"My own mother wouldn't recognize me."

"Neither would your father." And that was what mattered, at least in her mind.

He didn't believe it for a second. A dye job and a scar

might fool a cop in a patrol car, but it wouldn't fool his father. Despite his comment, it wouldn't fool his mother either.

Janis asked, "What are you thinking about?"

"Taking my face for a test drive."

She paled. "Why?"

"Might as well find out if it works, Jannie. Besides, there is still that thing."

"The one you won't talk about?" When he nodded, she ran for her purse. "I'm coming."

He nodded, but said nothing for a long moment. Then he cleared his throat and said, "Look, Jannie—"

"No. We will not talk about danger, Danny. We just won't. Two weeks ago, I was almost dead. My Mom is dead. My best friend is dead. All I have in the world is my new brother, and I will not let him talk about splitting up, so, no. Just forget it."

"Right." He couldn't escape her, but he'd keep her as safe as possible.

Once she had his agreement, she asked, "Where are we going? For that thing?"

"I want to get a feel for the city first." He left the house without a hat or his mask. He didn't even put his armband on. He felt exposed, almost naked. The sun and the breeze on his face felt strange.

They walked back toward Veteran's Memorial Park. He could have made better time if she'd been satisfied with holding his hand, but she seemed to need an arm around his waist. He decided speed was not critical at the moment and threw an arm over her shoulders. She wiped her face on his shirt and whispered, "I was afraid."

"I know." He squeezed her. "The posters say Julia Pinker was Gabriel, but even if she wasn't, they still want me for killing her."

Janis nodded slowly. "Maybe it would be worse. Everybody is happy Gabriel is dead. Lots of people think you should get a reward for killing her, but if you killed an innocent woman—"

"Right." Danny smiled grimly. "But not everyone is happy Gabriel is dead. The government wanted her in jail, or maybe in one of their labs."

"Is that why your dad hates you?"

He stopped walking and looked up, blinking rapidly. "He thinks I betrayed him. He thinks I spied on him for Tonys-Way."

"Did you?"

"I told Mike more than I should have. More than Dad could forgive. Damn it!" Danny slapped the wall beside him with the back of his fist hard enough to leave a little blood. "I had to, Emmie. Dad doesn't understand what is going on."

Janis stared at him. "You called me Emmie."

"Did I?" He licked the cut on his knuckles. "I'm sorry."

"It's okay." She turned and leaned against the building beside him. "So we run away?"

"We need allies. People we can trust to help us."

"But not friends? I mean, not TonysWay Friends?"

"They might be the ones who killed Pinker."

"Really?" She looked incredulous.

"They had Doctor Foreman in custody when the gangs shot him, and I'm pretty sure Mike killed Parker."

"Tony's pet dog?"

"Yeah." He held out his hand. "Come on," he said. "Let's keep moving."

He took a roundabout path toward the side street four blocks from the park where he'd left Mr. Massini's car. It hadn't moved, but finding it did him no good.

He didn't notice the stake-out until they passed a black Ford Explorer with heavily tinted windows and a pair of spotlights facing down the street. At the far end of the block two Friends climbed out of a van and started toward them, green bands conspicuous on their right arms. Danny edged closer to Jannie and lowered his voice. "Don't panic, Jannie, but my face is going to get its first test."

"What do you mean?" She looked alarmed.

He whispered, "You asked me for directions. You need to visit your mother."

She noticed the approaching Friends. Her eyes widened. They were Right Arms. She looked around nervously.

"If they take me, I'll meet you at your place as soon as I get free."

"You think they'll let you go?"

"With this disguise? No problem, twerp." He finally

noticed the girl watching them from across the street and added, "Remember, meet up at your place."

The friends were close enough to hear him. He forced a smile, pointed up the street past them, and continued, "It's only about a mile from here. Go on up five blocks and turn right, then left on Jefferson. You can't miss it. You'll see the crowd and—"

The shorter Friend, a stocky middle-aged woman, interrupted him. "What's going on?"

Danny nodded at her. "The young lady wants to find the crematorium."

She looked at Janis and asked, "Is that right, Miss?"

Janis nodded and licked her lips. "What's wrong?"

"Why are you going to the crematorium?"

Janis started to tremble.Then she stiffened and took a deep breath. "My mo—." Her voice hardened. "My mom is there. I have to see her before . . . before they do it."

The woman studied her. "Nobody sees anyone there. You know that, don't you?"

"Then I'll just sit with her." She blinked a few times, but she kept her emotions firmly in check. Danny was proud of her.

The friend remained suspicious. She glanced at her partner and nodded. He pulled an instrument resembling a cell phone from his pocket and scanned Janis' left arm, then nodded. "She's Pam Oliver's daughter, Janis. Her mother is at the crema—," and then he stopped. Maybe it occurred that he was being a little insensitive. "Anyway, she checks out."

"What about him?"

The man waved his chip reader over Danny's arm, waited a few seconds, and frowned. "He's one of us, a Right Arm. Anthony Messing." He stepped back and eyed Danny cautiously. "The history is incomplete, but it says he was in Atlanta."

On hearing that, the woman also edged away. She said, "Check his biometrics."

He held the reader toward her and said, "You want to take his print?"

She looked from the device to Danny and shook her head. "Photo should be enough."

"Yeah." Apparently the reader included a camera. He pointed it at Danny's face, pushed a button, and a moment later announced, "Confirmed, but Records has nothing more on his history." He addressed Danny directly. "You want to explain that, Friend?"

"Explain what?" Danny had listened to them with little hope, but his confidence increased as they grew more nervous. He remembered his conversation with the nurse at the gym. "I've been outside. They just confirmed and chipped me a couple days ago."

The woman lowered her voice. "Is it true about . . . you know . . . Belgrade?"

Danny looked away and said nothing. The woman waited long enough to take no answer for an answer. Then she sighed. Her friend abruptly demanded, "Why aren't you wearing your arm band?"

Every answer Danny thought of could arouse suspicion, so he said simply, "Orders. Talk to Mike if you have any questions."

That was good enough. The woman asked, "What are you doing here?"

"Like I said, talk to Mike." Danny looked around the street. The black SUV hadn't moved, although the engine was now running. Janis had shrunk back against a wall and was trying to look invisible. He saw a few pedestrians, but they'd all chosen the other side of the street. He answered the woman's question with one of his own. "What's going on here? Did I walk into something?"

"We're watching a car. If anybody approaches it, we hold them."

"You're watching a stolen car?"

The man shrugged. "I didn't say it was stolen."

"Why aren't the police doing this?"

"They get their orders. We get ours."

"Right." Danny studied the Friends for a moment, then said, "We better get back to work." He motioned Janis to follow him and started up the block.

After they turned the corner she said, "That was weird. They were waiting for us."

"Not for us. For Danny."

"That's you."

"Not any more." He shook his head. "They read my chip. I'm Anthony Messing now."

Janis thought about that as they walked. "Does it bother you?"

He didn't know what to say. He felt lost one minute, disoriented the next. Then he thought about all the people looking for a man who didn't exist any more and he wanted to laugh for the sheer joyous freedom. And then he thought about Emmie and if he wasn't her brother, who was he? He didn't know, so he shrugged and answered a different question. "It should make it easier to get out of the city."

"You really want to leave?"

"Too many people know me here. Someone will recognize me eventually."

They kept walking. It was a glorious day. The few clouds scattered over the sky floated on a sea of deep milky blue and cast only warm shadows in the midsummer sun. The air was sweet. A light breeze held no taint of automobile exhaust, and it came from behind as Danny and Janis approached the crematorium. It pushed the well-filtered haze and its hint of charred flesh away from the heart of the city, toward the asphalt and concrete plain of the airport and the ripe countryside beyond.

Danny didn't point out the funeral home and Janis didn't notice it until they were almost on top of the sign. When she stopped in front of it, frozen, he took her hand and led her gently around the building. Then she saw the refrigerator trailers and froze again. He had to pull her into the small crowd of men and women standing on a shaded knoll beside the parking lot. It was a quiet crowd for the most part. The time for wailing was long past and weeping silently was a talent everyone present had mastered.

Janis stared at the trailers. "Is she in there?"

Danny moved closer. His arm touched hers, but he didn't hug her. "She's in one of them."

"But she isn't alone."

"No. She has plenty of company."

"I'm glad. She needs people." Her hand slipped between Danny's arm and his ribs and pulled him closer. "She hates to be alone."

After a quick glance, he pulled his arm away and wrapped it around her. He held her close. They kept watch while two more names were called from the back door and added to the list. Lana Johnson and Amber Bishop. Jannie's fingers dug into his bicep twice, once for each name. The gurney shuttled two more bags from the trailer to the furnaces.

Janis leaned against him. She wasn't crying but her eyes were full and she blinked rapidly. She asked, "What if I'm too late? What if they already did my mom?"

"Let's go see." He pulled her to the building. A small group clustered around the clipboard hanging from a hook set beside the door, looking over the shoulders of a young woman who flipped through the five pages clipped to it and scrolled slowly down each page. Before she finished, one of the men behind her sighed and walked away. The others stayed for the last name on the list. Amber Bishop. Then the woman shrugged and muttered, "Maybe tomorrow."

Danny took her place and scrolled down the list, twenty-five hastily-scrawled names to a page, and Janis held her breath. When they reached Amber, she sagged back against him. He wrapped an arm around her to support her. After a minute, she said softly, "I'll be back tomorrow."

"I'll come with you." He examined the list more carefully. Each name was followed by dates of birth, death, and a cause of death. The cause was always blank.

The door opened and a friend pushed out an empty gurney. She took the clipboard and filled in another line while two friends from the trailer exchanged her empty gurney for one with a small bag on it, dark except where a patch of frost had begun to melt on the plastic. She called out the name she'd just added, Frankie Kamura, and then rehung the clipboard. She muttered, almost an afterthought, "Age five." Then she pushed the door open and pulled the gurney in.

Janis turned in Danny's arms and hid her face. He pulled her through the crowd, past the man and woman holding each other and weeping soundlessly, past the still form of Mike Massini, who watched him expressionlessly, surrounded by serious men with hard faces and tight green bands on their right arms. Mike shook his head as they passed and said,

"This needs to end."

He nodded and shepherded Janis away from the crematorium.

Chapter 29

They retreated to Janis' place. She headed for the couch and the sitcom channel while Danny watched a cup of coffee turn to sludge. He felt like a monkey in a shrinking cage, leaping from side to side, shaking the bars, desperate to find a door and not even sure there was a door. The only surprise about the warrant for his arrest was the lack of an arrest. He'd listened to his father talk shop for years. Once a person of interest was identified, capture became inevitable unless he escaped from the jurisdiction or disappeared.

Something was keeping Danny on the street. He should have been in custody hours after the warrant was issued, but he was still free over a week later. Why? He couldn't think of any reason the mayor or the federal agencies would want him free. That left Mike, who claimed that TonysWay needed the cachet that would come from capturing the man who killed Gabriel. Danny couldn't see it. The sketchy news filtering in from the outside world suggested that TonysWay was riding a green wave around the world. Friends were trusted for their generosity and helpfulness. They went where they pleased and, if you ignored the shadowy Right Arms, Greenies were universally regarded as benevolent. Danny himself might have joined if Mike hadn't framed him for the murder. Danny didn't even sip his coffee. His mouth tasted bitter enough without it.

Janis eventually came into the kitchen and banged

around. He didn't look at her until she set a plate of macaroni and cheese in front of him. She took the chair opposite him and waited. Eventually, she asked, "What's wrong, Danny?"

"Just feeling sorry for myself. I'll get over it." He took a bite of the macaroni. It was terrible. He swallowed and forced a smile. "Thanks for the food, twerp."

She brightened. "It's from a box. Mom always adds some milk to make it taste good, but everything is spoiled. I'll put milk on the grocery—" She remembered there would be no more grocery shopping with her mom and fell silent.

He stepped around the table and put an arm over her shoulders. She leaned her face against his belly for a moment. When she stopped shaking, he pushed her away. "What are you, Jannie? Fourteen?"

"Almost fifteen. Why?"

"Does your mom have any cards?"

"Cards?"

"Emmie and I used to play cards when Dad took us on road trips."

"You and Emma?"

He nodded. "It's a good way to pass time."

She smiled and hurried into the living room. When she returned with a deck, he dealt a hand and went over the rules for gin rummy. She caught on quickly and they played quietly. Danny noticed that Janis was crying silently. He didn't say anything and she stopped after a while. When he went out with a Gin and won the game, she called him a jerk and announced she was going to beat his butt. The rest of the evening passed smoothly.

When Janis started nodding off, he tucked her in and tried to get comfortable in her mother's bed. He woke on the couch again, this time to the smell of burning oatmeal, but Janis redeemed herself with a pot of very black coffee. They ate in silence until Danny asked what she was thinking about. He was surprised when she answered, "Soccer."

"What about it?"

"I really loved it, you know. Emma and I were a real team. We were going to be killer on the JV team and maybe make varsity when we were sophomores. That was the plan, anyway."

"They might still have school sports. Not everything will be canceled. Life goes on, Jannie."

"Not for me. Not here." After a moment she added, "When we got really sick, that first night at soccer camp, Emma wasn't scared. She said you'd save us. She made me believe it too. I knew Mom couldn't leave the hospital so I believed in you instead."

"Oh god." Danny felt like she had slapped him. He felt like slapping himself. "I came as soon as I knew."

"She just couldn't hold on any longer. She tried. It wasn't your fault." She put a hand on his cheek and turned his face. "I didn't mean to make you feel bad. I was jealous of her. I always wanted a brother like you. That's why I got so weird when you wanted to find that car. I knew you wanted to leave and I was afraid."

"I promised you—"

"I'm not stupid. You take me for a walk yesterday and we accidentally walk past a bunch of Greenies guarding a car? I don't think so. Why do you need a car, Danny?"

"We have to get out of the city. We have to find friends, and not the kind with green armbands."

She leaned forward. "What's wrong with my car?"

"Your what?"

"Mom's car is in the garage. I guess it's mine now. You can use it."

He felt stupid. Obviously, her mother had a car. He muttered, "Thanks."

"So where are we going?"

"I don't know yet."

"Do you know when?"

"After the memorial, if I last that long." He stared into his cup. "I've been lucky so far. I don't see how it can last."

"Nobody knows where you are. You can stay here. Inside. We'll load the car now. Then, right after the Service, we just drive out of town."

"Past the check points? The armored cars? The Right Arms?"

"They are going to cancel the quarantine. They said so."

"They canceled the cancellation, Jannie."

"They can't!" She looked shocked. He didn't say anything.

Eventually she pulled out a chair and sat beside him. "What can we do?"

"I need to know what's going on. Where the quarantine line is. How heavily it's guarded. What's coming in, and who's getting out. Who is checking the documents for the people cleared to leave the city." He slapped the table in frustration. "I need to know everything, and I don't know a damned thing!"

"Maybe I can help."

Danny stared at her. "How?"

"My phone is dead and my charger got left at soccer camp. Will you get my mom's charger." She muttered, "It's on her bedside table."

"Right." She couldn't go in there yet, not alone. "Let's get it together."

She nodded reluctantly and let him pull her up. She trembled when they entered the room, but once inside she seemed okay. She even remembered the car keys, and when they left she said, "It was easier that time." Then she went to work. Within an hour, she'd set up a teenage girl spy ring.

Danny watched her work her phone until hunger called him. Then he resigned himself to the kitchen and prepared two boxes of macaroni and cheese with a can of peas for variety. Janis nodded when he slid a plate in front of her, but she didn't stop taking notes until the dishes were done. Then she patted the couch beside her and began, "Okay, first, I got a picture of the latest map. The quarantine line only moved a couple of blocks in the last week. All three checkpoints are still active. There are crowds camped out at each one, real tent cities, but hardly anyone is getting out. Nobody knows why. There are lots of rumors and people are getting desperate. My friend, Celia—her dad works at the checkpoint by the freeway —says he told her only about half as many trucks are coming into town. She said they are taking names and sending lists of people who are cleared to the other side, but no approvals are coming back. Another friend said she heard shooting near the line this morning, so I called Bree—her mom is a nurse in Emergency—but she said nobody got shot. At least, nobody was brought to the hospital. Same thing, right?" She looked to Danny for confirmation.

He shook his head and changed the subject. "Tell me about the rumors."

Janis flipped back a couple of pages in her notes. "Most people think it's because some people outside hate the Greenies. They started here, you know, but they're getting pretty popular, and people are saying that if enough people get out of town, they'll drop the quarantine and then TonysWay will take over the country." She looked up. "What do you think?"

"It sounds far-fetched." He shrugged. "What else?"

"Well, one girl heard the government decided not to let anybody else out so everyone who is sick will be in one place is case they need to, you know, get rid of us. Her father said that was wrong. He said it was so everybody who knows how to make new germs will be in one place." She bit her lips. "That can't be right, though."

"It isn't. Gabriel told the whole damned internet how to edit bacteria."

When Danny didn't continue, Janis added, "They stopped taking the cots out of the gym."

That caught his attention. "Why?"

"Bree's mom didn't say. Bree doesn't think she knows, but she said she's acting really nervous tonight. She's drinking whiskey and writing a list of everything in the pantry."

Danny felt a chill. He asked, "What is her father doing?"

"She hasn't seen him for over a week." Janis leaned forward and peered into his eyes. "He left with the Greenies. She's scared her mom will leave too."

"She'll be okay." Danny tried to project confidence. "Her mom won't leave her."

"Yours did. Mine did."

"Christ." He scrubbed his eyes. "That whiskey sounds like a good idea."

"You want some?" Janis disappeared and returned with an unopened bottle of gin and two glasses. She set them on the coffee table and dropped the deck of cards beside the bottle. "What will it be, Danny? Gin, or Rummy?"

He laughed. "Where'd you hear that line?"

"I heard mom say it once when she brought a date home. She thought I was asleep, but I was spying, for pointers, you know?"

"On cards?"

"On dating. Don't be a jerk."

He grinned at her. "Which did her date choose? Gin or Rummy?"

"Well, the bottle is unopened and you had to teach me Rummy. You figure it out."

"So they went with plan C?"

"I wouldn't know. I went to bed." She bit her lips. "But Mom told me one time that a lady should always have a fall-back plan."

Danny stared at her a moment, then laughed out loud. "Your mom was a wonderful person."

Janis nodded.

He pushed the bottle aside and dealt the cards. She wiped her cheeks frequently for a few games. Then she settled down and concentrated on humiliating him. He was content to be humiliated until he caught himself wondering why he'd stopped playing with Emmie. Then he wiped his cheek and yawned.

Janis didn't mind quitting while she was ahead, but she put her foot down when Danny started to spread his blanket on the couch. "Not again," she said. "Use Mom's room."

Her permission made the difference. He slept in Pam's bed all night and didn't wake until Janis surprised him with a cup of coffee. She put it on the bedside table and said. "I didn't think I'd make it in, but it's your room now."

"I guess that's good." He lifted the cup, sipped, and made a face.

She said, "That was the last of the coffee."

"It's okay. The Memorial is next Wednesday." He added, "We say our goodbyes and then we drive."

She gave a quick little nod of her head and walked away. He cleaned up quickly and found her stirring a pot of oatmeal in the kitchen. She looked up when he entered and then stared intently into the pot. "It's gonna be hard, Danny. Really hard."

"It is the last thing we can do for them." Danny sighed, put a hand on her shoulder, and felt the corded flesh under her skin twitch. He didn't have to add that they'd probably never return once they left the city. She knew.

Janis shrugged off his hand and spooned the oatmeal into two bowls. Danny took one and looked into it suspiciously. "What are the brown things?"

"I found some raisins."

"I hate . . . ah . . . thanks."

A soft tapping at the door saved him.

Janis looked at him with alarm, then whispered, "You're not here," and started for the door. In the spirit of not being there, Danny scooped his bowl back into the pot and looked for the back door. There wasn't one, so he grabbed a butcher knife from the counter and put his back to the wall inside the kitchen door.

He stood there, feeling foolish, and listening intently to two female voices. He knew Janis, of course. When he recognized the other voice, he got rid of the knife and stepped into the great room. "Hello, Rosa. What brings you here? More threats?"

"Nice to see you too, Danny. Or is it Tony now?" She stepped around Janis and dropped onto the couch.

He tried to look confused. "Tony?"

"After I saw you at the Massini's car, I talked to our surveillance team. You changed your name, Danny." She shook her head. "Tony Messing. What the hell were you thinking?"

"I wasn't." He sighed and sank into the chair opposite her. "It was the only ID I had on me when the Greensleeves grabbed me at the gym. I was registered before I knew what was going on." He took a deep breath and waited, searching her face, then asked, "What now, Rosa?"

Janis had disappeared into the kitchen. She returned with two bowls, handed one to Danny, and walked around behind the couch to pass the other bowl over Rosa's shoulder. "Oatmeal," she said and remained behind Rosa.

"You'll like it," Danny assured her. "It's got raisins."

Rosa grimaced. "In a couple of months, this might be a feast."

Surprised, he asked, "What do you mean? The quarantine will be lifted eventually."

She shot a quick glance at Janis, then shrugged. "Did you hear what happened at the perimeter yesterday?"

"Only that shots were fired."

"Oh." She lifted the spoon from her oatmeal and began eating, raisins and all.

Danny watched her a few minutes before running out of patience. "Damn it, Rosa! You came here for a reason. Just spit it out!"

She took a couple more spoons of her oatmeal, then replied calmly, "You know that I'm facing the television screen, and it makes a pretty good mirror, Janis."

Danny sighed. "Bring me the knife, Jannie." To Rosa, he said, "She wouldn't hurt you. She's just anxious."

Rosa waited until Janis carried the butcher knife to Danny. Then she said, "I have a message from Mike, but I want to have a friendly chat before I give it to you."

"Go on."

"Those shots at the border yesterday were fired by the national guard. Refugees tried to cross the line at three different points." She watched them and waited.

Danny sighed. "So?"

"They weren't trying to get out of the city, Danny. They were trying to get in."

"What?" Danny jerked upright. "In?"

She nodded. "And sometime before midnight, the guard abandoned the perimeter. It is now manned only by the Right Arm of TonysWay."

Danny could think of nothing to say. Janis stepped close and put her arm around him. She asked, "What does that mean?" Her voice was shaky.

"Something is happening," he told her.

She asked timidly, "Something bad?"

"We had no advance notice." Rosa ignored her question. Maybe she felt it didn't require an answer. "Communications with our Friends outside have been difficult for the last few days. We've been able to rely on the existing channels, even after the Feds nationalized them, but they began to fail as the NOLA strain spread." She swallowed, then added, "Mike thinks we'll have reliable contact within a few days."

While Danny thought that over, Janis asked, "What's NOLA?"

"The first reports came from New Orleans," Rosa told her.

282

"We don't have a clear genotype yet, but it acts like a graft of Yersinia pestis onto pneumococcal bacteria."

"I don't know what that means." Janis spoke in a very small voice. It reminded Danny how young she was. Too young to know about these things, but if he was going to protect her, she had to know.

He said, "Somebody combined the plague, the Black Death, with pneumonia." He looked at Rosa. "What is the mortality rate?"

"Untreated, over eighty percent." Her face was expressionless. "The CDC thinks treatment might drop that to around thirty percent."

"Might?"

"They don't know. A lot of their staff didn't make it out of Atlanta. The last we heard, the CDC is running with about twenty percent of their people in makeshift laboratories. They don't have the drugs they need and they have too many new strains to test properly."

"My god." Danny sagged back into his chair and buried his face in his hands. After a few minutes, he felt Janis sink next to him. She wrapped an arm over his shoulder. That wasn't right. He was the brother. He should be protecting her. He looked up at Rosa and asked, "Is that it? Don't you have any good news?"

She lifted her eyes to the ceiling and said softly, "When I checked the database, I noticed that Tony Messing's record has been completed. He lived at your old address, the one before your father got promoted, and he has a new picture. His scar isn't too noticeable. He never went to college. It's pretty vague about employment before he joined TonysWay."

Danny stared at her. He said, "Thank you."

She nodded. "That brings me to the message. Mike said you are out of time. Come in tomorrow or he will come for you."

"He? My father?"

She shook her head. "There are only Friends in the city now."

He took a while to digest that before asking, "Why is Mike being so generous?"

"He isn't. There is a difference of opinion in the ranks.

Mike thinks capturing you will consolidate his control of the overseas Friends. Others think Gabriel's killer makes a better contribution as a symbol of justice, the strength of average people, and our ability to triumph over the evil unleashed by science."

"Where do you stand, Rosa?"

"With Mike, of course. I'm doing everything I can to bring Danny Murphy to justice tomorrow." She turned her gaze to Janis and continued, "Tony Messing is another matter. I have nothing against him. If he wanted to escape the city, it would be a good idea to leave while the situation is still fluid. The checkpoint on the freeway north will be particularly fluid until it is reinforced at midnight."

Danny jumped up and began pacing. "The guards wouldn't stop him?"

"They won't question a Right Arm on a mission. They'll be thankful they aren't going." With that, Rosa opened the door.

"Wait." Danny stopped her before she could step out. He approached her and asked, in a low voice, "Will you be okay here? I mean, with Mike?"

"I'll be fine, Danny. Mike's changed. We have all changed, but Mike. . . ," she hesitated, "Mike got lost, really lost. I'm scared for him."

He took her arm, just above her elbow, and squeezed. "Mike can take care of himself, Rosa. I'm scared for you."

"I'll be okay." She pulled her arm away. "He needs someone to keep him grounded. He keeps talking crazy, like he's running the world. I tell him he's not superman. I tell him . . . ," She took a deep breath and stepped through the door. Just before she closed it, she said, "I'm going to help him. At least, I'm going to try."

Chapter 30

After locking the door behind Rosa, Janis went to the kitchen and returned with a bowl. She spooned leftover oatmeal into her mouth and swallowed mechanically while staring at Danny. After a few seconds, he fixed a bowl and followed suit, matching her spoon for spoon. He said, "Good raisins."

She nodded.

"Pack the mac and cheese too."

She nodded again and asked, "How much water?"

"All of it. We don't know what we'll find out there."

She said, "Mom has a camping box. A little tent. Propane stove. Sleeping bags. I'll put it in the back seat."

"Good idea."

"We have backpacks. Suitcases might be too much."

"Probably."

"And all our canned food, and an opener, and—"

He said, "Jannie—"

"No!" She refused to look at him. She began to tear up. "You promised!"

He took her hands to calm her. She pulled away from him and dashed into her mother's bedroom. She threw herself on the bed, sobbing. He followed her as far as the door and tried to reason with her. "You heard what Rosa said. Someone brought the Black Death back. Have you heard about Belgrade? Flesh eating bacteria? And I have no idea what happened to Atlanta. Mike wouldn't tell me, but if people are trying to get back in the city, it is terrible out there." He walked into the room, sat on the bed, and hid his face in his hands. He spoke quietly. "I have to go, Jannie."

Janis wiped her eyes and focused on Danny. "It's because of the thing, isn't it?" she asked. "The thing the Greenies searched me for."

"Maybe." He shook his head. "I'm not sure what they wanted, but I promised Doctor Foreman that I'd carry something to his friend and I'm going to do that, no matter what it costs. No matter what," he repeated, looking very seriously at her. "But that's my promise, not yours, and I also promised to keep you safe. I wouldn't take Emmie outside and I can't—"

Janis didn't want to hear explanations. She demanded, "What is it?"

"An envelope." He paused before adding, "It doesn't make any difference what's in it. My promise—"

"Bullshit, Danny. Would you risk your life to deliver a . . . a birthday card?"

"It isn't a birthday card."

"Then what is it, Danny? Do you even know?"

He hesitated. "It feels like a letter and a thumb drive."

"But you don't know." She stared at him thoughtfully. "What do you think it is?"

"It's addressed to another scientist." Danny dropped his eyes to his hands, his tangled fingers, and added softly, "Doctor Foreman said it was his will, but I hope it is more. I hope it is an idea, some kind of solution. Something to end all this death. That's what I hope."

Janis asked softly, "Where is it now?"

"Parker is guarding it."

"Parker? Isn't he—"

"Yes."

She looked sick. "You told me where you found him and where you . . . put him."

Danny nodded.

She swallowed convulsively, took a deep breath, and repeated, "Okay."

"I have to get it before I leave." He bit his lip and added,

"It shouldn't take long, depending on where I have to deliver it. I should be back before the memorial is—"

Janis jumped to her feet and reached him in three long strides. She hit his head with a sweeping open-handed slap that rocked him back and left him dizzy, too shaken even to cover his cheek with his hand. She put her face directly in his and screamed at him. "I said NO, Danny! NO!"

He needed long seconds to recover. He stared with wide eyes into her face and said "Emmie. . . ?"

"No!" She swung her hand back again. Her shoulder was tight. "No!"

Anger flooded him. He grabbed her shoulders and squeezed and spun around, pushing her back onto the bed and kneeling over her. He stared down at her face for a few angry seconds before confusion overwhelmed him. Then hopelessness.

She winced. "No, Danny. Please? No."

He relaxed. Remorse overwhelmed him. When his grip weakened enough, he rolled aside, breathing heavily. She leaned against him. He suddenly found his arms around her shoulders and his eyes full. He hugged her tightly and said, "I couldn't lose you too. I just want to keep you safe."

"You can't."

"I know. I hate it."

Janis lay against him and whispered, "Celia texted me. The cremation truck isn't coming. It could be weeks before they have the memorial."

Danny closed his eyes while he digested that. One more hope slipping away.

She added, "I really wanted to say goodbye."

"Emmie—"

"You keep calling me Emmie. I can be Emmie if you need."

He shook his head. "If I think of you as Emmie, I protect you too much."

She pushed him back to arm's length and said, seriously, "You can protect me, but I'm pretty strong. I'll protect you, too."

"Maybe I need protection from you, Jannie. You've got a hell of a punch." He forced a smile. "Partners?"

She nodded solemnly. "Did you check what I packed?"

He hadn't, so they spent the rest of the morning unpacking, checking lists, searching the house for anything else portable enough and useful enough, and then repacking. They broke for a satisfying lunch of oatmeal with raisins, then played a couple hands of Rummy. When Janis began yawning, Danny suggested they get some rest and leave just after dark. His idea was to pass through the quarantine line just before the midnight shift change.

Janis closed her bedroom door while Danny retreated to the master bedroom. He wasn't tired until he lay down, but then he felt exhausted. He assumed it was emotional. The conflict with Janis. Letting go of Emma and Tony. His parents. His home. Doctor Foreman. He suddenly realized that he'd never get his degree. The magnitude of his loss overwhelmed him. His mind darted from anxiety to anxiety until panic settled into a nightmare and he awoke, startled by the fading light, and searched the house in vain for any sign of Janis.

She left no note, no explanation of where she'd gone, or why, or when she'd return. He paced the house, checked her room again and again. It felt emptier each time he poked his head through the door. The car still sat in the garage, loaded. Ready to go. She hadn't left without him. He finally sat in Janis' room. He felt closer to her there.

Her bed was made. There was a small indentation near the foot of the bed. He guessed she perched there, waiting for him to sleep and making her plans.

Plans to do what?

He returned to the garage. Her backpack was still behind the passenger seat. It still held her traveling clothes and she'd stuck her makeup bag back in it. He'd told her over and over that she didn't need makeup, but it kept showing up in her go-pile. He laughed and left it there.

He checked the ignition. The keys were missing.

They weren't on the floorboard, under the seats, in the door pockets, glove compartment, or center console, so he went back inside and tore the house apart. Her room. Her mom's room. Living room. Dining room. Both bathrooms. Every drawer and cabinet in the kitchen. She hadn't wanted him leaving without her.

Time passed. The sun set. It was full dark and he'd have to leave soon for the Massini house. If it was guarded like the car had been, picking up Foreman's envelope would be difficult.

Where could Janis have gone?

She'd be hungry when she got back.

All the mac and cheese was in the car. Their last supper in the city would have to be oatmeal, with raisins. He sighed and prepared to boil the oatmeal as soon as he saw her. That's when he found the car keys. They spilled out of the oatmeal carton into the measuring cup.

He put them in the middle of the table. Then he sat down and waited. He no longer doubted that she'd be back. He had other worries. Collecting Foreman's message. Reaching the checkpoint before midnight. Avoiding the Right Arms. Crossing the line. Keeping Janis alive. Finding a way to support the two of them. Avoiding the plagues.

Time crept. He stewed in a sea of indecision. He changed plans a dozen times and then, upon mature reflection, changed them back. By the time he heard a noise from the side of the house, all his plans had boiled down to one: get out of town and deal with whatever comes. When he heard the clatter through the kitchen window, he set the water to boil and opened the back door. Janis had pushed her bicycle into the yard. She wore dark clothes, jeans and a black hoodie. She dropped the bike and eyed him uneasily. He stood aside. "Welcome home."

She entered cautiously. "You mad at me?"

"I'm happy you're back." He waved at the stove. "I started supper."

She peeked into the pot. "Oatmeal. Yum." When she turned around, he was sitting at the table. She saw the keys and said, "I figured you'd find them."

"You shouldn't have felt you had to hide them. That's my fault. I'm sorry."

"You're forgiven." She glanced at the stove. "Did you cook all the oatmeal in the house."

"That's breakfast too. Maybe lunch. I don't know when we'll get another chance to cook."

She nodded.

"We're out of raisins." When she nodded again, he asked,

"Where did you go?"

Instead of answering, she pulled a baggie out of her pocket and dropped it beside the keys. Traces of dirt clung to the sealing strip and it smelled terrible. Danny stared at it. He swallowed and whispered, "My god."

"Why did you bury it so damned deep?"

"I hoped if anyone looked there, they'd stop when they found Parker."

"I almost did." She stripped off the hoodie and started washing her hands and face at the sink. She washed for a long time. The first few times her hands came close to her face, she gagged.

Danny's stomach turned. He carried the baggie into the yard, shook the envelope out, and waved it vigorously until he could sniff it without remembering Parker. Back in the kitchen, Janis had disappeared. Her hoodie was missing and the oatmeal had been turned off. He dished up two small bowls, spooned the rest into a baggie, and waited at the table.

The oatmeal was cold when she slipped into her chair with an embarrassed half-smile. He swallowed a spoon of oats before muttering. "I would have done that. You didn't have to."

"I had to show you. I can do what has to be done. I'm tough."

He nodded and said, "Prove it."

"What?" She looked surprised. "How?"

"Eat your oatmeal."

She snickered and picked up her spoon. She finished the bowl in a few minutes. She would have been quicker, but she carefully picked the raisins out of each spoonful before putting it in her mouth. Danny didn't say anything. He knew what they looked like.

When she finished, she collected both bowls and hand washed them. She gave the pot the same treatment. When she started scrubbing the counter, Danny told her to leave it. "We're not coming back, Jannie."

She spun on him, eyes blazing. "No! This is my mother's house and I will not leave my mother's house filthy. I will not!"

She turned back to the counter and resumed scrubbing it.

Danny watched her, stunned by her outbreak and appalled by his thoughtlessness. Her shoulders shook with the vigor of her strokes, and then he realized she was just leaning on the counter and her shoulders were shaking harder than before. He took the sponge from her hand and sat her at the table, then started scouring the counter top. It wasn't dirty, but he scoured it anyway. When he looked over his shoulder, she had a mop out, working on the floor. He finished the counter and started on the stove. She disappeared. He found her in the bedroom, stripping her mother's bed. He went back to the stove.

A few minutes after the washing machine started, Janis walked into the kitchen and told him to stop. She said, "This is stupid."

"It's not."

She sat, elbows on the table, forehead on her palms, fingers snaking into her hair. "Mom's dead," she said. "She doesn't care what the house looks like."

"We aren't cleaning it for her."

"It isn't for me."

"No." Danny frowned and took a seat opposite her. He spoke slowly, unsure of himself. "I won't say this right, but we're leaving tonight, probably forever. Everything we do is to wrap up this stage of our life. If we just walk out, we won't be finished here. We can't start clean if we end dirty."

She stared at him, wide-eyed. "You're crazy."

"Deranged. I know."

She took a nervous breathe and said, "You can't put it off any longer."

"Right." He started to push away from the table. "Let's go then."

"Not that." She shoved the brown envelope toward him. "This."

"It isn't mine. It's addressed to the Santa Fe Institute."

"Open it."

"No."

"Okay." She pulled the envelop back and ripped it open. A thumb drive fell onto the table. She slipped a single sheet of paper from the envelope, unfolded it, and began reading. Then she frowned. "This doesn't make any sense."

"What?" Danny couldn't tear his eyes from the note.

She handed it to him.

He read it twice before he thought he understood. Then he read it aloud.

"It breaks my heart that this has fallen to you, Julia, but apparently the best defense is still a strong offense. The final project report recommends another arms race, this time with bacteria and viruses. We will create the most virulent biologicals possible and release them automatically the moment we are attacked.

Did we really need another way to destroy the world?

Gabriel must be exposed. Use the proof-of-concept material if necessary."

Janis listened intently as he read. She frowned. "What does that mean?"

"It sounds like there was a biological warfare project. I'm not—" Then he turned the sheet over and stared at the line centered on the reverse: This Page Intentionally Left Blank. Above that, he saw the letterhead and the document classification. He bolted for the bathroom. He didn't make it to the toilet. He vomited into the bathtub.

Janis had followed him. When he finished and leaned back against the wall, swallowing convulsively, she waved the letter and demanded, again, "What does it mean, Danny?"

"Look at the letterhead on the back of the note."

She did and asked, "What is a DARPA?"

"The Defense Advanced Research Projects Agency."

"But the letter—"

Danny interrupted her. "It was written on a page from a classified report. Look at the classification level, Jannie."

"TOP SECRET — SPECIAL ACCESS REQUIRED: GABRIEL." She swallowed nervously. "It says Gabriel. Did Gabriel write this?"

"Gabriel isn't a person. It's the name of a top secret project at DARPA."

"A project?"

Danny nodded weakly. He started to wipe his face but changed his mind when his hands neared his nose. He started the cold water in the tub and spoke over his shoulder. "The note said the project recommended biological warfare.

Creating plagues, Jannie. The worst plagues possible."

"I don't believe it. America wouldn't do that!"

"We did it with atomic bombs. We did it with chemical weapons." The tub began filling up. The drain was clogged. He tried to force the vomit down it with his fingers. "It wasn't just us. Everyone who could afford it ran the same race. Do you have some cleanser? Or a plunger?"

She backed away. "Leave it, Danny. Just leave it."

"I can't." He cupped his hand over the drain, trapping some of the mess, and pushed. His palm made a poor plunger, but the drain began to gurgle. He did it again and then took his hand away. Water began circling the drain but the sour smell made him want to back away. "That's better," he said. "Pinker had something called proof-of-concept material. Maybe it was bacteria modified to make botulism. Maybe it was something else, something she could use to edit the bacteria herself. It doesn't matter what it was. She used it to make the poison chalk and kill Tony, and then she poisoned the money and killed Emmie." The drain had clogged again. He pumped it with his hand until the water started draining. He asked, "Do you have any air freshener?"

"No. Just leave it."

"I can't. That would be wrong." He found it hard to talk when he didn't want to breathe, but something had to be said. "The botulism toxin was just for attention, so people would take the threat seriously. The real threat was the name she used. Gabriel. She needed to publicize the project. Maybe she hoped that if people knew what the technology could be used for, they'd demand that it be outlawed."

Janis was struggling. "You mean Emma? Tony? Mom? Everyone?"

He shuddered. "They died for publicity. Just a publicity stunt."

"No!" Janis was crying. She shook her head violently. "It's too much! You have to be wrong. What about all the other cities? She couldn't do them. She couldn't even get through the quarantine."

"She didn't have to. Once the file was on the internet, people all over the world started working on their own germs."

"But why?"

"Why do people print 3-D guns when they can buy better weapons a lot cheaper?" The worst of the mess was down the drain. Danny started washing his hands. He used a lot of soap and scrubbed furiously, but he was feeling strangely dispassionate. Almost resigned. "Maybe they're crazy. Maybe we're all crazy."

"Mom wasn't crazy. Neither was Emma."

"Neither are you. Neither am I." He dried his hands and then held out his arms to her. She stepped into them and he hugged her. "But let's not trust anybody else."

Janis nodded and whispered, "Gabriel was a monster. I'm glad she's dead."

"There are monsters everywhere, Jannie. A couple weeks ago I was running around with a borrowed gun."

Janis released him and stepped away. She asked, "Why did your teacher want you to deliver his message? Why not do it himself?"

"He was being watched. Maybe he ran out of time. It doesn't matter. He asked and I promised." He looked around the room. "It is time to go, Jannie."

She sighed and followed him. Her head swung back and forth as she moved. She detoured into the living room and then into the master bedroom and walked slowly along the walls, stopping frequently at the framed pictures hanging there. She got as far as the garage door before she balked.

He asked, "Need a minute?"

"Yes." She mumbled an apology.

"I'll meet you in the car." While waiting, he rigged a green cloth to a broom handle and wedged it out the driver-side rear window. He fixed his arm band tight on his right bicep. He opened the overhead door, backed onto the drive, and waited. He didn't turn on the headlights.

When she finally slipped into the passenger seat, she was breathing heavily but her eyes were dry. She clutched an eight by ten picture frame to her chest. He looked at her cautiously. "You okay?"

She nodded.

He started to push the button to close the garage.

She said, "Leave it. Just go."

That surprised him, but he reversed onto the street. When he reached for the headlights, she said, "No."

He shrugged and started down the street. Halfway down the block, Danny Murphy pulled to the curb and Tony Messing stared in the rear view mirror at the flames filling the open garage behind them. He didn't say anything. He put the car back in gear and headed for the quarantine line. After a few blocks, he turned on the headlights. He wasn't sure they would help, but he was hopeful.

Other Books by Harlen Campbell

Monkey on a Chain

Nearly two decades after the fall of Vietnam, the knot of corruption and deceit that Rainbow Porter thought was safely buried in the alleys off Saigon's Tu Do street begins to unravel. A fortune is missing, a dead man has resurrected himself, and the heart of the storm is sleeping in his spare bed.

Jennifer's Weave

Most of us weave the fabric of our lives with strands selected from the seven virtues and the seven deadly sins. Jennifer Murphy found another thread, and when it began to unravel, she left a man with a knife in his chest on her kitchen floor in New Mexico and a cry for help on Rainbow Porter's door.

Sea of Deception

Nick Cowan lost his innocence and his wife in the Sea of Cortez. A small town in west Texas took a gamble on the future and lost everything. Paula Stafford lost her brother to Helen Daws, who never lost a thing in her life. And all of them are heading for a bloody rendezvous on the shores of the sea of deception.

PLENUM

Beautiful women. Brave men. Lonely machines. Terrifying aliens lost in a tunnel that connects every point in space and time. A ship that sails a universe so huge it can't be described in human words. A Lady who wants to be a mother. A true woman with a disturbing talent with an ax. And all hang on the courage of a hero who'd rather be in Chicago.